The jar was unusually light for a  than a potato. Even more peculia a mirror, yet offering no reflection whatsoever. If he didn't know better, Theo would have sworn that somebody digitally removed all the objects—his face, hard hat, the cave walls— that should have been reflected back. Either that or he was a vampire. Left only was the perception of dimension, an empty space. He just couldn't figure it.

Fixed atop the jar was a circular lid. It would not come off. Along the flat underside of the jar was a series of grooves. They were symbols, Theo guessed, though none he recognized. He ran his fingers over them. He started to feel woozy and disoriented just then, as if he had been drugged without him knowing it, which in a way, is exactly what happened.

There was a blast of white light. There were streaks of screaming fluorescent color. There was the sensation of being sucked through a tornado. And then there were stars. Lots and lots of stars.

Theo felt himself drawn beyond the glass edge, sucked through the surface. He felt like he had been swallowed by the Universe itself, zooming across a galaxy of everything that existed everywhere and yet nothing at all.

Acknowledgments

The re-launch of *Finders Keepers* comes at an exciting time in my life and my writing career. It took some doing to get this far, and it certainly didn't happen alone. My thanks go to Barney O'Neill, for his intense and thorough copy editing; Jim Chambers and Michael Wolfe, who both gave me critical feedback on the manuscript; Mike Rende for all things website-related; the boys at Crazy 8 Press, who think I'm their kind of creative madman, including my amigo Aaron Rosenberg, who invited me into their little world and provided the new interior layout; and to Rich Koslowski, for the tremendous cover, and for helping me bring *Finders Keepers* to life in the first place.

Crazy thanks go to Karl, without whom this wacky novel simply could not exist, and the sequels that I'm currently writing.

And, of course, to my wife Liz and our little ninjas, who fill my world with love and laughter and remind me why I write in the first place.

Matt-

FINDERS KEEPERS

A TALE OF COSMIC LUNACY BY RUSS COLCHAMIRO

Enjoy! :)

There are worse things to lose than your mind...

ICON
2017

Russ

CRAZY 8 PRESS

MATT-

Enjoy! :)

Russ

Nov
2017

To Liz—
You are forever my girl...

Prologue

The last thing Donald and Danielle ever wanted was to wreck their marriage, lose their jobs, get banished from Eternity and jeopardize the Milky Way galaxy. So much for hoping. They thought they had time to slink out of trouble, but thanks to that bonehead Milo and his spectacular fuck up, The Minder of the Universe opened a can of whoopass on the entire engineering department.

Each work crew was assigned a single jar of cosmic building material, or CBM—the core ingredient for construction throughout the Universe. In essence, it was the Universe's DNA. If not properly diluted, a single drop had enough juice to wipe out several star systems.

Lawrence, the CBM warehouse manager, stood behind the podium. He was pissier than normal. "The first time a portion of the Universe dissolved, I thought long and hard about your very *uncertain* status in Eternity." Images appeared on a screen behind him—shattered moons, comet sputum and asteroids turned to dust. "I'm still thinking..."

Danielle grabbed her husband's thigh. She dug in.

The second time a jar of cosmic building material accidentally spilled into the Universe, the Big Dipper almost shriveled up and died. The constellation originally consisted of more than eight thousand stars. Its current image came up on screen. "*Now* look at it."

Lawrence took a moment before continuing. His disgust was palpable. "The third time a jar of CBM was improperly discharged—and for your sake, the last—it sent the Hennoid galaxy into permanent flux." Milo, the engineer on duty, got drunk at the work site, and as a shout-out to his homies, spilled his entire CBM jar into the cooling galaxy below.

The overload induced a blast of white light. There were streaks of screaming fluorescent color. There was the sensation of being sucked through a tornado. And then there was lava. Lots and lots of lava.

Within minutes, there was another blast of white light. There were streaks of screaming fluorescent color. There was the sensation of being sucked through a tornado. And then there were flamingos. Lots and lots of flamingos. And then another flash occurred, resulting in cold, lifeless rock. Dead moons. And so it went. The affected planets remained in flux, jumping from one state of matter to another.

The engineering crew spent three eons trying to repair that section of the Universe, until finally they just had to wipe it clean. Permanent nothing. It became known as Milo's Smear.

Lawrence cleared his throat. He raised his voice. "The Minder of the Universe has made a *decision*," he said, almost smiling. "Trust me. You won't like it."

Though sitting among a hundred thousand engineers, Danielle knew the warning was all about her. Her heart raced.

The Milky Way, the glorious new galaxy with only one sun, was to be the prototype for millions more in the Universe. And the creatures that would become the dominant species on Earth—for a time, at least—were supposedly modeled after the very beings populating Eternity.

The Milky Way's public unveiling was more than a month away, but three days earlier, during Earth's plumbing phase, Donald and Danielle took an unscheduled, unauthorized break that wound up changing their lives—and the debuting galaxy—forever.

Rather than carefully inspecting installation of a drainage ditch, which became the Sea of Japan, they got naked on a platform overlooking the partially finished planet—still bright orange and smelling of scallion cream cheese—and engaged in some gettin' it on.

The newlyweds hadn't noticed that the glass CBM jar assigned to them was missing until Donald zipped his trousers and realized that one of them must have knocked it from the ledge.

After some initial panicking, they calmed down, rummaged through the bookshelf in their office and consulted page 40404 of the bound manual. They were not concerned that the Milky Way—or even just Earth—would be wiped out, as safety measures were in place. Gaffes such as losing a CBM jar were indeed uncommon, but they did happen.

The sealed jar, however, had plummeted into a cooling, frozen mass, one that became a 70 trillion-pound jutting glacier that tore up most of what is now Northern Asia. The jar had not been accounted for since the first Ice Age, and several hundred million years before Earth settled into its present form— somewhere in the early 21st century, although it was tough to be exact. The measurement of time on Earth was far different from that in Eternity; they did not run by the same clock.

Time in Eternity could speed up or slow down. It could leap ahead or jump back. It could travel in loops. It could bend (but not break). It could twist, flatten, knot and gyrate, as well as oscillate, pendulate, undulate and rotate. It could also whirl, purl, revolve, slant, spin, expand and retract, and—when it really got going—whiz, shimmy, shake, buckle, tangle, tremble, tread, roll, flip (although not flop) and even completely reconfigure. And it could all happen simultaneously or in any combination.

Tuesday breakfast in Eternity could unfold during 2 million B.C. on Earth, and lunch just a few Eternity hours later could coincide with 3223 A.D. Or vice versa.

But Donald and Danielle were not in charge of aligning time. Like all Eternitarians, they were at the mercy of a power far greater than themselves, and who—at least for now—had slowed their perception of time to synchronize with the pace on Earth.

They were also new to the job, and a blunder of this magnitude—losing their CBM jar—was not likely to go over well. Not to mention the recent memo passed along to all employees working on the single-sun galaxy project. It said that people— or humans, as they were being called—had been given an *existence extension*.

An existence extension meant that The Minder of the Universe, or The Big MOU, was intrigued by humans, and did not want anything to interfere with their evolution. Humans were to make their own way in the Universe, if they could make it at all.

The Big MOU—who seemed to have a reasonable sense of humor about a nickname that rhymed with cow, how, ow, wow and pow (pronounced The Big *Mow*)—was like that. You never knew what he would take an interest in next, or why. You just had to roll with it.

"*Any violation,*" the document read, "*will result in immediate redistribution.*"

Redistribution. They shuddered to think about it. Being reduced to your base elements, scattered throughout Eternity and then soaked into the cosmic fabric, reappearing somewhere, sometime—a part of everything, and yet the whole of nothing. Complete identity disintegration.

With the jar gone and no obvious solution for its retrieval, Danielle started to lose it. And when Lawrence called the department meeting, she knew they were fucked. "We're done! We're fuckin' done! The Big MOU's gonna make me a slug or some shit. Maybe a worm. They all slimy and live in the dirt. I can't be no slug. This shit's your fault!"

Donald ran his hand over his bald, white scalp. His graying blond hair along the sides and back was cropped. "How's it *my* fault?"

"How's it your fault? How's it your fault? You're the one with the, 'Ooh, Baby, you so beautiful. Ooh, Baby, I love you so much. You divine among the cosmic beauty n' shit.' You know I get all gushy when you say that kinda…" Danielle craned her neck and pulled Donald's lips to her chocolate skin. "Oh, come here and give mama the nibblin'." Danielle pulled it together, but her fear was ever present. Lawrence made sure of that.

"Now that The Minder of the Universe is approving new star systems again, he wants them *safe and sound*," Lawrence said. "So…for those of you working on the Urba, Fulmer, Lagronian, Yooshodo or Milky Way galaxies, there will be regular ware-house audits, which you *will* pass. Or you *will* be gone. And when I say gone, I mean *gone* gone. Redistribution gone."

Redistribution. Just like Milo.

Lawrence came out from behind the podium. The screen went blank. "Any questions?"

With Earth about to lock into its final form, humans couldn't be far behind. Which could only mean one thing. Trouble.

So while Danielle indeed had a whopper of a question, there was no friggin' way she was asking it. Instead, she turned to her husband, who had been infuriatingly calm since their jar went overboard. "I don't care *what* you say, muthafucka. We are sooooooo fucked."

PART I

THE MOMENT OF SPONTANEOUS MADNESS

Chapter 1
The Moment of Spontaneous Madness

Manchester, England—Heading Northeast on the M56
Wednesday, August 31, 2005, 9:41 a.m.

Jason Medley clung to the seat belt for dear life. Strapped into the left side passenger seat, he went nauseous and started to black out, certain that the oncoming cars in the next lane— *WHAM, WHAM, WHAM*—were going to crash through the windshield and decapitate him. After only twelve minutes, he hated England already.

Jean chuckled as they puttered along the M56, the major motorway to Manchester. It had many curves. "Relax, mate. Relax. You Yanks are so squeamish at first. You'll get used to it."

But Jason didn't want to relax. He didn't want to get used to it. And he certainly didn't give a horse's hairy nut about tea, cricket or if the Queen watched "footie." What he *did* want was to be back on Long Island, waiting tables at *Funzie's*, giving him enough time to search the online job postings again for a sign. A clue. A pigeon flying upside down and projectile crapping upward. Anything. A signal alerting him that there was indeed hope of a high school English teaching job for him with the New York City Board of Education, where he could then be persecuted for not properly educating his students. Hey. A guy could dream.

He also wanted to travel back in time to that regrettable moment of spontaneous madness, when he quit the restaurant on impulse, and then purchased the nonrefundable plane ticket that was now stuffed in his money belt.

But most of all, he wanted to take his bare hands and strangle Hank for convincing him to take this god-forsaken backpacking trip in the first place. Jason did not explore. He did not go on adventures. They really weren't his thang. The world was unknown to him for a reason.

"So, em...Jason." Jean was an attractive older woman, draped in a blue, acid-washed sundress and over-sized bracelets. Her long, gray hair was bunched in a rubber band. "Hank tells me you've been planning this trip for ages. He says you're quite the traveler."

"He said what? No, I..." An approaching four-door car spurred a near upchuck in him. The exit for Manchester arched toward the right. "He stuck a French fry in my face! He yelled at me to see the world before...*urrch, oh, god*...he told me I was hiding fro—"

"You took advice from him? Oh...Jason. Tell me you didn't."

"Well...I don't know. Maybe...? Kinda...?"

"Em...let me guess." Jean gestured with her free hand. "He said the world was chock full of possibility? That the more you embraced life, the more life would embrace you?"

Jason wiped the drool from his chin. "Actually...he did say that. Almost exactly."

Jean let out a controlled but exasperated sigh. "Don't be offended, because you seem like a nice bloke...but are you daft? He's divorced five times! He's a bloody ponce! He fills your head with hope and then leaves you to figure it out!"

"I know!"

"Then why'd you listen to him?"

"I don't know! Why did you? You married him." Jean was ex-wife number four. Jason forgot not to bring that up. Hank said they were still friends, but had some issues they never quite worked out. "So...," Jason said finally, changing the subject. "What are we up to today?"

"Oh...uh...sorry, luv. Hank said you were keen to fly into Manchester and then make a go of it on your own. He said London first and then the world was your oyster."

It took a few seconds for the message to compute. *Me no like these words. Words bad.* "Wait. What? Where are you *going*?"

"Em, right. We're off out to Scotland. Edinburgh, really, for the poetry festival. Be gone through the weekend." With her Mancunian accent, she pronounced it wheek-*end*. "We'll drop you at Piccadilly Station. Where's your first stop from London?"

From the moment Jason bought his plane ticket and Eurail

train pass he had mentally and emotionally anchored himself, if not to Jean then at least to the *idea* of Jean, so that when he first set foot on European soil, he would have someone to cling to, that he wouldn't be alone. And he believed those things because Hank told him so. *Settle in Manchester, Kid. Jean will take care of everything.* Jason ran off to Europe so quickly that he never considered how that might look—or what he was supposed to do—when he actually got there.

But he was now confronted with the reality that he was on his own, in a foreign country, with no place to eat, sleep or bathe, and no concrete ideas about how to make his situation better. Jason had the sudden urge to slip on his footy pajamas and watch *Finding Nemo.*

"I...uh...I'll just...head off...to...uh..."

"Rome is quite lovely."

"Yes! Rome. That's perfect!"

And to him, it *was* perfect. Jason felt a surge from testicles to torso. He was instantly re-energized, inspired. Although he spent more than five years at Buffalo State College, not once did he venture even so far as Toronto, a world-class city just two hours away. But now he was going to *Rome.* He liked the sound of it. In his mind he kept repeating...*Rome...Rome...Rome...*until a smile stretched across his face. And when Jean asked him what he was on about, Jason just looked toward the oncoming cars, almost daring them to come closer.

Okay, he said to himself. *It's go time.*

So when they sped past the sign for Manchester, Jason knew one thing for sure: With his new plan in place, he had it all under control. What could possibly go wrong?

They drove through downtown Manchester, along Oxford Road up to Piccadilly Railway Station. Thanks to the August humidity, Jason's clothes stuck to him already.

"You'll be in London in a tick," Jean said. "Rome will be a piece of piss."

Jason wasn't sure what she meant by that, but thanked her

anyway. He slung his rucksack over his shoulder. It was heavy. He held his knapsack by the strap. "Have fun in Edinborough."

"Cheers, thanks." Jean shook her head, chuckling at his mispronunciation. "Off you go."

As quickly as she came into his life, Jason was flying solo again. He ambled through the double doors, taking in the flow of morning commuters, each one looking more miserable than the last. Up until a week earlier he had essentially been one of them, dejected over his station in life. At twenty-four, he was $26,902.13 in hock to the State of New York Student Service Loan Center, $4,113.74 to VISA, and $9.12 to Roger's Rental Shack (although he held that charge in dispute, arguing that he did, in fact, return *Busty Babes in Toyland VIII* on time).

Jason was also living with his parents and their five cats, while his friends Reuben, Todd and Faye all had jobs in Manhattan. And Jill, his older sister by five years, owned a two-bedroom condo in Hoboken, New Jersey, with a great view of the Hudson River and the New York City skyline. That pharmaceutical rep money kept her in the good life.

Not to mention that Jason's waitress crush Lorna deflected his advances, instead getting jiggy with the bartender, and making sure to give Jason daily updates, seeing as how they were such good pals and all.

But those worries were lost to him. Jason smiled now, thinking about his final *Funzie's* lunch shift, when that silver-haired maniac really laid it on thick.

Hank was the oldest and considered the weirdest waiter on staff. Restaurant gossip had him as the CEO of a major corporation until its stock tanked after the Black Monday crash of 1987, with another tale circulating that he spent the latter half of the '90s in an Arizona psych ward. The dishwashers in particular appreciated his seemingly unlimited access to hallucinogenic mushrooms, while most everyone else dismissed him as a burnout loser.

"Get the fuck outta here, Kid. Quit. Just hop on the first plane to Guam or Lisbon or Tai-fucking-pei for all I care. You spend too much time up here," he said, pointing to his head with that blue cheese-covered French fry, "and not enough time out there. Besides, you have any idea how big this world really is? Big enough so that you can curl up to one woman a week, each one from a different country and it'll take five years before you need to start all over again. Shit. If I was twenty years younger I'd be getting a blow job right now from a Belgian maid, then move on to a German travel agent. I probably wouldn't be so particular after that."

With Belgian maids on the brain, Jason stood in line, humming to a Muzak version of the Bee-Gees. "...*More than a wo-man... more than a woman to me-eee...*" When his turn came, Jason slid his Eurail pass to the ticket clerk. He smiled wide. "London, please."

The clerk flipped through the booklet. He slid it back. "Ticket's no good, mate. Next."

"What?" Jason gaggled, shaking his head in mild horror. "What do you mean it's—?"

"Read the sodden ticket, mate. It's not valid."

Jason let out a whelp. Sure, he could have read his ticket before he left New York. And, okay, yes, he could have noticed... possibly...perhaps, that included with the booklet was a fold-out map detailing each of the seventeen European countries in which the ticket was valid—England clearly not among them.

But that would have meant thinking ahead, allowing for the outlandish possibility that a team of guides with maps, snacks and hotel accommodations might not be waiting for him on every street corner, of every city, in every country, to make sure he was supported, regardless of circumstance. He needed somebody to blame. *Jean...how could you do this to me?*

Jason looked through the glass doors toward the parking lot, hoping a whimpering puppy kind of hope that Jean had done her duty, one that should have been obvious, even though he just thought of it: Remain behind, just in case. *Come back.... Please?* His plan, such that it was, no longer seemed like a plan at all. Jason's newfound confidence was gone.

What do I do now?

"Oi! Keep it moving, mate."

"Wait. But I—"

Growing tired of their exchange, the clerk dismissed Jason in his best mock American. "Dude," he said. "Have a nice day."

Chapter 2
The Search for Beet Root

Germany—30 Miles Southwest of Berlin

Wednesday, August 17, 2005, 1:54 p.m.

Theo Barnes hadn't slept in the same bed more than four consecutive nights since he left home. After nearly six months, he was still looking for proof, for an answer. At the rate he was going, Theo figured he could squeeze out another month, maybe two, but he wasn't heading home until the last dollar was gone. He would sort the rest out later.

Theo was stretched out on the padded bench extending the length of the compartment. He leaned his head beneath the window. Locks of his brown hair, lightened from long exposure to the European sun, fluttered as the German countryside whisked by the speeding train.

The distorted landscape was a familiar blur, a streaking of trees, mountains, houses, cars and phone lines, as if the fabric of the world stretched out like putty, as if existence was elastic, malleable...constantly reshaping itself, reforming...cosmic molecules able to reassemble themselves in an infinite number of possible incarnations.

Maybe we see what we think we see, Theo thought. *Maybe we're the ones in flux.*

Ever since that day in the mountain's still waters, underground, wonderful little creatures his only source of illumination, Theo had been sleeping more deeply, more intensely. His dreams had been vivid, almost tactile experiences. They left him with an incisive imprint, as if he had been branded. Awakened. Changed.

He drifted off again, his arms hooked through the loops of his battered green rucksack. Theo thought of his dad, Oscar, wondering if he would have lived a different life, chosen another path, if he had been afforded the same opportunities thirty years ago that Theo had now. If Theo would even be Theo. If anyone would be who they are.

Theo had been saving his New Zealand dollars for two years, and at twenty-three he was eager to explore the great nations, to leap from his little country at the bottom of the world and see what the fuss in other time zones was all about.

Not to mention what was concealed in his knapsack. As a precaution he had taken several pictures of the jar he found, one that gave him intense, space-soaring hallucinations, driving him to the brink of madness. He wasn't about to hand the actual item to just anyone.

But as he zipped along from one European city to the next, his life before he departed on Kiwi Air seemed to him an amalgam of one long day.

Theo thought back to that late February morning, when he bobbed along the kitchen floor, naked but for his gray cargo shorts. He instinctively kept his bare heels from touching the floor, as if making contact with it would somehow cement him in place, trapping him forever.

Sunshine streaked across the ranch-style house, common to the suburbs of Auckland. With New Zealand in the southern hemisphere, the summer was almost over as February came to a close.

"So whudduya say there, Dad? Gonna fire up the old birdie today? The helicopter is starting to look good. Choice day for it."

Theo didn't normally talk much, and it wasn't because he had nothing to say. But he often felt that being asked to mine his thoughts—to make sense of all the questions he had from all the noise in life—was just more effort than it was worth. He preferred the quiet of his greenhouse, which he built by himself. He wasn't just collecting plants, he was *cultivating a garden*. And that takes time. And patience. Not a lot of talk. He left that to his brother, Roger.

But Theo would be leaving soon, so he offered his father some breakfast small talk. Burly and almost bald, Oscar

Barnes was hunched over the kitchen table, reading *The New Zealand Herald*. Just a few strands of white hair clung to his dome. "Oh, yeh, what's that?"

Theo disappeared behind the refrigerator door as he held it ajar, placing a physical barrier between father and son. It was an intuitive gesture honoring their unspoken agreement that their level of interaction would emphasize hobbies, not chores; adventures, not responsibilities.

The Barnes men shared a genial acknowledgment that, sure, it would be just peachy if we could connect on a deeper level, where we have the father-son chitchats and maybe even give a good hug in there now and then and all that other cute koala crap. But, yeah right, mate. Yeah right. The day we start sharing our feelings is the day the dolphins start talking back. If you don't bust my balls, I won't bust yours.

"So whens you off to Waitomo then, Theo? Gotta get back in those caves, yeh?"

"Beet root, beet root," Theo muttered from his side of the door, searching for his favorite condiment. "Ah, there you are. Oh, dunno. Few days. Not sure yet." He stood up just then and looked toward the dining room window. His father's bare legs were crossed beneath the table. "You still got that big red ax, Dad? I get the weirdest feeling I'm gonna need it."

Chapter 3
Floating Solo in the
Rappelling Cave

Otorohanga, New Zealand—Approaching the Waitomo Caves
Tuesday, February 22, 2005, 11:09 a.m.

Humming along to Ben Harper's *Please Bleed*, Theo motored his black '96 Toyota Hilux Surf 4x4, pulverized from years of off-roading. Beneath the cloudy sky, he headed southbound along State Highway 1 until Hamilton, and then State Highway 3, the major motorways ranging the westernmost third of New Zealand's North Island.

Theo admired the herds of cows grazing on the dairy farms, New Zealand predominantly an agricultural nation. He spotted one plant after another along the fields, thinking they would make fine additions to his greenhouse.

But he needed to improve his knowledge about *Frangipani*. There was a demand for the tropical plant, rare in New Zealand, one that can grow up to forty feet high and half as wide. To Theo there was nothing quite like its fragrance, gleaming with jasmine, citrus and gardenia.

Yet Theo had more pressing concerns. He wasn't officially due back in Otorohanga for another four days, but he was eager to romp around in the Waitomo Caves, about 175 kilometers south of Auckland.

This was his last chance before the new tourist season started to explore the underground passages alone—a major no-no according to the employment agreement he signed with *KiwiFun Adventure*. You followed the buddy system, or you didn't go down there at all. Safety first.

Theo parked his truck on the dirt road beneath the hillside. There he changed into his wetsuit and slung a little pack on his back. He tied the laces of his rubber, watertight boots and fastened his hardhat. The miner's light was in front.

After tightening the rappelling harness around his waist, he hiked up to a wood platform bolted into the hillside. It overlooked a hole boring through the rock. With a *clack*, Theo attached his safety line to a metal hook drilled into the platform. He turned so that his back faced the cave entrance. And with a hard push of both feet against the rock side, Theo began his descent.

As his hands slid down the nylon rope, he felt a great surge of apprehension. The thought indeed crossed his mind that a bad fall would leave him injured, if not dead, and without any realistic chance for medical attention. But he quickly dismissed such conjecture as crazy talk.

Slowly, Theo spun three hundred and sixty degrees clockwise, hearing the rope twist and tighten, and then unspool in the opposite direction. He had undergone six months of training, led or accompanied one hundred and thirteen guided tours, and made at least a dozen solo journeys through the caves, all without ever suffering so much as a twisted ankle.

Theo thought about the first time he went down there alone. He had imagined himself as a James Bond-in-training, set to infiltrate the secret mountain hideout of the bastards plotting to overthrow New Zealand. But not on his watch. *Barnes. Theo Barnes. License to thrill.*

The light from Theo's headgear cast dim shadows on the rocky walls beneath the Earth's surface. The hillside's underbelly was rust colored and damp; there was a coldness he never got used to. The fear wouldn't last long, but he couldn't help wonder if ghosts were down there.

Theo stared off into the black expanse beneath him, which, from his vantage point, was a bottomless pit. He then glanced up, focusing on the sunlight peaking in from the cave entrance. It was now a tiny point two hundred feet above, making him feel very small indeed. He finally touched down on a reinforced wood platform, and removed his rappelling gear.

Theo then grabbed an inflated rubber tube from a nearby alcove. He tossed the tube into the murky water three feet below, and dropped into the cold stream, submerged up to his nipples. He shuddered. He wriggled his toes. He took a look around. *Nope. No ghosts.*

Theo climbed onto the tube, and dropped his bum in the center hole. His hands and feet drooped over the edges. The air was cold and dank. Yet smiling and with eyes closed, he drifted comfortably in the chilled waters. "Yeh," he said. "This is the life."

The cave walls narrowed as the ceiling slanted downward so that it was less than five feet above him. He was now more than a thousand feet diagonally from the cave entrance and three hundred and fifty feet below the surface.

Theo drifted along the calming waters and into the recess of his thoughts until he found that gentle rocking he longed for, letting his awareness fade into a dream state, so that he was neither awake nor asleep—alert yet oblivious.

Weightless and peaceful, he floated quietly along the dark tunnels. The pull of the Earth's gravity comforted him, extending a connection to the spirit of all living things. It was a feeling, Theo imagined, that must have been like those nine glorious months in the womb.

And while drifting through the cave, Theo smiled again. Aware without having to look, he knew that in his subterranean world, clinging to the walls, there was life as perfect as he had ever known. He was not alone.

Chapter 4
The Five-Minute Rule

Manchester, England—Piccadilly Rail Station
Wednesday, August 31, 2005, 11:09 a.m.

Jason's impulse was to wet his pants in protest and then cry a little, but he figured there had to be a better way. Still, he flitted back and forth on his heels, peeking around strangers in the hope there would be a sign flashing: *Jason Medley. Relax. We're Here To Solve Your Problems.*

"Oh, shit. What am I gonna do? I don't even know where—"

"Where you off to, son?" Jason had his spaz attack interrupted by an older gentleman in a gray suit and tie, standing in line behind him.

"Rome. I mean, London. I mean—"

"Easy, mate. Easy. Next train to London leaves in…," Gray suit checked his watch, "…in five minutes. You can buy a ticket right here. If you hurry, you'll just make it."

Jason wanted to throw his arms around Gray suit. "Thanks so much. Thank you." He turned to the ticket clerk. "London, please. One way."

The clerk growled. "Forty-eight quid."

"Forty-eight? What's that for me? Like twenty bucks?" *And what the fuck is a quid?*

"'Ats about ninety dollars," Gray suit said.

"Ninety? That's like three days travel money! I can't afford—"

"Better hurry, son. Train's leaving the station."

Jason relinquished his VISA card, flooded by visions of having to sleep under a bridge in order to recoup some of the extra money he was forking over. Unable to stand still, he glanced at his purple T-shirt. It had a pink dinosaur decal and the lettering *Death to Smoochy.* He rubbed his hands together nervously.

"Sign," the clerk instructed.

"Where? I don't see—"

"On the sodden line, mate. The bottom."

Jason scribbled his name, shoved the ticket into his front jeans pocket, and then reached for his crotch. Moneybelt check. Because you never know. Hank told him to guard that money belt with his life. Since the pouch contained his passport, credit card, cash, traveler's checks, Eurail pass and return plane ticket, it seemed like sound advice, even coming from Hank.

Jason hauled ass, bags in tow. "London, London…" He studied the electronic message boards posted around the station. "London! Track six!" He bolted down the corridor past Track 3. Track 4. Track 5. "Six must be…" Jason scanned the entranceways. "There!" He ran down a short flight of stairs and spotted his train, which hissed, huffed and then lurched forward.

Shhhhhh!

Perhaps it would have been prudent had he waited for the next train, which, had Jason bothered to investigate, was due to leave the station less than an hour later. He didn't *have* to get to Rome that day, that week…or ever. It's not like he would have been forced to toss a salad if he changed plans. But he was tired of waiting, tired of maybe and tired of tomorrow. The weight on his back was like the weight on his life—humping around what he was told he needed without ever questioning why. Now that he had Rome in his sights, it wasn't just any destination, it was the *only* destination.

He isolated his possibilities: he could be the same old Jason, or the Jason he wanted to be. He remembered the exact two words he uttered when Hank first told him to take the trip: *I can't.* And when Hank asked him why not, Jason's impulse was to retort—short and powerful like a boxer's jab—ending the discussion, not just then, but forever. But he didn't.

Why not? It was the question fundamental to his stunted evolution. *Why not forget Lorna and flirt with the other waitresses? Why not get my own apartment rather than bitch about living at home? Why not network with established teachers? Why not why not why not?*

"I don't know," he told Hank, and with that admission, it dawned on Jason that he really *didn't* know. That nothing except a knee-jerk reaction to say *no* had kept him from saying *yes.*

That a prolonged habit of denying his desire was a sabotage of his own design. He was a card-carrying NO person being challenged with YES.

Believing there must be a way to bridge the divide between his two inner selves—poised and confident Jason; rattled and intimidated Jason—he looked at the train before him and knew that he had a choice to make. He could give in or go for it. Time was up.

Shhhhhh!

Dashing frantically, Jason threw his arms out, and leapt— short in distance but enormous in stature. His hand grasped a metal bar, and when he landed safely, the steady, confident pull of the train smoothed him away.

"Well, God damn." His hand shook a little, but he didn't mind. He just stood there feeling connected to the train's vibrations and the breeze on his face, until finally, signifying that he was really on his way, the Manchester platform shrank from sight. Jason finally said *yes*. And it felt damn good.

The English countryside whisked by. Jason leaned his head against the window, staring at the hills and fields. At cows and horses. At shuttered houses and cobblestone walkways. Having shifted modes of transportation yet again, he longed to be on foot, to escape the confinement of planes and cars and trains. He had a desire to explore, to touch and smell and feel the outdoors, to be a part of something.

But London was two hours away, and from there he still had a long ways to go. Jason finally nodded off—it was a hard sleep—and though he was out for most of the trip, it seemed to last only minutes. He woke hungry, thirsty and in need of a shower. He had skank breath.

With London fast approaching, Jason did an inventory check, amazed at how much he'd been able to cram into his bags. As his guidebook instructed, he secured a knapsack for day-to-day sightseeing, and a rucksack for his main gear. Stuffed inside were: jeans (1 pair); shorts (2 pairs); sneakers (1 pair); boxers (10 pairs); socks (6 pairs); T-shirts (4); sweatshirt (1); towel; washcloth; rain slicker; umbrella; laundry bag; shaving kit; flashlight; batteries; Swiss army knife; camera; MP-3 player; European adapter; playing cards; and a photocopy of the front page of his passport.

Also tucked away were his address book, pens and one box of condoms (Hank suggested six). Although, Jason left his cell phone behind, reasoning that he didn't have an international plan anyway, and calling cards were just as easy, and one less thing to lose.

Jason stepped off the train, in awe. Unlike the claustrophobic hellhole that is New York's Penn Station, London's version was clean and open and encased in glass. He could see the sky. Announcements came over the loudspeaker. Commuters were full on.

Wow, he thought. *I made it.*

Rome, however, was another matter entirely. With his timetable open, Jason approached a conductor. "Excuse me. I'm going to Rome, and I see there's a connecting boat to France. How do I get there?"

The conductor nodded toward a glass doorway. "Bus to Folkestone."

"Where's that? Where do I go?"

"Over there, mate. You have about five minutes 'til it's off."

Jason checked his watch, which he kept fastened to a front belt loop. "And the bus after that?" He cringed, hoping his demeanor might somehow influence the answer in his favor. *An hour an hour an hour an hour an hour...*

The conductor adjusted his silver belt buckle. "Tomorrow."

Jason nodded patiently, thought for a minute, and then scratched the scar on the underside of his elbow. "Yep," he said. "That sounds about right." And with the acceptance that a meal and a piss would simply have to wait, he begrudgingly sprinted through the open-air corridor, hoping to make his next connection in time.

Chapter 5
The Big Bang Theory

The Northern Sphere of Eternity—CBM Training Center
Milky Way's Public Unveiling: T-Minus 37 Days (Eternity
Standard Time)

Donald may have kept his cool, as he was an optimist by nature, but there was no getting around that he and his wife were in deep, murky puddles of cosmic excrement.

With the Universe in a constant state of upgrade and repair, he knew that any damage resulting from the missing jar wouldn't affect Eternitarians on a day-to-day level—they didn't live *in* the Universe; they only worked on it. But the poor bastard responsible for such a mess? Yikes. Not good.

As Eternitarians, Donald and Danielle existed on a plane outside the constraints of the metaphysical Universe, in a sphere of possibility not reachable by scientific methods. There is no such planet called Eternity. There is no galaxy. There is no solar system.

Eternity is a realm made real only by being in it. But to those outside Eternity it appears as nothing more than a glimmer, a possibility, a dream…a sense in those unknown parts of the mind and soul that there just might be something out there beyond us—a feeling with no label. It is not magic; it is more than hope. Eternity is that call to reach beyond ourselves, to become more than we are or think we can be.

And yet Eternitarians don't concern themselves with the plight of non-Eternitarians. If they sat around worrying about all the creatures of the metaphysical Universe, they'd never get anything done. Eternitarians have their own problems. Most have occupations fulfilling the needs of their everyday lives—bankers, teachers, cab drivers and the like—but they almost all support Eternity's leading industry: Universe Design, Maintenance and Expansion, or UDME.

The Big MOU had never divulged the reasons behind such extensive development of the Universe outside Eternity, as the hours are long and the payoff debatable. But planets, galaxies, solar systems, stars and other cosmic debris don't simply appear. There was no Big Bang. There was no *poof!*

They are commissioned, designed, approved and constructed—some more successfully than others. The planning stages often drag on and on, but once a project gets green-lit, immediate progress is expected.

Donald and Danielle, like all project development teams authorized to work on specific parts of the Universe, were assigned a specific jar of CBM. Each jar is engraved, the symbols denoting the particular elemental base of CBM contained within. No two batches are exactly alike. One project, one batch of CBM.

Donald thought back to that first day on the job, when Lawrence, the CBM warehouse manager, gave him a personal walk-through of the facility.

"We certainly have some space in here," Lawrence said, "but the system is really quite sophisticated. Don't worry. I'm sure… ahem-ahem…you won't screw up." He looked Donald over. "Your qualifications are…well…I'm sure you'll find your way."

Inventory, Lawrence explained, is tracked through a standardized bar coding system, with each jar stored in its designated slot on the shelving unit, one that extends the equivalent of 4,113 Earth miles in length and 74 Earth miles high, about average for a warehouse in Eternity.

"The Universe is a considerably large canvas," Lawrence said, "and The Big MOU likes to experiment. But then, you already know that."

Donald was not the paranoid type, but it was difficult not to notice that Lawrence was giving him the stink-eye something ferocious.

Lawrence further explained that outside the CBM warehouse, the jars were indestructible. Moreover, they did not respond to light, pressure, temperature, gravity or any of the other 96 basic forces known in the metaphysical Universe outside the realm of Eternity.

"And there is no way to open these," he explained, yanking on the lid, "except with this." Lawrence handed Donald a specially coded high-frequency harmonic key, shaped like a stick of gum still in the wrapping. Blowing into the harmonic key produced an ascending, and then descending, series of notes, sounding like clicks from a calypso bell, only squeakier.

"Each jar gets its own harmonic key," Lawrence said. "You wear it around your neck at all times. Don't take it off. At the beginning of your shift you pick up the jar," he said as if Donald had been dropped on his head and needed instructions repeated to him slowly, "and the key," which Lawrence also held up, "and return both at the end of your shift. Pick them up, bring them back. Think you can handle that?"

Of course, Donald had said, no problem at all. Pick them up, bring them back. Don't take it off. The instructions seem simple enough. Donald smiled when he spoke.

Lawrence rolled his eyes. "Yes, well...my ex-wife said the same thing when she signed the divorce papers. She suspected I was gay when we got married. It's just like her to believe she can have everything her way if she just wills it so. But then, I let her try, so I guess that's my bad. She can be quite persuasive. But me with boobies? Mmm...not so much." Lawrence shook his head. "Sometimes," he said, moving closer, "we do really foolish things and then try to hide from them, even though they stare us right...in...the face."

Donald stopped smiling.

Initially, Donald and Danielle hoped their missing jar of CBM—the Universe's DNA—would just turn up, or else the problem would go away on its own. But when neither miracle fell in their laps, Donald knew they had to make a decision, and they had to make it fast.

Inventory inspectors were due for their regular CBM warehouse audit, and if they were to find even one jar missing, it would be bad news for everyone. Donald didn't even want to think about what would happen if, somehow, some way, that jar actually cracked open on Earth. It would be a real mess. "Yep," he muttered to himself. "We are most definitely fucked."

Chapter 6
Cold Drinks on a Hot, Hot Day

Yuma, Arizona—The Desert Back Roads
Wednesday, August 17, 2005, 1:54 p.m.

Underneath a hazy sky, Emma sipped lemonade, made the way it was intended: cold, satisfying and utterly disgusting.

Lex, a brown Labrador, lay in the pool of Emma's ever expanding shade, lazily tossing his tail about this way and that, and wondering how much longer he would have to remain a dog.

"Hey, boy." Emma wiped the tart residue from her lip. "What would you say to a couple of steaks and a couple of cold Buds?"

Paws beneath his chin, Lex answered in his usual aloof manner. "Woof...fucking...woof."

And with equal aloofness, Emma shaded her eyes from the blistering Arizona sun, then took another sip. "Yeah," she said. "Me too."

Relentless and punishing, the raging fireball above had just winked at her, Emma was sure, a reminder that her present situation was not of her choosing and not hers to choose. But if she wanted to change her destiny, go right ahead. Give it your best shot.

Emma had contracted the sun, *that* sun. Her signature was on the order form. She had copies in her office. In triplicate. The original blueprint called for three smaller suns, and, if you could stomach it, four moons. *Four.* But what did she expect?

All those teenybitcher designers with their tight asses, silk thongs and overglossed lips, sticking their tits out like that meant something, groping to get their *style* in the papers. To make a name for themselves. A brand. Not one to shy away from stardom herself, Emma was all for making a mark, a lasting impression. But three suns? Back then? Please.

And this is the thanks I get for keeping the wannabes in check. For

reminding investors what a real galactic designer is all about—that
substance makes the style, not the other way around. For designing an
atmosphere emphasizing class and possibility, a galaxy built to last. The
Milky Way. You sell the sizzle, sure. But you have to give them the steak.

Emma curled her pudgy arm, raising the cool glass to her
forehead. A rusted Winnebago sat motionless behind them like
the barely functioning piece of crap that it was.

"The big bastard sure has a sense of humor all right." Emma
shifted in her chair, giving herself a wedgie. With some not
inconsiderable maneuvering, she dislodged the yellow, flowered
housedress, which tugged at her throat. "Yuma, Arizona. The
garden spot of Suck-Ass, U.S.A. I got bad knees, bad B.O. and
my gums hurt. I used to be hot. Way hot."

"Your breath could use some work..."

"Oh, go lick your balls."

Lex rolled his eyes.

"One hundred and seven degrees," Emma said. "One-oh-
seven." She shook her head, and then set the empty glass on the
white, plastic table. She reached for her walking stick. The former tree branch nearly snapped under the stupendous weight it
was now supporting.

As usual, business at her roadside stop had been slow. There
are only so many rattlesnake hides and coyote skulls you can
sell in a week. A month. After almost two years in the desert—
two long Earth years—Emma figured there wasn't much left to
understand about being stuck in the middle of nowhere.

And while she could appreciate the cosmic irony of being
banished to this very planet, she had no idea why it had been
at this particular point in its history, when any other had been
equally plausible. Emma concluded that there was either no
rhyme or reason at all, or else a very specific reason indeed. She
still hadn't figured out which.

"Let's get inside, see if we can get that fan working. We
should be getting the call any time now. Angelique has a lead
on that fucking jar. *My* jar. Our ticket out of this dump." Emma
accidentally kicked the table on its side, knocking the glass
before Lex, who let out a *woomph*. His chin never left his paws.

"And believe me," Emma said, "when I find the numb-nuts

who's got it, he's going to discover long, slow and hard just what the end of the world is all about."

Sizzling ground chuck seared against the pan as the burner spouted a blue flame. Emma hung up the phone. "Angelique says a skinny, white bastard with a chirpy accent came in an hour ago. Looks like he's the one. He's got the jar."

Lex was curled on the Winnebago's plaid couch, snug against the wall. He nibbled the end of his tail. "Sweet. It's about time."

Emma grabbed the plastic spatula, and fueled by an urgent, erotic rage, leaned into it with all her might. Her small, pink nipples hardened at the thought of the crumbling chuck crying out in agony, begging for mercy while she punished it for winding up in such a precarious situation. For being a victim. For being weak.

Emma clamped her lips together. "Yes, indeed." Her rotund face trembled purple with insidious delight. Her eyes bulged. "Yes, in...deed."

Boiling grease splattered on her housedress as Emma thought back to that day in Eternity, at the gates of Titan Hall, the media capital of the Southern Sphere. She was there to announce her landmark deal—three new galaxies of her design—but also to unveil her recently completed Milky Way galaxy. And her arrival as a star.

Titan Hall was a rectangular marble building marked by four fluted columns in front. Leading up to Titan Hall on both sides was a stupendous marble staircase, curved along its wide edges and narrowing to a stage at the top. Between the staircases was a lush, green lawn.

Centered in the lawn was Titan Lake, a sparkling blue body of water, from which large bubbles emanated, releasing wisps of an opiate-based gas. There were many visitors. Twice each day, at dusk and dawn, a school of dolphins leapt from the lake in graceful arcs, splashing down in the lake, releasing a flurry of the pleasure-inducing bubbles.

Given the inherent nature of Eternity, the sky rotated through each nuanced tint of the spectrum once per day, the changes imperceptible by the second, but noticeable by the hour. At the time, it was aquamarine, just beginning its fade into yellow. The air carried a faint lemony base. And though the physical temperature hadn't changed, there was a feeling that the morning had grown warmer.

Standing on the platform overlooking Titan Lake, the publishers of *Top Galaxy Design*, *Cosmic Designer Digest* and *Galactic Fabric Review* had all begged could Emma please please please grant them an exclusive interview following the press conference? Just five minutes alone with the blue-eyed, raven-haired beauty that single-handedly revolutionized the art of galaxy design, including the yet-to-be-seen Milky Way. The galaxy we're all dying to see. The reason we're here.

"Even after the Blue-Bubble Nebula and the twin moons of Dimitri Minor," the reporters asked that morning, "how did you land the Milky Way and a three-galaxy contract extension? It's unheard of."

The Blue-Bubble Nebula was inspired, for sure. The massive cloud of gases was shaped like an eye deep in the cosmos, with its black pupil, indigo iris and magenta flecks around the outer edges—a nod to the Andromeda galaxy, yet mesmerizing on its own merits.

But the Milky Way? Wait 'til they get a look at this baby.

"If you're dying to know," Emma began, "and I know that you are, I can tell you this: It helps when you're simply the best. Not that the so-called *competition*," she said, making quote marks with her fingers, "makes that distinction particularly meaningful."

Emma smirked and then fanned her eyes as a dozen comets tore across the heavens like a salute to her glory. The crowd responded to Emma's effrontery with a mixture of *oohs*, *aahs* and coy laughter. They clapped.

"Besides." She placed her hands on her hips and tossed a wink to the cameras. "I'm the hottest piece of ass in the business…and everybody wants a slice. You can quote me on that."

But that was when Emma was still glamorous, svelte and fabulous. When she was the queen of galaxy design, when her place in history could not be denied. Before she made one lapse in judgment. Before she was banished to the back roads of Arizona, sentenced to a body—a flesh and blood prison—unworthy of her beauty, talent and pizzazz.

Lex yawned and let out another *woomph*. His floppy pink tongue dangled over the ridges of his teeth. "So the jar's in Amsterdam. Red Light District. Nice."

Emma cranked the rusted, iron handle above the sink—overrun with unwashed dishes— and opened a small, rectangular window. The beef-flavored smoke escaped.

"No. He's on his way to Venice. The sap." Emma ran a towel under the faucet, and then rubbed at the splatters on her frock. "Chirpy's one of those backpacking morons. Angelique is e-mailing us a picture. We'll have to drive into town. They have one of those cyber cafés. What's wrong with these nitwits? Why isn't the whole planet synced for free?" She shook her head. "They're fucking Neanderthals."

Still adjusting to a canine existence, Lex lifted his hind leg and scratched at his ear. "You believe her? I always get the feeling Angie's holding back. Like she's hiding behind that makeup in more ways than one."

"Yeah, I know." Emma drained the grease into an old Folgers can. She looked out to the desert. "Angelique's no gem, but she's a drag queen with a dream, and I'm the one doling out the wishes."

Chapter 7
My God, It's Full of Stars

They glowed.

Slinky, fingernail-sized creatures lived among the rocky surface. They illuminated the otherwise lightless underground passage in a fluorescent barrage, like billions of stars against a distant sky. Theo chuckled as a single glow-worm, clutched to the ceiling, threaded down a thin strand of web. "Devious little fuckers, aren't you?"

According to Theo's trainers, the glow-worms had lived down there for millions of years. The tiny creatures attract with their body light hordes of unsuspecting insects that become caught in dangling webs, winding up, literally, as worm food.

Theo paddled with his hands, maneuvering the windy passageway. The living, glowing flecks around him formed thousands of constellations along the ceiling and walls. One cluster of glow-worms connected into a fin. "Oh, big fish," he said, although to an ear unaccustomed to New Zealand dialects, *fish* sounded like *fush*.

Theo leaned back. Reclined, he noticed along the ceiling what looked like a long, green arrow. Curving left, it disappeared around the next bend. He leaned to follow it, but as his weight shifted, the tube shot out from underneath him and landed several feet away, leaving Theo facedown in the water. A mouthful channeled down his gullet.

Theo coughed and wheezed as the cold air and water tore at his chest. He splashed about, finally regaining his composure. He leaned against the moss-covered wall. "Fuckin' hell." His hard hat bobbed away from him. He felt one of his watertight boots coming loose.

Leaning over to adjust the strap, he slipped, once again

ending up facedown in the water, coughing and hacking, only this time with greater impetus and fervor. He shouted various curse words between gasps. Propelled by his thrashing about, his hardhat and inner tube bobbed deeper into the cave. He waded after them, but after a few steps, set foot on an unstable surface, sending him on a third and final plunge.

In a fit of anger, Theo reached down to show the troublesome rubble just who was boss. Only when he stuck his hand below the surface and removed it, he did not come up with the rock. Instead he clung to a pear-shaped jar with a flat bottom, in wet if not pristine condition.

Theo finally caught up to his hardhat. He placed it back on his head, and then turned on the miner's light. He offered a look of befuddlement. "What the...?"

The jar was unusually light for a container its size, no heavier than a potato. Even more peculiar was its surface—silver like a mirror, yet offering no reflection whatsoever. If he didn't know better, Theo would have sworn that somebody digitally removed all the objects—his face, hard hat, the cave walls—that should have been reflected back. Either that or he was a vampire. Left only was the perception of dimension, an empty space. He just couldn't figure it.

Fixed atop the jar was a circular lid. It would not come off. Along the flat underside of the jar was a series of grooves. They were symbols, Theo guessed, though none he recognized. He ran his fingers over them. He started to feel woozy and disoriented just then, as if he had been drugged without him knowing it, which in a way, is exactly what happened.

There was a blast of white light. There were streaks of screaming fluorescent color. There was the sensation of being sucked through a tornado. And then there were stars. Lots and lots of stars.

Theo felt himself drawn beyond the glass edge, sucked through the surface. He felt like he had been swallowed by the Universe itself, zooming across a galaxy of everything that existed everywhere and yet nothing at all. He soared with a bewildering warmth and familiarity, as if his spirit had been set free to roam the infinite landscape of forever.

He hurtled through the expanse, rocketing beyond the boundaries of time and space and dimension. Theo was enthralled, his senses simultaneously electric and soothing. His propulsion through the fabric of existence exceeded even his wildest sense of dream. Theo wasn't sure if he had tapped into a spirit world beyond life or death, consciousness or pharmacopoeia, when on the periphery of his awareness he heard a distant mumble. Again he felt woozy and disoriented.

"Wrrr-wrrr wrrah wrrooo?"

There was a blast of white light. There were streaks of screaming fluorescent color. There was the sensation of being sucked through a tornado. And then there were glow-worms. Lots and lots of glow-worms.

Theo was confused and weak in the knees, but returned to the darkness of the Waitomo Caves. He heard the noise again. "Theo, is that you? It's me, Lea. I got Hal with me, yeh?"

"Uh, yeh, yeh," Theo said. "Just me."

Lea floated on an inner tube. She also was in a wetsuit and hardhat. "Theo. You're gonna get busted, yeh? You keep coming down here alone. You parked your truck outside."

Lea was Theo's supervisor and sometimes girlfriend, a relationship that suited them both, except when Theo wanted to be unencumbered, which was often. Lea was surprisingly strong for having such a petite frame, and though Theo never told her so, he took a certain comfort in how her smaller curves seemed to fit into his more awkward frame just so.

Hal was a big ox of a friend. "What's you got there, mate? You're not taking any glowies back are you? Do a little smoke and watch 'em bug you out? Get it? *Bug* you out?"

Theo was oblivious to Hal's humor. "Huh? Oh, no. It's nothing." He directed his miner's light at the jar, at his mates, then back at the jar, which remained a mystery. Theo dropped it into his backpack. "Let's get a feed. I'm starving."

Chapter 8
Where's the Fire?

Waitomo, New Zealand—The Off-Road Motel
Tuesday, February 22, 2005, 6:07 p.m.

Naked and face up on the bed, Theo thrust his pelvis once, twice and then thrice. He felt woozy and disoriented. There was a blast of white light. There were streaks of screaming fluorescent color. There was the sensation of being sucked through a tornado. And then there was pleasure. Lots and lots of pleasure.

Lea screamed with violent exaltation, writhing atop Theo's midsection, leaning forward while grabbing the headboard. The setting New Zealand sun jutted in through the curtained window of his rented, second-floor room overlooking the parking lot. Soggy clothes were strewn about the floor.

"Oh, god." Lea extended upright and pulled at her pointed breasts. "I'm on fire!"

With each carnal hump, Theo felt himself rocketing across the white expanse. Eyes shut, he pawed at Lea's sweaty thighs, digging his fingertips into her flesh.

Theo didn't love Lea, but he cared about her, wished her a pleasant life, albeit one that would almost certainly unfold without him. But while penetrating her, Theo started to wonder if there wasn't more to his sex partner than he had ever given her credit for, revealing a passion he never realized. Yet somehow he knew that his unprecedented level of ecstasy—an intensity he was unsure his physical body could sustain—was not an extension either of himself or Lea, but the result of some external force.

He knew they were passengers only, on a spectacular ride for sure, but journeying down a path over which neither had any control. Careening along the blurred, streaking inroads deep into consciousness, Theo felt his body peel away.

Is this my spirit? Is this the pure me?

The color spectrum engulfed him, into infinity. Feeling resistance against what should have been his face, his spirit accelerated through the limitless immensity.

Theo reached around Lea's gyrating waist and grabbed her small, white ass, one cheek in each hand. He pulled her forward, and with one final undulation, arched his back. With the great release, Theo fell into the mattress. He felt as if he had experienced more than a physical climax, but an orgasm of the spirit—as if his very essence had ejaculated.

There was a blast of white light. There were streaks of screaming fluorescent color. There was the sensation of being sucked through a tornado. And then there was sweat. Lots and lots of sweat.

The exhausted lovers were naked. Lea was on top of Theo, her hair ragged and sweaty. Her sticky, white bum obscured Theo's spent noodle. The sheets were soaked and torn from the bed. The headboard was cracked. Lea sighed her hot, limp breath. "That was...I'm just..."

With the little energy he could muster, Theo nodded in agreement. It was then that the door to his rental unit came crashing down.

Hal panted, wielding a heavy, metal smashing tool. "Everybody okay? I heard somebody yell *fire*. I took the ax from your truck." He then offered an embarrassed grin, letting the head of the ax swing toward the floor. "Oh. Fire. I get it. I heard the screams..."

Theo brushed Lea's hair from his face. "No worries, mate." He was nearly out of breath. "Now fuck off will ya? I gotta sleep."

Chapter 9
The Brigsby Effect

The Eastern Sphere of Eternity—Horizon Terrace
Milky Way's Public Unveiling: T-Minus 36 Days (Eternity
Standard Time)

"Are you outta your mind, muthafucka?" Danielle pointed at Donald. "Fuck that shit. I ain't goin' nowhere."

After nineteen months on the waiting list, since before they were even married, Danielle was not about to leave their two-bedroom condo in Horizon Terrace now that she was settled in. No fucking way.

Horizon Terrace was considered *the* upscale apartment complex on the Eastern Sphere of Eternity, the only region offering unobstructed views of the Andromeda galaxy and the comets that spiraled through its center.

When they moved in, Danielle had plush carpeting installed throughout the apartment and ordered a glass coffee table to complement the tiger-striped sectional. But what she bragged to her friends about most was the six-foot grapefruit tree, complimentary to all new owners, blooming out on the balcony.

"Danielle. Honey." Donald offered a smile. Sunshine beamed through the sliding glass door on the 491st floor, just 717 floors below the penthouse. "I know it's not optimal, but—"

"Optimal? Optimal? What the fuck you mean, optimal?" Danielle threw her hands up as she paced along the leopard-spotted carpet. The multicolored beads in her hair clacked. "I can't, I can't. I just can't."

Donald and Danielle moved from Industrial Row, leaving behind their dark, cold, one-bedroom basement apartment with leaky faucets, cockroaches and view of a brick wall with the permanent urine stain.

They had been able to obtain and afford their new abode thanks only to Brigsby himself. The host of *Breakfast with*

Brigsby—the top-rated daytime talk show—was an old friend of Donald, and a Horizon Terrace board member. Brigsby owed Donald a favor, and so he arranged for a friendly purchase price when a unit suddenly became available in the sold-out building. But Danielle didn't trust Brigsby. She had issues with Brigsby.

Four inches taller than his bride, Donald was a white pear of a man, oddly thick in the middle, but not fat, with strong arms that almost, but not quite, seemed too short for his body. He took small, cautious steps toward her. "Look, sweetie...I know you love it here. So do I. There's no place I'd rather be than right here, in this apartment, with you." Danielle watched her husband brace for the outburst he likely assumed was coming. "See, the way I'm thinking about it is...we're going to find the jar, we're going to bring it back, and then we're out of this racket. We're not cut out for this kind of work. You know that, I know that. Heck." Donald smiled. "I'm pretty sure they know that."

Donald and Danielle first met at the Galactic Particle Plant, or GPP, where Donald was the shipping supervisor and Danielle was an administrative assistant in his office. But in order to justify their residence at Horizon Terrace, Brigsby had a friend six times removed hire them as junior-level engineers, prestigious positions that came with a significant upgrade in pay and social status indeed.

They would never become Grade-1 galaxy designers—they knew that—but the chance to manufacture landscapes and some life forms, at least in theory, beat office and warehouse work any day of the week. Especially with the way things were going at GPP.

But the first major planet they were assigned to—Earth—was posing more trouble than they anticipated. Not only was the galaxy designer a real piece of work, but The Big MOU was particularly interested in the final product.

Danielle took in her husband. Bright solar light brimmed along his edges. His smooth, white pate glimmered like the eyes of a saint. *I'm a lucky woman,* she said to herself. *I know that.* She composed herself, collected her thoughts. *Just so damn lucky.* She heard every word he said, and knew just how to respond. "Eat shit, muthafucka! I'm stayin' home."

Several afternoons later, after Danielle locked herself in the bathroom threatening never to come out, Donald finally made some progress.

"Honey, really, let's think it through. The inspectors are coming next month, so we know they're going to find out. Okay, fine. But a month up here is like a *billion years* down there. We'll have all the time we need."

There was silence, save for some gentle tapping. Donald assumed Danielle was clinking her heart-shaped perfume bottle against the zebra-striped vanity top.

"Possibly," she said from her side of the door. "Possibly."

Donald nodded at the first sign of Danielle's weakening resolve. "Plus...every moment in the Universe exists at all times, like a calendar that goes back and forth. You know that. We just have to choose which moment we want...and then show up. And with the key as a locator...," he reached for the silver harmonic tab that hung from his neck, "...it shouldn't be *that* hard to find. More or less."

Danielle rebutted. "But we go down there, we're on their time, too. Their turf, their rules. We get old like them, sick like them. *Die* like them. Hell! We have to be in their bodies n' shit. What if I get all fat eatin' their crap-ass food? Are you gonna just leave me down there?"

Donald often felt guilty about his inability to erase any misgivings Danielle had about her looks, as if it were actually within his power to do so. Channeling his love, he pressed his open palm against the closed bathroom door as if it were the contour of her cheek. "Listen, Honey. I know you're scared. But we've got some vacation time coming. So we'll just take it earlier than we thought. We'll go down to Earth, we'll find the jar, then we'll come right back. It'll be like we never left. Really."

And even though he was forty-three, and nine years Danielle's senior, Donald often felt that being older—on a cosmic scale—than most planets outside the realm of Eternity was inconsequential to how young and stupid he could feel when his wife was upset with him.

Danielle answered in her soft, baby-talk voice. "You sure?"

"Absolutely. We'll be back in no time."

"Really? A hugsy-wugsy promise?"

Donald nodded. "Yes, Baby. A hugsy-wugsy promise."

There was silence. Donald was struck by Danielle's sudden calm.

"And if we don't find the jar, The Big MOU won't turn me to no slug, right? That's what you said? No slugs?"

Donald dropped his shoulders, and sighed. He had another tough sell on his hands. "*With* the jar it's a return trip," he said assuredly, although he had no idea what would become of them even if they *did* manage to find it. But he was assuming the best. "No problem. We just activate the bar code and it'll send us right home."

Donald was repeating what he read in the employee handbook, but since there were no documented cases of successful returns, theory was all he had. He also knew that the problems they faced were compounded by the rules governing the Universe, and Earth specifically, which were different from the rules governing Eternity. Traveling on Earth was subject to the physical limitations of its inhabitants.

Standard public transportation—including but not limited to buses, trains, cabs, and sea and air ferries—was readily available within each of the Nine Spheres of Eternity. But the cities, complexes, oceans and mountain ranges did not all physically connect. Rather, the nine spheres eventually drifted into Infinity—an all-encompassing cloud with no discernable top or bottom, beginning or end.

To travel from one Sphere of Eternity to another, you had merely to enter the limitless ether of Infinity, and think yourself—to let your feelings dictate a path—to your destination. You could walk, or even drive your car along the highway into Infinity, in your mind's eye see where you wanted to end up, and without incident, simply arrive where you needed to be.

Eternity listened to you.

Traveling in this fashion—traversing the limitless ether of Infinity—was no more unusual to Eternitarians than it was for people on Earth to step into an elevator on one floor and get off on another. Eternitarians left the mechanics to The Big MOU.

Donald took a deep breath. He clenched his teeth. The next part would be tricky. "But if we leave the complex unauthorized and *don't* find the jar, we're stuck down there. On Earth. For good. That jar's our only ticket back. Says so right in the manual."

There was a long pause. "Okay," Danielle said finally. "I understand."

Donald was confused by his wife's unexpected poise. "Are you sure?"

"Yes, Baby. I'm fine now."

Donald heard his wife open and then close the medicine cabinet. And if he knew Danielle as well as he thought, she faced the mirror, applied a powdered pad to her nose, staring blankly at her reflection. It was her early stage of denial. She didn't do well with bad news.

*Anger...Fear...Silence...Powder...*Donald then heard his wife gasp, snort, and with a thud, pass out....*Collapse.*

"Danny...you okay in there?" Donald knocked repeatedly. "Sweetie?"

Using the good butter knife to jiggle the door open, he found Danielle sprawled out on the floor, her left foot in the bathtub. He leaned over to check on his wife. She was all right.

Donald sat on the closed toilet seat. He examined the bent knife, a wedding gift from his mother-in-law. He tried to force it back into its normal shape. "Damn. I'm never going to hear the end of this."

And while waiting for Danielle to wake up, Donald wondered if a life on Earth wouldn't be quite as bad as he imagined.

Chapter 10
Who the Fuck Is Alice?

Amsterdam, The Netherlands—The Ball and Tickle
Thursday, August 18, 2005, 2:29 a.m.

Angelique was draped in a black sequined gown with a slit up the right leg. Black pumps were like vices against her feet. Her wig had long black curls. She sat before a mounted mirror with globed lights around the edges. She stared at her reflection, and rubbed peach body lotion into her forearms. A mustached lip grazed the back of her neck.

"Always with the naughty-naughty," she said in Dutch. Angelique smiled at Andre, her bare-chested lover dressed in black leather, including chaps, vest, boots and beret. A silver hoop pierced his right nipple. "Be a gem and get me a seltzer? I need to strap on my garter before I go on." Angelique winked into the mirror. "Maybe you can unhook it for me later."

Andre opened the door of the back-room office and disappeared into the *Ball and Tickle*. Orange and green neon signs provided the brick tavern's only illumination, with messages such as *Wet Lips*, *Tug My Nugget*, and *Ball and Tickle*.

The crowd guzzled Belgian ales, puffed on German cigarettes, and riding the appropriate cues, shouted the chorus to their favorite polka pub song blasting through the overhead speakers: *Who the Fuck is Alice?*

Taking a short reprieve before her second set began, Angelique closed the door, encasing herself in silence. She billed her weekly performance as a one-woman cabaret, and though she recited more so than sang, rarely was there an empty seat in the house. "Where else," she began each show, infusing a French accent upon her sexiest, deep-throated Dutch, "can you have your tits and balls under one garment and be cheered for them at the same time?"

Despite her outward public persona, however, Angelique was

discrete in private, when he went by George, his given name.

George owned a small, respectable art gallery across town, but he was best known among the locals as a facilitator, a liaison. He was people who knew people, if he were the type to speak of himself as such, which, when George, he was not. Blessed with a quiet confidence, facilitating acquaintances was easy enough. The true skill, George discovered, came in knowing when and where to introduce one party to another.

Selectivity was key. Some people were better off never meeting, a lesson he learned the hard way. Tailors, lawyers, artists. Line cooks, drug dealers, garbage collectors. Politicians. A pawnshop owner, a pharmacist. Bartenders, warehouse managers, prostitutes. Street cleaners, pastry clerks. George knew all kinds.

Yet they all had a common agenda: to satisfy their particular lusts and desires—the deep, dark longings revealed only under the most intimate of circumstances.

On Earth, George helped facilitate the process. What he got out of introductions, he said, was the betterment of others. What he actually got out of them was something else entirely. And since the people on this new planet looked and behaved much like those he knew from Eternity, he saw no reason to change. It was what he did best.

Before his banishment, George heard the rumors.

Eternitarians impudently denied even the slightest similarity between themselves and the Earth cretins, physical appearance being the only exception. The people trudging along the Earth were said to evolve painfully slow and possess only the most petty and selfish instincts. Worst of all, they seemed insistent not only to repeat their mistakes no matter how many generations were afforded the opportunity to make adjustments, but also to increase the depth and breadth of the blunders.

Conventional wisdom held that littering the metaphysical Universe with humans, or pseudo-Eternitarians, or pseudo-Es, or PEs—considered the origin of the word *peon*—would be a colossal waste of time. Along the cosmic scale, PEs were considered by Eternitarians to be a slug-like, unorganized bunch, and not expected to last.

And yet tales circulated that The Minder of the Universe, otherwise known as The Big MOU, had larger plans for PEs. Some had them eventually developing the technological means to travel the Universe in search of new inhabitable planets, seeing as they were on a clear course to overpopulate and devour their own.

Other versions had PEs developing telepathy, only to destroy themselves soon thereafter in a heated battle of *I can read your mind faster than you can read mine, so nyeh.*

But the most troubling incarnation was that PEs were not actually peons at all. Rather, this edition had The Big MOU ingraining PEs with the innate possibility of elevating themselves beyond even Eternitarians—if they lasted long enough to evolve, and were able to forgo material trappings for an existence far more spiritual.

Eternitarians dismissed any such talk—they were the ones populating Eternity, thank you very much—but when it came to The Big MOU, nobody really knew anything for sure.

And the single-sun galaxy projects would mean a plethora of new jobs and craters-full of available funds ripe for the pilfering, so those who had influence over such matters were only happy to oblige. If The Big MOU wanted to indulge his whimsy by experimenting with peons, indulge away. The more the merrier.

On Earth, George had been allowed to retain much of his previous form, a rarity among the banished. At no other time had it helped more to know people. When you were sent into exile, you were all but guaranteed a new form you would find to your utter dissatisfaction, each case of remodeling, of course, dependent upon the individual. The more extreme banishment came in the form of redistribution.

Reduced to your base elements, scattered throughout Eternity and then soaked into the cosmic fabric, reappearing somewhere, sometime—a part of everything, and yet the whole of nothing. Complete identity disintegration.

After converting Eternity measures to those governing Earth, George was only five feet, five inches, with the facial features of a forty-one-year-old Taiwanese man. He wore his straight black hair with a swoop in the front, highlighted with slight blonde streaks. He looked a decade younger than he was, although the hint of weariness behind his eyes suggested an undercoating of heavy mileage. Just how much mileage, however, was far beyond what anyone on Earth was likely to comprehend.

What most endeared George to people was that he was an attentive listener, although he was equally adept at leading a conversation in the direction he most wanted it to go. And yet for the countless secrets and burdens others shared with George, he wanted others to know as little about him as possible.

If George knew anything about secrets, it was that the more you talked about them, the more diluted they became, until that vital element of your personality dissolved into a distant memory. And George didn't want to let go of his secret. He would have been lost without it.

Yet when assuming the Angelique persona, she often told people that she was a caramel-colored goddess. When you're fabulous you should *mm-mm shout it, tout it and flaunt about it. Tss!* Angelique was a sharer, and the best thing Angelique had to share was...Angelique.

George removed a laptop computer from the top drawer of the makeup counter. While assuming the George persona, an opportunity presented itself, just as he figured it would. He had a plan for getting back home, to Eternity. An image appeared in the upper right corner of the screen. Underneath the image was a name: Theo Barnes.

But feeling more comfortable as Angelique during these communications, she contacted Emma earlier that morning. Angelique started a new e-mail now, attached a digital photograph of Theo, and keyed in directions:

Em—

This is the one with the jar. Should arrive Venice two
weeks. Send the girl. He's ripe for the plucking.
—Angie

p.s. Say hi to Lex. Love his big balls.

Chapter 11
Number Nine

Paris, France—The Downtown Subway
Wednesday, August 31, 2005, 10:46 p.m.

Panic. Jason was becoming well acquainted with it. After the London bus to Folkestone and then the hovercraft across the English channel, he barely made his connecting train from Boulogne-sur-Mer to Paris. The Medley logic in full force, Jason decided it was *the* train to Paris, which would drop him off within feet of his connection to Rome. He would simply get off on one track, walk across the platform and board a new train on the opposite track. That his train schedule said otherwise was another matter.

After rectifying his train blunder, Jason switched to the subway—a French teenager with long hair used a particular finger to direct him. But for reasons Jason could not quite indentify, he only took the subway as far as the *Gare d' Austerlitz* stop, when he needed to be at *Station de Lyon*. Despite its regard as one of the most efficient, easiest-to-navigate in the world, the Paris underground system simply baffled him. He finally jumped in a cab instead, and with a lack of nuance, announced to the driver where he wanted to go—and when the trip should begin.

Jason was unimpressed with the cabbie, who tried playing it all tough and cool, smoking away on a stinky brown cigarette, like he had all the time in the world, when obviously there were important matters that needed immediate resolution. But Jason showed him what was what. A fat wad of bills put the insolent a-hole in his place, oh, yes, it sure did. Although, Jason was a bit surprised at just how quick the trip from the station where he started—to the station where he ended up—turned out to be. He tried not to consider the possibility that he had just paid ten times what the trip should have cost.

Besides, he couldn't even understand the money. He'd had

to convert American dollars to British pounds when he first arrived in Manchester, and then convert the British pounds to Euros, the currency in Europe, except, of course, in Britain, which rebuffed the Euro on principle. But how many Euros to a British pound to an American dollar, he couldn't even compute.

And all he'd eaten by then was a heavily mayonnaised roll with what was advertised as bacon, but was in fact pure bacon *fat.* So he had that going for him.

But now that he was so close to finding his train to Rome, Jason only had minutes left to actually board it. Posted on an overhead message board was a row of horizontal slats. The fifth slat from the top read: *22:56: Roma: Track 9.*

Two dozen trains lay in wait beneath the cool night sky. People people people were going this way and that, with brief-cases and rucksacks and suitcases, all headed somewhere.

Jason had decided that Rome would be his initial destination, and though he would come to acknowledge that he just as easily could have stayed in Paris, or gone to Amsterdam, Berlin or any other city, getting to Rome was the only acceptable outcome. Why? Because it *had* to be that way. That's just how he was. Hank laughed at him often for being so rigid. "Relax, Kid. Relax. Life's more fun when you let it flow. Don't force it so much. Just let things happen."

Let it happen? Sorry, dude. No time for that now. I gotta make it happen.

Jason sought out Track 9. Each platform had a signpost with its corresponding number. Track 2 was directly ahead. Then Track 4, Track 6. Track 8. All even numbers. He checked his watch: *10:49:04.*

Jason followed another series of platforms. Track 1, Track 3. He smiled, knowing he was close. Track 5. Getting closer. Track 7. He smiled again. *10:51:32.*

And finally he came upon his destination, hallelujah. Track 9. Except that it was empty.

"No fucking way." The arch of his back whimpered, struggling beneath the weight of his supplies. He ran to a conductor flipping through pages of a leather-bound pad. "Excuse me. Train to Rome? Did it leave?"

"Moved," he said in English, without looking up from his pad.

"Moved? You mean to a different track?"

The conductor flipped a page. Flipped again. Flipped again.

"To another track? Which track?" *10:53:11.* T-minus three minutes.

The conductor looked up. He had barbs in his eyes. "Don't know."

"But where—?"

"Don't know," the conductor repeated sternly, and then walked away.

Oh, God. This isn't happening.

Jason ran along the platforms until he came across an information booth. Two men were sitting on stools, reading the newspaper. "Excuse me. Look. Train to Rome. It was supposed to be on track nine, but it's not. Do you know which track? Do you know where it is?"

The first booth worker grumbled, and then stormed into the back room. *Slam!* The second winged his newspaper, creating a distinct barrier, preventing eye contact. Smoke floated up from behind the paper.

Great. More cigarettes. Stinky French fuckers.

"Sir! Train to Rome. It leaves in...," Jason checked his watch, "...in less than three minutes. Train to Rome. Which track? Do you know which track?"

The cigarette fucker wrinkled his paper defiantly. He turned his back to Jason.

"Excuse me, sir. *Please.* Can you help me? Train to Rome..."

Jason fantasized about jumping over the counter and clubbing the cigarette fucker with a bacon-fat baguette until the right answer popped loose, but instead the clock in his head clanged away like an ancient gong, one second at a time.

10:54:03...*Clang!*

10:54:04...*Clang!*

10:54:05...*Clang!*

The cigarette fucker looked over his shoulder. "Three," he said finally.

"Track three? That's the one to Rome?"

The cigarette fucker stormed into the back room. *Slam!*

Jason cringed at the rattling door, and then made a decision. *Fuck it. Track 3 it is.*

He sprinted along the platform, straining to see through the train windows. Compartment after compartment was filled with passengers. Not an empty seat to be found.

An awesome *clang!* echoed in his head at the tick of 10:55:27. The train was about to pull out of the station. Jason heaved his rucksack onto the next car, conceding that his wish—to be selective when it came to choosing a seat—was no longer an option.

He jumped on the stairs, but tripped over his bag, his foot caught in the straps. He dented his shin on the doorframe. *Ow! Shit!* Leg throbbing, he pulled himself up and limped along the narrow hallway. Light came in through the windows. The first compartment was full. Same with the second, the third and the fourth. He was getting anxious now, covered in a film of sweat and anxiety that soaked through his clothes. He itched in that dirty, uncomfortable way from the back of his kneecaps to the bottom of his tackle, afraid he would have to stand the entire fourteen-hour trip to Rome. When he came to the last compartment, it was marked by a small, rectangular sign. A single message was draped in shadow.

The compartment was fitted with two padded benches, facing each other. There was just enough room for six passengers, three to a bench. There was one spot available, the middle to his right. "Train to Rome?" He looked to a twentyish knockout with long black hair and a white ruffled blouse. There were dark bags under her eyes. "Sí," she said.

Jason forced his rucksack between the other bags on the overhead rack, then squeezed himself between two strangers. Six sets of interlocking knees now occupied the small common ground between the two sides.

As the train pulled away from the station, Jason drew both hands down his face. Opposite the sliding door, a shutter covered the small window. It shrouded the compartment in darkness, blocking the moonlight. The overhead light was off.

Every fiber in his body ached, and he didn't care. Rabid dogs barked within his walking boots, and he didn't care. He hadn't eaten a solid meal in nearly two days, and he didn't care. He hadn't showered in just as long, and he didn't care.

Jason was grateful just to have reached the end of one of the longest days of his life, one that spanned three nations, two oceans and thousands of miles, a day whose beginning he could no longer remember or even care to recall. He was sitting down, and would remain so for quite a long while. He reached for his crotch. Money belt check. Because you never know.

And it wasn't until after the train settled into a cruising speed that Jason finally realized what was posted outside the door: *Smoking*.

The sleep never came. Jason pinned his shoulders against the seat back so he wouldn't invade the personal space of his fellow travelers. But more than the desire for physical freedom, he sought refuge from the moldy cavern of his own mind. He wanted to feel like a whole person again, to make a connection. "Hi," he said to the guy sitting next to him.

Jason's new bud rubbed his scraggly beard, adjusted his glasses, and then swept the long hair from his face. "Uh...sí, hello, yes. You America, no?"

"Yeah, America. From New York."

"Ah! New York! Sí, sí. Antonio, Antonio." Antonio then introduced Sonja, the black-haired knockout to Jason's left, and then facing him Christi, René and Angelina, three twentyish girls, pretty and without makeup, dressed in jeans and ragged shirts, backpackers all.

The six compartment mates took turns in the bathroom, a tiny closet at the end of the car. They watched each other's belongings, a gesture for which Jason was extremely thankful.

He stood before the mirror, and cringed. His complexion was sickly yellow under the dim light; he had dark bags under his eyes. Exhausted, he could feel the seams in the railway tracks groove beneath the locomotive as it rumbled toward Rome.

...*clug-lug...clug-lug...clug-lug...*

"I look like ass," he said, and then had an *aha* moment in regard to his dinosaur T-shirt. "Nice wardrobe, stud. Way to make an impression." Despite the tight quarters, Jason managed to wash his face, brush his teeth, gargle with peppermint Listerine, and then spritz each armpit with deodorant. The spray was cool. It stung.

Perked, but not perky, Jason walked in on his Italian friends. They were using their knees as tables, sharing a box of crackers and a brick of chocolate. They passed around a water bottle.

As if slapped in the face, Jason couldn't believe his stupidity. Among his forty pounds of gear he hadn't packed the most important item of all: Food. Not a cookie, not a sandwich. No candy, no fruit, no drinks. Nothing. Not even an Altoid. *Holy shit. I'm gonna starve to death.*

He all but collapsed into the fetal position and started to cry—*I brought a fucking laundry bag, but no food; nice job, dumbass*—when Christi smiled at him. Frilly blonde hair draped over her shoulder. A cross hung from her neck. "Hungry, yes? Eat. You receive good deed, you do for someone else. Is the traveler's karma. You'll see."

It took all Jason had from hugging her senseless. *You're an angel.* But gratitude aside, the starving coyote in him was ready to rip the throats from anyone who came between him and the sesame crackers, including licking the crumbs off the cellophane wrapper. Jason surveyed the food, let out a short sigh. "Thanks," he said finally. "I could eat."

Bellies satisfied and with the overhead light switched off again, Jason and his new friends tried to sleep, a jumble of limbs strewn about. They made stops at Lyon and Modane, and as the eyelids of the morning sky began to open, they crossed the French border into Italy.

Jason looked upon his now-slumbering mates, and in his mind thanked them all for their generosity. For treating that compartment as their home, and for making him their most welcome guest. And as he thought about the days ahead, he wondered if he would meet anyone even half as nice as they were, and if he could do so without completely losing his shit along the way.

Chapter 12
Bottom of the Bag

Waitomo, New Zealand—The Off-Road Motel
Thursday, February 24, 2005, 8:12 a.m.

When Theo finally woke after two consecutive days of motel slumber, he was alone save for the pungent reek of damp sex soaked into the walls, sheets and blankets. He pulled back the curtain, and squinted at the steady drizzle. He was naked. Hungry.

Lea had been with him...he remembered that...he could still smell her on him, could almost feel her *in* him, although he couldn't figure out how that could be so. From within the dresser, he removed a clean pair of boxers and a towel, although he didn't remember unpacking his clothes. Maybe it was Lea. She was always doing things like that, taking care of him whether he asked her to or not.

Theo reached into the stand-up shower, turned the spigot and then stood beneath the hot water until it was exhausted. He dressed, including his brown, tattered moccasins he wore rain or shine, at the beach, hiking or out to dinner.

Pressed into his knapsack was a half-full bag of mini pretzel sticks, his wallet, a week-old newspaper, a Rotorua map, and stashed at the bottom, his newest possession—a small, glass jar.

Theo let the pear-shaped object weigh in his hand. Having endured what he could only assume were hallucinations, he now felt a sense of importance handling the item—a solid, three-dimensional glass container he could touch. He put the jar to his ear like listening for the ocean spirit in a seashell. Nothing.

He twisted the top. It would not open. The ridge marking where the lid should come apart from the neck was easily identifiable, but after soaking in that murky water for weeks, months or, Theo theorized, even years, the pieces had probably cemented together. *In time they'll come loose,* he thought. *In time.*

A melodious beep came from the dresser drawer. Theo dug beneath his boxers, the last pair white with little red hearts on them. His mobile phone was ringing. "Yeh," he answered in his soft Kiwi accent. A voice came through the other end.

"Dickhead. You wanted to meet me at Cook's Beach. I've got the Jet Ski, yeh?"

Theo had absolutely no memory of making such a request, although he *did* want to see his younger brother. "Hey, Roger? When did I ask you? Like, what day did we discuss it?"

"I don't know. Whenever. Who gives a rat's fuck?"

Theo was still a little woozy. "Never mind. So you got the Jet Ski, yeh?"

"Are you a fucking egg? I just said that. Wait...did you drop acid again?"

Theo put a think on it. "Um...I dunno. Maybe." Had Theo been certain that he actually *had* dropped acid, and he wasn't sure that he hadn't, he would have felt a whole lot better about the previous few days. But since they were still a blur, he was left with an uncomfortable sense of curiosity and doubt.

Barely seventeen, Roger was annoyed, as he often was. "Just stop fuckin' about, asswipe. I'll see you midday. I think Carla's gonna give me some. It's about time. Bye-bye virginity, hel-lo titties. Gonna be sweet sweet sweet."

Momentarily woozy, Theo was overcome by overbearing sexual intensity and feeling as if he were about to pass out. He sat on the edge of the bed. "I hope you're up to it."

"Are you kidding? What the fuck are you on about?"

"Never mind," Theo said, thinking that perhaps drugs and sex didn't quite mesh as well as he was led to believe. "You'll find out soon enough."

Chapter 13
The Cost of Fabric

The Labrador *woomphed!* at two desert bunnies as Winnebago backfire echoed throughout the narrow ravine.

Before redistribution, Lex couldn't remember having paid even the slightest attention to animals leaping across the road, but then, neither could he remember a time when he *hadn't* thought about it. He was a dog now, so an adjustment period seemed reasonable. New body, new sounds, new smells. Only the longer he remained a dog, the more it seemed...natural. Normal. Not that he could forget what their life used to be like, or what it took to get as far as they did.

Before their banishment to Earth—before there even was an Earth—Emma was just another struggling galaxy designer buried six-deep on a staff that offered no immediate hope for promotion given the firm's politics. This was before Lex ever heard of the Milky Way, before he had any idea just how much his life was about to change. He remembered that night like it had never ended, which, in a way, it hadn't.

Lex was called into the owner's office, a glassed-in cage in the far corner of the dark basement warehouse. Jerry sat behind his desk, twirling a sleek, silver pen. "Take a seat." Jerry was slight, with thin hair and wore round, frameless glasses. "Let's discuss this fabric business. Seems we have a situation."

Having spent numerous weekends snowboarding Mount Kilejo, Lex was trim and well conditioned, standing nearly six feet tall, with spiked, black hair. He pulled his fingers along his chin whiskers; he was otherwise clean-shaven. "What situation?

I'm...not sure I follow."

"That's disappointing, Lex, seeing as how you're the purchasing officer. Four of the nine shipments of galactic fabric we used to touch up the Big Dipper have tears in them. It's a real mess. We're going to have to redo the whole repair job—at our cost."

Lex sat up in his chair. "What? Are you sure? I inspected the lots myself. The fabric was top-notch. There's got to be a mistake."

"You are correct." Jerry did not blink. "A big mistake."

"Oh...then...I...don't understand."

Profits had been up for six consecutive quarters, all since Lex came on board. His initial few months consisted of consolidating a few troublesome accounts and reorganizing the delivery routes, steps that enabled the tripling of inventory without needing to increase staff. Yet he now had the most awful feeling that his good works weren't totally appreciated.

"It's been going on for some time." Jerry shook his head. "I didn't want to believe it, but now I'm sure."

Lex was now officially concerned, if not perplexed, and though his instincts told him he would be better off anywhere in Eternity than where he was, he asked for clarification anyway. "Sure...about what?"

"I was hoping you would be more honest, although I'm not surprised." Jerry shifted in his chair. "I was never sold on you."

"Am I in trouble?" Lex knew he was, although he couldn't figure why. "What's—?"

"Normally we would have you arrested and sent down with the other scum, but we don't need the publicity right now. There's no point calling attention to ourselves, what with the extra revenue from the big contracts allowing us to expand. But I'm sure you know that."

Jerry stopped twirling his pen. He leaned forward in his chair, which squeaked. On the blotter pad was a single sheet of company letterhead. He rotated the document to face Lex, and then pushed it across the desk. Jerry handed over the pen. "Make this easier on everyone." He glared at Lex, and then through the glass door behind him. "Especially you."

Trembling, Lex peeked over his shoulder. Standing outside were a pair of tattooed brutes with shaved heads and massive forearms. Lex read from the top. The document began:

This letter stands as my resignation from Quality Galaxy Fabrics (QGF). I acknowledge that my personal greed, lack of dignity, and contempt for ownership fueled my implicit quest to undermine the firm; I renounce all rights as an employee; and I agree to vacate the premises immediately and not ever return, or else be subjected to criminal and physical proceedings far beyond the fullest scope and extent of any known laws.

"Wait. What? I don't understand. What do you think I did?" Jerry explained. Dumbfounded, Lex slumped in his chair.

"Sign at the bottom. We'll mail you your copy." Lex did as instructed. Jerry placed the signed confession in his top desk drawer.

Lex looked to Jerry just then, hoping to claim at least a sliver of self-respect before they shredded its remnants, much as Lex was sure they did with numerous documents. "Can I at least clean out my desk? I'd like to collect my things."

Twirling his pen again, Jerry leaned back in his chair, and as much as it seemed within him, relaxed, then shook his head playfully. He offered Lex a smile.

"No."

Chapter 14
Creative Accounting

The Eastern Sphere of Eternity—Wally's Bar & Grille
Milky Way's Public Unveiling: T-Minus 228 Days (Eternity Standard Time)

Six days later, Lex awoke facedown on a skanky barroom floor, with broken peanut shells stuck to his face. *Yank My Comet* was grooving on the jukebox.

Lex plucked a shell fragment from his eyebrow. Bleary-eyed, he looked up, only to find a slender, raven-haired knockout with short, firm calves and yowsa cleavage standing above him. He couldn't help but notice the garter belt hugging her upper thigh. Lex pulled himself up, then sat at the table. He rubbed his face. "Fuck. What day is this?"

"Tuesday." Emma sipped her drink through a straw. "Tuesday night, actually."

"Really? I got canned last *Wednesday.*"

"You've been on the floor since then? Impressive."

"Last thing I remember was being thrown into a gutter and then a wino taking a whiz on my leg. Although…I do seem to recall standing on a table, probably this one, and then grabbing my crotch and screaming. Other than that…"

"You do nice work."

"Thanks." Lex held up the silver peanut dish, and checked his face for bruises. "I haven't seen you since the trade show."

Emma had stopped by the booth to pick up a sample catalog for an asteroid project she was developing. Although they worked in different departments at *Quality Galaxy Fabrics*, Lex and Emma crossed paths now and again. Lex even thought about asking her out to dinner once, but dismissed the idea when she called him Leonard—twice—even though his convention name badge said otherwise in block letters.

"How's the design department? You running the place yet?"

Lex looked himself over. "Wow. I'm a mess."

"Nothing gets by you."

"Be nice. I'm not having my best week."

"You've had worse?"

Lex smirked. "Hardly."

Emma reached over and pulled a peanut shell from his ear. She ran a finger through the top of his scruffy sideburns, and then up to his earlobe. "Look," she said. "Let's get you cleaned up and see if there isn't something we can do?"

Lex tilted his head. "We?"

Emma nipped at the straw. "Sure," she said. "Why not?"

After a hot shower, shave and change of clothes, which Emma said belonged to her ex-husband, Lex sat on her black leather couch. He followed Emma's shapely hips as she lowered them into a matching chair opposite him. She flipped off her open-toed shoes with the sides of her pedicured feet, and draped one leg across her knee.

Lex explained the terms of his dismissal.

"Somebody, most likely that pinhole, Jerry, submitted phony billing slips to the clients, charging at least double what the original fabric orders called for, and then somewhere during the delivery process, switched the quality stuff I ordered with old, useless fabric." He continued. "Jerry then pays the supplier the inflated amount, and gets some of the refund as a kickback, making himself rich. He then resells the quality merchandise for an added profit."

Emma nodded. "And since your name is on every purchase order..."

"Bingo. Paper trail leads to me. They probably got greedy, and drew attention from the accountants. I'm the perfect scapegoat."

"Yeah, but if the order forms are fakes, they shouldn't be hard to find. That's one thing my ex always said. No matter what gets recorded on the balance sheet, make it your business to know exactly how much you've got of what, where it comes from...and where it goes. Records aren't for you. They're for show."

"It's why they wouldn't let me back in my office. They obviously have my signature on file, and made the switch. I'm sure the originals are gone."

Lex walked toward the window of Emma's one-bedroom apartment.

Almost a foot shorter than Lex, Emma came up beside him. Her breasts pressed against his ribs. Her nipples were erect beneath her red, silk blouse. She put a hand on his shoulder. She whispered. "I have a confession for you."

Lex turned and looked down to face her. "Oh, yeah?"

"I quit today."

Lex licked his lips. "Really? Why's that?"

"I figured...why give them my best work when I can keep it for myself and then...offer it as it suits me?"

"Huh. You starting your own firm?"

Emma leaned in. "Long overdue."

Lex wrapped his arms around her waist. He lowered his mouth to her neck, breathing in her perfume. "Good," he said. "Fuck 'em."

"Actually." Emma rubbed her bare foot against his leg. "I'd rather fuck you."

Emma was naked, laying face down on the bed, arms pillowed beneath her head. Moonbeams cross-hatched on the wall. "Two hands are better than one," she said.

Lex rubbed his palms into Emma's taut tush. "I *am* using two hands."

"Not my ass. *Starlight Designs*. The business."

Lex looked up. A horizontal box of moonlight painted across his eyes. "What? You mean...like partners?"

"Mmm...something like that. I've got an idea for a new galaxy. I'm calling it the Milky Way. At the core will be a star system with nine planets, a lot of moons and only one sun. A yellow sun. We'll make room for life on some of the planets, with the others for decoration and balance. I haven't figured out which ones will be which. But the third planet—my favorite— will get the love. It'll be a hit. I just need the capital."

Lex drifted into fantasy just then. He sat behind his own desk and had *his* goons pummel Jerry into a soggy eggplant. "Good, boys, good. Just like that." Lex put his feet up. He flipped open the top of a silver-plated lighter, waved the blue flame beneath a cigar. "Break as many bones as you can find." He blew out expanding gray halos. "Start with the little ones."

Returned from revenge fantasy, Lex found Emma rubbing the bottom of her foot against his tingling grape sack. He wasn't a designer himself, but he knew how to supply them, getting quality materials at a good price. He never went cheap, but he knew how to find a deal. "Okay," he said. "Yeah. When do I start?"

Emma turned over beneath him. Her breasts jiggled. She let her knees fall open. "Right about," and she pulled Lex on top of her, "now."

"I gotta ask," Lex said as he inserted himself into Emma. "Is this part of the job?"

"Do you...*uhn*...want it to be?"

Out and in and out and then in again, Lex plunged deeper inside Emma, not simply as a means to an orgasmic end, but to demonstrate his abilities as a man, to prove that he wasn't the drunken loser she scraped off a barroom floor.

Lex pulled himself completely out, supporting his torso above her, his arms braced into the mattress. He gazed into the crystal blue eyes staring up at him and wondered if what he saw in them revealed what was actually there, or if he would ever look into those eyes the same way again. Lex thrust into her with an extra jolt.

Emma yelped.

Back in revenge fantasy, Lex chomped on his cigar, watching a screen mounted on his office wall. The video surveillance revealed Jerry lying motionless in a hospital bed, his body wrapped in casts and bandages. Tubes were stuffed into his nose and mouth. Next to the bed was a small monitor. A green, wavy line flowed across the screen.

...*bleep...bleep...bleep...*

Lex considered Emma's proposal. "It would be a serious...*uhn*... oh, fuck, yeah...upgrade from my last position. Would I...*uhn*... have my own office?"

"Of course." Emma groaned beneath him. "As soon as...oh shit, right there, fuck!...the space is ready."

Lex moaned. His sweat dripped onto the sheets.

"Harder," Emma instructed.

Lex thrust faster.

"Harder!"

Thrust after thrust, Lex wondered if he was hitting the mystery spot, or if she was testing him, trying to find out just how dedicated he was to getting the job done right. But since he was about to blow a load inside her, he was going with his being a great, big stud. His arms quivered. He squinted. His body clenched. Lex exhaled a series of short, staccato breaths and then released a long, puckered one as if trying to extinguish a candle. "*Uh-uh-uh...ohhhhhhh.*" He rolled over on his back.

"Mmm," Emma said. "That was nice."

"Fuck, yeah, it was." Lex patted her thigh, then wiped his face with both hands. "So," he said, still out of breath. "Are we doing this?"

Emma rolled back on top. "That depends." She pinched his left nipple.

"Ow. On what?"

"On how much you've got left in the tank there, big boy.

Once may be good for you, but I'm just getting started." Emma straddled him, sitting upright, streaks of moonlight draped across her face. "I'm tough to please."

Lex let out a deep breath. "I'm getting the idea. So why'd you get divorced, anyway?"

"Because," she said, "only one of us should've been sleeping with men...and I'm certain that should've been me."

As the sweat rolled down Emma's glistening body, Lex found it difficult to look upon her with anything less than a twang in his loins. Yet he couldn't deny the sliver of suspicion needling him as he considered what he was agreeing to. "Was this part of the interview?"

Emma reached behind her. She cupped his marbles. "Does that bother you?"

Lex grabbed her thighs as he thickened up. "Nope. Hands down. Best. Interview. Ever."

With his finger Lex drew a smiley face around Emma's taught, sweaty breast, dotting her nipple like the nose on a snowman, and admitting to himself that he didn't trust her at all. That aligning with Emma would be a very big mistake indeed.

And that he was therefore doing it anyway.

Chapter 15
Ask Me If I Care

243 Miles North of Rome
Thursday, September 1, 2005, 8:04 a.m.

Jason was marinating in his own juices. He needed to get up and stretch. It was only eight in the morning but the temperature was already over ninety degrees. He stopped at the end of the car, by the doors. The next car rumbled behind him. He caught the breeze, watching the sun light up the countryside.

Rome was still hours away, so he just stood there, staring out the window. He leaned his shoulder against the door, taking comfort in the train's rhythm. There was something about the thrust of motion, the repetition of it all.

...clug-lug...clug-lug...clug-lug...

Jason's eyes were heavy. They hurt. He closed them for just a few...minutes? Seconds? He couldn't tell. Time on the road seemed to jump ahead in flashes, or drag on, or even just stand still. Was he awake? Asleep? Eyes still closed, he shrugged, answering his own question. *Does it matter?*

And when he opened them again, the train *whooshed* by white, stone apartment houses, at least forty deep, big and small. They were clustered together, all with orange roof tiles. And then there were low-lying mountains in the distance. And maybe he drifted off, maybe not, but there was a valley, and then a field, and then trees. And beyond them was a farm, and a slope, and then more apartment clusters until finally Jason could almost feel the centuries of history soaking into his skin that was just so...*Italian*...without even knowing what that meant.

He put his hand up against the window, for the first time since he left New York realizing just how much he *wasn't* in America anymore. Not that Europe was necessarily better or worse, but different. There was something in the air, something in the vibrations that told him he was someplace else, with its own rhythms. Its own mojo.

Jason reached into his pocket to dislodge a crumpled receipt. His fingers brushed against a square edge. He removed the object, only to find himself staring at a keychain his sister gave him. He had forgotten all about it. On the end was a yellow tag that read: *ASK ME IF I CARE*. It was an old joke between them.

For years, Jill had pushed him to travel, even offered to lend him money to do so, but he always resisted, still stuck on *no*. And now he was watching the other side of the world go by.

From there, Jason's memory leapt to his student teaching days, in Buffalo, when he would climb up on the desk tops and scream lines from *Julius Caesar*, his students' mouths agape at his Shakespearean antics...which finally led his mind to that Wednesday night at *The In-Between*, his favorite college bar. Two-for-one Molson Lite bottles, Quiet Riot's *Cum on Feel the Noise* on the jukebox.

Beer in hand, Jason was talking to a blonde cutie with a flat chest and a great smile. When he felt a tap on his shoulder. He turned around. A pack of his eleventh grade students stood there, with drinks in their hands.

One of his students approached—he couldn't remember her name—but she had long, brown hair and sat in the first seat by the window. *That* he remembered.

"Mr. M," she said. "What are you *doing* here?"

"What am *I* doing here? What are *you* doing here?"

"You have homework tonight, and I know, because *I* gave it to you."

Jason couldn't wait for class the next day. And when he saw those kids with their heads buried, slumped in their seats, knowing they were totally busted...he owned them for the rest of the semester. But when he moved on to another school, he really missed those kids. They had a daring streak he just couldn't find in himself, as much as he wanted to.

But those days seemed like lifetimes ago. Jason was excited now, finally leaving behind the *getting there* phase of his trip and closing in on *being there*. He put the keychain away, and when he returned to the compartment, his mates were wide awake. They smiled at him the way people do when they're truly glad to see you, when there's just no way to mistake the greeting for anything else. Jason smiled back. *Ask me if I care.*

It was a damn good question.

Chapter 16
Magnetic Driving

New Zealand's North Island—Cook's Beach Parking Lot
Thursday, February 24, 2005, 12:38 p.m.

Theo slobbered down two jumbo hamburgers while sitting in his truck, stuffing in his mouth the overflow of onions, lettuce and beetroot. His stomach grumbled as if it hadn't been satisfied in two days, which it hadn't. But he hungered not just for food, but for answers. For clarity. Theo had the strangest sensation just then:

As if he spread his mouth open like the South American anaconda, his jaws unhinged so that the two halves of his face lay flat. As if with miner's hat and pickax, he wriggled feet-first over his own tongue, past his epiglottis and through his esophagus, tunneling into some unknown region of himself—a corridor that wouldn't show up on a medical X-ray. As if he carved through his center, uncovering a dimension he always suspected might exist but never knew for sure. A beacon leading him away from one path and toward another.

But leading where? And why now?

Theo had cruised the 360 kilometers, first heading north on State Highway 3 to Pokeno, due east on State Highway 2, and then along the northeast coast past Pauanui.

As he drove through the farm country, he passed a series of small ponds and then along a windy stretch of hills that always made him a little bit nervous. The trip to the northeastern shore took nearly six hours total, where, in typical New Zealand fashion, it rained for twenty minutes, became sunny, then windy, then calm, and then rained again before settling into a clear blue sky.

But when Theo pulled into the Cook's Beach parking lot just moments before and cut the engine, his mind raced. It was filled with flashes of color and whiteness. Of Lea. Of the Waitomo

Caves. Bits and pieces only, but no whole. Nothing concrete to latch onto.

Theo still had no idea why he had rushed off to Cook's Beach, or how he even knew the eastern shore of the Coromandel Peninsula was where he was supposed to be. His hands indeed had been on the steering wheel and his feet had operated the pedals. Yet Theo hadn't felt as if he were driving, only that he had been the conduit for motion. That the truck had been maneuvered by remote control. That *he* had been maneuvered by remote control.

While he was uneasy about the lack of influence he had over his trip to Cook's Beach, he also felt an intriguing sense of freedom. Thinking had been rendered unnecessary. Theo didn't know *why* he was doing what he was doing, but then, he had no doubts regarding the veracity of his actions. He was a passenger in his own life, a magnet pushed and pulled toward a destination that seemed arbitrary, yet specific.

Theo was taking his rightful place among the order of things, although what that place was or what purpose it would serve, he couldn't even imagine. Literally. His thoughts were like a batch of eels, slipping through the fingers of his mind. He just couldn't hold on.

A kaleidoscope of color.

Squish.

Streaking whiteness.

Squish.

Tiny green glows.

Squish.

Maybe I took a hit of acid after all, he thought. *Maybe I just forgot.*

There was a tap on the glass.

"G'day, Dickhead." Roger wrapped his knuckles on the driver's side window, and then pointed to Theo's Jet Ski, perched on the trailer attached to their father's truck. "You getting up, or am I yanking you out by your short hairs?"

Chapter 17
The Smoking Cove

The Barnes brothers tore across the ocean on their way to Cathedral Cove. The Pacific stretched out from the coastline until it narrowed to a point in the distance. The whipping wind behind them, Theo could feel the solid mass tucked against his back as he clung to Roger's waist.

Theo trusted Roger more than he trusted anyone, and if he couldn't trust him with this, if he couldn't tell *somebody*, he would go absolutely mad. Roger still had that prickly teenager attitude—as his sworn duty lobbing sarcasm grenades at even the slightest hint of hypocrisy—a check Theo was counting on to be kept honest.

"Yo, fuckface," Roger hollered over the Jet Ski. "Are you in love?"

Theo hollered back, his bare feet wet along the baseboard. "What?"

"Love, dickhead! Love!"

"No!" *Not love. Something else.* "Why?"

"No reason, mate. You're just...different!"

Theo looked toward the distant beach and the massive, white rock formation set upon it. Green treetops, like heads of broccoli, sprouted up from the rock. Roger banked right to enter the inlet, navigating them around the smaller rock formations leading to shore. They finally slowed to a putter, dismounted in the shallow water, and beached the Jet Ski.

Theo had been to Cathedral Cove dozens of times, to relax, to be away from expectation. But the massive tunnel boring through white rock—leading from Cathedral Cove on their side, to Mares Leg Cove on the other—now seemed like a cave of doom.

In the shade, Theo knelt in the cave's cool sand, and slid the backpack from his shoulders. He reached for the jar. But with his hand inside the bag, he hesitated. Waves oozed onto the beach, fizzled into foam, then retracted to sea. *Am I really doing this? Am I sure?*

His heart pounded. Theo let out a breath, slow and measured, like he was about to cut the red wire—and hopefully the correct one—just seconds before a ticking bomb finally blasted his eroding sanity to smithereens. He exhaled and then presented the jar to his brother, who toked on a joint. Sweet as brown sugar, smoke wandered from the lit end.

"You should grow this shit in your greenhouse, mate. You'd make a killing." Skinny as a post and three inches taller than Theo, Roger rambled on about the first time he got high and ate a bowl of crispy wheat lathered in their aunt's breast milk. "Still, you do have to be careful. I mean, you smoke bowls every day, it's like, you're not doing them. They're doing you."

After watching Roger exhale, Theo took two short puffs and then one longer one. He was uneasy about how Roger might react, but he needed to know if he had actually stumbled upon something extraordinary deep in the Waitomo Caves, or if he needed a CAT scan.

Roger glanced down at the jar. His eyes were glossy, bloodshot and half open. "So...," he said. "What the fuck you got there?"

Chapter 18
Luxury Sweet

The Western Sphere of Eternity—The Brockryder Hotel
Milky Way's Public Unveiling: T-Minus 31 Days (Eternity
Standard Time)

Donald led Danielle through double doors with brass door-knobs, polished to a shine. "Okay, now, Sweetie. Open your eyes."

Danielle would call her husband by his actual first name only three times during their lengthy relationship. This was the second. "Oh, Donald...a suite at the *Brockryder!*"

Sexed out an hour later, Donald and Danielle draped themselves in their complimentary silk robes. They laid face up on the canopied bed, made up with silk sheets, gold-plated bed-posts and a piece of imported chocolate on each pillow.

"So why all this, Baby?" Danielle snuggled into the nook, resting her cheek on Donald's chest. She played with the curly hairs on his stomach. "It ain't my birthday or nothin'."

"Well, you've been such a dream about this whole jar situation. I figured you deserved a great send-off. It's the best room in the hotel."

Danielle went quiet and still. She rolled on her side, facing away.

Donald knew he had done something wrong, but after playing his best card, was at a loss as to what the terrible deed might be. *Think! Damn it! What did I say?* "Honey?" He reached for his wife, who pulled away. "Sweetie? Is everything all right?"

"You said I should be getting' a great send-off 'n shit."

"That's right, my angel. The very best."

"But you said *me*, not *we*. *Me*. You sendin' me away. You dumping me down there. You kickin' my ass to the curb."

"Oh, no, Honey. No, no. No." He chuckled. "Not at all."

Danielle sat up. "Oh, so now you laughin' at me? You think

this shit is funny?"

Donald learned early on in their relationship that it was best to accept responsibility as often and as thoroughly as he could, or else he would be in for a long, excruciating evening. His next few words would be critical. "You're totally right, Honey. Right as rain. It's my mistake. I'm sorry for my choice of words. I don't know why I said them. I completely understand why you are upset, and if I were you, I would feel exactly the same way."

"You're not gonna...you can't just..." From her side of the bed, Danielle looked down at the floor. She rubbed her toes into the padded carpet. She peeked up at her husband. "You would? You are?"

"*We*, Baby. We. *We're* going. You and me. Together." Donald smiled as Danielle unclenched her fists.

"Really?" she said. "Mean it?"

Donald nodded. His voice was gentle. "You and me. Like always."

Donald let out a long, silent sigh as Danielle returned to the nook. He then changed the subject, fabricating a laugh.

"What?" Danielle asked with a toothy grin. "What you on about?"

Donald stared at the white netting draped across the bedposts. "Oh, I was just thinking about those early days. When we got assigned to surface development, before we got transferred to plumbing and drainage? That was something, wasn't it?"

"Yeah. That was some fun shit...'til you messed it up."

"Me? How did *I* mess it up?"

"How? Think about it, fool. Dinosaurs. Fuckin' dinosaurs. We got the ultimate shit, the top chronic, and you go and make dinosaurs."

"So? What's wrong with dinosaurs?"

"Uh, let's see. Slow. Stupid. Too damn big to fit anywhere." Danielle smiled. "They just like you, ya big hairy muthafucka."

"Hey." Donald smiled back. "I'm not hairy. I'm cuddly."

"*Tsch.* Cuddly, my ass. You hairy."

"I bet The Big MOU liked them. He thought they were cool."

"Ha! He pissed his pants he saw that shit. They go and give us the juice, right? What they call it now? The primordial ooze, or some shit like that? They say, 'Go wild, see what you can come up with, and we'll check in later.' So *I* bust out with the oceans and rivers and every damn flower I can think of. And what do you start with? Mud. Mud! Big MOU laughed ten million years straight when he heard that shit."

"Birds were mine."

"See? That's what I'm sayin'. You *gots* good ideas, you just go and fuck 'em up. You come back with beaches to go with my oceans. Now *that* was some good shit. Remember how we tried 'em out? Come here, Baby." Danielle grabbed his cheeks. "Then I bust out with fish, and you come up with dolphins, and some damn nice ones, too. But then you gots to be a big mutha-fucka, go and get all *I'm da man* 'n shit. Frogs. Toads. Lizards. What the fuck? Then you keep pushin' it. Takin' 'em outta the water, makin' 'em bigger and louder until you got these big-ass muthafuckin' dinosaurs stompin' over everything until there's no place left to put 'em."

Donald nodded. "Guess I got a little carried away."

"A little? They took over the whole planet!"

"Still," Donald said sheepishly, "you didn't have to drop a meteor on them. They would have died out eventually."

"Eventually? Eventually? Don't be givin' me no eventually shit, muthafucka! I ain't got time to wait around 'til those clunky-ass freaks finally fuck each other up. Besides," she said, "I filled out them forms. Came back all approved. You know what that means? Means, wipe them fuckers *out!*" She laughed. "Gotta admit, though, I ain't mean to fuck up Mars with that first batch. I wrote down the wrong quadrant. Knocked out the core, drained the water system. Just ain't fixed it yet. They said not to worry, though. Gonna be a dumpin' ground anyway." She shrugged. "My bad."

Despite his bladder-busting urge to do so, Donald refrained from reminding his wife that it was her meteor incident that got them transferred in the first place. But he did let a mumble slip, one he regretted even before his lips finished moving. "Try shutting up for once."

"*What's* that?" Danielle snapped to her knees. "You got somethin' to say? Come on, tough man! Come on, muthafucka! You done? You through?"

"Yes, Dear. Sorry, Dear." Donald hung his head. "You're right, Dear."

"Damn straight you through. First you say we gots to go down to that tub of crap planet. Make that *sneak* down. Then you drag me to this fancy-ass room just to get me all in the mood 'n shit. And now you givin' me lip for sayin' what's what. For talkin' truth. You jus' wait till I get your ass home. Mm, you in trouble." Danielle stood beside the bed. She clenched a pillow to her chest. "And don't even *think* about putting that hairy back near me, muthafucka. Your ass is sleepin' on the couch."

Chapter 19
Table Manners

Yuma, Arizona—The Sunshine Spa
Monday, August 29, 2005, 4:18 p.m.

She lay face down on a matted table. Oil was being rubbed into her calf. A white, cotton sheet was draped over her naked body. Her round, freckled breasts were pressed beneath her. There was a calming *whoosh* of distant waves. The room was cloaked in shade.

Her name was Lilly Opadopolous. She was Emma's best chance.

Lilly groaned, drifting into fantasy. There was a white, marble gazebo perched at the tip of an Italian villa. It overlooked the Mediterranean Sea. The gazebo was ornamented with a spectrum of lilacs, tulips and roses.

Jamila kneaded Lilly's thigh. "That's good, sí?"

"Oh, yeah. Fantastic. Maybe a little lower down…"

Jamila dug her thumbs into the underside of Lilly's foot.

On the verge of orgasm, Lilly felt a tingling undulate down her body and then between her legs. Her nipples were at full arousal. "Oh, God. That's…" Led away by the firm rubs, Lilly drifted back to her Italian villa, where she cooed at the lapping waves in her mind, unaware just how close to her dream she would soon find herself.

Emma wanted to talk, that's all Lilly knew.

Lilly's paintings weren't selling as well as she would have liked…they never did…but when she puttered into Yuma four months before—after the trouble she'd had in San Diego—she sensed that her luck was finally on the upswing.

At the *Gas 'n Snack* on South Main Street, where they met, Emma had filled a 60-ounce cup with blue slushy, Lilly's favorite. Lilly reached for a pizza roll, only to trip over Emma's walking stick, spilling the cup. Lex licked the slushy off Lilly's face.

Lilly knew it was fate, as she had grown to anticipate the rhythm of her destiny: Good luck, bad luck. Good luck, bad luck.

There was something about Emma. Lilly could tell. She could always tell. Those special passions people possess but don't nurture, crying to break free. If you want to be a fireman...do it. Get divorced. Open a dog-grooming salon. Motorcycle across Canada. Plant tomatoes in your backyard. Just don't look back and say, *what if? You might never get another chance.*

But Lilly didn't consciously seek out these undeveloped spirits in Portland and Reno. In San Francisco and Santa Fe. In Eldersburg, Maryland. In Toledo, Ohio. In Charlotte. Yet no matter where she landed, fascinations were amplified, aspirations enflamed. And then somehow, as if jinxed by the gods of spite and envy, her fortunes would take a tumble.

"That was wonderful," Lilly said. A white cotton robe was loose about her short, stocky frame. At twenty-seven, her chestnut eyes still filled out her face, round and cute-sexy. Her thin brown hair was curled behind each ear. "I'll have to come back soon."

Jamila rubbed a finger against her lip. "Oh," she said. "I much certainly hope you do."

Chapter 20
Motivational Techniques

The purple shadow of descending night fell on Downtown Yuma. Lilly leaned against a three-tiered fountain. Street lamps, topped with halogen bulbs shaped like little flying saucers, marked the fountain's perimeter. They thrust a glow upon the greenery that flourished in Yuma's desert air. Yellow clouds drifted before the full moon.

Lilly lit a cigarette, took a puff, but then dashed it out with her sneaker. She smoked only when she was nervous, horny or on her period, so she felt that keeping herself to a four-butt-a-day habit was worthy of a pat on the back and another cigarette.

Meet me at eight, Emma had said. Don't be late.

Lilly was fascinated by Emma, as if there was a sexy little firecracker buried somewhere in that roly-poly frame. As if Emma was somehow trapped in a life that seemed so far removed from where she would like to be or perhaps once had been.

Woomph, and then *woomph, woomph* came from the darkness. A hefty figure with a staff approached; a four-legged companion was close behind. Lilly could hear the *tap-tap-tapping* of claws against the asphalt.

"Hey, Lex." Lilly knelt down and rubbed her balled-up fists into the Labrador's wrinkled cheeks. His nametag clacked. "Did-you-watch-some-ten-nis-to-day? Did-Ve-nus-win? Did-she?"

Emma handed over a photograph. "You see this guy here?"

"Hey, Emma." Lilly stood up. She wore denim overalls and a blue, short-sleeve shirt. The words *Star Attraction* curved around her breasts. "Nice to see you."

"Yeah, yeah. Nice to whatever. The picture. Look."

Disoriented by Emma's abruptness, Lilly held the sheet

beneath one of the flying saucer streetlamps and examined the photograph. She squinted.

"Well," Emma said, "what do you think?"

"Well...what do I think, what?"

"You like him?"

"He's pretty cute. Why?" Lilly thought a moment, then crinkled the paper. "Wait. Is this guy your brother or something? Are you trying to fix me up? I told you. I really just want—"

Emma guffawed and then dropped her chin toward Lex, who *woomphed*.

"No, no! He's a...friend of a friend."

"But you want to set me up with him, right?"

Still laughing, Emma wiped away a tear, and then took a deep breath. "Wooooo. Oh, that was good." She held her hands against her stomach rolls. "No. Not exactly. I want you to go on a little trip for me. I want you to find him, and then bring him here. I want to talk to him."

Lilly looked at Emma, at Lex, and then back at Emma again. "Wait. I'm confused—"

"Yes, dear. I know, but that's a life thing. You need to focus on what I'm saying. All you have to do is meet him, and then bring him to me."

"What do you mean, bring him here? Who is he? I don't understand. How am I supposed to get him here? Why don't you—?"

Thwack! Emma crunched her walking stick against the fountain. The vibrations echoed like a musket shot. Recycled water spritzed down from tier to tier. Lilly shook.

"Listen, dear. *Why* I want to speak to this chirpy little fucker doesn't concern you. That I *want* to, does. We both know your way with men, and from what I can tell," she continued, and then looked Lilly over, "perhaps women, too. Yuck, but *C'est la vie*. But either way, you meet him, you do that thing you do, and bring him back here. That's all."

"What do you mean, way with men? It's not like I'm some slut or—"

"*Listen to me.*" Emma dug the tip of her walking stick into Lilly's bare shin. "You are uniquely talented when it comes to motivating people. Best I've seen in a long time. You get these douche bags riled up so they'll do all the things you don't have the balls to try yourself. Oh...you tell yourself that it's just sex, that you don't mean to lead them on. But, no, no, no," Emma said, waving her finger in Lilly's face. "You bask in their passion, and just when they start to really believe in themselves, when they start thinking you're their...soul mate,"—Emma made a gagging noise—"you run like the cowardly twit that you are. You can't help yourself."

Mouth agape, Lilly was speechless. Her eyes welled up.

"So...you're going to meet this fucker, and you're just going to be you. You're going to smile and show off your tits and be all into whatever he likes, and then you're going to suck his cock, suck his elbow...suck his fucking eyeballs for all I care. But when you're through, you're going to *bring...him...here.*"

Lex yawned. A wad of white drool hung from the side of his mouth.

"Now," Emma said, softening her tone, "just to show that I'm not a total bitch...those paintings of yours, well, they're good. I know someone who owes me a favor. He's got an art gallery in Amsterdam. You do this for me, I set you up. And your trip? It's to Italy."

Lilly lifted her head.

"Yeah. I figured you'd like that. To Venice. You know, romance capital of who-gives-a-crap. You go, you ride a fucking gondola, you find this guy. And then you bring him here. That's it. Nothing sinister about it. I just want to talk to him. I'd go myself, but as you can tell," she said, looking at her walking stick, "it isn't easy for me to get around."

Emma handed Lilly an envelope. Inside were two open-ended airline tickets. "One for you, one for him. You land in Rome, then take the train to Venice. You leave tomorrow."

"Tomorrow? But—"

"Or..." Emma took Lilly's face, "...I tell your little tennis buddy from San Diego where to find you. And I promise...it will be one visit you can't escape."

Emma released Lilly's face, handed her a tissue. "Clean yourself up."

Lex raised his ears at the sound of a coyote baying at the night.

"It'll be okay." Emma smiled, took hold of Lilly's shoulder and then gave it a nurturing shake. "Really. It'll be fun. It's fucking *Italy* for Christ sakes. You'll love it."

Lilly wiped her eyes. "Yeah, that's true." She cried a few short huffs, and then smiled as a stream of mucus dribbled down to her upper lip. "Italy's cool."

"See?" Emma took a breath and then looked toward the heavens in a way that virtually no one on Earth ever could. "There's something in this for everybody, right boy?" Lex yawned again. He licked his chops. "Now pack a fucking bag. We're leaving. Now."

Chapter 21
The Son Also Rises

The Western Sphere of Eternity—The Brockryder Hotel Milky Way's Public Unveiling: T-Minus 31 Days (Eternity Standard Time)

They came mostly at night. Donald had another panic attack, that utter sense of helplessness, of humiliation. He was camped out on the sofa in the *Brockryder* suite, while Danielle snored away in the bedroom, sounding like the spine of a stallion was being ripped out one vertebra at a time.

Still plagued by years of office politics, as if he had never actually escaped them, anxiety thrust Donald back to more than a year earlier, to the torment of his old job with the Galactic Particle Plant. To that day when he had been summoned to the lobby of Dünhauser's executive suite, offering the most spectacular view from any building in the GPP arsenal.

And how he called Brigsby that night, begging for help.

Donald paced back and forth in the Industrial Row apartment, and then swallowed a pill from Danielle's *SnoozyDooz* bottle. He threw scotch down his throat. He winced. "Brigs. You've got to help me. Get me out of this place.."

"Now, now," said Brigsby, who let out a dry, falsetto hiccup. "Tell Brigsypoo your tales of woe and fro and the silly little world of GPP."

Donald heard Brigsby sip his drink—a blue martini, always a blue martini—and could almost see him lean back in that enormous whirlpool bath. It was set beneath a diamond-shaped skylight with a view of the Andromeda galaxy and Milo's Smear— that permanent nothing. The speakerphone was as clear as if

Donald were right there with Brigsby, bubbles and all.

"Come on, Brigs. I know Dünhauser Senior pulled some strings for you in the beginning, and you feel loyal to him. I respect that. But since he retired and put his son at the helm... it's a nightmare. Junior's a spoiled punk playing games with us."

"Isn't that why we're here? At the whim of someone's folly?"

"Oh, don't start with that 'we're just the product of Eternity's imagination' crap. This is real. More than thirty thousand people work for GPP, including me and Danny, and most of us have been there a lot longer than Dün...damn it! Come on, Brigs. Talk to the old man. He listens to you. Help us out."

Giggling came through the speakerphone. Donald heard at least two other voices.

"Brigs...I left early today. I've never done that before. Ever." Donald pinched his eyes. He sighed. "Last week, he fired three hundred and twenty-seven people from the cleaning staff. They'd all been here at least seven years. Some of them almost twenty." The scotch was sharp against his lips. His breath was acidic. Bitter. "And you know what the little weasel did with the savings? He built a glass room in the lobby to park his motorcycle. He doesn't even drive! And now this! I don't even want to tell you what he said to me today."

More laughter came from the speakerphone, followed by a *splash*, and a *spuh-lunk bloop*.

"I love you, Donny. You know I do. Young Dünhauser is not the finest kind, I agree. But even I don't ring up billionaires and tell them that their sons, no matter what kind of spandex they might wear, are inappropriate for the ball."

"Spandex? What you talking abou—"

"Darling...think for a moment, shall we? You want me... moi...to call Dünhauser Senior, my friend, and say something along the lines of: 'Oh, you dear chap. I'm indebted to you for launching my career, but your only offspring, your heir, is...or so I hear...a pathetic, bratty twit who will become the greatest embarrassment in your otherwise proud legacy. So why don't you send him on permanent sabbatical?'"

Donald slugged down the rest of his drink. "Yeah," he said. "That sounds good."

"Donny, Donny, Donny. You're sweet. Truly. But calling Dünhauser Senior won't help you, and it certainly—and more importantly—won't help *me*. He knows his son is excrement in a milk saucer. But he's going to let the little didderbug do his own thing." There was a sipping of martini. "I feel your pain, Donny. I do. Well...perhaps not really. Although I must say, it does sound quite yucky. Just awful. But wherever you are, it's where you're supposed to be. You know...that Eternity nonsense again."

The tranquilizers were taking effect. Donald leaned back in his chair. He poked at his face, now rubbery and numb. And despite a buzz creeping along his spine, he was feeling a sense of helplessness and defeat. Brigsby was his last best hope.

"Although," Brigsby said, "there is something you can do for me."

Chapter 22
Whose Life Is It Anyway?

Rome, Italy—Pensione Abruzzi
Thursday, September 1, 2005, 6:42 p.m.

Pensione Abruzzi overlooked a cobblestone street that stretched into the distance. Lilly leaned on the edge of the second-floor balcony. A blue, creamsicle backdrop was smeared across the sky. The sun dipped toward the horizon.

Pedestrians ambled in and out of shops, among them a locksmith, a bakery, and a tailor, all, Lilly fantasized, passed down through the generations. She could almost hear the jingle of small, copper bells as the doors opened and closed with friendly exchanges of "Ciao, ciao." And the shops would have old family names like Gianni and Corsillo, stenciled on the store windows, displayed with a carpenter's pride.

This is how we should live. No worries. Nothing to run from.

Lilly shaded her eyes, and followed two silhouettes as they approached the hostel, with rucksacks strapped to their backs. They stopped out front, and shook hands. The lanky, long-haired silhouette wandered down the road; the other disappeared into the building below.

Having arrived two days earlier, Lilly shared a wide room with a high ceiling and three sets of bunk beds. Hers was the top bunk nearest the door leading to the hostel's common room. Sunshine streaked across the floor.

She climbed up top and lit a cigarette. Emma or no Emma, Lilly was going to enjoy Italy the way *she* wanted. She would meet this whoever, this Theo Barnes, okay, fine. But not the way Emma said. Lilly wasn't like that. "I'm my own woman," she said, and then shuddered at having uttered her thoughts aloud.

Feeling exposed and vulnerable, Lilly took a defiant drag on her cigarette. She imagined herself lying on the manicured lawn

of her fantasy villa. "Maybe it's not my dime...but it is my life."
She heard voices in the next room. Emma would have to wait.

"Hi," Lilly said to her newest roommate. He took the final bed,
the bottom bunk opposite her, nearest the balcony.

Even as he sat down, Lilly thought he bestowed upon her
an intimate look of recognition, like he was flipping through a
scrapbook of his life, searching for a time or place they had met
before. Like he knew her. That in some way, he knew her well.

"You're American?" he said.

Lilly nodded. She blew smoke out of the corner of her mouth,
toward the ceiling. "You, too, huh?" She felt an unexpected
bubble of joy, piqued by his pleasant, smiling stare. "There are
a few other Americans here, too. In the other rooms. They're
doing the Rome thing today."

"I never thought I'd miss hearing an American accent," her
roommate said. "I've only been on the road two days, but it
feels like two months." He dropped his rucksack, rubbed his
face and let out a long, relieved sigh. He was wearing a purple
dinosaur T-shirt. "I didn't think I'd ever see a real bed again."
He stretched out. "I'm Jason."

"Lilly," she said, and as the greeting came out of her mouth
she felt herself staring at him, although she didn't know why.
And yet she couldn't stop. She was drawn to his square jaw,
the sprouting of a goatee, the slope of his nose, the scar on the
underside of his elbow. Other than a slight belly, he was stocky
and fit.

Lilly knew trouble. Jason wasn't trouble. He was something
else. She could sense it. She just *knew* it. He was honest, safe,
and yet...something more. She could almost feel their auras
embrace, their molecules mixing together. The hairs on her
neck stood up. Her breasts tightened.

Aware that she was gawking, Lilly took another drag. She
turned her head to discard the smoke, the perfect excuse for
breaking eye contact. "I was just about to get dinner." Relieved
to have spoken clearly, she nervously rubbed her small, bare feet

together as they draped over the edge of the top bunk. "You hungry?"

"Starving. But I gotta shower first. I don't even want to think about what I smell like."

"Yeah. I didn't want to say." She smiled. "It's a long way from...?"

"New York."

"New York," Lilly repeated, then smiled again, although she reined in her grin, thinking Jason's purple dinosaur T-shirt was dorky, but cute. "Thought so."

Jason raised his eyebrows. "That obvious?"

"Your accent's not *too* bad." Lilly hopped down from the top bunk, then sauntered past him, brushing her bare shin against his leg. She went out to the balcony, leaned on the ledge and tossed her cigarette. She watched it fall precipitously to the street. Her calves were stretched tight beneath the orange dusk. She held her pose, waiting...waiting. Waiting.

"Can you give me twenty minutes?" she finally heard him say.

Not wanting Jason to find her smiling, Lilly bit the inside of her cheek. Hard. She could taste the salt of her blood. She turned to face him. And with the sun in her face, she squinted, brushed hair from her eye, then curled her fingertips behind her ear, and along the nape of her neck. "Sure." She looked side to side, and then straight at him. "I know a good place."

Lilly sipped red wine, hoping that Jason found her sexy beneath the crescent moon. The breeze was warm. Outdoor café. Table for two.

Lilly was aroused by Jason's muscular calves and taut arms, imagining him grab her by the shoulders and pull her in close, his hands strong and firm, but not forceful, exerting pressure, influence, but without demand. Much to her satisfaction, Jason had changed out of his dinosaur clothes and into a pair of olive green hiking shorts and a black T-shirt.

"What? So you just decided one day...that's it, I'm off to Europe?"

"Yeah, I know." Jason chuckled in deep, staccato bursts. "It's totally not like me at all. I've never been anywhere before. I don't know what got into me. I guess it was time."

Drawn to his soft gaze and unabashed smile, Lilly fought her impulse to float away into the recess of his brown eyes. The kind of eyes you only get by knowing things. By getting knocked around and picking yourself up with a smirk on your face, knowing there's some sort of plan to this crazy, fucked-up world. That there's a reason for the things we do.

Lilly caught another glimpse of the scar on the underside of his elbow, and thought about the incision and the stitches that came with it. He said it was a baseball injury. Very painful. She dipped her fingertip into the glass. The wine was thick and red. Slowly, she pressed it to her tongue. "Time for what?"

Jason swallowed hard. And much to Lilly's delight, he was unable to avoid staring at her mouth and down to her breasts, which were hoisted beneath a white, cotton blouse. The top two unfastened buttons allowed for ample cleavage.

"I guess...I don't know." Jason smiled, raised an eyebrow, and then took a sip of wine. "It's like...you know how, when people fantasize about winning the lottery, they imagine how great their lives would be?"

Lilly nodded as a couple sat at the next table.

"They think about all the places they'd go, the things they'd buy, the freedom they would feel? Like all their troubles would suddenly be solved? But some of the same people never even buy a ticket. Do you know what I mean?"

Lilly nodded reflexively, enraptured by his intensity. She wasn't sure what he was trying to tell her, but he seemed to really believe it, and that was good enough for her.

"It's like they live inside the fantasy, only, if they ever actually bought a ticket," Jason continued, gesturing as if he held one in his hand, "this real, tangible item—with the numbers all picked out—will impede on the fantasy, because deep down they know they won't win."

Lilly stiffened. *Wait, this is me. How does he know this?*

"So the dream, the fantasy...it gets them through the day. They wait for miracles...but don't do anything to make it happen."

"Yeah," Lilly said, as if she needed to justify herself. "I guess I know the type. But—"

"*I'm* that guy." Jason pointed to himself. "I have all these dreams, all these things I could try, but I've been hiding from them because...*pfff*...I don't *know* why. It's like with me being a teacher. I love it sometimes, but do I really want to spend the next thirty years within the walls of a high school? I mean... *thirty years...*"

Lilly rubbed her feet together beneath the table. Her heart pounded.

"I've been waiting my life out, like one day I'll just wake up to find I really did win the lottery. Forget that I never bought a ticket, but you'll see. Somehow I'll win."

Lilly loved the way Jason chuckled, how he tipped his head back. How his hands opened up like he was catching a basketball.

"It's so easy to be adventurous and confident all the time... when I'm in my head. When I don't have to actually *do* anything or take any real risks. You should see me in my own head. It's quite impressive. I'm so *totally* the man." Jason unholstered his finger guns and cocked his thumb triggers. "Watch out, boys and girls. Big J is on the scene." He made the *chk-chk* sound.

Lilly laughed a frothy, rippled laugh, then took a sip of wine.

"But out here, in reality...," Jason leaned back in his chair, drawing the waiter's ire, "it's not so easy. I finally got tired of waiting. It was time to buy a ticket. Play for real."

Lilly watched Jason gulp down his wine, cringing at the aftertaste.

"Oh, good God. Woo." He wiped his mouth. "Did I just totally lose it? Don't listen to me. It's a bad habit, I know. I rant when I'm tired. I'm a maniac. I'm sorry."

The waiter brought the check. Jason reached for his money belt.

"No." Lilly patted his hand gingerly, wanting to lean across the table and taste the sweet red wine on his lips. "Take another drink. You're not crazy at all."

Chapter 23
Floral Arrangements

Rome, Italy—Pensione Abruzzi
Friday, September 2, 2005, 12:21 a.m.

Jason and Lilly stumbled back to the *Pensione Abruzzi*, arm in arm, laughing. They were drunk. "Thanks," Lilly said, just lovely in the moonlight.

Jason leaned down and sank into her as she hugged him, holding him close. Their cheeks pressed together. Lilly's warm, tender breath tickled his ear. It set his loins on percolate.

"I had a great night," she whispered. "One of my best."

"I had a great night, too. Really." And Jason held her. And held her. And held her. "So I guess...," he finally said. As they eased apart—his hands still snug around her waist, her hands pressing his lower back—they separated just enough so that he was locked into her gaze, like examining a glass slide beneath a microscope, magnifying her golden irises.

"Yeah." Lilly smiled. "I guess..."

She kissed his cheek, then walked upstairs. She glanced back.

Jason needed a few minutes in the night air to let a certain bulge deflate. But when he finally made his way up to bed, Lilly was already asleep on her top bunk, facedown, in the dark.

Sleeping on the top middle bunk was Victoria, a twenty-year-old brunette from Scotland, while her cousin Katherine, a nineteen-year-old Scandinavian blonde goddess, was passed out on the bottom. She wore a string thong. She was topless.

Yet in his wine haze, on his back, Jason stared only at Lilly. And in a flash, in a blast of utter genius, it came to him. He had a plan. A wonderful drunken plan.

As part of this plan, he would wander down to the *Termini* train station, find a florist and buy Lilly roses—big, red roses. Then, under the cover of night, he would slip back into the hostel undetected, tiptoe into the room and leave the flowers on her pillow, his heart detonating against his chest.

As part of the plan, Lilly would awaken the next morning with the roses by her side, the sun beaming in through the balcony window. And with the sun on her face she would smell the roses and know they were from Jason. That he had thought of her. That his desire was pure. And her heart would swell, watching him sleep, touched by his romantic spontaneity. And when he woke they would embrace, the beginning of their glorious new beginning together.

Jason loved this plan. He really did. He loved it so much, in fact, that just before passing out, he almost ran out and did it.

Chapter 24
Do You Sea What I Sea?

Theo was alone. Figuring that he must have passed out, he stepped from the cave and into the sunshine. He walked on the sand with the bouncy stride he had, as if the surface beneath his feet was always made of foam. Theo once wondered if his gait had anything to do with his craving for spontaneity. As if walking with an even, firm stride was a form of conceding to commitment, which he believed was just another word for forfeit.

Theo dusted himself off, and in salute style held a hand above his eyes. He found Roger facing the cave, whizzing on a shrub. Theo strolled over to the surf and rubbed the ocean waters on his arms, hands and face. He closed his eyes, shaking his head.

"G'day, mate. Feels good, yeh?"

"Yeh, yeh," Theo said. "Long week."

Roger walked up beside him. "Who you talking to, ass breath?"

Theo rubbed the back of his neck. He stared at the shallow layer of ocean water creeping up to shore. "You. Who else?"

With the back of his hand, Roger slapped Theo on the leg.

"Quit it," Theo said.

Roger slapped again.

"Roger, I said qui—"

The brothers stood side-by-side, mouths agape. Before them was a bottleneck dolphin, which, like an aquatic Jesus, extended its body above the water. Its underbelly flippers were chubby and outstretched. The bottom of its tail was still beneath the water.

The horizon faded off in the distance so that Theo and Roger were engulfed by the cool expanse of the dolphin's silhouette. "Uh," Theo said to his brother, who responded in kind.

"Whuddaya say, mates?" the dolphin said. "Ready for a ride? Grab on, yeh? Don't worry about the air. We're all set."

"Uh," the brothers said in unison.

There was a blast of white light. There were streaks of screaming fluorescent color. There was the sensation of being sucked through a tornado. And then there was water. Lots and lots of water.

Theo and Roger looked up, only to find themselves submerged so far beneath the ocean surface they could only assume that Cathedral Cove was still somewhere nearby. They vomited chunks and sputum, which floated away among the crystal blue waters.

"Nasty," the dolphin said. "Let's go."

The brothers instinctively coughed, gagged and thrashed about, as experience had taught them that oxygen was a requirement for remaining very much not dead.

Roger panicked as they plunged through the ocean at forty kilometers an hour. "Holyfuck holyfuck holyfuck holyfuck." Theo nodded in agreement.

"Relax, mates. Relax. No need to piss yourselves." The dolphin steered with his stubby pectoral flippers, and then looked back at his passengers. Their faces were streaked with the kind of terror typically reserved for first-time skydivers whose parachutes don't open. Drifting behind the Barnes brothers was a cloud of urine. "Well, for future reference..." The dolphin led them deeper into the sea and then swam along a rock ledge. "Okay, boys. Off you go."

The brothers sat with their backs against the poking, porous rock wall. Their feet dangled over the edge. The ocean floor was buried in darkness.

"All right," the dolphin said. "I'll be right back."

"WHOA! WHOA! WHOA! WHOA!" the brothers shouted. "Don't lea—"

"Relax, mates. Relax. I just gotta get my stash. Sheesh. What a bunch of babies."

Staring at the vast ocean world, the brothers held their breaths until their cheeks turned purple. Theo was the first to exhale, and though he was actually unaffected by the natural forces of sea water, he expected the change in pressure to crush his lungs like an anvil on a kiwi.

He thrashed about, choking and gasping, pounding at his head as if attacked by hornets, praying that he would wake up. Literally tearing at his hair, Theo knew he would be dead in minutes, if not seconds, which he started to think was just the inevitable end to his steady decline toward insanity. His mind drifted into a black recess of nothingness. *Maybe this is the final step. End of the line.*

Roger exhaled a stream of bubbles, and then breathed in, realizing that his lungs were not filling with water. "It's okay, it's okay. We're not dead. We're just totally wasted."

"You got that right." The voice was hefty, like deep tenor chords oozing from a cello.

The Barnes brothers stared into an eyeball the size of a sewer cap. Their hearts pounded. Blood rushed to their faces. But the true terror was yet to come. They shrank beneath a blue-gray goliath the size of a jetliner. It had gray spots and a flat, elongated head. Its mouth was large enough to swallow an ambulance in one gulp. It had two blowholes near the top of its head.

Theo and Roger felt puny and insignificant in the presence of such a spectacular beast. "That's uh," Theo said. "That's uh…"

"A blue whale," the dolphin said. "Sharpest coral in the reef, you are. He's Howard. I'm Ira." Ira looked at Howard, and then at the brothers, who were about to crap themselves. "Don't worry, mates. He's harmless."

Ira shoved stringy, red seaweed between Howard's gum and upper lip. He did the same for himself. "Oh, yeah. That's the stuff."

Grinning like a drooling sea otter, Ira stuck his nose inches from Theo's face, apparently unaware just how close he was.

"You guys want some? We'll be wankered for hours. Hell, I'm wankered already."

Howard's eyes glazed over. "Right back atcha, slick."

"Oh, no thanks," Theo said. "We're good."

"Suit yourself," Ira said. "But there's plenty more if you want."

Roger let out a restrained chuckle at the thought of explaining this to Carla. "So, like, uh...dude. I mean...Ira." Roger exhaled freely. "Man, that's weird. So, uh..."

"Go on," Ira said to Howard, who stared at a starfish. "Tell him."

"Whoa...they're like, sooo cool," Howard said. "They're so...pointy."

"Howie!"

"Oh, shit. Right. Sorry." Howard's grin was wider than the length of Theo's truck three times over. "Jump off," he said to Roger. "Go ahead."

"What?" Roger looked down. He couldn't see the bottom. "Jump where?"

"Just jump," Howard said.

"Fuck that, mate. You jump."

Ira turned to Roger. "Seriously, mate. Just give us a jump, yeh? It'll be fine. Trust me."

Roger turned to Theo, who shrugged. Roger looked around, and then took a slight breath just to make sure that he wouldn't suddenly choke to death. When his lungs didn't implode, he stood up, cautiously, and then waved his hands to clear a space for himself. "Well...here I go." With a strong heave he launched above the cliff and floated like a man in space. "Holy crap. This is awesome! This is amazing! This is so fucking grea—"

Howard's gargantuan jaws snapped shut, encasing Roger whole.

"So..." Ira said to Theo, who, with mouth open and eyes wide, exfoliated another yellow cloud. "Your turn."

Ptwey!

Howard shot Roger out of his mouth and sent him tumbling

end over end until he sank to the ocean floor. As Roger lay discombobulated in the sand, a school of goatfish sniffed him and giggled. Marked with pale blue spots, vertical brown stripes and bright red fins, they suddenly turned the color of sand, and vanished.

"What the fuck, mate?" Roger held up his arms. Howard's warm, salty saliva coated him like spoiled brine on a Sunday ham. "Oh, man. I'm covered in whale spit!"

Howard let out a baritone belly laugh, one so deep and polarizing that Roger thought it could have been the voice of God, once again sending him head over feet over head.

"Howie! Dude!"

Howard chuckled. "I never get tired of that."

Ira navigated Theo through a forest of white coral. "Don't worry. Roger's fine."

Theo clung to Ira's dorsal fin. "You sure about that? I mean—"

Ira laughed. "Howie's always pulling that stunt. I know it's a slap in the balls, but I gotta admit...the look on your face..." Ira plunged with his passenger toward the bottom of the coral. "Listen, mate, you mind if I do a little business? There's some killer shrimp down here."

"Go ahead. I could use a minute."

"Sweet. I'll be back in a sec. Wait here." Ira started away, but stopped. "Howie would've loved that one. Stay here." He chuckled. "Like you have a choice."

Theo looked around, hidden from the beach and the sun and the trees and the sky. No matter how far he swam, Theo felt that he would never reach the surface, marooned in a watery desert. He began to process:

I'm talking to a stoner dolphin.
Check.
I'm breathing underwater.
Check.
Roger was gobbled up by a whale.

Check.

I'm alone on the ocean floor and have no idea what's happening to me.
Check.

"Uh...," he said.

Roger used a horn-shaped crab shell to scrape Howard's spit from his arms and legs. He rubbed against a cactus-looking plant to shave the goop off the back of his shirt. "I thought you guys were, you know, like...extinct."

Howard dug his tongue between two teeth, freeing some plankton. "Do I look extinct?"

Roger gawked at the enormity that was Howard. The whale's dark shadow spread across the ocean floor like an oncoming eclipse. "Hardly, but...what happened?"

"Humans. Bunch'a bloody tossers. But us blueies...we've been swimming the oceans for forty million years, mate. *Forty million.* Not bad."

Roger nodded, still unconvinced that his lungs weren't about to implode.

"And then in what, like, a hundred years, you're gonna wipe us off the planet?" Howard opened his eyes like a pair of spotlights shining on a stage. "Really? You sure?"

Roger shrugged.

"Don't be a wally. If I called all my mates over here, you'd crap so high you'd drown in your own shit." He paused. "Hey, I didn't even mean that one. Drown. Get it?"

"Uh...yeah. Swell. But everybody thought—"

"Hey. I'm not saying you wankers didn't do some real damage, because you did. And let me tell you, we're pissed." Howard glared down on Roger, who wanted to cower inside the crab shell he just used to scrape the whale scuzz from his flesh. "But we figured it was better to hang out down here and trip our spout holes off until you idiots figured out that messing with us was a bad idea...or you killed yourselves off. You know, nukes, polluted air and whatnot." Howard chuckled. "Current odds are that you won't make it another decade. I think you might go a bit longer, although it depends on a lot going your way. But from the looks of it, I wouldn't hold my breath." Howard thought a moment, smiled. "Hey. I did it again. Get it? Hold my breath? I'm a whale? Get it? Oh, man, I crack myself up."

"Look, mate. My balls are tickled piss pink that you give yourself the shits and giggles. But is there any chance you'll stop blubbering about and get on with it?"

"Get on with—?" Howard paused. "Wait. Blubber. I get it. Good one."

"Yeah, mate. Great. Thanks. Now can we—?"

"So tell me about this girlfriend of yours," Howard said. "You into her or what?"

Theo picked up a handful of sand, then opened his fingers, watching it float away. He wondered if the world's secrets and memories were imbedded in the grains.

Ira swam from the far side of the coral.

"Whoa!" Theo pointed at a four-foot snapping turtle. "Look at that!"

"Larry? Funny bastard. Never says a word, which is pretty weird, since he's in charge of the eggs. Like nobody else can handle it." Ira swam closer to Theo, and whispered. "It's the quiet ones, mate. They freak everybody out."

"Um," Theo said. "Is there...I dunno, like...why are we down here?"

"Oh, I just like to shrimp out and watch the coral go all supernova. It's way cool."

"No, mate. I mean, why am *I* down here? Why me?"

"Oh, right. My bad." Ira slurped down a finger-sized shrimp. "Listen, mate. Your life has been getting pretty strange lately. Let me give you some advice."

Chapter 25
Knock, Knock

Cathedral Cove, New Zealand—Somewhere Beneath the Ocean
Thursday, February 24, 2005, 1:53 p.m.

Deep down in the ocean waters, with Cathedral Cove nowhere in sight, Theo and Roger started to feel woozy and disoriented. There was a blast of white light. There were streaks of screaming fluorescent color. There was the sensation of being sucked through a tornado. And then there was sand. Lots and lots of sand.

They sat up in the cave, looked at each other, and then out toward the ocean. The orange summer sun reflected off the waves. They threw up.

"There's no way." Roger wiped vomit from his chin. "Did you, I mean...did we...?"

"There was a dolphin, yeh?" Theo buried his puke. "And a whale?"

"Fucking too right there was a whale! Covered me in spit! So gross."

Theo felt his clothes. They were dry. The jar was still screwed in the sand between them. He checked his watch. *1:53 p.m.* They had only just arrived. *I don't know if I can handle this.*

Roger picked up the joint. It was still burning. He tossed it. "I'm off this shit for good." He stood up just then, but stumbled, and fell back down. "Or...maybe I'll just sit a while."

The sand was cool beneath them as a breeze brushed in, reminding them that they were breathing oxygen again. That they were back where they belonged. Theo looked at Roger. Roger looked at Theo. They both looked at the jar, at each other, then out at the water. And they broke out laughing.

Roger pounded the sand. *"Phaaaa ha ha ha ha ha!* Oh, God, oh, man..."

Theo drooled with laughter. His stomach hurt. *"Pha ha ha ha ha!"*

"Wait, wait. *Ha, ha, ha*...no, wait." Roger kept laughing. "No, check it out. *Ah uh uh uh...Knah...*Knock-knock."

Theo burst into more convulsive laughter. "Wha...what? *Ah ha ha...*"

"Knock-knock," Roger laughed, kicking spastically. "Knock-knock."

"Who...*ah ha ha...*?" Theo managed to eek out. "Who's there?"

"Whale," Roger snorted.

"Whale?" Theo uttered between belly laughs. "Whale who?"

"Whale spit," Roger said, his feet kicking. "*Phaa ha ha!* Whale spit."

Theo held himself in push-up position. His head hung forward. "No, stop. I can't take it. Oh, wow...whale spit. Oh, shit. *Ooooooh.*"

Roger held his stomach, took a deep breath, exhaled. He did this once more, then again. "*Whew.* Killer, mate. Killer. So what now?"

Breathing more steadily, Theo stood up and brushed the sand from his shorts. He stepped out into the sunshine. "I have to go."

Roger followed Theo onto the beach. "Go? Go where?"

"Amsterdam. The *Ball and Tickle*. I need to find a guy who's not always a guy."

"What the fuck does that mean?"

Theo picked up a twig and waved it like a magic wand. "No idea."

"Okay," Roger said. "I'll bite. What's the *Ball and Pickle*?"

"*Tickle*," Theo clarified.

"Tickle, pickle. Whatever. Why there?"

Theo snapped the twig, then tossed the halves into the water. An oncoming wave pulled the broken pieces out to sea. "Ira told me to."

The brothers looked at each other, and with a rush, were again rolling in the sand.

"Listen...listen," Theo squeezed out between howls of laughter. The surf rolled over his legs. "I need...oh...ah...hoo...I need a favor."

Roger pounded his fists. White foam splashed on his back. "No problem," he said, and then rolled over. "I'm sure it'll be a *whale* of a good time."

Swells of laughter rose above the rock line and the broccoli trees and up into the sky. As the brothers giggled themselves silly on the beach, the glass jar remained in the cool, white sand, all alone, in the cave. And if only for a moment, Theo and Roger forgot all about it.

Chapter 26
The Eternal City

Rome, Italy—The Spanish Steps
Saturday, September 3, 2005, 9:34 p.m.

Lilly took in the nighttime crowd from atop the Spanish Steps. Below, on the street, was Fontana della Barcaccia—*Fountain of the Old Boat*—spouting water from bow and stern. She had spent the day with Jason at Vatican City.

"Michelangelo is the Babe Ruth of art," he said. "Incredible."

There was a purr of voices, with bodies bodies bodies, interlocking fingers and snuggling shoulders, so close and warm on the massive stone steps, from the upper platform to the cobblestone street. The three-tiered staircase sloped from twin clock towers.

And yet even with the Spanish Steps, the starry night... even with a cone of strawberry gelato, Lilly was depressed, worried. "I guess," she mumbled, feeling compelled to respond. "It wasn't bad."

Jason carried on, raising his arms like she had just accused Batman of being an inferior breed of superhero to the Wonder Twins. "Not bad? It was incredible! That ceiling...the Sistine chapel. My God. It was so lifelike, so real. Almost three-dimensional. I don't know how he did it. That dude's my hero."

This should be my fantasy realized. A dream come true.

But riding the subway to Vatican City that day, with Jason poring over baseball scores in the European edition of *USA Today*, Lilly was baffled at how deeply she had let herself grow accustomed to just being with him. As if his companionship was supposed to be part of her life, but hadn't been until then. Suddenly she realized—with the clarity of a cast-iron bathtub crashing on her skull—that she wanted to tell Jason something she had only told once before, and got burned for it. How she'd gone home to make amends, but as usual, turned hope into disaster.

That the thought of staring into Jason's eyes again, those kind, strange eyes, made Lilly want to cry, her tears flowing in a wave of guilt and fear and panic. That maybe she was ready to admit what she had done that day as she leapt through the air. How she came crashing down. And how she ruined so many lives because of it.

Lilly realized that she needed Jason. Absolutely *needed* him.

But she wasn't ready to need him that way. Not anybody. Especially with Emma hovering like a hawk over a field mouse. Instead, Lilly withdrew from Jason, desperate to stay distracted until the anxiety passed and her memories could sink to the bottom of her mind's muddy ocean where they belonged. She had to get away from him. For good.

"There's this superstition," Jason started. "If you throw a coin in the Barcaccia Fountain, it guarantees your place in the Eternal City. Now...I'm not sure what the Eternal City is, but it sounds pretty cool. I read about it," he said. "In a pamphlet."

Lilly could feel the pulling in his voice, trying to regain the closeness he wasn't wrong to believe she had been sharing with him, but was now retracting, without explanation or warning.

"Wanna chuck a coin?" he said. "I'm buying."

Standing side by side, Jason snaked his head out in front of Lilly, the first time their eyes had met in hours. His gaze delved into hers in a way that made her nervous. The parade of voices below melded together in a constant hum. A collective presence.

He wants something from me. If it were just my body, he could have me. Again and again. But he wants something I can't give. To anybody. He thinks I'm somebody I'm not.

"I'm actually meeting a guy," Lilly jabbed sternly, sucker-punching Jason. It filled her with a fleeting twinge of empower-ment and relief. "I'm going to Venice. Tomorrow morning."

"No way!" Jason took hold of Lilly's arm, startling her. "Me, too! That's awesome! We should go together."

Unprepared for his response, Lilly was overcome with anxi-ety. Another glint of nausea kicked up. "Yeah," she blurted impulsively, honestly, because she *wanted* to be with him. As much as she fought her longing for Jason, for that one instant

Lilly let herself feel the depth of his emotional embrace. And it was wonderful.

But atop the Spanish Steps, surrounded by the energy of a thousand lovers present and past, Lilly smiled wistfully beneath the night sky. And then she retreated into the recess of her heart and mind, far beyond his reach.

Chapter 27
The Sounds of Silence

Italy—On the Train from Rome to Venice
Sunday, September 4, 2005, 7:21 a.m.

Despite the familiar, reassuring weight of his rucksack, Jason was nonetheless confused, anxious and even a little bit angry. His heart beat fast and heavy.

Guhn-glon, guhn-glon, guhn-glon...

Lilly had barely spoken to him on their way to the train station. Initially, Jason chalked it up to the early hour, but Lilly's distance felt more...distant...than merely being the by-product of the early morning grouchies.

"Ooh," Jason said. "This is nice. Better than the last train I was on." The 09:23 to Venice was an air-conditioned express train, with padded bucket seats, two seats to a row on either side of the aisle. The train was more than half full. The bright reach of the morning sun found its way through the windows. "This is much nicer," he repeated.

Face pressed against the window, Jason felt a surge of adrenaline kick in, excited to be on his way to Venice. He loved being off on another adventure, headed someplace that he just knew would be great. He was also relieved to leave Rome behind, although he wasn't sure why.

Feeling the worst kind of isolation—together but alone, purposefully shut out—he turned to Lilly, who leaned back in her seat, eyes closed. Jason had to try something, to recapture the togetherness that seemed, inexplicably, to be slipping away. "You want a piece of bread?"

Eyes closed, Lilly shook her head, in silence.

Guhn-glon, guhn-glon, guhn-glon...

After an hour racing through Italy at a hundred miles an hour, Lilly still hadn't uttered a word. Jason felt the panic beating inside his chest. His hands trembled. He squeezed them into tight fists, camouflaging his awkward distress before Lilly could notice. Or did she already?

When the train pulled into the *Santa Lucia* station in Venice, Jason grabbed his bags and stepped around Lilly before she rose from her seat. The sun was hushed, unlike the brutal sun of Rome. "Can't you just feel it?" he said to Lilly, who came out behind him.

They walked through the lobby of the station's small main building, bright and airy with large windows. Shadows streaked across the floor as people whisked to and fro, buying tickets, asking directions in English and Italian. German and French. Japanese and Spanish.

But it wasn't until they made their way out to the other side when the true amazement of Venice shone through. They stood on the stone staircase, staring out at the Grand Canal. The waterway snaked through the heart of the city. He dropped his rucksack beside him. "Will you look at that."

Small buildings lined both sides of the canal. The water lapped right up against the base of the doors. Gondolas and water taxis were a regular sight, yet on the streets, there was not an automobile to be found. Hank was right. He told Jason that Venice would be the turning point for him, that it would get him thinking about things he hadn't considered before. When Jason asked why, Hank answered in typical Hankonian fashion.

"You're a sucker for love, Kid. Don't know why, it's just the way you are. You chase the ones you can't catch so you can sulk about it later. After Venice, you'll see things differently. It's your kinda town. Trust me. You'll see."

A pungent breeze came off the canal. Jason squinted, chuckled. "Wow," he said, thinking that Lilly would eventually say something. "I've never seen anything like it. Have you?"

But continuing her code of silence, Lilly kept her thoughts to herself. Not a sigh, not a *hmm*. Nothing. But not, Jason discovered, because she was rude, indifferent or unable to speak.

Because she was gone.

Chapter 28
Poker Faces

Yuma, Arizona—Top Joe's Finest Motel
Friday, September 2, 2005, 7:48 a.m.

Lex urinated on a *Tow Away Zone* signpost in the parking lot of *Top Joe's Finest Motel*. There was some cloud cover in downtown Yuma, even a threat of rain, but the heat was rough as ever.

"What if she finds out you bluffed?" He quickly nibbled his right testicle. "You have no contact with San Diego. You only saw the postmark on the envelope. You really think—"

Emma was irritated. "Take your tongue off your balls when you're talking to me. My ex had a fondness for that area. That's why he's my *ex*-husband. Although, I suppose we owe him."

Lex looked up at his beefy companion, his tongue literally an inch from his scrotum. He held his stare, thinking about how many more laps to give the old boys. It wasn't a bad perk, all things considered.

Emma was holding out on him, Lex knew that. She always did. But how could he blame her for it now, after all they'd been through? As if a setback such as theirs—getting banished to the most famous planet in a galaxy Emma designed—would be enough for her to actually change her ways. To show some humility. If Lex had learned anything about Emma, it was to fear her most when she was getting slapped around.

But he sensed the faintest wisps of doubt were beginning to sink in, that maybe Emma had bludgeoned Lilly because it made her feel important again, like she was in charge of her own destiny. If he was ever going to pry something loose, now was the time. "You know Lilly's a flake. Can you really trust her with this?"

"That little slut fears nothing more than confrontation."
Good. Let's see that temper of yours. Keep talking.
"She'd rather give a foot massage to a leper than take

responsibility for herself."

"True. You read that right away. You definitely called it." He watched Emma rub her neck. "But what if she *can't* get the Barnes kid back here? I mean, what if? I'm just saying. That jar's our only chance out of here."

Thanks to her ex-husband Lawrence—the CBM warehouse manager in Eternity—Emma knew how to activate the jar's bar code, and send them back home. Instantly.

Emma stared at Lex. He could see that he got to her. Her eyes drifted just a millimeter, avoiding him. Tipping him off. He could actually *smell* her fear, like a sweet tinge of sugar and concentrated bacon grease.

They both knew Lilly might not pan out, that a contingency plan would be reasonable, if not prudent, although Emma had never admitted to one, and Lex had never asked. As always, they were engaged in the dance of revealing and concealing.

"I guess you're right. I mean…why wouldn't the Barnes kid go with her? She's good-looking, must be dynamite in the sack… not unlike *somebody* I used to know," Lex added, and with his big brown paw, rubbed his big brown face. "And if it turns out she can't get it done, there'll be other chances. There's always a way." Lex suddenly, urgently, nibbled his back. "And if it turns out that we're stuck on this planet for good…if there's just no way out of this…we'll make do. You always make the best of it."

A slight rain fell. One heavy drop at a time.

"But that's why you're you," Lex said as he started back toward their motel room. He flipped his tail from side to side, daring her to follow. "And I'm me."

Draped in an aqua blue housecoat with little yellow Tweety Birds, Emma dropped the tweezers in the bathroom sink. She tried again. "Come on, you snaky little fuckstick. Come on!" Sweat saturated her trembling hand as she squeezed the delicate apparatus tighter and tighter.

On the corner of her chin was a flesh-toned mole the size of a gumdrop. Sprouting from it was a single hair, mocking her transformation from beauty to beast.

"Wait-wait-wait...got it, got it..." She gave a yank. "Sonuva fuck! Ow!" Emma grabbed her face, now covered in red, sweaty blotches. She crashed into the toilet, knocking her walking stick to the floor. "Shit. Just fuck me in the kidney." She removed her hand, gritting her teeth. "Where's that God-damned tweezer?"

After another thirty-seven minutes of plucking and yanking, her chin was a flabby ache. She gave up, not something she was prone to do.

Ever since being dumped on Earth, Emma had tried to look at herself in the mirror, tried to make eye contact with herself. But how could she accept that the reflection staring back had anything to do with her? Even for another week? Another day? Another hour?

And after the call—that amazing, unexpected call—after she realized that someone had come to help, someone she needed more than anyone else, Emma had to find herself again. Had to. She reveled in the idea of seeing him. But she feared it just as much. He would understand or be repelled, but either way Emma couldn't let vanity deter her from getting home.

Eyes closed, she leaned on the sink with both hands. *This is just a disguise, just a picture they've pasted on. This is only temporary.* Emma opened her eyes, seeing in the mirror a bizarre, awful imposter—a phony—where she should be. "I'm not gone," she said. "I'm not gone."

Reflected in the mirror, Emma could see Lex curl up on the bed. He *woomphed,* and then settled off to sleep. Emma pulled the bathroom door closed behind her. She stared at that fake, that fucking phony. *Is this my fate? What if I'm like this forever?* Bubbling in each eye were salty pockets of sputum and resentment. They broke open and oozed down her face.

And then the old fire burned in her eyes. "What the fuck am I on about?" Emma slapped her face—*Whack!* Then the other side—*Whack!* "Don't get all weepy on me, you stupid cow." She let out a sly grin. "I'm not done. Not by a fucking long shot."

Emma bowled out of the bathroom. The door slammed against the bedroom wall. *Wham!*

Lex's head snapped up. He was startled, if not truly frightened.

"Don't worry about me, you mangy little fleabag." Her smug confidence coated the room like stale sex. It was the best phone call she ever got. She wasn't going to let him go. Not again. "Everything's under control. Backup's on the way."

Chapter 29
Take a Bow

Amsterdam, The Netherlands—The Ball and Tickle
Friday, September 2, 2005, 1:36 a.m.

"Mm-wah, mm-wah, mm-whah." From the stage of the *Ball and Tickle*, just two weeks aftere-mailing Emma, after helping orchestrate a rendezvous in Venice, Angelique threw kisses at an audience who cheered and laughed and demanded more. More, more, more. "No," she smirked with mock indignation. "No."

Angelique curled her shoulder to the audience. She stepped so that the profile of her face, dolled to the max, was all that remained in the spotlight. She folded her gloved hand at the wrist and dropped her chin. "Stop it. You embarrass me." She wrinkled her nose, and gave a Wonder Woman twirl, exposing caramel skin from shoulders to the arch of her rump. Her small, muscled frame was elevated on high heels.

The audience roared: *"An-gie! An-gie! An-gie!"*

Angelique pirouetted to face her devotees, taking her rightful place as the center of their spotlight moon—the brightest star in their sky. "Oh, who am I kidding? Embarrass me," she said. "Embarrass me."

She winked at the audience and laughed, a rehearsed moment cueing them to cheer and cajole. Only her laugh—a laugh she had delivered many times before on that very stage, at that exact moment, during that same routine—wasn't so rehearsed this time. Her practiced guffaw now carried a sparkle of sincerity, a twinkle of genuine emotion. She couldn't deny it. She was going to miss the fans.

Only two weeks earlier, while trimming Angelique's wig, George had a visitor. A young man had come a long way.

"Um...hello," he said. "I was told that...uh...you could help me."

Caught in the shadow of his two personalities—one, reality; the other, fantasy—George was becoming less and less certain which was which, or if they were even beginning to merge. Sitting in his chair, he returned the wig to its ceramic head. He wasn't ready for Angelique. Not yet. "Well," he finally said in English. "Might I ask your name?"

"Theo," the visitor said, standing inside the doorway. "Theo Barnes."

"Well, hello, Theo. My name is George. It's very nice to meet you." George stood up and extended his small hand. "If you don't mind...may I ask who sent you?"

Theo chuckled. "I dunno...it's...hard to explain."

George was used to new acquaintances guarding their requests, fearful of divulging too much too soon, of exposing themselves. After all, they came about private desires. Fantasy. The barriers didn't always come down so quickly. George offered a smile. "What can I do for you?"

Theo reached into his knapsack and removed a clear plastic sandwich bag containing a series of photographs. "Do you know what this is? Like I said, it's...I dunno. Have you—"

"May I take a look?" After gazing into Theo's hands, George felt inexplicably possessed, as if by the soul of the gods.

"Are you all right, mate? You know what this is, yeh? It can be overwhelming."

George rubbed his forefinger in a gentle motion around the smooth, glossy edges of the first picture. "Yes, Theo. I can help."

Neither George nor Angelique could disappear without arousing suspicion. But now that plans were set, the celebration was under way, at Angelique's favorite venue: On stage.

"Mm-wah, mm-wah. Mm-wah. Keep all the lovely yum-yums coming, my sweethearts. Angeliquey will be gone for a few days on a very important trip, so get her in now. Angeliquey loves you. She just absolutely loves you."

Chapter 30
Instructional TV

The Western Sphere of Eternity—The Brockryder Hotel Milky Way's Public Unveiling: T-Minus 30 Days (Eternity Standard Time)

"Honey!" Donald shook Danielle. "Come inside! You're gonna miss it!"

She grumbled from beneath the bed sheet. "Huh? 'm sleepy, mutha fuh'er. 'm sleepy..."

Donald grabbed her by the hand. They sat on the couch where he spent the night thinking about their predicament. The television was on. "Watch. Look. This is it. We got it." He turned up the volume just as the studio audience's laughter was dying down.

"It's happened to us all, hasn't it?" Brigsby wore bell-bottom slacks, a paisley blouse, black zip boots and a cinnamon-colored scarf, knotted in front. Oversized, tinted glasses camouflaged his wrinkles. His bowl-cut toupee was so bad it was almost endearing. Almost.

He rested his slight frame on a stool against a black-lit stage. There was nothing for the camera to focus on but Brigsby. The star. He leaned one hand on his knee, and waved the other so that his palm was open.

"Oh...now don't lie you turdy birdies. You know you've done it. We've all done it. Oh, darling, we've done it," he said with a twinkle in his eye. "We've all survived a horrible cocktail party with one too many martinis, one too many powder puffs with a nameless *squire*," he continued, making quote marks with his fingers. "Hell, they all have names...but who asks?"

More laughter.

"We've all had one too many throws in the rolls...and my-oh-my, you've knocked over a picture from your host's wedding. But there's no *shiatsu* to blame."

"That's our topic on *Breakfast with Brigsby*," the emcee announced: "*I Ruined Something Special...And Got Away With It!*"

Brigsby posed a question. "Are we naughty? Perhaps. But that's what keeps us fabulous. So how should we handle a social whoops-y-do? Do we apologize? Do we confess? Oh, you jest. Confession may be good for the soul...but it's not my *soul* I'm worried about."

More laughter.

"So, you broke the picture frame," he said. "Should you hide it?"

"*No!*" the audience shouted.

"Should you camouflage it?"

"*No!*" the audience shouted again, only louder.

"Should you...replace it?"

"*Hell, no!*" the audience shouted a third time, loudest of all.

"Oh, you are so good. The secret," he said, and then stood up as he raised his voice, "is to be the first to do your worst. If you knock over a glass giraffe from your host's little collection...break four. When you destroy something pretentiously precious...the divas are grievous, the queens are mean. But when you destroy with style, you ascend a mile. Your host will swoop and swoon for pity and condolence—and get it—forgetting about that horrible little tchotchke you broke in the first place. Your hosts have moved on to better things. Themselves!"

The audience oohed and aahed.

"Say it with me: destroy with style, ascend a mile."

"*Destroy with style, ascend a mile!*"

"I can't hear you, darlings."

"*Destroy with style, ascend a mile!*"

"Once more with love."

"*DESTROY WITH STYLE, ASCEND A MILE!*"

Donald was beaming. "Don't you see? Isn't this great?"

"Ain't what great? That fool says to go break a bunch of shit. What kind of crackhead logic is that?"

Donald faced his wife. He kissed her hand. "The kind to set us free."

Chapter 31
Allergic Reaction

Venice, Italy—Santa Lucia Train Station
Sunday, September 4, 2005, 11:27 a.m.

Jason jostled up and down the stairs. He ran back into the lobby. When Lilly wasn't there, he ran out to the platforms. He even convinced a portly Italian woman to look in the ladies' bathroom.

Guhn-glon, guhn-glon, guhn-glon...

He made his way back through the lobby and out the other side, facing the Grand Canal.

God damn it! Where the fuck are you?

Jason knew he couldn't just stand there and do nothing, hoping on some crazy kind of miracle that Lilly just might turn up. He needed a plan, and he didn't give a horse's hairy nut if it was through some newly developed powers of mental telepathy, spy satellite or getting *I Dream of Jeannie* to do that blinking head bob thing she did. Just so long as it worked.

But instead he forced himself to remain where he was, sitting atop the stone steps facing the canal, figuring that the best thing to do was sit tight. No point in getting lost. So he waited.

One Mississippi...I can handle this.

He felt a warm breeze on his skin.

Two Mississippi...That's it. Waiting's not so bad.

He squinted as the sun reflected off the water.

Three Mississippi...Nope. It's not bad at all...

Until he just couldn't take the swirling madness in his heart even one fucking Mississippi longer. He literally tried to shake the jitters off him, like a dog coming in from the rain. Jason looked side to side. In front of him. Behind. Across the narrow section of the Grand Canal.

But after almost another twenty minutes searching the crowd, Jason decided it was time to face facts. There was no point in denying it. He would simply have to wait longer.

And then he remembered something Hank told him just a few nights before leaving for England, sitting in *McDougal's*, a pub down the road from *Funzie's*. "You're going to meet a lot of new people, Kid, so don't get attached. You hook up with someone in one city, lose them in the next. Don't try to figure out why. It's just the way it is."

Most importantly, Jason started to think, was Hank's advice about women. "Find yourself a nice lady friend to hang out with, but whatever you do, don't...fall...in love. Got that? No love. Just enjoy people while they're around and the rest will take care of itself."

Jason considered the canal and the crowds and the sunshine. He took a deep breath, then let it out slowly. Again. And once more. He finally shook his head and chuckled, unable to hold back a goofy little smile. And then reluctantly for sure, Jason picked up his rucksack and holstered it on his shoulder, relinquishing his search for Lilly. *Okay, Hank. You got me.*

From there Jason wandered along the Grand Canal, passing vendors who sold postcards and T-shirts, maps and vanity plates, fruit and trinkets. There were smaller canals ahead where it looked like little side streets should have been, but were not, giving Venice a dream-like quality.

Still rattled by Lilly's vanishing, Jason tried to convince himself that it was just an honest mistake, that they had gotten separated accidentally, and that they would find each other again. That while he was looking for Lilly, she was looking for *him*. After all, he reasoned, they had just arrived. How far could she have gotten?

Jason stopped at a vendor's cart and bought three red apples and a bag of pistachios. He wasn't getting stuck without food. Not again. He tore into one of the apples with pride, as if the crackle of the breaking skin had announced his arrival. He had a Bulgarian couple take a picture of him with the apple in his mouth.

Needing a place to stay—a dwelling with a bed, a shower and a locker for his bag—Jason consulted his guidebook. Somewhere nearby was a hostel converted from an old church, run by young nuns. The doors opened at one o'clock. Jason checked his watch: *12:47 p.m.*

He found his way through a series of narrow alleys. Cool and shaded, they were crowded, leading him away from the Grand Canal. Once through the alleys, several arching bridges took him over even smaller canals.

After making his way through a courtyard, Jason looked up to a third-floor balcony with an iron rail. A beautiful pregnant woman stood, barefoot, staring as tourists and locals flowed through the alley. She had long black hair and wore a white sundress. She waved.

Jason got so excited just then he nearly pissed himself, thinking maybe Lilly was up there too, and that he should go to her. Lost in the fantasy, Jason even hoped—like in a dream, where the rules of logic and physics don't apply—that she would morph into Lilly somehow, that she was carrying *his* baby, and that she was waiting for him. Her true love.

So Jason waved back and walked faster and faster toward the mother of his fantasy child, up ahead, just a few doors down. But then, as if someone had called to her, she looked back into the apartment, and slipped inside. Deflated, Jason could barely carry his feet forward. Someone bumped him from behind and then disappeared into the crowd. Jason looked back at the high balcony, thinking maybe...

He finally came upon a large, shaded courtyard leading to the church. At least thirty other backpackers were already waiting. He searched among them for Lilly, hoping that she had been waiting there for him all along. That he had let himself spiral into Hell for nothing.

No go.

Jason stood against a railing. Another backpacker was just a few feet away. He wore gray shorts, a gray baseball cap, a turquoise T-shirt with a *Motocross '02* logo on the front, and a pair of battered brown moccasins with no socks. He seemed harmless. And with the Lilly fiasco still raw, Jason figured, how much drama could one guy really bring in comparison? Besides, he knew Hank would bust his balls mercilessly if he just sat there and did nothing.

"*What* am I doing?" Jason shook his head. "This is ridiculous." He pushed off the rail—forced himself—and approached the backpacker. He needed to make a friend, although reaching out still took some convincing.

I don't want to let go.

—Shut up, you loser.

But I—

—Do it now!

"Hey," Jason finally said. "You waiting to get a bed here?"

"Yeh, yeh," the backpacker said.

Jason reached into his pocket and offered the bag of pistachios.

"No, thanks. I'm allergic. My throat'll blow up," the backpacker said, pronouncing throat as *froat*. Jason couldn't place the accent, soft and mumbled, with a British quality, but not quite.

"Oh, well, I guess you shouldn't have one." Jason offered his hand. "I'm Jason."

The backpacker took it. "Theo."

Jason nodded, and figuring he had nothing to lose, asked Theo if he wanted to drop their stuff inside, and then walk around together. Although as soon as he made the invitation, Jason sensed that he had done something significant.

It didn't take long to get an answer, but in just those few seconds, Jason waited hopefully, watching Theo as he shifted along the rail, looked away, and then back again.

"Yeh, yeh," Theo said. He took hold of his bag. "Let's go."

PART II

WANING DAYS
OF THE DYNAMIC DIPSHITS

Chapter 32
Always Bring a Wipey

Venice, Italy—Draper's Pub

Sunday, September 4, 2005, 10:36 p.m.

Jason was shitfaced. Room-spinning, word-slurring, on-the-verge-of-blacking-out-and-puking shitfaced. Five hours guzzling *Peroni* will do that to a guy. Ordinarily, he would have thrown in the towel, but whereas the pub was crowded, loud and smoky, Katja was blonde, blue-eyed and Swiss. And leaning against him. And holding his hand. She had a soft German accent.

"How 'em, did you get that scar? On yours elbow."

Stacy's Mom by Fountains of Wayne came through the jukebox.

Drunk off his nut, Theo wrapped around Michelle, a red-headed Irish knockout with long legs and small breasts they met at the topless beach earlier that day.

"Yeah, mate." Theo slapped Jason's back playfully. "How *did* you get that scar?"

Like flipping a switch, just as Theo's hand made contact with his back—*slap*—Jason saw a blast of white light.

There were streaks of screaming fluorescent color. There was the sensation of being sucked through a tornado. And then there was garbage. Lots and lots of garbage.

With *Stacy's Mom* still ringing in his head, Jason was drawn to that night two weeks earlier, slumped over in *Funzie's* back alley. The experience was so real to him now, as if he was living that night all over again.

One hand against the dumpster, Jason retched beneath the crescent moon shining over Long Island. Even at half-price with an employee discount, the sweet corn chowder didn't seem worth it. He flicked a yellow niblet from the corner of his mouth.

Jason had been working at *Funzie's* for nearly four months, feeling like his past, present and future were all the same—just screws, embedded in a wall of disappointment, which would never come loose. One part of him wanted to blame the gods for punishing him, for dumping him in that stupid suck-ass job with those stupid suck-ass uniforms and stupid suck-ass managers with their stupid suck-ass nametags.

But there was a voice that insisted he face facts—that his predicament wasn't because of fate, bad luck or karma, but because he had made a series of decisions that landed him there. He could blame anybody and everybody he wanted, but there was no escaping that he got exactly what he asked for.

That voice was Hank. The restaurant's elder statesman lit a cigarette, and then shook out the match. He lurched forward so as not to stomp in Jason's chunder.

"Kinda squeamish there, huh, Kid?"

Although physically unable to utter the warning, *say another word and I'll shred your small intestines with a cheese grater,* Jason's glare seemed to convey the sentiment.

Hank raised a hand in protest. Red ash burned at the end of his Camel Light. "Okay, o-kaaay. I see you're busy here. I'll come back when you're not such a cranky pants."

Hunched over a puddle of his own splatter, it was difficult for Jason not to consider that when he graduated college and set out for a career as an English teacher, this wasn't exactly what he had in mind.

"Hey." Hank flicked his butt to the asphalt. "You need a wipey?"

Jason sighed, and then brushed the sweat from his brow. He offered a weak smile. "Yeah...that would be good."

Hank nodded. "There's some in the office. You should probably get one."

Jason rolled his eyes. His hair was cropped short. "Thanks. You're a champ."

"Sheesh. *Just kidding.*" Hank handed over a moist napkin. "This is quite a life you've carved out for yourself there, Kid.

Putting that degree to good use. Well done."

Jason wiped his mouth. "Thing is, I used to laugh at those jackasses who graduate college and then never move on to real life. Staying in limbo, jumping from one crappy job to another, avoiding responsibility. Refusing to grow up." He shook his head. "Now *I'm* the jackass."

Only moments earlier while bussing tables, Jason discovered that a gooey, saliva-coated booger was stringy between the bottom of a fajita tray and his left hand. It sent him running into the alley and puking his guts out. Working in kitchens taught him to be afraid.

Just thinking about the mucous spurred more upchuck, and while Jason lurched forward, he recognized with regurgitated clarity that whatever he intended for his life, he was starting to think that maybe...possibly...it was time to reevaluate his plan for getting there.

It was then that Hank busted Jason's balls in the very manner he liked to dish it out. Hank unholstered his finger guns and pointed them at Jason. "Watch out, boys and girls. Big J is on the scene." Hank cocked his thumb triggers and made the *chk chk* sound.

Jason looked up from his yak. And there he saw Hank as some distant version of himself, the senior Jason having come back in time to warn his younger self about wasting opportunities, about where he might end up unless he did something about it lickety-split.

Commotion came from inside the restaurant. Hank put a hand to his ear. "Ah, yes. I hear the distant song of another dissatisfied customer. You coming?"

Jason pulled a final corn niblet from his tongue.

The future has to look brighter than this, he thought. *It just absolutely has—*

There was a blast of white light. There were streaks of screaming fluorescent color. There was the sensation of being sucked through a tornado. And then there was beer. Lots and lots of beer.

Snapped out of his drunken memory haze...*what the hell was that?*...Jason shook his head and blinked hard, realizing that Katja had been talking to him all along. "I, uh, it was...what?"

Katja turned up his palm, and then ran a finger along the underside of his elbow, like a psychic reading his lifeline. "This."

"Oh! My scar. That." Jason chuckled. "It, uh...it's a baseball injury. I blew," he said, and hiccupped, wishing he hadn't physically and metaphorically choked at that particular moment of the story. "I blew out my elbow."

Only when Jason described it as baseball, he meant Whiffleball. And when he said league championship, he meant one-on-one tournament against his buddy, Reuben. And when he said Wantagh Park, he meant in the driveway, at home, pitching against the garage.

After throwing a slider those seven years earlier, Jason turned around and dashed after the batted ball. With his head craned back while running, he looked up, inches from an over-the-shoulder catch, Willie Mays-style. But just as the ball was about to land in his outstretched hand, Jason felt a blast of pain in his foot as he tripped over the curb, breaking his big toe. With a loud, unsophisticated *aaahhh!* he landed on his elbow, breaking that as well, requiring surgery and a cast. The first recorded injury in Whiffleball history.

But Jason assured Katja that the pain was manly and baseball and all things tough and proud and American.

"Oh," she said. "That sounds much horrible."

Hoping he wouldn't topple over, Jason fell back against the bar, and then looked to Theo, who was lip-locked with Michelle. And just as he thought that his experiences since meeting the quiet Kiwi were getting progressively bizarre, Katja slipped Jason's hand inside her back pocket.

"Well," he said, "recovery *was* tough." Jason glanced at her cleavage. "But I got over it."

Chapter 33
Phone Sex

"Starlight Designs. How can I help y—?" The phone went dead. Wearing a cordless headset, Lex leaned forward at his new desk. He looked up to see Emma's finger depressing the hook switch. Dusty beams of sunlight oozed through the crescent moon window.

With eyes wide and mouth closed, Emma offered what appeared to be a look of patient but stern encouragement. "Hi." A shiny silk blouse revealed borderline slutty cleavage. Her long, black hair was in a ponytail. "I thought we talked about that. How do we answer the phone?"

Lex stiffened, feeling as if he was being interrogated about the cucumber-scented hand lotion next to his bed. "What do you...I don't...Oh! Shit. Yeah. Okay, okay. I got it. Sorry. I got it." Answering the phones, his was the voice of the company. This was his first day on the job, and no time for distractions. He was an almost partner, after all. He shifted in his chair. "Okay." He cleared this throat. "Here I go."

"I'm wet with anticipation. I'll try not to cream myself."

"Starlight Designs," Lex orated proudly, and perhaps not coincidentally, like a puppy dropping the morning paper at his master's feet. "How can I help y—?"

"Lex!"

"What? I thought...oh, son of a bitch! I did it again. Fuck." He rattled off the greeting. "I know, I know, Starlight Designs. This is Lex. How can I direct your call?"

Emma sat in his lap, wrapped her arms around his neck. She sucked on his bottom lip like it was a butterscotch candy. "See, Pumpkin? You just need to relax."

Lex groaned as his bulge inadvertently poked her in the no-no spot.

"Oh, you naughty boy." Emma wrinkled her nose, pressing her breasts against his chest. "But as far as you're concerned, that's a one-way street. Exit only." She licked his upper lip, depressing her tight booty on his lap. "For now."

Mouth agape, Lex gawked at Emma's nipples, erect beneath her blouse. He was oblivious to the phone's rolling, muted tone and a small green light flashing next to *Line 1*.

"You can talk into my tits all you want, but the phone doesn't work that way."

"Huh? What?"

"That ringing? The phone? You know…your job?"

"Oh shit, right." Lex tried easing Emma to her feet.

"Uh-uh." Emma unbuttoned her blouse. "Go ahead. Answer."

Lex gasped and then puckered his lips. He wanted to wipe away the single bead of sweat that seemed to find every irritated pore. "But…are you…?"

Emma tongued his earlobe, whispered her hot breath. "Answer."

Lex pressed the *Talk* button. "Starlight Designs. How can…? This is Lex. How can I direct your call?"

He listened to the voice on the other end of the phone. Emma lowered her brassiere, and with her naked breast in hand, rubbed her nipple against his cheek, like writing her name with frosting on the top of a birthday cake.

"Ye…yes," Lex said, barely holding back a series of pants. Erotic swells of anxiety pulsated from balls to lips. "I think she's still…mmh…here. Let me…mmh…see if she's available." He clawed for the *Hold* button, and then rammed his tongue down Emma's throat. His hair was mussed. His tie was yanked to the side. "It's Jack Appledouche."

Emma raised an eyebrow. "Apple *who*?"

"Appledouche." Lex shrugged. "The guy said Appledouche."

"Lex. What the fuck is wrong with you? Nobody's name is Apple*douche*."

"Well, I don't know. He's got a weird accent. He said—"

"Oh," Emma said, buttoning her blouse. "Ah-bla-dooh-zjay? Abladeujé?"

"Yeah," Lex said. "That must be it. Abladeujé. Right."

"And it's Jacques, you pinhead. Not Jack." Emma chuckled. "Jacques. Well, well, well. I knew he'd call. He wants to back the Milky Way. But really, he just wants to fuck me, which is okay. He's got a shitload of money and likes to throw it around." She nodded at the phone. "I'll take it in my office."

As he watched Emma saunter away—her office door was frosted glass, her name along the crescent-shaped company logo—Lex knew that his would be a job like no other. That it would take him further, and drive him madder, than anything he had ever done before. And that when it was all over, he would never look at his tiny little life quite the same way again.

"Oh, and get that phone bit straightened out," Emma called back, poking her head out from behind the door. "I can't have you fucking up my office."

Chapter 34
Taking Care of Business

Thunderstruck, Lex was in mid-crap. *Maybe it's a dog thing,* he thought, *maybe it's an Earth thing,* but more and more Lex found himself doing some of his best thinking while taking care of business. "You're sending Rufus, aren't you?" He squeezed out the rest of his brown, curly-cue dookie. "It's Rufus, isn't it? I knew it."

Leaning on her walking stick, Emma grabbed the stinky load with a plastic *Arby's* bag left in the motel parking lot. The late morning sunshine peaked over the rooftop.

"Oh, fuck." Lex walked in a circle, his tail whipping to and fro. "Rufus? Really? Oh...not Rufus. Not *Rufus.*" Lex looked up at Emma, hoping he might be wrong. "Rufus?"

Emma smirked as she chucked the knotted bag into the dumpster. "Why? Do you have a problem with Rufus?"

Of course I have a problem with Rufus, you fucking ox!

Lex let his head drop with well-rehearsed precision to an inevitable question. With each day on Earth, Emma treated him more and more like a dog, as if he had lost his humanity. His soul. Although it was clear to Lex that Emma was the one whose humanity seemed to be slipping away. Yet she also failed to appreciate that as a canine, his senses were far more acute than even he initially realized.

Just days earlier, the low muffled ring of the motel phone woke him, even though he had been asleep in the bathroom, curled up next to the bathtub. From the other side of the door, he heard Emma's conversation, as clear to him as if the voices had been shouted directly in his eardrum, rather than whispered in the next room.

Lex was finally starting to decipher the multitude of sounds, tones and pitches inundating him—footsteps; cell phone ringers; vibrating pagers; scurrying mice; yelling; laughing; grinding teeth; gurgling ulcers; screeching tires; the crackle of a candy wrapper; the whine of other dogs. It was like listening to a hundred radio stations all at once, only with each passing day he was better able to simultaneously distinguish and compartmentalize each one from the others.

"My Emma," Lex heard through the phone, and while the voice did not resonate with the sultry timber he remembered from Eternity—it now carried a hesitant Jamaican inflection—it was unmistakably Rufus. "I am here to help you."

Even from the other side of the bathroom door, Lex could hear the creak of the chair as Emma leaned back in it. He could hear her quivered breaths. He could hear the slight chafe of the spiraled receiver cord as she twirled it around her finger.

Lex could also smell the heaping sorrow that oozed from her pores, the desperate, salty isolation as pungent to him as the plume of an agitated skunk. And Lex could hear her cry. And listen. "I saw Lawrence," Rufus explained.

Lex immediately figured the rest, detecting the glint of recognition in Emma's whimper. As the CBM warehouse manager in Eternity, Lawrence was in the unique position to arrange for Rufus' banishment to Earth. And as Lawrence's ex-wife, Emma understood the reach of his influence, information she must have confided to Rufus long before her own banishment.

How Lex knew about Lawrence's prominent standing in the greater scheme of Eternity—more important than even Emma realized—was another matter entirely.

"It took some persuading," Rufus told Emma, "but Lawrence...he was willing to put reason aside and make an exception. I did not think he would." Lawrence told Rufus that a CBM jar had gone lost on Earth, and that if Emma could actually get her hands on it, she would know how to get them back home.

Lawrence didn't know exactly where the jar was—they were

far more difficult to track outside Eternity—but he could locate it within a few thousand miles. Not bad, considering that in Earth measures there wasn't an equation sophisticated enough to quantify the immensity of the metaphysical Universe.

And much to Rufus' surprise, Lawrence also knew precisely where Emma was. When Rufus asked how he had come upon such particular information, Lawrence merely smiled, and said that Rufus had asked for enough favors already, and was in no position to ask for another.

From the other side of the bathroom door, Lex heard Emma sniffle and cry into the phone again. He then heard Emma and Rufus agree to communicate by e-mail only from then on—until they found the jar. Emma barely got out a trembling whisper. "It's too much to hear your voice," she said. "Go to New Zealand. I know where to look."

But that was three days before. Emma had since been her typical, haughty self, although mixed in were the first glimmers of trepidation Lex had ever seen in her.

Walking across the motel parking lot now, Lex stared at the *Arby's* sign hovering over the service road. While pretending to be upset with Rufus' return, he was enraptured by the aroma of greasy, onion-slathered roast beef. Lex *was* upset. It's just that he already had a few days to get used to it.

Emma looked over her shoulder. "Let's head over to the library and check the e-mail. Lilly should have some news by now. Maybe she won't be worthless after all."

Lex wanted to reach up his hind leg and scratch the inside of his right ear just then, but his heart was a heaping spoonful of sorrow. Never before had he regretted his decision, when he gave up the opportunity to follow one distinct path so that he could follow another.

My life didn't have to be like this. No Rufus, no Emma. It was up to me. It was my choice.

"Well," Emma called back. "You coming or what?"

Staring at the bitter, three hundred-pound pear that Emma

had become, Lex's grief lifted suddenly—the fuzzy gray head of a dandelion scattered in the summer breeze. "Yeah, yeah," he said. "Don't get your nipples in an uproar."

Lex shook out his fur. His metal tag jangled. And then a mischievous smile overtook his face. A wry, cagey glint twinkled in his black eyes. He smiled again because he was sure that Emma noticed, and that for a moment, she was worried. Because Lex had a secret of his own. A secret that went beyond Lawrence, way beyond Rufus and even the missing CBM jar itself. Lex knew the biggest secret in Eternity. The biggest secret there ever was.

And he wasn't sharing.

Chapter 35
The Morning After

Venice, Italy—Piazza San Marco
Monday, September 5, 2005, 11:05 a.m.

Jason and Theo wandered through the Piazza san Marco, an enormous square in Venice, adjacent to a wide berth off the Grand Canal. Gondolas floated side by side, tied to wooden posts.

The crowded square was overrun by pigeons as Jason and Theo snapped several pictures of the *Basilica di San Marco*, the cathedral of Venice. The exterior brickwork was laid out in three levels, with large archways, copper doors and mosaics on the lower, topped then by smaller and larger domes. Bronze horse statues lined the entranceway.

"Where's what's-her-face?" Jason struggled for the name. "Michelle?"

"Yeh, dunno, mate. She was with me when I passed out." Theo chuckled. "Where's your friend?" He pronounced it *freeend*. "She was foxy."

Squinting beneath the morning sun, Jason's head throbbed like a punk band's bass drum. "We, uh...she..." He shrugged.

Theo chuckled again. "Women, yeh?"

"Yeah," Jason said, but he didn't mean that women confused him, which they did, or that he was indifferent toward Katja, which he wasn't. But he was conflicted about their rendezvous the night before, which included a moment he wanted to Photoshop out of existence.

After leaving the pub, Jason and Katja slipped into the courtyard behind the hostel, where they dove into a kissing frenzy. Only instead of gettin' busy, Jason suddenly recused himself. He claimed to have been too drunk to stand up, let alone engage in any activity requiring timing and finesse, leaving Katja confused, if not just a little bit insulted.

But Jason hadn't removed his hand from her left breast because of anything she did. And he hadn't passed up on almost guaranteed sex because he thought it improper or ungentlemanly, seeing as how they only just met. Jason left Katja with her honor intact because, in his drunken, convoluted logic, having sex with *her* would have meant betraying *Lilly*, even though she had deserted him with no warning or explanation.

Aware that he had whacked the logical side of his brain with a shovel and locked it in a tool shed, Jason was convinced— just absolutely certain—that he and Lilly would find each other again, sometime, someplace, and that when they did, it would be worth the wait.

He also considered another possibility. It had been more than a year since his last night of partnered naked time and was out of practice, something he did not want to demonstrate. But he rejected it on the grounds that destiny was a far better excuse than him being a complete wuss.

"So...I'm off to see this...," Theo said, and then hesitated. "Actually, it's...no. Forget it." Jason watched him look toward the canal and back again. "Oh, fuck it. I'm looking for this guy, yeh?"

Theo unfolded a note. He showed it to Jason, who was indeed curious. Part of the note read: *Vincenzo Antiques. Venice. Ask for Pietro.*

"My mum," Theo said, although Jason sensed awkwardness in his manner, like Theo was embarrassed about something, "she just got this old jar, yeh? It was...buried in a closet. I dunno. It's been in the family for ages. We're trying to find out where it came from."

From inside his knapsack Theo presented the plastic sandwich bag containing six pictures of the jar, one each from different angles. "This guy, yeh? Pietro? He's supposed to be an expert. Antiques. Stuff like that. I dunno. I got the address from...someone I met in Amsterdam." Theo shrugged. "You want to come? It's close. Then we can get a feed."

Surrounded by tourists, Jason stared up into the bright blue sky. He followed a pigeon as it soared over the sparkling canal, and then swooped back, perching on a cathedral tower. And as his eyes drifted off into the distance, there was no Hank or Katja or Lilly to confuse him. *Do I want to come with you?* Jason turned to Theo, and smiled. *Hell yeah, I do. Absolutely.*

"What are we waiting for?" he said. "Let's go see about this jar of yours."

9-05-05

Hi Mom,

Just spent four days in Rome and now I'm in Venice. Rome was kinda cool, but I was soooo tired by the time I got there, it took me a day or two to unwind. Traveling is hard work!

Met this nice guy from New Zealand, and we're off to get some breakfast. It's like cheese every meal. You should see this place. No cars! There's water instead of roads. Pretty weird. You see it in the movies, but when it's right in front of you...Love you, mom.

Jason

Chapter 36
Who Watches the Watchman?

Venice, Italy—Vincenzo Antiques
Monday, September 5, 2005, 2:33 p.m.

Maroon curtains aligned the front window of *Vincenzo Antiques*; only a faint whisper of sunlight stole through. The shop was filled with vases, necklaces, watches and clocks, displayed in dusty glass cases, and on dark, wooden tabletops with scratches in the finish. As Theo approached the counter, Emerald shards of light from a glass ashtray refracted into his sight line. A discarded cigarette burned in the receptacle.

Jason stood by the front window admiring a black vase with the bust of a naked woman.

A barrel-chested man appeared from behind a maroon curtain. He had salt-and-pepper hair and gray stubble. "Can I help you, yes? What is I can do for you?"

Theo immediately felt a tornado of anticipation. After months searching for the source of his wonder and confusion, he was finally going to get some answers. And yet Theo treated his jar like a Picasso—a rare item that only a select few had the expertise to authenticate. The pictures enabled him to screen anyone who claimed interest in the jar. Theo didn't know what the jar was, where it came from or what it contained, but he clearly understood there was no way to describe it to someone who didn't already have a pretty good idea of what it might be. Either you know or you don't.

Theo proceeded with extreme caution. Pictures first. Then maybe...maybe...he would produce the jar. If he could actually find someone who had information about it, he needed to look them in the eye.

In Amsterdam, Theo had shown the pictures to George, who gave reasons to believe that his information was on the level. George said that whoever held the jar had inexplicable dream-like hallucinations, although he wouldn't offer specifics.

But Theo's instincts, perhaps much like George himself, were in conflict. Standing in the *Ball and Tickle* dressing room before show time, Theo believed that George was an okay guy, or woman...*or whatever*...but knew more than he was saying.

"Are you Vincenzo?" Theo's soft voice was firm except for an unexpected quiver at the end of his Kiwi lilt. "Is this your shop?"

"No, no. I am Alberto. There is no more Vincenzo. Mi fratello. Poor Vincenzo...he is dead from the stroke." Alberto held his head in silence.

Wobbled but undeterred, Theo looked back at Jason. The silence allowed his whirlwind of emotions to settle. Thoughts finally coming together, Theo extended his hand. "I'm Thee—"

"But this is no time for sadness, sí?" Alberto detonated his hands in a clap, then sprang from behind the counter, sending Theo back a step. "We come here to make our acquaintances... and maybe some biz-i-ness, yes?"

"Uh...actually," Theo began. "I'm looking for Pietro. Is he here?"

"Oh, Pietro? Pietro!" Alberto's laugh was hearty. "No, no. My nephew is no here now. You tell Alberto, sí? I maybe help you."

As Theo reached for the pictures, he felt himself hurtle through that multicolored vortex, much as he did in the Waitomo Caves, except that as he *whooshed* through the great expanse he thought he saw Jason hunched over and throwing up in the back alley of a restaurant, an event that was simultaneously familiar and unfamiliar. *Have I seen this before? No. I don't...think so, but...wasn't there a cranky, old fucker, smoking a cigarette and...?* To Theo it was like a dream he wasn't sure was really his, which only added to his mounting paranoia.

Since arriving in Venice, Theo felt as if he were under surveillance, if someone was just a few steps behind him. He snapped out of it. "When's Pietro back? I got something here, yeh?"

"Oh, you no be shy, yes? You show Alberto. Come. Show."

Theo took another step back. He looked to Jason, who shrugged, and then nodded. Doing as suggested, Theo emptied his bag.

"Oh." Alberto's eyes drew wide. "Sí. Yes. Pietro would much love this piece. It is very beautiful. Are you to sell? Do you have? I give you good price."

"No...I dunno," Theo said. "Is...do you know when Pietro will be back? I'd rather talk to him, yeh? I was told he knows about this?"

"Sí, sí. Pietro makes the glasswork. He...how you say? He gives blow to glass. No, no. He blows. Sí, yes. He blows it." Alberto nodded. "Pietro is the best at blowing. But Alberto...I prefer the watches. Time is both enemy and friend, yes? You listen to what Alberto tell you."

Theo nodded agreeably, although he wasn't sure why.

"Time is glorious to chase, but it bring much sadness when it chase you." He pointed at his crow's feet. "You never know how much you have left, only how much is gone. Do while you can, because once time chase you, it never stop."

Thundering like a quartet of trumpets, Alberto unleashed a septic cloud more potent than a tank of piranhas. *Hraaamp!* Recoiling from the toxic fumes, Theo instinctively put his hand up near his face. Jason covered his mouth, holding in a chuckle.

"Oh, scusami, scusami," Alberto said. "Too many anchovies. They are my weak-i-ness." But time is good, yes? I have many watches for to buy. Come. You see."

"Uh...no thanks." Theo tried not to gag on the gnarly mist. "I think I'll wait for Pietro, yeh? When will he be back?"

"Oh, Pietro no be here for four, maybe five months."

"Five months?" Theo sunk, feeling insignificant in such close proximity to his gassy host. "Do you know where he is?"

Alberto explained that Pietro spent half the year at *Vincenzo Antiques,* and the other half at *Vincenzo Italia,* a second store in

Barcelona, where he would reside at least until Christmas, if not longer. "He leave yesterday," Alberto said. "Should arrive Barcelona, maybe two weeks. Go see his famiglia first, then to store in Barcelona. You can visit him there, if you like."

Theo stared at the ashtray, following the smoke as faint swirls slowly dissolved.

"But now I show you nice watches, yes? I give you good price."

Chapter 37
Aquariums

The Southern Sphere of Eternity—The Aquarium
Milky Way's Public Unveiling: T-Minus 28 Days (Eternity
Standard Time)

Rumor had it that Brigsby himself would be in attendance, which was true. Rumor had it that Brigsby was going to quit his talk show, *Breakfast with Brigsby*, to launch a monthly lifestyle magazine, *B*, which was false. Rumor also had it, for those who knew how to listen, that Brigsby was making inquiries—quietly—about galaxy design. George knew how to listen.

It seemed as if Brigsby rolled into the converted warehouse on a platform, neither in step with the music nor out, but with a smooth confluence of motion and beat. He seemed to glide through the slalom of martini drinkers and pill poppers, blondes and brunettes, bisexuals and transsexuals, money makers and money grubbers, those with power and those without. A party like all the rest and a party like no other.

The music pulsed. *"Twice in one...twice in one...mmm-mmm... yeah."*

George felt a slight tapping on his shoulder as aqua blue neon lights sparkled throughout the *Aquarium*. The marine-themed club was designed as if a rectangular box of air had been carved out from the deep sea and then encased in glass. Behind the walls, floor and ceiling was an array of exotic sea life, including hammerhead sharks, mantas and jellyfish. Centered in the fish tank of people was a black, oval bar with a smaller, cylindrical aquarium wrapping around its base.

"Hey," a young man said. "Is that Brigsby? He's so...puny."

"Yes," George said above the pulsing, electronic baseline. A tall redheaded woman and three young men in black T-shirts surrounded Brigsby. "That's him. That's his secret. It isn't that he's small...but he knows how to make others feel big."

"Nice. I know someone who could use that advice."

"Oh?" George was impressed with the young man's sleek physical prowess, although he surmised quickly that his new acquaintance was interested in women only. "Who's that?"

"Nobody," he said. "It's nothing. I'm Lex."

"Well, hello Lex. It's nice to meet you. My name is George." They shook hands. "Might I ask...are you looking for someone? You look lost."

"I'm supposed to meet my part...," Lex began, and then shook his head, "...my boss. She says if we want to land the big accounts we have to, you know...meet the right people. Well, that's not exactly the way she said it, but...you get the idea."

"Yes, yes." A tiger shark swam beneath them. It snapped at the bottom of their shoes. "I understand. And you think this is the place to...meet the right people?"

"Honestly, I have no idea. But Emma, my part...damn.... My boss, Emma. She has very...particular ideas about how to achieve success. Actually, she has very particular ideas about success, now that I think about it."

"Really? What are *your* ideas about success?"

"Me? Shit. I...*pfff*...good question. I'm not sure."

"That's understandable. Success can be quite confusing. So many ideas about what's important. Would you like another beer? I could use a drink myself."

Having downed another two cocktails apiece and working on a third, George led Lex to a semicircular booth. Its clear fiberglass cushions were filled with blue-tailed goldfish. Before them was a glass table, also a fish tank. "So tell me about *Starlight Designs*." He rested his drink above a school of needle-fish. "It seems fascinating."

"It is. Kinda. I mean...we do get our hands on the fabric of the Universe, so that's pretty cool. Right now we've got a few smaller projects—comets and whatnot—plus we just finished something pretty big, although it's still hush-hush. Emma's such a secrecy nut. 'Control the spin.' That's what she says. We're putting out a press release about the unveiling. She's been working on it for weeks."

"I'll be on the lookout."

"Thing is, the Universe isn't exactly, you know...what I expected."

George leaned forward, distracted by some laughter. "How so?"

"Well, it's so, I don't know, it's so...temporary. I mean, all you really need are the right materials, which...granted, are not easy to come by. But once you've got them, you can build or destroy virtually anything. I mean...anything. It's pretty simple. Not the design part. Naturally...you have to have good ideas about shape and texture and proportion..." George nodded. "But once you've got the blueprint—"

"It's just work?"

"Exactly. It's a job, it's work....There's tons of paperwork, and there's the contractors, suppliers and zoning commissions. Everybody's got their hand out. And then there's..."

George watched Lex retreat into his beer. "Go ahead. It's all right."

"I really shouldn't complain. I mean, like I said, it *is* pretty cool. Plus, eight months ago I got fired from my job and now I'm sitting inside a giant fish tank with...Brigsby." Lex looked around. "Well...he was here a minute ago."

"He left after five minutes," George explained, having decided that Lex would be perfect. Just perfect. "Once word spread that he was coming, the whole world showed up. He can usually keep it quiet, but I'm sure you can imagine how that goes." George sipped his drink. "Would you like to meet him?"

"Me? Really? You know him?"

George chewed on a pineapple sliver. He nodded. "We've met."

"Yeah. Emma'll flip. Oh shit. There she is. Let me go get—"

"I've got a better idea." George put his small hand on Lex's shoulder. "Brigsby's having a little get-together tomorrow night, and I'm sure he'd be interested to meet you."

"Really? Why?"

"Because you're smart, decent and curious. Brigsby likes that."

"He does? I mean...I am?"

"Certainly. Don't you think of yourself as being smart and decent?"

"I...don't know," Lex said. "Maybe...? I guess...? I'm not sure."

"Well, then. It's time we got you to think about it. And I can't imagine anyone who would agree more than Brigsby."

Chapter 38
The Rainbow Connection

The Eastern Sphere of Eternity
Milky Way's Public Unveiling: T-Minus 27 Days (Eternity
Standard Time)

Six prodigious rainbows equidistant from one another arched over Willow Park. They intersected at their zeniths like a spectacular troika of multicolored wishbones.

Danielle reclined in the grass and leaned against a Keiko, one of nine seven hundred-foot fig trees with raspberry-colored bark and a bushel of yellow leaves at the top. Except for three others in the dense forest region of the Western Sphere, these were the only Keikos in Eternity.

Gazing up at the sky, still holding onto its mid-range blue, Danielle admired the orange sunlight draped over the rainbow arches. It created a translucent, tangerine dome.

She felt insignificant in the shadow of the Keikos, which seemed insignificant beneath the mile-high apartments making up Willow Towers, which again seemed insignificant beneath the meteor shower alighting the heavens. "I can't, I can't. I just can't." She scratched her forearm, leaving white streak marks. "It's all my fault. I fucked it up. I did it."

Danielle held her silver wedding band between two fingers. A tear rolled down her face. "I remember how you proposed, Baby. We was holdin' hands, makin' sure we underneath the rainbows, like now, and I was all annoyed 'n shit because you was actin' uptight." Danielle chuckled, wiped her eye. "And then you took me here, under our tree...with them little figgy things way up tip-top and you said, 'Danny, you my life and my love. And I ain't never want to think about a life that ain't with you.' And then you got down on one knee, like all romantic, and before you even took the ring out I was sayin' to myself...nah, I was *screamin'* to myself, 'Oh, yes, Baby. I'll marry you any time, any day."'"

Danielle looked up to see Donald walking across the grass, beneath the tangerine dome. It left her with a bittersweet pang in her heart. He smiled, waved. "And now I messed it all up. It was me that knocked over that jar. I should'a fessed up before, but I can't live like this no more. I love you, Baby. I'm gonna put this right. You'll see."

Donald leaned over. His shadow crosshatched on her face. "Hi, Sweetie." He kissed her cheek and then laid with his head in her lap. He said he had the missing jar situation all worked out. As if Brigsby and his nonsense could actually provide a blueprint to their freedom.

But Danielle had made a decision of her own. And if Donald found out, he wasn't going to like it.

Chapter 39
The Great Pretender

The Southern Sphere of Eternity—Brigsby's Loft Apartment Milky Way's Public Unveiling: T-Minus 27 Days (Eternity Standard Time)

"Don't spit in my face, Brigsby. I'm beggin' you, and I ain't never begged for nothin' in my life. Donnie don't even know I'm here. He thinks I'm at the movies."

Danielle stood before Brigsby in his second-floor loft, an old pool hall converted into one of his hideaways. Contrary to his primary abode, this sanctuary was sparse, with a leather couch, glass coffee table and stand-alone bar decorating an otherwise empty room. Looking at Brigsby in the vast space, holding up his martini glass as if it were a medallion to ward off evil spirits, Danielle was reminded of just how small and fragile he was.

"So, yeah. I'm scared and it's my fault. Why you makin' me say it?"

"Darling…of course, no one knows better than moi…you are most definitely your own woman. I can't *make* you do anything."

"Don't mess with me, Bri—"

"Yes, Danielle. You're right. You want my reaction? Fine. Here it is. The two of you are in more trouble than you can possibly imagine. And whether you want to believe this or not, I'm putting myself in very real danger just talking to you at all."

Danielle stared at the aging talk show host, with his sagging, sad-frog eyes, lopsided toupee and scrawny arms, seeing him not as a celebrity, but as the mere outline of a man wistful about his obvious mortality. A man with fear.

"Yeah," she said. "Okay." Danielle turned away from Brigsby, although she wanted to face him. "But where else can I go?"

"I don't know what you expect, Danielle. This is stunning, even for me. Sure, I play my little games to get what I want, but this is no game, and certainly not one I can win. If you told me sooner what you'd done...and what madness Donald has in mind—"

Danielle spun around. "Sooner? Sooner? I been in shock, motherfucka! How can I tell this shit to anybody? 'Oh, excuse me, but...me and my husband lost one of them jars that can create or destroy half the Universe. You got a spare?'"

Brigsby raised his eyebrows. "Well...you got me there."

Danielle sighed. "You my last chance, Brigs. We got no one else. Donnie won't listen to me. You know how he gets. Always gotta be responsible for everything. But not this time. I gotta take the hit for this one, and you can make it happen."

Danielle held herself, watching as Brigsby eased his head back and forth. "Ain't nothing you can do? I know you got friends with the company."

"This goes far beyond knowing people. This isn't just misplaced company property. That material can alter the predetermined order of things. Did you ever think that you were *supposed* to lose that jar? That this is just the way it was meant to be?"

"Meant to be? Are you outta your muthafuckin' mind?! This was an accident. An *ax-i-dent*. We don't deserve this kinda trouble just for one stupid mistake. It ain't fair. It ain't right."

"Maybe," Brigsby said. "Maybe."

"Maybe?" Danielle said. "Maybe wha—?"

"You need to accept some responsibility Danielle. I didn't force that condo on you, or that job, either. And I *certainly* didn't force you to fellate your husband on a platform overlooking the very planet you were supposed to safeguard, having a very real say in matters of life and death." Brigsby put down his blue martini, spilling some on the coffee table. "Donald asked me for help, so I did. I helped him because he's my friend. My best friend."

Danielle brushed her humiliation aside. She would be humiliated later.

"Friends? You don't know Jack about *havin'* friends because you don't know Jack about *bein'* a friend. Yeah, you got groupies comin' outta that skinny white ass of yours, but that's all you got. You need groupies to *worship* you so they don't ever get to *know* you."

Danielle closed in on Brigsby, who seemed to shrink and dissipate as she approached, as if he were just a mist held together by poofy clothes.

"Who you kiddin'? You didn't do any of this for us. For Donnie. You hooked us up with that apartment...the job...to keep him close. You figure he's always gonna feel like he owes you. Like it's an obligation 'n shit to be your little nurse. And the sad thing is...that's exactly what happened. Donnie ain't never leavin' you because ain't no one more loyal." She pointed at him. "You want your cake and now you're chokin' on it, too. Donnie's your friend when it's convenient and a groupie when it ain't."

Danielle reached for the doorknob, but turned, lowered her voice.

"I never say shit to him because it ain't my place to come between folks. He's gotta figure this shit out for himself. But you...*tsch*...you know better. *Way* better. Donnie's your friend, that's for damn sure. But you ain't his. He's gonna wreck his life—our life—if you don't do somethin'. You got the juice to make it right. And if you don't use it for somethin' worth doin', then you're every bit the dog you say you ain't."

Danielle went to the window and looked at the quiet street below. She turned to face him. "Your move, Mr. Celebrity. Time to be a star."

Brigsby stood before her. He said nothing.

"You gotta choose what kind of man you're gonna be, Brigs. You don't find a way to connect with somebody...connect for real...then your life's nothin' but one big distraction. At least us regular folk admit we got problems. Our hearts break. We're afraid. You stand up on that stage every day, always pretending."

Brigsby put his glass on the windowsill. "I think...," he said.

Come on, Brigsby. I know you in there.

"Maybe...," he said.

That's it. You almost there...

"Can I...call you a cab?"

Danielle closed her eyes. She thought of her life with Donald. And her life without him. "No," she said. "I'll walk."

"Are you sure? It's quite a long way."

"Yeah, it is," Danielle said as she pulled the door behind her. There were two men at the bottom of the stairs, on their way up. "But I got a lot on my mind."

Chapter 40
A Convincing Argument

Venice, Italy—Vincenzo Antiques
Monday, September 5, 2005, 3:17 p.m.

As they spilled back out into the stark Venetian sunlight, Theo and Jason gasped for any air not contaminated with the defiled vapor of festering ass crack, unaware that a phone call was being placed from within the shop, and that the recipient of that call was delighted to receive the news.

But pacified that there would be at least one more leg to his search, Theo gagged and then staggered over to a bench facing the Grand Canal. He never expected his trip to be easy. Which is the way he liked it. The bigger the challenge, the bigger the fun.

Jason sat beside him. "Listen...you've got at least, what, like...two weeks until Pietro is in Barcelona?" He sniffed his T-shirt. "Good God, we should burn these."

Theo nodded. "Yeh, about two weeks."

"So you won't be able to find your jar guy until at least then, right?"

Theo nodded again, sensing that Jason wanted to ask him something.

After a pause, he did. "You want to go to Budapest? And then maybe Prague? We could leave today."

Neither of them had plans to go there, until the day before, when Theo's redhead made a convincing argument. While topless. Rubbing suntan lotion on herself. Neck to bellybutton. She pronounced the cities *Budipist* and *Proog*. "They're fuckin' brilliant, mate. Fuckin' brilliant."

Theo considered Jason's proposal. It was one thing to sightsee with a virtual stranger, or even just knock back a few beers. But it was something else entirely to travel in tandem, sharing sleeping quarters and food, forgoing total independence in exchange for companionship, putting trust in someone you barely know, and accepting some in return.

And it wasn't that Theo didn't want to go—he had secretly hoped Jason would ask. But after months of travel, Theo lost urgency about his jar, at times forgetting about it completely. Since leaving New Zealand, he had zigzagged across Europe, including stops in Oslo, Helsinki, Copenhagen, Stockholm, London, Amsterdam, Berlin, Hamburg, Frankfurt, Brussels, Zurich, Geneva, Zagreb, Lisbon, Athens, Corfu, Paris, Florence, Milan, Tuscany, Rome and now Venice.

Theo immersed himself in the adventure of backpacking—meeting new people, crossing borders. But he felt again much as he did that one extraordinary day, deep beneath the ocean off Cathedral Cove.

Seeing Alberto—giving form to both a quest and a question that had transmogrified into a hazy, dream-like memory—Theo became mesmerized, thinking finally that he would meet with relief from the peculiar, mind-boggling itch that for the past six months had driven, confused and fascinated him.

Now that those emotions had erupted again, Theo wasn't quite sure how to handle them. He felt guilty about lying to Jason, but what choice did he have? *Hey, mate, I found this jar in an underground glow-worm cave—maybe it's alien, maybe it's magic, I have no idea—but it makes me hallucinate as I go insane. Wanna hang out?*

Theo let out a sigh, looked at the sparkling waters, then at Jason. "Yeh," he finally said, and smiled. "Let's go to Budapest."

Jason smiled back. "Really?...Cool."

For reasons he couldn't pinpoint, Theo started to laugh just then, and as he laughed, Jason laughed too. It was a loud, cackling laugh that inspired more laughter from Theo, and then more again from Jason, two young men from opposite corners of the world acknowledging without words that a friendship had formed.

That while neither of them understood why they seemed to click so well, they appreciated that such connections weren't made often. That they shouldn't be taken for granted. And that there would be no going back.

05-09-05

G'day Roger,

Been having any more dreams? I've had a few, but not in a week or so. Still...

Seen some really cool churches and buildings, although I know you don't care about that stuff. A lot of really hot birds, though!

Was on with a girl from Brazil about a month ago, but I've been traveling with this guy from New York the last few days. He's a bit high-strung, but a super nice guy. He's like cousin Phil, only way more fun. We're actually off to Budapest next. Never thought I'd get there!

Stay out of that cave...freaky, man.

Theo

Chapter 41
A View from the Bridge

After rolling into Vienna, Jason and Theo still had several hours before their connecting train left for Budapest. They wandered through the downtown, stopping in a small park. Red, yellow and white petals popped against the swaths of grass. In the distance, over the treetops, were four pointed towers of a white stone building. Birds chirped.

They breathed in an invigorating tonic of crisp morning air, a most welcome respite from Italy's stifling, muggy heat. They exhaled, took another breath, then another.

Theo was still groggy, but he started perking up at Jason's enthusiasm, something he was beginning to anticipate. Once Jason got going, there was no stopping him. Theo told him about New Zealand and its great beaches, which got Jason all riled up about New York.

"Yeh, yeh," Theo said, wearing a blue-and-green pullover his grandmother bought him in Mexico. "I bet it's mad there."

"You gotta visit. I'll show you the best view in the city. My dad used to take me when I was a kid." Jason flicked his eyebrows. "It's not what you think."

Theo was getting excited, wanting to make his way to America. Like most Kiwis, he was fascinated by New York—a giant, fast-paced metropolis compared to every city in New Zealand, even Auckland, with a million residents of its own.

No matter what New York City was actually like, forever embedded in Theo's mind were the news reports he saw as a kid, hearing about how violent New York was. How it seemed to be a ruthless gangland—the Wild West of present day America. But its metamorphosis since then compelled him to go there someday, to see if the city lived up to its legend.

Theo guessed. "Top of the Empire State Building?"

"Great view...but that's not it." Jason offered a mischievous smile. "It's from the middle of the Brooklyn Bridge. Once you walk up there, you never see the city the same way again." Jason pointed, giving a tour. "You've got the Manhattan Bridge on one side, the Statue of Liberty on the other. It connects Manhattan and Brooklyn over the East River, which is amazing when the sun hits the water. It was better before the Towers went down...," Jason paused. "...but it's still awesome. And if you stand in just the right spot, you can see the tip of the Empire State Building way off in the distance. The view'll just knock your socks off."

"Oh, yeh?" Theo said. "That sounds..."

And for some reason, Theo found himself remembering the waters at Cathedral Cove just then, with a dolphin named Ira looking right at him.

"Once you walk around down here," Ira had said, underwater, "you never look at the ocean the same way again. You sure you don't want some shrimp? The buzz'll knock your socks off."

"No, I'm sure," Theo said. "Where's Roger?"

"Don't worry, mate. Howie and Roger are just having a little chat. He's fine."

Standing on the ocean floor—not breathing air, but not *not* breathing either—Theo was surprisingly comfortable. "It's so warm," he said.

"Could be, or could be you're in shock." Ira shrugged. "Either way."

"You're really starting to fuck me off, mate. Are we doing som—"

"Let me ask. You find anything recently?" Ira scratched his belly. "Something you can't describe? Kinda...different?"

Theo would have held his breath just then if there was breath for him to hold. He eyed the dolphin suspiciously. "What do you mean?"

Ira bounced Theo's jar between his flippers. "Look familiar?"

Theo was speechless, yet there was so much to say.

Am I dead? Am I crazy? What the fuck, mate?

"This is more than meets the eye." Ira swam in a circle, his powerful tail coming within inches of Theo's face. "But then... maybe it's less."

"I've been having these dreams," Theo admitted. "Like I'm—"

"Breathing underwater and talking to a dolphin?"

Theo nodded, feeling like he was testifying in court, the lawyer presenting questions to which he already knew the answers. "Well...yeh. Kinda."

"Getting more intense? More real?"

Theo nodded again.

"Supa-dupa. Then I guess you're ready."

I don't think I am.

"You are," Ira assured him.

"But how..." Theo stopped, confused, angry and just a little bit terrified that Ira knew so much about him, and seemed to be able to read his mind. Theo wanted answers and he wanted them now.

"Don't worry." Ira swam in a figure eight. He spiraled once and then again. "I can't read your mind. I just guessed. Seemed like a reasonable conclusion."

For that at least, Theo was grateful.

"So what are you ready for? That's what you want to know?"

Of course, you fucking nimrod! What else?!

Ira turned to Theo. "Hey. No reason to get snarky."

Theo tilted his head, and was about to speak, when Ira interrupted.

"When you wake up from this...and yes, let's just assume that you do wake up; you can relax now...will it really matter if being down here is a dream or hallucination? Or nervous breakdown? Or even if it's real. Will it matter if you *imagined* being down here, or if you were *actually* down here?"

For the moment, Theo didn't care if his underwater experience was induced by drugs, magic or the all-fucking-mighty, just so long as he would wake up, his life would be just the way he left it and he would be at least reasonably sane when he opened his eyes again. And yet there was a part of him that didn't want the hallucination to end. "I don't know," he said. "I'm not sure what to think."

"Fair enough. But more significant...is how you'll handle things once you *do* wake up." He tossed the jar to Theo. "I can help you figure out what this is."

Theo held the jar. It felt heavier somehow. "You could just tell me."

"I can't, actually. We have rules about that sort of thing."

"What do you mean you can't—?"

"I can give you the name of someone...or I can give you nothing. Your call."

Theo ran his fingers along the ridges, feeling subtle impressions he hadn't noticed before. "I'll take the name....You're a crazy fucker, you know that?"

"Not so crazy...but I can see why you think so." Ira shoved another shrimp between his gums. His eyes glazed over. His body went limp. "Oh...and whatever you do, don't lose that thing. Keep it safe."

Theo shrugged. "Like where?"

"Ask Roger." Ira spiraled on his back and floated away. "He'll know what to do."

"Do about what?" Jason looked confused. "The Brooklyn Bridge?"

"What?" Theo blinked hard, seeing the *Südbahnhof* train station up ahead. "Oh, uh...no. You want a feed first? Might be a while before we, uh...get a chance to eat."

"You know," Jason said, "I've got a bizarre craving right now for shrimp cocktail. Yeah...like that's in our budget." He offered a quick laugh. "Wishful thinking, right?"

Theo had a dulled look. A flock of pigeons scattered from the train station rooftop. He let out an uneasy smile. "Yeh," he said. "Wishful thinking."

Chapter 42
I Always Feel Like Somebody's Watching Me (Tell Me Is It Just a Dream?)

Austria—Downtown Vienna
Tuesday, September 6, 2005, 12:17 p.m.

As morning rolled into early afternoon, their enthusiasm had somehow morphed into a curious suspicion. Lost in conversation, Theo and Jason looked up to find themselves in the shade of St. Stephen's Cathedral, a gothic church with a latticework spire that pierced the sky.

They held their cameras steady, gawking through the viewfinders. But they were unable to depress the buttons, as if snapping the pictures was forbidden somehow. They could almost feel the sad survivor's pride soaked into the soul of the city, as if it was eager to break free from its tormented past, yet still not convinced the roots of a new beginning had taken hold. Despite a crowded city square, there was almost perfect silence.

"Do you notice...?" Theo started. "...It's so quiet, yeh?"

Jason nodded. "It's freaking me out. If there were this many people in Times Square, you wouldn't be able to hear a fleet of tanks. But here, it's like they're all looking over their shoulders, afraid Hitler is still watching. I'd be scared shitless, too. That dude was fucking crazy."

"Yeh, true, true. But...I dunno. It's been sixty years."

"I know, but to the old-timers, it probably feels like it was yesterday. You should hear my grandmother tell stories." Jason shook his head. "They still creep me out. I mean...how do you forget fear like that? It's like being sprayed with pure evil. It never washes off."

Theo rolled his shoulders. His neck was stiff from accidentally sleeping on a water bottle on the train ride from Venice.

"Yeh. I dunno. Maybe they're waking up, though. I bet they will. I never underestimate people. We always find a way."

"Really? You think so? I always want to believe that...I really do...but when you think about all the shit out there...bombs going off, planes flying into buildings...people starving to death...sometimes I wonder...what's the point? Why bother?"

"Neh." Theo squinted. "I never worry about what's gonna happen. Not global warming or nuclear war or what fucker is running for president. We climbed out of this tiny little mud hole billions of years ago and now we're cloning animals and sending spacecrafts across the universe. That's pretty wild, yeh?"

Thinking about what he just said—wondering how much of it he actually meant, and how much was just having something to say—Theo was drawn to his glass jar, believing that maybe, in some strange way, it had come to him for a reason. That had he never gone off on his own in the Waitomo Caves, and then fallen from his tube, he wouldn't be standing there, in Vienna, with Jason. That they never would have met. And what a shame that would be.

"There's something about people that keeps us moving forward, yeh? We might fuck up like mad bastards, but I think we're amazing. We'll keep on going. We always do."

They traded cameras, and then took pictures of each other standing before the great spire. Jason turned to Theo. There was the hint of a smile. "Maybe...," he said. "Could be."

"You're here now. That's pretty awesome." Watching Jason look up into that blue sky and take a breath, Theo felt his own lungs fill with the purified Viennese air.

Jason exhaled, then smiled. "Yeah," he said. "It kinda is."

Theo stared at his reflection in the spit-shine floor of the *Südbahnhof* train station, wondering if there were actually two of him—the Theo he knew and the Theo he might someday become. While able to glimpse both his present self and potential self, one at a time—individually—he couldn't catch them together, no matter how quickly he jostled from one eye to the other, even though the two Theos appeared to be standing side by side.

Present Theo. Blink left. Vanish. Reappear.

Potential Theo. Blink right. Vanish. Reappear.

And then back, and then again. And then back, and then again, when really, he hadn't moved at all, causing him to shudder.

There was a strangeness about Vienna. Not just the silence, but an internal confrontation elicited by it, a poking around in places better left undisturbed. Amid the quiet, Theo caught up with Theo. No matter what he said about his faith in humanity, he couldn't shake the feeling that someone might be stalking him. But after those words echoed in his mind—*I'm being followed; someone is after me*—he chuckled and then shook his head. *Easy, mate. Easy.*

Seeing a shrink isn't looked upon in New Zealand like in America. With the Kiwis, if you have a problem, you deal with it yourself, and if you can't figure it out, well…maybe there is no answer. Life's just funny that way sometimes.

But Theo was starting to think that maybe Freud himself—whose home was preserved as a museum a kilometer away—was sitting in a straight-backed chair in the next corridor, patting his leather couch, saying, "Zit down, Mr. Barnes. We have much to diz-cuzz."

Theo never denied the awkward distance between himself and his father, or his mother for that matter, but he suddenly felt like he would break down and cry right in the middle of the station if he kept thinking about his parents. And for some reason, he couldn't stop.

Had Freud's couch actually been within crawling distance, Theo just might have draped himself across it, letting his fears and shame come blubbering out like the sad bastard he was.

Feeling vulnerable just then, Theo became anxious. "When's that train get here?" He was instantly embarrassed, startled by his unintended sharpness, afraid that Jason may have taken it personally. Theo looked at the board. 13:25. *Budapest Keleti pu.* Track 7.

Appearing unphased, Jason flipped through his timetable, tattered from constant use. The cover page held on by its last staple. "Wait a second. It's not the thirteen twenty-five," he said. "That's the train *from* Budapest. We want the twelve twenty *to* Budapest."

They looked at the board overhead—12:20—and then heard a nearby hiss of steam. An announcement came over the loudspeaker in a German cadence. Their train was leaving. Now.

Running toward the track, Theo followed his friend and leapt onto the train as it pulled out of the station. Only Theo was now lost in the fog of his own mind, questioning his deep faith in humanity's adventurous spirit, wondering whether he was actually more cynical, bitter and lonely than he had ever wanted to admit or believe.

Sensing again with a type of neurotic radar that someone was watching him, and that he would find out who it was soon enough.

But after finding an empty compartment, Theo offered an exhaustive sigh of relief. He looked to Jason, and took comfort in that big American smile staring back. Theo shook his head, hearing his brother's voice, as if Roger were sitting right there.

Don't be such a scrotum. Get a grip on yourself, dickhead. Get a grip.

With the train rumbling along the Austrian countryside, Theo chalked up his paranoia to adrenaline, a wonky diet and lack of sleep, satisfied that his emotions had simply gotten the best of him. That he wasn't being followed. That there wasn't anyone to worry about.

Which, of course, there was.

Chapter 43
Moonlight Drive

The Southern Sphere of Eternity
Milky Way's Public Unveiling: T-Minus 27 Days (Eternity Standard Time)

Lex sank into the leather bucket seat, speeding against a nebulous midnight, driving one of only eleven Portal-Smyths ever constructed. He wondered what Brigsby was thinking about, sitting quietly in the passenger seat of his own car.

The winding road led to a bend overlooking the Lambert Falls Dam. The roadster hugged the tight curve. The motor was powerful.

Still unsure as to where they were headed, or for what reason, Lex leaned forward and peered through the windshield, struggling to find his own center. His eyes darted to the rearview mirror and caught his reflection, as if he was watching some poor, clueless chump who looked an awful lot like him, but just couldn't *be* him.

I have no idea where I'm going. I'm lost.

"You see," Brigsby said, "I *love* cars. Just love 'em, love 'em, love 'em. But I don't know how to drive. Go figure. Oh, I suppose I could learn, but that would just be one more little annoyance that can easily be handled by someone who isn't me. Besides, I'd much rather watch a fellow such as yourself control the stick. My, your hands are strong."

Lex was quick to change the subject. "Who was that woman? The one with all the beads. She barreled past us...just before. When we came up to see you. Remember, George?"

"Mm," George said from the backseat. "Mm-hm."

"Yes," Brigsby said, "Well...as I'm sure you can imagine, I get approached by a great many people, big and small and fools and all. Even at my secret apartment, which, I'm finding out, isn't so secret."

Lex observed George through the rearview mirror.

"Which is why I never buy off the rack. Everything—and everyone—is handpicked. You have to be discerning about the company you keep, Lex. Who knows what kind of trouble it can bring to associate with the wrong people."

Lex agreed.

"Good," Brigsby said. "Good. If you learn nothing else tonight, I hope you come away with the idea that whomever you *choose* to spend time with will dictate whom you *get* to spend time with." Brigsby wrapped a silk scarf around his neck. He shivered. "Never give up your solitude, Lex. If you can't block out all the nitwits yammering at you day and night...you'll never know who you really are. *Their* nonsense becomes *your* logic."

"So who was that wo—?"

"Oh, just another dissatisfied customer. Everybody wants something. Which, to be fair, is the way it should be. Don't you agree that it's good to want things?"

"Sure," Lex said. "I guess."

Brigsby shifted. "Believe me," he said. "*Be-lee-heeve* me, it's good to want things. But more important, it's good to *let* yourself want things. It's just that people rarely take it well when the answer is *no*."

Lex gripped the wheel as they came out of the turn.

"Head through that tunnel. I want to show you something."

They drove through a long, narrow passage underneath the Lambert Falls Dam, and as they emerged, took a dirt path that ran off the main roadway. It curved along the lake. Across the water shone the sparkling lights from the Wrolen Library of Organic Beauty. And to the north was the Midwestern Sphere, leading into the ether of Infinity.

"Wow," Lex said as they exited the car. He dug his fingertips into the door handle, just to make sure he wasn't dreaming. "I've never seen the library from here."

Brigsby took Lex's arm, leading him to a grassy patch. They stretched out on their backs. The talk show host pointed, first at the waters of Lambert Lake—still, like a blackened mirror—and then gestured up at the most immaculate creation in Eternity.

Dominating the heavens, the Andromeda galaxy seemed close enough to touch. Lex had never considered before that the tremendous swirl was a living, breathing element with a pulse and soul of its very own. Its power was massive, its force undeniable.

There was also a low, distant rumble, like two stone gears in constant motion, grinding just so. The sound was so faint as to barely be noticed, yet offered a nuanced tremor that touched Lex's very center. Some thought it to be the language of Eternity—the hum of everything.

"Holy fucking crap," Lex said. "H-h-oly..."

"Well said, my friend. Well said." Brigsby pointed to the brightest concentration of magenta gases above them. "This is the closest point to the Andromeda galaxy within a thousand miles of here." And in the distance was Milo's Smear—that permanent nothing.

Lex was terrified. Mesmerized. Enthralled. His heart thundered.

"Can you feel it tugging on your soul?" Brigsby said.

"Yes," Lex said in unison with George.

"Can you feel it pushing you, pulling you, tumbling you around?"

"Yes," they chanted.

"Can you...feel its glory?"

"Hell, yes," Lex said.

"Well, good then. I want you to enjoy this moment. George and I are going now. And when you're done here, when you find your way back, ask yourself just what you're after—and why. Then come see me again. We'll talk."

"Wait." Lex stood up. "You can't leave me here. How do I—?"

"Don't worry." George looked up at the mammoth swirl and then toward the boundless ether of Infinity. He smiled. "It's easier than you think."

"Stay awhile," Brigsby said. "Stay. You've got potential, Lex. You really do. That's why I brought you here. But unless you rethink some of your choices, I'm afraid you'll end up just like that woman tonight—angry, bitter and utterly disappointed.

But never mind. You'll see."

"I don't understand why—"

"I'm on the air in fourteen hours," Brigsby said. "Need my beauty sleep and all." George and Brigsby drove off, the hum of the sports car fading beyond the bend.

Lex stood in the black of night, the Andromeda galaxy swirling above him, tugging, as Brigsby said, on his soul. Lex leaned back in the grass, pillowed his hands behind his head, and let himself be swallowed up by the warmth and energy from above. When he listened carefully, he thought he could hear the faintest beat of a distant drum, the beat of time, as if he had picked up on the pulse of creation.

Lex was joyous in his solitude. And for the moment, he wouldn't have it any other way.

Chapter 44
Rasta Bond

Wellington, New Zealand—Wellington Harbor
Monday, September 5, 2005, 9:38 a.m.

"Well, *all* right," Davey said as they drove from Wellington International Airport, although Rufus wasn't in the mood for chit-chat. He needed to focus. Emma was counting on him. "Rufus. Rasta Bond. Been a while, yeh? Glad to be away from all them stinky Aussies?"

Crisp, frenetic wind thrashed against the car like a shark in bloody waters. Rufus rolled up the passenger-side window, his enormous hand black as a minor piano key. "Fucking too cold, man," he said, still frustrated by the unfamiliar twang in his voice. "Too cold."

Davey grinned as an unlit cigarette dangled from his lips. "Windy Wellington, mate. Cold as a witch's tit when the wind blows like this. But you'll see. Warm up soon as we get out of the harbor, yeh? Nothing to worry about."

Pulling out of Wellington Harbor, on the southwestern tip of the North Island, they were still 485 kilometers south of Rufus's final destination—Auckland.

When Rufus finished this deal, he would be done for good. He didn't traffic marijuana because he wanted to. There was a bigger issue at stake. "Just take me to the stuff. I've got a meeting up north."

"Hey, look who you're talking to. It's me. Davey. Relax, mate. relax." Davey steered with his elbow as he lit a cigarette. "It's a long way from Jah-maaykah, mahn. You should spend more time with us Kiwis. Nothing here but beautiful beaches and beautiful *bitches*."

Six-foot-three with a short mop of dreadlocks, Rufus's skin was darker—much darker—on Earth than in Eternity, and when he caught his reflection, he would take a second look, as if he were his own stunt double.

But most of all, Rufus missed his baritone voice. After the virus scarred his vocal cords, when there were no more nights on stage, no more club owners trying to sign him to a recording contract. Rufus mumbled now in an accent even he could barely understand. After more than a year on Earth, he still felt alienated from himself, a self he had just started to make peace with in Eternity. When Rufus heard this new voice, aware that he was moving his lips, he still had the very real sense that someone else was controlling the tone and volume. Hearing himself talk was like a splinter in his soul, lodged at an angle he just couldn't get to. He couldn't rip it out.

Rufus said: "Make sure there's a tank full of gas. I don't want any delays." But what he heard was: *Mayk shur dares a tahnk fulla gahs, mahn. I dohn wan no dee-layz.*

"What's with you?" Davey blew smoke through his nostrils. "Got some good ass lined up? That's it, yeh?"

Earth was lonely for Rufus, who realized immediately upon arrival that he had made a big mistake. Rufus owed Emma, owed her huge. She didn't just save his life—she saved his soul. But the truth was that he didn't belong on Earth. It had been a long year indeed.

"I knew it," Davey said. "Rasta Bond's always on the prowl. Gets more play than a fucking theater group, yeh? Stick with Kiwi girls, mate. They're just like the fruit. Sweet, juicy and always in season."

In all, Rufus figured it would take ten days to load up on product, make his key stops, and then meet with his seller in Auckland, Davey's older brother, Aputa—a serious dealer in his own right, and nobody you wanted on your ass.

Rufus wanted to maximize on dollars, as there was no better way to negotiate than with bundles of cash. And if he could deal for Emma's jar, he would give up every last dollar on Earth. He would never need money again. He'd be able to go home.

All he had to do was find a certain young man. They had much to discuss.

The first and most obvious strategy Rufus could come up with was to ransack the Barnes' house and find Emma's jar. Having spent years in nightclubs, he knew well that people hide what is most valuable—often as close to them as they can—even under their pillows or wedged in their underwear. As if *watching* something was the same as *protecting* it.

Rufus also knew that something worth possessing was something worth stealing. And something worth stealing was never safe, especially at home.

He thought back to that night on stage in Eternity, when he locked eyes with a brown-skinned beauty, imagining his arms wrapped around her, her face pressed against his. He saw a life with this woman unfold over the years. And Rufus sang:

"...Too many nights have passed me by..."

"...When I whispered your name and wondered why..."

So that when he looked out at the crowd he saw her smile, as if she were thinking what he was thinking. That in a darkly lit club, late at night, without even knowing her name, they had made a connection. That they belonged together. And Rufus sang:

"...Too many nights have passed me by..."

"...Knowing it should be you and I..."

So that after his set, when Rufus stepped off the stage and into the shadow of a soft light, this young woman appeared to him even lovelier still. Her name was Vanessa. They retired to his apartment, sipped his wine. Vanessa hadn't been the first woman to find his bed, but Rufus hoped that she would be the last.

Yet when he awoke to find his glands swollen and his voice rough and hoarse, when the doctors diagnosed him with an adenoidal virus, when they traced it back to his new love, Rufus knew without having to be told. His voice would never be the same.

Only Emma didn't believe his voice was truly gone. She'd been to the club many times. She'd heard Rufus sing. She often sat off to the side, studying him. Watching.

When Rufus returned to the stage after the illness passed, when he tried to force out notes that just wouldn't come, Emma was the one who kept him pushing on. "There's nothing left in me," Rufus said that first night back, when the crowd broke early. When his voice was no longer a force of gentle power. "It's gone."

"No it isn't. It's just a little rough right now. It'll come back. You'll see."

"The doctors told me not to hope," Rufus said. "The doctors said—"

"Screw the doctors. How can you survive without hope? If you can't see yourself smiling tomorrow, how can you smile today?"

Rufus indeed smiled that night, as Emma took him into her bed. But it was the last night he would smile without help for a long, long time. He found solace in Emma, but without his music—without his voice—he was a star with no galaxy, with no purpose. Just a heft of burning gas waiting to be extinguished. His thoughts betrayed him.

Why would anyone want me when I have nothing to give? What use am I?

"You don't need this junk," Emma would say, night after night, as he injected the brown narcotic into his veins. "There's nothing in there for you. It's a lie."

"But there is," Rufus would say, his eyes red and glazed, unable to express his love and anguish in any other way. When his deep, soothing voice was reduced to sandpaper. When he had been knocked off that stage for good. "My voice is in here," he said, tapping his finger on the needle. "Just follow a new song."

"No," Emma said again and again, refusing to give up on him. She would press her small hand against his chest, feeling his heartbeat. "Your voice is here."

Finally, before he disappeared permanently in that river of narcotic dream, Rufus left the junk behind, waking each day with Emma's words swirling in his mind, until the voice, indeed, became his own again.

"My voice is where? You okay, mate? Jetlag must've fucked you big style."

Rufus looked over at Davey and wondered how a young man with no purpose, with no apparent future, could find such happiness in the moment. "It's nothing," he said. "Just drive."

Rufus didn't know the first thing about violence. He was gentle by nature. But he knew this: if he ripped the Barnes' house apart and didn't find Emma's jar, he would call attention to himself. And if that happened, things were sure to get messy. Rufus had been given a second chance. He didn't want to waste it.

He had learned to accept a life without *his* music, but not a life without any music. When he got back to Eternity, he would open his own club. He already scouted new talent. He would protect them. His new dream was to help others live theirs. He was reminded of Emma's words. *If I can't see myself smiling tomorrow, how can I smile today?*

Breaking into that house would be a calculated risk. So when Davey announced that he wanted to see his mate Roger Barnes, Rufus no longer had to make a decision. The decision was made for him.

Chapter 45
Waning Days of the Dynamic Dipshits

Budapest, Hungary—Your Best Days Hostel #14

Tuesday, September 6, 2005, 11:22 p.m.

Your Best Days was a chain of hostels scattered throughout Eastern Europe. The particular hostel Lilly was staying in, the hostel Theo and Jason were staying in—hostel #14—was converted from an old, rickety brothel.

There was a dingy bar in the far corner, welcoming patrons with a sea of light, red as a fireman's globe. Beneath the crimson fog, Lilly sipped her drink at a small table in the back, set on a raised platform. She could see out over the tavern, but tucked away near a support beam, no one could see her. She sat alone.

It wasn't lost on Lilly that she was hunkered away in an old bordello, the smell of sex and smoke and alcohol soaked into the walls. The aura of salty red lust oozed from the lights. A lit cigarette dangled from her lips. Her foot ached. Midnight approached.

Lilly scribbled with a fluorescent yellow highlighter on the back of a purple flyer. There was a common theme: *Fuck Theo Barnes. Fuck Jason Medley. Fuck Emma. Fuck Me.* Like her dad, Lilly didn't ordinarily say *fuck*, but no other word so precisely captured her predicament.

Yeah, she wrote in bubble letters. *That's right. Just absolutely fuck me.* Next to her *Fuck* list she doodled a stone bridge. The walkway was lined with tennis balls, chalk lines and racket strings. Forehand grunts flowed down the river and through the stone arches beneath the bridge. Lilly took another drag. The Beatles' *Birthday* was playing.

The tequila went down hard. Two double shots to go.

After the long trip from Vienna, the Budapest sun was

ablaze, the humidity awful. Lilly had felt like a foot trapped inside a sweat sock. *So, yeah*, she thought. *Fuck me.*

Lilly lost Theo and Jason in a sea of agitated backpackers, having followed them from a train car's length behind—close, but not too close. She was then accosted by a twenty-year-old Hungarian wearing a T-shirt with *Your Best Days* printed in red letters. His dark hair was slicked back. He grabbed Lilly's hand, all but rubbing his erection on her leg. She was a young woman alone in Eastern Europe. *So, yeah*, she thought. *Fuck me.*

Lilly ripped herself away from the welcoming committee, and then jumped into a beat-up cab, following the shuttle bus transporting backpackers to the hostel, including Jason and Theo.

Keeping up with the Dynamic Dipshits, as she started thinking of them, had been far more difficult than she prepared herself for. In Venice, Lilly nearly missed the train to Budapest, as the dumbasses apparently didn't know how to read a timetable. Having to run after them, she not only tripped on the stairs, but almost dropped her rucksack on the tracks as the locomotive pulled away, straining her ribcage in the process. Lilly had a black-and-blue welt on her hip the size of a leopard's paw.

She'd also had to keep them within sight while on the train, as she had no idea where they were going until she overheard them, at which point she trusted that they would actually end up in Budapest. Lilly even told a family of three that Jason and Theo might be following *her*, but couldn't be sure, so could they keep an eye out for them?

And outside the hostel, waiting behind thorny bushes while said morons checked into the old whorehouse, Lilly tripped on a stick, slicing open the bottom of her big toe. Wearing sandals wasn't working out quite like she planned. *So, yeah*, she thought, *Fuck me.*

As such, Lilly came to a conclusion, irrefutable by philosophy, faith, fact or logic: The Dynamic Dipshits were done for. She was going to split those nitwits up. She was going to get Theo alone. And she would get him back to America. To Yuma. But not the way Emma said. Lilly had an idea of her own. A good idea. Emma was all for it.

Lilly watched Theo and Jason sit at the bar beneath the dirty red light.

"Drink up, boys." Lilly tipped her glass. "Drink up."

Things were in motion. It was just a matter of time.

"Flowers?" Emma had shouted through the phone just hours earlier. "You're telling me he's into fucking flowers?"

Huddled in a phone booth outside the hostel, Lilly waited for Theo and Jason to check in. Her big toe bled. "Plants *and* flowers," she said. "He has a greenhouse. I heard him talking about it on the train."

"Are you...sonuva...are you fucking kidding me? Barnes is a pansy? He's a fucking pansy? Why didn't I know this? Angelique, you bitch. I knew you'd screw me."

Lilly interjected, feeling strangely protective of Theo just then. "He's not a...no. Why do you have to say that?" She leaned against the side of the phone booth, cradling the receiver. She lifted her foot, squeezed her big toe and then flicked the brick red droplets to the ground. She winced, wrapping her toe in a napkin.

"Wait! Wait. You fucked him? You went for his cock?"

"No!" Lilly held the phone away, giving it the finger, hoping the message made it all the way to Yuma. She nodded to three female backpackers filing into the hostel. "No. But—"

"What do you mean, no? It's been three days. You know about this flower crap. Why haven't you blown him? Oh, wait! Oh...ohhhhh. I get it. You *blew* him. Well...that's okay."

Lilly rolled her shoulders. "I didn't...you know...blow him." She heard Lex *woomph!* A sigh came through the receiver.

"Look," Emma said. "You found him in Venice. So that's good. And to be honest, I don't really give an iguana's asshole why you're in Budapest. It's just that...now...my only real question is...WHEN THE FUCK ARE YOU BRINGING HIM BACK?!"

Maybe it was the distance, maybe it was the heat or her bloody foot, or maybe it was just a rare and unfamiliar surge of self-respect coursing through her veins. But Lilly made a decision: It was time to fight back. Somewhat. Kinda. A little.

"*Look*," she said, mocking Emma. "I *mentioned* the flowers *to* bring him back." There was silence, except for Lilly's thundering heart. She let out a long breath. *Breathe. Control the panic.* "I figured," Lilly continued, quivering at first, "you could...you know...get, like, a Web site set up. You could be this rich benefactor and I could be one of the artists you sponsor."

Lilly paused, waiting for a reaction. More silence. *Okay. Maybe.*

"I could get him talking about his greenhouse, and, like it's a total coincidence, mention that you're looking for a gardener with knowledge of exotic plants. I could tell him that you're willing to spend big money. Cash up front."

Again there was silence. So Lilly waited. There was even more silence. So Lilly waited. And then finally, a low grumble came through the phone. "Hmm."

Oh, thank God.

"We could call it Emmaline Estates dot com. I'd believe it, especially if the site has a nice-looking home page. You could take a photo of the fountain in Yuma. He'd never know."

Yet again there was silence. So Lilly waited. And finally, a low grumble came through the phone. "Hmm," Emma said once more. "That's not bad. That's not bad at all! I like it. No. Fuck that. I love it. Go with it. Sell it. Give me two days. We'll be ready."

Lilly took a strange sense of pride in her plan—and that she hadn't peed herself pitching it to Emma. "You'll have to wire me some money, though. I'm running low."

There was more silence. So Lilly waited. And then finally, a low grumble came through the phone. "How low?"

"Well..." Lilly was as shaky as a *Jenga* tower. "I...don't know how much to offer him. Like..." She closed her eyes and clenched. "...two thousand?"

"Two thousand?! Are you out of your fucking mind? I'm not—"

Lilly heard a *woomph!* and then another *woomph!* And then, "I'm not going to—" And then *woomph!* And then *sigh...*"Fuck."

And then, "tell him...one thousand now...a thousand when he gets here, and then we negotiate the rest. But that's it. Got it?"

Confidence restored. "Yeah," Lilly said. "Got it."

Lilly heard another *woomph!* "And you sure he's not a pansy?"

"Jesus, Emma. He's not a pans...he's not *gay*. Trust me. He's not."

"Okay," Emma said. "Call me in two days. But one more thing."

Confidence rattled. Pride shaky. Lilly held her breath. "...Yeah?"

"Close the fucking deal. You're sure flower boy's no homo... suck his green thumb." Emma paused. "Swallowing optional. Don't forget to rinse. Ciao."

Chapter 46
Catch Me If You Can

San Diego, California—UCSD Medical Center
Thursday, April 25, 1991, 2:28 p.m.

Catch me, Daddy! Catch me!
I love you, I love you, I love you.
Get ready, Daddy! Here I come.
I miss you, I miss you, I miss you.
Oh, no, Daddy! Are you okay?
Don't ever leave me again.

Lilly's braces were tight around her teeth. A large red pimple was plump behind her right ear. It hurt. She clutched the chair's thin, metal slats, as if it would protect her somehow, peering from the safe side of chaos while her world spun out of control. She was twelve.

Bright California sunshine gleaned off the white walls of her father's hospital room. The University of California at San Diego Medical Center was the best for what he needed.

The medial collateral ligament of the right knee, the orthopedic surgeon explained to them, had completely ruptured. "As you can see here...," he said, pointing to an X-ray, "...there is total separation from the thighbone, so you've got no stability to the inner side of the knee. We'll do laparoscopic surgery to repair the damage, and then you'll need about six months of physical therapy. After that, you should regain most, if not full, function of your knee. I wouldn't worry. You'll be fine."

"See, Lollipopolous." Lilly's father sat up in bed. "Popidopolous will be a-okay."

Lilly watched her father, a gentle warrior reduced to a hospital gown, smiling the kind of smile only her daddy could smile. She resented it, a smile more severe than punishment, more hurtful than betrayal.

Just let me own it. It's mine. Just let me own it.

Even more than the smile, Lilly hated her mother's worry and Billy's sulking, as if his dreams, and not her father's knee, had been torn to bits, leaving a mess for someone else to deal with. Billy. Daddy's trainer, but no friend at all.

"So, Doc." Billy tugged nervously at his goatee. "Can Marcus get back on the court? Will his knee hold up?"

"Well," the surgeon said, "with the advances we've had with this procedure, there's a good chance he'll get back to full strength. That said...this is a particularly severe injury. It's been degenerating for years. And he is thirty-one. As a matter of everyday function, Marcus should have an unrestricted life-style. As a matter of profession...only time will tell."

"Hey, guys," Lilly's father said. "Hang on a second."

Peeking over the top of the chair, Lilly squeezed the slats.

"Lollipop." Her father smiled that damn smile again. "Sit with me."

Lilly knew what was coming. She *knew* him because she *was* him. As she let go of that chair, it was as if she had let go of her life, watching the only world she ever knew vanish before her eyes.

"You guys are my family," Marcus began, and then let out a smile and a subdued *hmmph*. "Well, not you Doc." He winked. "Truth is, I've been thinking about this, and, you know, like Doc said, my knee was bound to give out eventually. I think God's trying to tell me something."

Shaken, Lilly felt her father give another squeeze, could see her mother, Audrey, balling up with anger and resentment.

"I had a good run. I never got a title, but I came close a few times. It just wasn't meant to be. And now...I'm tired. This bum knee...*hmmph*...it just makes this easier. It's time for me to retire. I've been away too long. It's time to come home."

Catch me, Daddy. Catch me.
I'm falling.

Chapter 47
The Manual of Why

Auckland, New Zealand—Barnes Residence
Friday, September 9, 2005, 12:23 p.m.

Out in the backyard, Roger ran his hand along the dome of his father's helicopter, a giant locust with massive propellers on top and a smaller set at the tail. Oscar Barnes, who had been tinkering with the whirlybird for almost three years, was on his back now, working with a wrench beneath the monstrosity. It was warm for early spring in Auckland.

"Looking pretty sharp, Dad. When'll she be airborne?"

"Hey there, Roger." Oscar reached out his burly right arm, a formidable appendage, even at fifty-seven, after almost three decades as a medical equipment technician. "Hand me that rag, yeh? Got a bit of oil down here." Roger obliged. "Ah...maybe in a month or so, maybe never. You never know with an old girl like this."

While the neighbors thought Oscar Barnes was a crackpot for renovating an XR-5 World War II helicopter, Roger understood the determination. His father probably never expected it to fly, but that was all the more reason to try. What else was retirement for?

His father had his mechanics, Theo had his greenhouse, which sat not twenty feet behind the helicopter, and Roger... he had surfing, spending almost every free moment he could on the waves. Although he hadn't had quite the same balance since Theo left for Europe, never quite sure if the forthcoming ground beneath his psychological feet was solid or merely a thin layer of dirt covering a bottomless pit in his mind.

Staring at Theo's neglected greenhouse, Roger leaned with his back against the helicopter hull. He broke a twig in small pieces and tossed them at the grass. "So, Dad, yeh? You ever..."

Lose your mind? Hallucinate so badly you can't tell what's real?

Roger hadn't been able to stop thinking about that day at Cathedral Cove. In the waters *beneath* Cathedral Cove. When in a dream—Roger was certain it had to have been a dream—a blue whale named Howard challenged him with the onus of responsibility.

"So is this weird for you or what?" Howard had said in the ocean after gulping Roger into his mouth and then spitting him out. The heft of Howard's deep tenor voice reverberated like a concert cello. The whale spoke slow and powerful. "Pretty cool, right?"

Roger stared down the length of the blue whale's body. It stretched longer than three oil tankers lined end...to end...to end. "Weird? Yeh. Cool...well, I'm not—"

The whale produced an item. "You mind telling me what you boys are doing with this?" Howard tossed it with one enormous flipper—sending the jar arching through the Kiwi waters—and then back with the other.

Roger was perplexed. Howard had in his possession what seemed to be the very jar Theo had found. "Hey. How'd you get that?"

"I think the better question is: how did *you* get it? And maybe an even better question is: what are you going to do with it, now that you've got it?"

"Wait," Roger said. "You know what this is?"

"Of course I know." Howard rolled his eyes. "Heh. This kid is too—"

"Howie!"

"Oh, right. Sorry. My bad." Howard focused back on Roger. "Me knowing about this jar is beside the point. You have it now. And that's something."

Roger fell back, sat on the ocean floor. A school of sea horses eased up to him, nodded to Howard, and then went on their way.

Seeing Howard with Theo's jar connected Roger with dry land—*above* water. It sent him into a panic, overcome with the urgency to breathe again, to have oxygen filling his lungs. When it didn't happen, Roger began to hyperventilate. He started pacing, kicking up a cloud of sand. "I'm gonna die! I'm gonna die!"

"Mate," Howard said. "You're okay. You're o—"

Roger threw up a chunky cloud.

"Feel better, mate? Wow, you guys really puke a lot."

"What do you want from me? How could you have that thing?"

Howard looked at Roger. "Let me ask you something." The whale's cello voice resonated in long strands. "Have you ever met someone that you connected with immediately, but couldn't explain why? That sort of inexplicable magic?"

Roger immediately thought of Carla. "Yeh. So?"

"Picture that day in your mind. You're off to school, or the beach...do you ever stop and think that if you had done anything differently right before you met that person...that if you had left the house five minutes earlier or later, or took just five *seconds* even, to tie your shoelaces...that maybe you wouldn't have met that person just then? Or ever? Or that maybe by doing exactly the things you did that day in the exact sequence you did them...that's what set your timing in motion so that you *did* meet?"

Roger saw a series of moments unfold in his mind, an elaborate set of dominoes toppling over. "Yeh," he said. "I think so."

"When they do happen...when you make these connections...does anybody hand you a manual with the reasons *why* you met, and at that very moment?"

Roger shook his head, feeling foolish, and a little angry. "No."

"Do you know *why* nobody gives you a reason?"

Roger shrugged. "Because there is no reason?"

Howard opened his eyes as wide as they would go. "Who said there's no reason? I didn't say there's no reason. Listen to this kid..."

"Is there?"

"Aha!" Howard's awesome tones reverberated across the ocean floor. "Now we're getting somewhere." He sent the jar floating above them until finally it landed at Roger's feet. "Only, that's for me to know...and you to find out....It's okay. Pick it up." Roger complied. "Your brother is going to make a request of you. It may not seem significant at the time, but it will be extremely important. I think you should do what he asks."

"How will I know? Theo's been asking me some weird shit lately, even for him."

Howard smiled, and offered Roger a squint. "You'll figure it out."

"But I thought—"

The blue whale turned his tremendous torso away from Roger. His winged tail arched up and down. The force of it shoved Roger back a few feet. "Watch who knocks on your door," Howard called back as he disappeared into the watery shadows. "Introductions are key."

"Introductions to what?" Roger shouted. "Introductions to what?"

Oscar Barnes extended his arm again from beneath the helicopter. He hung the oily rag on a metal bar. "What's that? Who you bringing by?"

"Uh...nobody, Dad. Nobody."

"Ah," his father said. "Got yourself a girlfriend, yeh?"

Even though Roger could feel the sun's warmth on his skin and inhale the plume of an easy breeze, he shuddered, as if he were still beneath the ocean waters, engulfed by the presence of the great whale. "It's nothing—"

"Women are like this birdie here." His father tapped the side of the helicopter. "You can tinker with them all you want, but unless you spend the time to find out what's messing up the works, they're never gonna fly. Maybe you should ask your mother about this one, yeh? I got my hands full."

Chapter 48
Girl Trouble

Roger was quiet, but serious. "Hey, Mum? Can I ask you something?"

Shocked as if a polarized copper wire were squirreled up her rectum and surging with the wicked blue spark of electricity, Lydia Barnes dropped a dirty plate into the sink. Her hands were covered in soapy water. Her apron had little yellow ducks on it.

The men in Lydia's life rarely solicited her opinion. She felt removed from them, the lone woman in a house full of boys. Whether they kept their distance because of her worrying, or she worried because of their distance, Lydia could never quite tell. Still, she knew they considered her the glue of the family—so long as everybody came home before dawn and not bleeding from both eyes, equilibrium had been maintained.

The truth was, she forced herself to *assume* they loved her, but she figured that when you don't get the words, you fill in the blanks however they suit you best. Lydia snuck a deep breath.

I lay awake at night just waiting for the day somebody asks me something that matters, thinking about how I could be a totally different person, a more dynamic person, if only they'd let me. Iif only they'd look at me with wider eyes. And now I'm fifty-two and that day is here and I'm up to my elbows in dirty water and there's only one cinnamon apple muffin left in the tray.

Okay, Lydia thought, and then exhaled. *I'm okay. I'm ready.*

"Of course. Yeh. What's that, Roger? You can ask me anything."

"I was just wondering, yeh?" Roger looked at the floor, swayed his foot. "Like, did you ever...I mean...like way back... like *way* back...when you were my age..."

Lydia was suddenly aware of the vivid sag of her artichoke-shaped breasts. How the wild gray strands had infiltrated her blonde hair. How her pale skin was marred with purple clusters of varicose veins. And that despite still being a size six, she hunched a little when she stood because her back ached and her knees throbbed. *They never used to, but they do now.* Lydia wiped her hand on a dish towel. "Go on. What's that?"

"It's...well, I've been...hanging out with this...girl, yeh?"

Lydia watched her son. She watched him trying to open up to her, as if he were removing the dome of a serving platter, uncovering the true Roger. *Her* Roger. She watched him trying to overcome his father's silence, passed down through the generations.

Lydia watched Roger stare at the kitchen floor, a floor that still needed mopping. And she watched her youngest son tick nervously, until finally he raised his eyes, although not his head, to ascertain how well she was receiving him. "Carla? The girl who's been calling?"

She watched her son as he blushed. *Roger* was asking *her* for help. With something that matters. *He's so tall these days, but he's still such a little boy.*

"Yeh." Roger nodded. "That's the one."

Lydia turned off the water and faced him. There was a baking tray on the counter. Roger pried loose the last apple cinnamon muffin, the one Lydia had been saving for herself.

I bake and I bake but I never get a muffin.

"Are you having a fight with her? Is something wrong?"

"No, not exactly," Roger said. "It's just...you know...well...you know how girls are, yeh? How they like it when you say nice things to them? And how, like, when you, I dunno...bring them little presents, you know, nothing big, but like some sticker she saw at the shops, and then like a month later you give it to her and she's happy because she knows that you listened? That you're really paying attention, even when it doesn't seem like you are?"

My lord. He's such a sweet young man.

"Yes, that's quite nice to do something like that." Lydia's heart swelled with a mother's pride. She fought the tears. *He needs me. He needs me to be strong for him.* "That's very nice."

"Well, what if you do it, yeh? And she doesn't...you know... get excited?" Roger tore off another piece of muffin, put it up to his mouth, but didn't bite. "What if you do all the little things, yeh? And then she acts like it's not important?"

We're going to make a connection. I'm so happy I could tinkle.

"Have you done this for Carla? Did she—"

The phone rang in a muffled tone. Lydia wanted to rip it from the wall, and with a hammer from her husband's shop, unleash her fury upon that ringing nuisance. But instead she watched in silence as Roger snatched the receiver. She watched him nod and then listen. "Yeh, okay," she heard him say. "I'll get right over."

Lydia watched Roger hang up the phone, as if hanging up on her. And then she watched her youngest son, her baby boy, head for the door. Anxiety circled her chest like soapy dishwater down the drain.

Like anyone would even care if I just disappeared, except for the laundry.

Roger called back. His hand was on the doorknob. One foot was outside. "Hey, Mum? You like whales? You think they're all right?"

"Um." Lydia stepped into the living room. A breeze crept in as Roger held the door open. "What's that? Whales? I don't—"

"Never mind," Roger said as he disappeared into the sunlight. "See ya."

And as the door closed, Lydia once again felt left behind, standing alone on a gorgeous afternoon, with a wet dish towel in her hand, left to clean up the little messes, the stuff that really doesn't matter. Remaining quiet when there was so much to say, when she could be doing so much more with the days she had left. When she could know the men in her lives, and they could know her.

"Love you," she said to an empty room. "Love you."

Chapter 49
The Unbearable Lightness of Being Naked

Budapest, Hungary—Your Best Days Hostel #14
Friday, September 9, 2005, 9:42 p.m.

Jason slugged down the rest of his beer. His eyes burned from the smoke as it swirled beneath the red light. His skin smelled like chlorine. The image of naked flesh was burned into his brain. It made him shudder.

Jason and Theo had spent the day exploring Budapest, which, they discovered, was actually two separate cities—Buda and Pest. The Danube River snaked between them; Buda to the west, Pest to the east. Jason and Theo were dazzled by the marble buildings downtown and the area's business vitality. But as they came to an old woman, kneeling, begging with her hands squeezed together—as if she were not just praying for a nickel, but for her soul—they were reminded that like the two cities, there were two worlds.

And during a wander through the hilly residential section, they passed a series of houses that still bore tank blasts from the Nazi occupation of World War II. Jason put his hand against a mortar scar larger than his head.

While crossing the Chain Bridge on their way back to *Your Best Days*, Jason and Theo ran into Sven, a law student from Ringsted, Denmark, a small town 40 kilometers south of Copenhagen. Sven had blue eyes and short blonde hair. He wore wire-rimmed glasses. His ambition, he said, was to get a law degree and work in New York City for five years, and then return home.

"To humble you Americans," he told Jason, laughing genially. Sven pointed to a stone lion carved into the entrance of the Chain Bridge. "Americans." He shook his head as the river flowed beneath them. "They think they are center of everything."

Jason raised his eyebrows. "We're not?"

"Ha! Only of trouble. You pick too many fights."

"Yeh," Theo agreed, smiling. "Everyone does kinda hate you guys."

"Yes, yes," Sven mocked, waving his finger. "Didn't your mommy teach you? You make friends with the huh-ney, not vin-uh-ger."

"Don't you want us to be your friends?" Theo asked. "Are you lonely?"

"But," Jason said. "But…"

In the hostel bar, they toasted with bottles of *Dreher*, a Hungarian beer brewed in Budapest, and only $1 U.S. per pint when converted from the Hungarian forint.

"That place was nuts," Jason said, with no pun intended, and for some reason he found himself thinking about the Karikari waterfall in New Zealand just then, even though he had never been there, as if Theo's stories had transported him half way across the world. Jason passed the beers. "I can't believe we did that."

Sven, who was also staying at the hostel, had led them to a Turkish bathhouse, which, much to Jason's surprise, was not the seedy dump he envisioned, but a high-end health spa.

Beneath the smoky red light and facing the pool table, Theo laughed and then pointed to Sven. "Yeh, yeh. You really told off that old guy. He was a real nutter. I dunno…"

"It's thermal *bath*house," Sven said. "Not *whore*house. You're supposed to cover up your balls, yes? Not hold them like a baby."

Before entering the steam rooms and heated pools, guests were required to change into loin clothes, which Jason, Theo and Sven did—reluctantly—leaving them bare-assed and giggling like five-year-olds. The small cloths barely covered their giblets.

Trouble ensued when a prune-butted old man lifted his covering and asked Sven to check for birthmarks. It was then that Jason realized the difference between regular locker room naked and Turkish bathhouse naked. "Those wraparounds," he said. "They didn't leave much to the imagina—"

Jason went suddenly silent. His eyes fixed on the Mona Lisa. Not *the* Mona Lisa, but a watercolor copy on the wall, adjacent to the bar. It was a respectable likeness, except for Mona's unibrow and elongated fingernail on her right pinkie, groomed, it appeared, for sniffing opium.

Still, Jason was transfixed on Mona, as if she were looking right at him, telling him to listen. Carefully. The Romantics' *Talking In Your Sleep* was playing.

Theo was on the next stool, laughing, and Jason couldn't hear him. Sven was laughing in deep waves, and Jason couldn't hear that either. It was as if he was alone in the darkness. Staring at the Mona Lisa, just not *the* Mona Lisa, Jason was caught in a daze. An answer he had been desperate for became suddenly clear.

"Oh my God." Jason spilled beer down his shirt. "It's her."

"What's that?" Theo laughed. "Sven? Another pint, mate?"

"Yes, yes. Another. I buy this time. My turn to—"

"It's her," Jason said again.

Sven looked to Theo, who shrugged, smiled.

"Who? Who are you—?"

"Lilly," Jason said. "It's Lilly."

Jason told Theo and Sven about Lilly. How they'd met in Rome, how she disappeared in Venice. How he couldn't get her out of his mind, no matter how hard he tried.

"And she's here?" Theo said. "I gotta see—"

"No," Jason said. "She's not here."

"Wait." Sven turned toward the back of the bar, covered in a haze of pot smoke. Beneath Mona, three Canadian hippies were selling Ecstasy to a French waif and her chubby German boyfriend. "You just said—"

"You don't understand. When we met, we had that thunder-bolt moment, you know? That *kablam!*" Jason slapped his hands together. "What's been killing me...I felt like I knew her, like we'd met before." He shook his head. "And now I know where."

Jason had been harboring a secret—not because he didn't want it known, but because he hadn't realized its significance. Until now.

Uli, a twenty-two-year-old opera singer from Hamburg they met the night before, passed a joint. *Dude (Looks Like a Lady)* by Aerosmith came screaming through the speakers.

"Did you ever have...?" Jason started, and then toked on the joint.

Theo looked to Sven, who shrugged.

Jason sighed, then sipped his beer. "I had this dream once..." He shook his head. "No. It was too real for a dream, but...I read this book about past life experiences..." He looked to Theo, Sven and Uli, waiting for them to roll their eyes and laugh like drunken hyenas. He could hear their thoughts: *Past life experiences? Yeah. Okay, mate. Riiiiight.*

Only they didn't mock him. They listened.

"I'm not saying I had one...a past life exp...but...*pfff*...I don't know what to call it, so I'll just call it a dream." Listening. Still listening. "It was hundreds of years ago. And we were in France. We were fruit merchants, with a cart in town. And one day after breakfast, I come in from outside, and Lilly is at the table. She's not saying anything. Neither am I."

"Lilly had a miscarriage. Her third."

"And in the dream, we're not talking, just looking at each other."

"The pain of losing another one is too much to bear."

"The grief is driving us apart. We have no kids. We're not going to make it."

"That was it. I hadn't thought about it in years, but I never forgot it. Now I know why."

"That must drive you mad, yeh?" Theo gulped his beer. "And you just figured it now? That Lilly, the girl you met, was this...I dunno...this girl in your dream?"

Jason was stoned and woozy. "Yeah. I don't know why. It's freaking me out. It makes no sense, but I keep expecting to find her. Like she's right in front of me—like right there, just ten feet away—and I just don't see her."

"She probably thinks the same about you," Sven said.

"Don't say such things." Uli inserted herself between Theo and Sven. She wrapped her arms around Jason. Uli was short and curvy, with black hair in a bowl cut. Her breasts pressed against Jason's chest. "You poor thing. If she runs away like that...she doesn't deserve you."

Jason didn't know Uli from the Mona Lisa, but figured it wise to agree. Theo and Sven both flashed him huge, toothy grins and the silent, go-for-it thumbs up.

Uli led Jason from the smoky red light. And as they crossed the hostel lobby he thought, if only for a few seconds, that he caught a glimpse of a young woman he had met long ago in a strange, strange dream. That from behind, as that silhouette walked into the black of night, she looked just like Lilly. That if he hadn't known better, he would have sworn it was her.

But with his mind abuzz from the intoxicating troika of skunky Euroweed, Hungarian beer and Uli's perfume, Jason wasn't going to make the same mistake twice. There was sex to be had. And whatever he thought about Lilly, he knew one thing for sure.

She was long gone.

Chapter 50
Remembrance of Things Past

Yuma, Arizona—Top Joe's Finest Motel
Saturday, September 10, 2005, 5:23 p.m.

Emma sat at their motel room table. The blinds were drawn. She slobbered on a loaded hot dog. Sauerkraut, onion and chili juices leaked down her forearm. Three wet clumps fell to the carpet. "Listen to me, you mangy little fuck stick. You're wrong. You got that? You're fucking wrong."

Sitting by her feet, Lex lapped up the fallen chow. Only he wasn't wrong. In fact, Emma couldn't remember him ever being more right. And that was something she just couldn't allow.

"You have to admit." A sauerkraut string dangled from Lex's mouth. "I didn't...*mmph*...good...I didn't think Lilly had it in her. I thought she would fold like a house of cards. You leaned on her pretty good, and she bounced back. I'm impressed."

Emma was acutely aware that Lex was staring at her half-eaten hot dog, her third. "We'll see," she said. "We'll see. It's one thing to devise a little plan. It's another to pull it off. Let's see how the skank does from here."

"Give her some credit. On the fly she comes up with this Web site scam. She's pulling the strings like a pro. Even you said so. It's not bad."

Emma pulled the hot dog stump from the roll and then chucked it by the bed, as if it were no longer worthy of her attention. Lex pounced on it.

"I don't have to admit anything. There's nothing to admit."

Staring at Lex as he now eyeballed the empty bun, Emma realized just how far he had fallen. That every day Lex was becoming more of a dog—a nonperson—and therefore should be treated as such. Emma dangled the mustard-covered roll. Lex made a slight move for it. "That's right." She looked down at Lex until he begged like the dog that he was. "Now sit!"

"Oh, come on. Gimme a brea—"

"Sit, fucko. Sit."

As it had been throughout their relationship, Emma barked an order. And as it had been, Lex did as she commanded. Sitting upright before her, Lex *thwapped* his tail and let out a whine. He chopped his teeth. Emma dropped the roll into Lex's mouth. "There you go."

Lex immediately stole away, curling up on the side of the bed. His front paws encircled the half-eaten bun. He licked off the mustard smears, and then munched it down.

"Let's be clear about something." Emma wiped her face. "The only thing Lilly *has* done...is *not* do the one thing we know she *can* do. Fuck. So unless this Kiwi jerk-off shows up here... *with* the jar...the little whore has done nothing except waste my fucking time and money."

Lex stared at her.

"What?" she said. "What?"

Lex smirked. "You know, in a way...she kinda reminds me of you." He licked his paw. "Once upon a time. If you remember."

Emma leapt with an agility fit for her smaller self. The floor creaked. The farmhouse pictures shook. Lex cowered in the corner. And with her enormous gait behind her, Emma swung her tree trunk of a leg into his ribs.

Lex jumped, let out a high pitched *whelp* and then scurried toward the bed. "What the *fff...uck*? Shit. What's your pro... *cough-cough*...problem? It was a compliment, you lunatic. It was a fucking compliment."

Emma's face was clenched so tight that she was seeing double. "You bet your ass it was." She dropped her massive torso, pinning Lex between her stomach rolls and tricep. Lex *whelped* again, breath forced from his body. Emma dug her fingers into Lex's brown, clammy gums. He frothed. "To *her*," she corrected, gritting her teeth. "To her it was a compliment. But to me...it was a fucking insult."

Emma glared into Lex's eyes as they glazed over. His tail

flopped from side to side. She could feel his canine heart *thwapping* beneath his chest. He had no choice but to listen.

"Don't ever fucking compare *me* to *her*. Got that? *I* design galaxies," Emma said, jerking Lex's face to one side, "she's a fucking whore." She jerked his face again. "I'm a winner, she's a slut. Got that?"

"Rysh."

Emma stared into Lex's eyes as they fell back. "What?"

"Rysh. Yes...*cough, cough*...My bad. Right. You design galaxies. She's a whore. Winner. Slut. No comparison."

Huddled in the gutter between the wall and the bed, Emma looked up at the digital clock, sitting on the nightstand. She caught her reflection in the plastic guard, seeing herself not as she wanted to be, but as the woman she had actually become—gluttonous, bitter and vain—literally squeezing the life out of a dog. Out of Lex. Emma rolled to the side. She let him up.

Stunned, Lex lay there, taking short breaths.

With some difficulty, Emma pulled herself atop the mattress. Her face flush and sweaty, she breathed heavy, then looked upon her massive, slumping body and its remarkable contours. And then she saw Lex, curled up in a ball, in the corner.

Winner. Slut. No comparison.

"I...," she began, and shook her head. "I didn't mean...I'm just..."

Except for their breathing and the hum of the clock radio, the room was silent. Finally, after a time, Lex spoke softly. "Crazy times," he said.

Surprising herself, Emma cried. Surprising herself again, she laughed, dumbfounded, not by Lex's fall, but her own. "When did I become this horrible? This isn't how I planned it."

Lex nodded. He stared at his genitals. "Quite honestly... I didn't really see this coming either. Man, those fuckers are itchy."

Emma laughed, more of relief than humor, remembering why she had been attracted to Lex from the start. "She really is a sweet piece of ass. Lilly. You know."

Lex lifted his head. "Well...," he said. "For a whore."

Emma took him in just then, ashamed not only for how

she had treated him, but for how she had been treating herself. "Well...yeah," she said, and for a moment, remembered how she had been not so long ago—a talented, sexy woman, sitting behind her desk at *Starlight Designs*, at the beginning of her journey, and not the end.

"For a whore," she said, and cried again. "For a whore."

Chapter 51
The Great Viking Hangovers

Budapest, Hungary—Keleti Pu Train Station
Saturday, September 10, 2005, 8:34 p.m.

Navigating the crowded *Keleti Pu* train station was proving difficult, as by the fifth night in Budapest, Theo was feeling rough. Unfortunately for Jason, he looked far, far worse.

Despite their bold proclamations to the contrary, they discovered that there really was a limit to the amount of alcohol, marijuana, girls, churches, museums, shops, bridges, monuments, hills, bath houses and cheap food they could handle.

That first night at the *Your Best Days* bar, as they spilled beers down their shirts, laughing like crazed Vikings on the warpath, nothing was beyond them. *More chicken! More wine!*

Jason in particular had an especially good week. His realization about Lilly—that she had actually been in his dreams years before ever having met her—opened his mind to the possibility of fate, and that maybe Hank's advice had been right on the money. Uli smothering him in some serious *bowm chicka wow wow* only cemented those ideas. But that was then.

For young men, Theo and Jason were feeling an oldness beyond their years—their backs and shoulders ached, their knees throbbed, their heads were heavy like sacks of potatoes—confessing that perhaps...possibly...their fathers weren't as totally lame as they wanted to believe. That they just might have exaggerated—although only by an itsy-bitsy, teensy-weensy smidge—the mythic tales regarding their own invincibility. Anybody, they reasoned, can be off by a teensy-weensy smidge.

Not only were Theo and Jason crumbling like sandcastles beneath the waves of high tide, but Sven had moved on to the Swiss Alps, while Uli was on her way back to Hamburg, to begin rehearsals for Mozart's *Die Zauberflöte*, an opera about three ancient Egyptian women and a giant snake. Constant drizzle had rolled into Budapest.

The cab ride to the *Keleti Pu* station had been no plate of fish sticks either. Theo was still hung over despite twenty hours of sleep. Jason, meanwhile, had already puked twice. At least the driver pulled over to let him spew out the door. He mostly hit the street.

Their plan was to catch the 21:20 train northwest through Hungary, cross the Slovak Republic, and then make it to the Czech Republic, finally arriving 6:29 the next morning at the *Praha Holesovice* station in Prague. They would spend a few days there, and then leave their fates up to the gods. As if they had a choice.

Inside the station, Theo stopped along the busy corridor, stuck behind an old Hungarian man with short, spotty whiskers and a black eye.

Scanning for their train—Theo could see nine in all beneath the dim, overhead lighting—he wondered just how many stations he'd passed through since leaving New Zealand. There was a constant, familiar murmur that resonated throughout the railways. Nameless faces. Strangers. The motion of people, the buzzing of time. Theo knew this sensation as the marker of transition. The end of one experience, the beginning of another. Departures and arrivals. Change.

Jason bent down on one knee. He took a deep breath. One train pulled in along the track behind them. Another hissed and then rolled away, expelling a trail of steam.

"Are you okay?" Theo said. "You don't look so good."

"I think I'm getting the flu." Jason closed his eyes. His face was sweaty and pale. "Don't worry about it. I'll sleep on the train."

"You sure, mate? I dunno. We can always go back."

"Really," Jason said. "New day, new place, yada-yada."

"Yeh. Okay." Theo figured a long night's sleep would do them both some good. "There it is, mate." The locomotive's front end extended just beyond the corridor and into the damp, night air. "Train's right here. Track eight. I'm just gonna piss first."

Theo pointed to the *WC*, or water closet, opposite the train. Two soldiers sat at a security desk. One surveyed the crowd while the other nodded at a teenager speaking in Hungarian.

Jason stood up, grimaced. "Rock on."

On his way to the *WC*, Theo wondered if Roger went back to Cathedral Cove, if their Dad was tinkering with that busted helicopter. Theo wasn't one to get homesick, but he smiled at the thought of that metal eyesore, a plate of his mother's roast chicken, and spending days and days in his greenhouse. With nothing but his plants. And the time to watch them grow.

Jason grabbed him by the arm, and though it lasted just a few seconds, Theo felt a blast of white light. There were streaks of screaming fluorescent color. He wondered if Jason felt it, too. It didn't seem so.

Jason squinted. He swallowed uneasily. "I gotta lie down. I'll just grab a compartment. Meet me inside."

"Yeh, yeh. I'm totally fucked, too. Back in a minute."

"I'll be," Jason began, then waited for an elderly Hungarian couple to pass in front of him. He pointed to the third car. "In that one. Right there. If I can't find an empty compartment, just keep walking 'til you find me. I'll keep the door open."

"Sweet." Theo said. His bladder was starting to throb. "I'll…"

Jason was already off, the back of his rucksack bobbing up and down.

"…see you in there, mate. I'll be right there."

After relieving himself, Theo went to the sink and splashed cold water on his face. The bathroom walls were dirty and cracked. He looked in the mirror. The bottom left corner had been smashed away. Staring at his reflection, Theo zeroed in on the large, black rings under both eyes.

I'm wearing down. I'm losing it.

Sooner or later, he would have to go home. But not yet. He slapped his face, chuckled. "Come on, ya little fucker. Off you go."

Crowds mushroomed at the ends of each car as the train to

Prague filled up. Heading to the train, rucksack in tow, Theo stepped over a girl sitting against the wall as her mother rifled through a yellow handbag. "O-kay." Theo counted the cars, searching for Jason. "One, two—"

Ooof!

Theo crashed, knocked over, crushed between his rucksack and a young woman laughing uncontrollably. He reached for his head, which hit the floor. Hard. "What the...?"

"Oh, my God," she said, clearly an American. "Are you...are you okay? This little boy was chasing me." Lying on top of Theo, her breasts jiggled beneath her short-sleeve shirt. She rolled to the side, pointing behind her. "We were playing a game."

Shhhhhh! The train to Prague was preparing for departure.

"Yeh," Theo said, struggling to get up. "But my train's..."

Still laughing, the American seemed in no rush to extract herself. *Star Attraction* was printed across her chest. "My foot," she said, her legs tangled with his. "It's caught in the straps."

"THEO!"

Theo scanned the train. Passengers were waving from the open windows, reaching out to friends and family as they waved back from the platform. He finally spotted Jason.

"Theo, come on! What are you doing? Let's go!"

"Yeh." Theo said, "I'm—"

"Here," the American said. "My foot. Wait...wait...no, I think..."

Get off me, you stupid cow.

Theo heard the first locomotive chug. His heart sank.

"I think I got it," she said.

You're fucking me off. I have to...

Theo wanted to make a run for it. Except he wasn't going to make it.

"THEO!" Jason shouted again. "MEET ME AT..."

Theo could barely hear over the constant murmur. The blended voices. Departures and arrivals. Change. He unhooked his bag, leaving it unattended. He ran toward the train, making his way through the crowd.

"CHARLES BRIDGE!" Jason shouted from the open window. "NOON!"

Theo shook his head violently. He still couldn't hear.

The front of the train slipped into the darkness. "CHARLES BRIDGE!"

"Yeh, yeh!" Theo shouted back. He nodded sharply. "Noon."

Jason leaned on the open window, extending his hand. The train pulled away.

Theo stopped running. He waved to the empty track. Partly to acknowledge Jason. But mostly to say goodbye. "Charles Bridge," he said.

"Here's your bag." The American grimaced. "It's heavy. Was that your friend?"

"Yeh." Theo nodded quietly. "My friend."

"I'm really, *really* sorry," she said. "I didn't mean...oh, crap. I'm Lil...Liz," she said. "From America. I didn't do much for international relations just then, did I?"

Theo nodded again. "Yeh," he said. "From America."

The constant murmur. Blended voices. Departures and arrivals. Change.

Helpless, Theo watched as Jason's train sped up through the darkness, the roar of motion growing louder, louder, and then sadly quiet. And like even the best of memories, Jason vanished from him, fading into the distance.

Fading.

Fading.

Gone.

Chapter 52
Catch Me If You Can (Redux)

San Diego, California—UCSD Medical Center
Tuesday, September 10, 1991, 8:33 p.m.

The year it all went to hell, Lilly heard the rumors. That her father, Marcus Opadopolous, the No. 26-ranked tennis player in the world at the time, had visits from female admirers while he was on the road.

Lilly was only twelve, but she knew what that meant. She knew what it meant to have curves, to look different from boys, and that boys looked at your curves, even if you didn't want them to. And that sometimes they wouldn't look even when that's exactly what you wanted.

Lilly also knew that her parents were talking less. That they were laughing less. That her mother would huddle at the table with her coffee and notebook and red pens, studying the sports pages like stock reports, because there was no other way to stay connected to her husband.

And Lilly knew that she couldn't bear another year with her daddy gone seven of those months, when she had so many fears, so many questions.

Lilly rooted for her daddy to win each and every match, but she didn't need him to be champ. Lilly rooted for her daddy whether he played on grass or clay, day or night, in the U.S. Open or a local match, but she didn't need him to be a hero. Lilly rooted for her daddy whether he was the favorite or the underdog, but either way, she just needed him to be home. She just needed her daddy.

So when she came home from school and saw him sitting there, back from the road three days early, with his sore knee taped up, legs hidden between the footstool and couch, she ran across the sun-soaked living room like she was jumping over the net.

And when her daddy stood up to greet her and his eyes exploded like the lights on center court, Lilly jumped through the air and into his arms and smothered him with all the love and joy and desperation and confusion coursing through her pubescent veins.

As she hurtled toward him, Lilly could feel her destiny unfold.

Catch me, Daddy! Catch me!
I love you, I love you, I love you.
Catch me, Daddy! Catch me!
I miss you, I miss you, I miss you.
Catch me, Daddy! Catch me!
Don't you ever leave me again.

In the months that followed, when her daddy told her not to worry—that his injured knee was really a blessing in disguise—Lilly knew better. The ruined knee had ruined them all. When the doctors said that the injury was inevitable—Lilly knew better.

After his knee started to heal and he retired officially, Lilly's mother moved into the Laguna Beach apartment. Lilly would never forget the date: *September 10, 1991.*

And even though Lilly's parents said they had been drifting apart for years, that they would be happier being friends—and her parents—but not being married anymore, that their divorce, like her daddy's knee, had nothing to do with her, that it would have happened no matter what, Lilly knew better.

Lilly destroyed her father's career. And with it her mother's dreams. With nothing left to hold them together. The end of her father's career wrecked her parents' marriage.

Of course they blame me. They just don't have the guts to say it.

And when her parents said that they both loved her very much, that nothing would ever change that, Lilly knew better, too.

They say they love me, but they secretly hate me. Parents always think they know more than they do, and that kids know less.

And when they told Lilly that accidents happen, that sometimes the unexpected can lead to a better life, that she shouldn't blame herself, Lilly knew better. Because Lilly knew what they didn't. What they could never understand. That when Lilly saw her daddy's weak knee taped up like a mango, she knew it was her best chance at knocking it out once and for all. At keeping them a family. Instead of ripping them apart.

Lilly would spend the next fourteen years petrified at the mere thought of confessing her sins, when absolution was the one thing she needed most.

Catch me, Daddy. Catch me.

I'm falling.

Chapter 53
Consolation Prize

The Southern Sphere of Eternity—Starlight Designs Milky Way's Public Unveiling: T-Minus 19 Days (Eternity Standard Time)

"Listen. Doug, dude. No can do. You gotta drop the price by ten percent or no deal." Lex leaned back in his chair as one set of contractors took measurements for his corner office. The others installed four new desks, one for each of Lex's staffers, new hires who were answering the phones or at least trying to look busy.

"Look...I don't...well...this isn't *last time*. This is *now*...Yeah, yeah. Emma said, Emma said. New day, new rules." Lex looked toward Emma's office. The door was closed. "Emma knows design," he said into the wireless headset, "but she doesn't know pricing. I do. So either give me a real rate on the nebula paste, or I'll give Bernice a call. She swears up and down that she'll take care of me." Lex smiled. "Yes, I know she's a crackpot. But if you're okay telling your boss that you lost your best new account to her...well, hey...I'm okay with it, too."

Lex leaned forward at his desk. He motioned to Tyler, then covered up his mouthpiece. "Did they start my office?" Tyler shrugged. "Doug, hold on a sec. Tyler. Look. I know it's your first day, and..." Lex felt a change in the air just then, a ripple through his heart. The elevator door opened into the office. A stranger approached. "I understand if...you know...you're feeling a bit...awkward."

"I don't feel awkward," Tyler said.

Lex smacked his lips. Standing before him was a large black man who smelled of hand-rolled cigarette confidence. Lex leaned on the arms of his chair, but his left hand slipped. His body fell to the side. Feeling that he had lost stature in this relationship already, Lex straightened himself, and then stood up.

His eyes were even with the stranger's chin.

"Can I help you?" Lex said in his deepest, manliest voice.

The stranger looked down at Lex, and then toward Emma's office. "No."

"Well," Lex inquired, "why are you—?"

"Rufus." Emma called from outside her office. "Excellent. Come." She nodded to Rufus, who brushed past Lex in long, powerful strides.

"Whoa, whoa." Lex ran over to Emma. "Who, uh…who's this?"

"Don't worry about it. He's helping me with something." Emma raised her hand before Lex could interrupt. "I need you to cancel tomorrow's dinner at Forté."

"Uh…o…kaaay," Lex said. "What, uh…why?"

"Change of plans. Rufus, go on in. I'll be right there."

Lex looked away as Rufus walked passed him—into Emma's office. "So Appledouche backed out, huh? That happens."

Emma raised her eyebrows. Lex held his defiant composure. *What the fuck are you up to? And who the fuck…is Rufus?*

"Yeah, yeah," he said finally. "Abladeujé, Abladeujé."

"No, he didn't back out." Emma followed Tyler's butt across the office. "In fact, I bet he wants to sign another deal before anyone else can lock me in. A much. Bigger. Deal. It's just like I said, pumpkin. The Milky Way's my ticket to the big time."

A contract with Jacques Abladeujé would mean big things for Emma. Perhaps not for Lex, but for *Starlight Designs* to be sure. They were still working out the kinks on the Milky Way center-piece—the irrigation system on Mars was a bust, Pluto was having trouble qualifying as a planet, Mercury was way too hot and the atmospheres on three of the Jupiter moons were converting oxygen to a form of space mucous—but the announcement had gone out as planned.

The Milky Way's official unveiling was less than three weeks away. The phones rang almost nonstop. And no matter how cool Lex tried to play it, he was getting more frazzled by the day. He had no idea how Emma managed the stress.

"Hey, not bad. Okay. Nice. Three for dinner. Where should I make the reservation? Oooh…how about Somberosa? They make a mean mai tai."

"Jacques is taking *me* out. He's got something very...*big* to show me."

"But..." Lex's heart gagged as his new assistants, the contractors and the janitor all pretended not to listen. "...I thought you wanted me there, to...you know..."

"*Tsch.* Don't be disappointed, sunshine. Jacques asked just for me."

Lex squinted hard. "I don't remember putting that call through."

I don't remember a lot. Why'd I let her talk me into all this? I'm such a doofus.

"Of course you don't. I gave him my direct line."

"You said you don't want anybody to *have* your direct line."

"Noooo. I said I don't want *you* giving *out* my direct line." She looked into her office. "I, on the other hand, can do whatever I want."

Lex took Emma's elbow. He whispered sternly, closed her office door. Rufus was on the other side. The inside. "Listen. I'm getting tired of this. You said we were going to be partners. You focus on design, I handle the day-to-day. Who the fuck is Ruf—?"

"Actually." Emma removed Lex's hand as if it were a pair of dirty underwear. "I said we'd *sort of* be partners. And, yes. I focus on design, you handle the day-to-day. But *I* sign your checks," she said loud enough for everyone to hear. "And while I'm sure you're quite the Trader Joe with your little buddy, Doug, I'm sure I can get...," Emma snapped her fingers as she fumbled for the name, "...Tyler, there...to pick up the slack in no time. See? Once he figures out the copier, I won't be able to tell you apart."

Lex was a giant teardrop. Lex was a dirty mop head.

"Oh, don't be upset, sweetie. You still get your own office, as promised, and you get to boss around all these hungry little monkeys. And don't be threatened just because they all want your job. They're not up to it." She opened her office door. "Not yet."

Lex was back on the floor with peanut shells stuck to his face.

Emma took her finger, lifted his chin. She offered a slight smile. "I'm going to the top. Whether you come with me or not...that's up to you."

Lex was his mother's child, a son between worlds, watching as Emma smiled at him. She straightened his tie. She smoothed the wrinkles on his chest and then held her hand there. "Think you can handle it? It's gonna happen fast."

Breathing in her perfume, Lex simultaneously felt empowered and powerless. "Yeah," he said. "No problem."

"Oh...it'll be a problem. But you just might handle it anyway."

Chapter 54
Holy Ring of the Talisman

Eastern Europe—Somewhere Between Budapest and Prague
Saturday, September 10, 2005, 11:51 p.m.

The overnight train to Prague rumbled through the darkness. Jason hadn't been on his own since Jean dropped him at the Manchester station almost two weeks, five countries and several thousand miles before. And now that he was solo again, lying face up in the small compartment, he was nauseous, achy and burning with fever.

Raging with flu, he felt like a backpacking orphan, abducted for reasons unknown to him, shuttled off in secret, in the dead of night, heading deeper through Eastern Europe and into the arms of any number of foster guides who, at best, might provide a bed and a meal, and at worst, would be treacherous and evil.

Still, when he made it to Prague he would wait for Theo on the Charles Bridge, although even he knew there was virtually no chance in the many levels of Hell that they would reconnect. Not having a cell phone, Jason finally acknowledged, was a real pain in his nut sack. Paying for the international activation fee would have been worth every penny.

While feeling safe and protected under the umbrella of constant companionship, Jason gladly forgot what it meant to carry the entire burden of responsibility. But he was struggling now to accept that it was for him alone to make it across the continent.

Since he didn't have a reliable plan for getting himself from place to place, his emotional and psychological weariness was greater than his extreme physical discomfort. He felt isolated, as if the floor had turned to putty, like a cartoon picnic blanket sunk into Bugs Bunny's rabbit hole, swallowed into the earth, and him with it.

On the platform, right before he got separated from Theo, again Jason felt a blast of white light. There were streaks of screaming fluorescent color. There was the sensation of being sucked through a tornado. Was it exhaustion? Fever? Spiked Euroweed? Was it God setting him straight for being a non-believing weenie?

Jason couldn't even call himself a lapsed Jew because he hadn't lapsed—he had never invested himself in the first place. In that regard, Jason followed his father's lead, impudently rejecting all organized religion. But also like his father, Jason overlooked the spiritual aspects of Judaism, absent from him not only in his outlook on life, but also when he needed it most.

Jason had no faith, no sense of cosmic or even cultural belonging to help get him through times of crisis. So as he often did when faced with struggle, he embraced worry—not because it helped solve his problems, but because it was easy, accessible and familiar.

And most ironic for Jason, he started thinking just then about Jesus, of all people, and his lesson about the fish: Give a man a fish and he eats for a day; teach a man to fish and he eats for a lifetime. Jason was starting to realize just how much that idea applied to him. Receive a guided tour and journey for a day; learn to *be* a guide and journey for a lifetime.

But being as he was, Jason once again clung to the rhythm of an overnight train gliding over the seams in the railway tracks.

Clug-lug, clug-lug, clug-lug...

Ideally, he would sleep until Prague, but he struggled on these overnight trips, in constant fear that he would miss his stop, get robbed...or worse.

He reached for his crotch. Money belt check. Because you never know.

Jason rubbed his temples. His glands were swollen. His skin was hot and clammy. The thought of food only intensified his queasiness, but it would be at least another four hours until he reached Prague. He levered down his knapsack from the overhead rack. He would force down the bread and Swiss cheese if he had to. And he would have to. He fished through his bag. "You know..." He sighed. "Crap."

Jason forgot to load up on food. Again. He ran his fingers through his sweaty hair.

What am I gonna do? I've got no food or water. I'm alone I'm sick it's the middle of nowhere it's two in the morning I can't speak the language and they have guns and wars and there's no real police and I can't trust anybody I'll get robbed lose my passport my money I'll get dumped by the side of the tracks and the werewolves'll eat me alive and I'll be a carcass bleeding in a ditch and I'll never—

He squinted hard, put his hands out. "You're losing it, dude. Just breathe...breathe..." He followed his own instructions. And then once more. "Okay. I've got to calm down, just cool myself down." Dehydrated, Jason considered licking condensation off the dirty compartment window. Instead, he changed into his shorts and then removed his gray pullover, stripping down to his white cotton T-shirt, soaked through with sweat.

Forgoing all hygienic concerns, he laid down on the floor between the padded benches. His head was beneath the window, his feet near the sliding compartment door.

His bare skin was probably pressed up against flecks of animal manure tracked in from the muddy farms of Eastern Europe, and he didn't care. He was undoubtedly lying in drops of drool and sneeze and dirty sex residue, and he didn't care.

Skanky or not, the floor was cool and soothing. Jason let out a sigh of relief. He smiled, laughed a little. He closed his eyes. And then he heard the voices.

Jason's eyelids snapped open. His eyes shifted. He heard whispers beneath him, below the floor. Voices, definitely voices. "What the...?"

He got up and looked into the hallway. It was empty. The Hungarian countryside whisked by in the darkness. The breeze whistled through an open window. An older couple with a small child slept in the compartment to his right.

Jason returned to his own compartment. Sunk in his seat, he rubbed his eyes. He wiped the sweat from his brow. "Don't freak out, dude. You're fine. You're totally fine." He laid down, his ear against the cushion. Only he wasn't okay, he wasn't fine. Jason felt that his spirit, adrift in its own darkness, was following the true destination of the train, which he came to believe was the murky, steaming underworld of the Devil and his minions. He heard more whispers, more voices. Only now they were clearly coming from beneath the cushion.

"All right." He jumped up. "I totally heard that. I..."

Jason put his fingers beneath the edge of the cushion. It gave. Before prying it up, he considered what might be underneath.

Vampires? Cujo? Satan?

"Nah. Couldn't be."

Jason breathed, exhaled. He closed his eyes and lifted. Peeking first through one eye, then the other, he found a storage compartment beneath the cushion. Reluctantly, he reached in up to shoulder, more than just a little worried that whatever was in there would yank him down with it. He hit bottom. He wriggled his fingers.

My arm's still attached. Cool.

Jason replaced the cushion, sat on it. He rubbed his temples in concentric circles, as if he could rub the voices into oblivion. "They aren't real," he whispered as the train slowed down. He breathed in, breathed out. "It's the fever. I'm delirious." And again. "They aren't...real."

The train gave a final lurch forward, and then stopped. *Krr-psshh.*

Passengers exited, boarded. Shadows and silhouettes passed by the window. Jason heard the voices again. The presence beneath him. His compartment door opened.

I don't like it here. I want to go home.

Shivering with fever, he nodded uneasily at his compartment mate. She was a gumdrop of an old woman with penciled-in eyebrows and a scowl that would make the Devil cry for his momma. She wore a fur hat and clutched a handbag to her chest.

The conductor inspected their tickets, punched Jason's passbook. The old woman eyed the conductor with disdain, handed over her ticket and then snatched it back. She shoved it into her purse, which she clasped shut. She mumbled in Hungarian.

Clueless as to what she said, Jason agreed anyway. "Yeah," he said. "Me, too."

"Ahhh," the old woman said. "America? U...S...A?"

"Yes," Jason said. "I'm American. From..."

The old woman reached into her purse, although careful to make sure that only she could see inside, as if she were hiding a secret—like latex gloves, a rusty hatchet, spiked dildo and a bottle of ether.

Jason shifted in his seat. His breaths shortened.

The old woman looked at Jason, her hand still buried within her purse. She stood up, reached for the compartment door and slid the metal bolt, locking them inside.

Jason quickly fell back into his fever fantasy. He stiffened.

I knew it. She's going to rip my throat out bathe in my entrails and chop my lungs into a chunky stew. I'm going to be human stew! Human stew!

The old woman looked at him, wet her lips. She removed her hand from he purse. Only instead of a meat cleaver, she produced a large silver hoop with religious trinkets. Angels, saints, prophets. Silver crosses. Gold-plated crosses. The Virgin Mary. Baby Jesus. The Virgin Mary cradling Baby Jesus. She shook the holy ring at him. "Tahleesemahn!"

Oh, God.

Jason grimaced politely, his intense, antireligious instincts mashing against his need to be polite to an old woman.

Oh, good God.

The train rumbled through the night.

Chapter 55
The Greenhouse Effect

The Auckland Museum was set on a hill overlooking the sparkling waters of Waitemata Harbor. Two rows of trees, parallel to one another, lined a walkway up to the museum. The branches and leaves formed a wide, arched canopy, encasing the grass in shade.

Lydia Barnes was right where George thought she would be, staring up at an old tree, where she had been every morning at 11 a.m. for the past three days. Right on time. It hadn't taken George long to figure out how to find her. And finding Lydia was the key.

When Theo sought him out in Amsterdam and produced pictures of the jar—but not the jar itself—George deduced that Theo left it with someone he trusted.

Smart. Never carry the item with you.

While in the *Ball and Tickle*, George asked Theo if he had a twin sister—telling Theo that he carried a knowing sort of wisdom that only comes from sharing a womb, as if embedded within each twin is a swath of the sibling's soul.

When Theo said that, no, he didn't have a sister—unable to hold back a smile...*Vanity. Nobody can resist a compliment....*but did have a younger brother in New Zealand—George knew just where to look for the jar. George had learned long ago that finding out secrets was simply a matter of knowing when, and how, to ask.

So George sent Theo southbound to Venice and then west to Barcelona—away from the jar—while George took a flight southeast to New Zealand—toward it. Alberto was an old friend who owed George a favor, and was happy to misdirect Theo to Spain.

George spent his entire life helping *other* people get what *they* wanted. But now it was his turn to be selfish. And if that meant using Theo, so be it. One of the joys of Angelique was never playing second fiddle to anyone.

Yet getting to New Zealand was only part of the problem. George also had Emma to contend with. Out of necessity, they had agreed to pool their resources. On Earth, only a handful of people knew the jar even existed, but for those who did, it was their only chance for getting back to Eternity—and a long shot at that.

George and Emma agreed that whoever came into possession of the jar would contact the other, and together they would take an express journey through the cosmos.

Not that George had many options. Without Emma, the jar was all but useless to him—for getting home, anyway. Given that Emma had once been married to Lawrence, the CBM warehouse manager in Eternity, she knew how to activate the bar code, sending them back from whence they came. George, however, did not.

Even with the jar, he was at Emma's mercy. And George had no allusions about her. He was convinced that if Emma obtained the jar first, she would leave him behind. George therefore had to obtain the jar before she did, yet he needed Emma just the same.

So after seeing the pictures, George informed Emma that Theo was in Europe—which was true—and that he had the jar with him—which was not. This kept her focused away from the very item she was after, while giving George extra time to find it himself.

He also factored in Emma's paranoia and manipulation, assuming that she would never willingly stake her success on the efforts of anyone who wasn't in her back pocket. Therefore, George also assumed that Emma sent someone to New Zealand to find the jar on her behalf, excising him from the deal. George had to act quickly. And what better way to get to a young man than through his mother.

Lydia gets me to Roger. Roger gets me the jar. The jar gets me home.

Lydia may have been staring up at the tree, but her attention was elsewhere.

"He's quite an interesting little fellow, don't you think?"

"Oh, what's that?" she said. "Who's that now?"

A well-dressed Taiwanese man with a Dutch accent pointed to a red-crowned parakeet with green plumage, perched on a low branch. "Look there. He blends right in."

Sunshine sparkled through the leaves, as if refracted through a diamond.

"My oldest son...Theo...he comes here a lot. Bird watching. I always thought, you know, he meant girls." Two inches taller than her visitor, Lydia blushed, patches of her pale face turning red. "But I guess a mother never really knows her own sons. It's a terrible thing. You want to know them...but they don't let you."

Although she ordinarily felt it embarrassing to be so familiar with a stranger, Lydia knew it in her bones that he was someone to confide in. She didn't know why. Holding her loneliness inside was causing her body to sag. It was time to let it out.

"Oh," he said. "I would guess he meant both."

Lydia's skin went flush with goose bumps as her new acquaintance moved closer, yet still keeping a respectful distance. He stood directly beneath the small green parakeet, no larger than a pear. A patch of red feathers marked its tiny forehead.

The stranger's own hair—black with a swoop highlighted with blonde streaks—had gray flecks along the sides. "Birds *and* girls, that is."

Lydia watched him look to the top of the old tree. The weathered brown bark was rough and chipping away, much like Lydia's resolve. She felt like George could read her slumping body language. *I'm so lonely. Someone listen to me. Please.*

"This *is* a lovely spot," George said. "I see why Theo likes it."

Lydia held her forearms, hugging herself. "Yeh, I see it, too. Theo's always been mussing about with plants. He has a greenhouse in our yard, yeh? He gets lost in there for hours. When you call him, he doesn't hear you. Then he'll take off for days just to find one flower. He's always so...by himself. Like his father."

It wasn't difficult for George to see that Lydia lamented the loss of innocence—not just of her children, but also in the way they saw her. But what struck him most was her unconscious at work. Lydia seemed unaware that she exaggerated her maternal anxiety to camouflage that she might even resent her sons for possessing the youth and promise she felt had long passed her by.

"Theo sounds like an interesting young man."

"He is," Lydia said. "I just wish I knew more—"

"And I think," George said, raising a hand, "if you'll permit me, that you probably know him better than you think. Sons are an enigma, but not such a mystery." He led Lydia around the tree. "Oh, they put on quite a show. Demanding, impudent... trying to prove their parents are old. Dense....Useless."

George smiled. It was time to tell a tale that needed telling, regardless of its authenticity.

"But deep down they treasure your experience. They're counting on it. Where else can they turn when disappointment sets in? When I brought my first...boyfriend home...and later when it soured, I was more nervous than you can probably imagine. But my parents surprised me. Even with all my secrets... they were good about it. They made it okay to be who I was."

George introduced himself. Lydia did the same.

Lydia gets me to Roger. Roger gets me the jar. The jar gets me home.

Ohhh. He's a...well...you know. Realizing that George was of no sexual threat, or temptation, Lydia found her emotions unspool.

"I used to climb this tree when I was a girl. If you can believe that, a woman my age." Lydia reached for two branches stretched out in opposite directions. "My mum...she would never allow it..." Lydia shrugged. "...I did it anyway. Something about kids, yeh? They always want to be someplace else…someplace hard to get at, but never right where they are."

The parakeet hopped to a higher branch. A twig bounced in its wake.

"What about your other son?"

"Roger?" Lydia pronounced it *Rahja*. "Oh, yeh. Quite a mouth on that one. But he still never says anything you can understand. Nothing *I* can understand, anyway. Always in riddles. And now with his girl—"

"Ah," George said. "Young love. So much passion."

"But why is it such a secret? Why does he hide it from me?"

"Young men are forced to take such risks. They keep their hearts locked up—"

"Yeh!" Lydia grabbed George by the hand. "They do, they do!"

"Because they think they're sup*posed* to. But it isn't natural. They fight themselves and torment, but the heart will lead a young man 'most anywhere. Give it time. If Roger loves her, he'll share it with you."

"He's so confused. I could help if he'd let me."

"Or perhaps…," George said as the bay shimmered in the distance. "No. Never mind. It's not my place."

Lydia almost passed out with anticipation. "No. Tell me. Please?"

George clasped Lydia's hand. Her fingers were long and weak.

"Mothers. They share a common fear. That sooner or later a young lady will come along and steal their position in their son's heart. That they'll be replaced."

Lydia dipped her head. Her hand dropped. She looked away.

"Impossible. Young love is but a fragile thing. But a son *always* needs his mother. It is the way of things, Lydia. Have faith. Roger will come to you. When he's ready."

"But how do you know?"

Lydia gets me to Roger. Roger gets me the jar. The jar gets me home.

"Because they always do," he said. "Because they always do."

Chapter 56
The Prophet of Doom

Eastern Europe—Somewhere Between Budapest and Prague
Sunday, September 11, 2005, 1:47 a.m.

"Tahleesemahn!" the old woman shouted at Jason. "Tahleesemahn!"

Despite her insistence otherwise, Jason struggled to explain, without being rude, that he was not a disciple of the Lord. He pointed. "Me. Jew." He looked up and pointed toward God. "No Jesus." He shook his head, pointed to himself again. "Jew."

"Tahleesemahn!" She shook her holy ring of the Jesus clan. "Tahleesemahn!"

"No," Jason repeated, feeling an unexpected connection with his roots. As he unraveled physically, emotionally and psychologically, he found that clinging to the tiniest threads of his religious background made him feel slightly more whole. More him. "Me. Jew. No Jesus." He shook his head. "Jew. Understand? Jew."

"Ahh," she said, offering a gesture of recognition. She smiled.

Finally, Jason thought. *Finally*.

The old woman removed a silver pendant from her over-sized ring and then stuffed it into a pocket of Jason's knapsack. She zipped it closed. "Tahleesemahn," she said.

Jason reached for his bag. "No. I—"

She slapped his hand away. "Tahleesemahn!" But then she patted that same hand, like a grandmother would. His Hungarian grandmother. She smiled at him. "Tahleesemahn."

Jason nodded. There was no use fighting it. "Yeah," he said. "Okay. Talisman."

Eighteen miles from the *Wien Südbahnhof* station in Bratislava, the train slowed, and then came to a halt, leaving Jason somewhere between Budapest and Prague. He looked at his Hungarian grandmother. He shrugged. She did the same.

A drunken tenor boomed from the hallway. "We die! God's warriors will slit our throats!"

Jason's Hungarian grandmother clutched her bag, rocking in place. "Tahleesemahn," she said, then kissed one of her many crosses. "Tahleesemahn."

Jason went to the door, looked down the hallway. Other passengers did the same. A large, middle-aged Hungarian man clutched a brown bottle. He reeked of whiskey. Droplets glistened in his scraggly brown beard.

"You." He pointed at Jason. "We die. The army of darkness has come."

Jason slammed the door, locked it. His Hungarian grandmother clutched her bag closer. They waited. And waited.

Finally, the train lurched forward, rolled a bit, then stopped. And again. No information, no explanations. Stopping, starting, pushing on for minutes—sometimes just a few seconds—and again sitting motionless. On and on they went for almost two hours, finally passing over the Slovac Republic border, and toward the Czech Republic.

At the next stop, Jason's Hungarian grandmother left him to fend off the prophet of doom on his own. She patted his leg and smiled. "Tahleesemahn," she said. "Tahleesemahn."

The comfort didn't last.

"Blood will spill," the Hungarian doomsayer whispered in the hallway. "The serpents of God have come. Our souls will drown in Hell."

"Please," Jason whispered from inside his locked compartment. "Just shut up." He didn't have a gun, flamethrower or *Ghostbusters* nuclear apparition-doohickey to protect himself. And he had whizzed on the concept of God enough times to rule out getting divine intervention now that a pack of demons was outside his window waiting to rip off his spiritual gonads. All he had now was the Jesus lady and her holy ring of the talisman. "Please, just stop."

And then the voices returned, only more clearly. Frantic. Jason pried up the cushion, put his hand against the metal base. He felt movement beneath him.

The Hungarian doomsayer ran across the hallway. "Like rats, they come for our flesh..."

Jason heard multiple voices now, not underneath the train, but outside. He snuck into the hallway, where two other passengers were already ducking beneath the windows. Outside in the darkness, Jason saw six men in coats and hats marching single file, hands behind their heads. Their boots scraped along the pebbled roadside.

From behind them, three soldiers pointed machine guns. One soldier cocked his weapon. His gloved finger curled around the trigger.

"They smuggle across the border," someone said. "We are fine. We go."

Smugglers. Huh. Better than Satan.

The train proceeded without further incident, speeding along into early morning. And as it passed through Romania and into the Czech Republic, Jason sat alone with the door locked from the inside. Dazed and delirious, he reached into his knapsack. He rocked back and forth on the bench, rubbing the silver pendant. His Hungarian grandmother had faith—or a wicked case of the bingo bango bongos—but either way she believed in God, something big and mysterious and powerful, and put her trust in that. In lieu of his own god to believe in, Jason would take any faith he could get.

After twenty-four years he was finally starting to think that he might have been basing at least some of his values on a very big mistake. Sure, he had no proof. Or did he?

Rather than rejecting all thoughts of God and religion as if they were one and the same, maybe he could believe in some idea of God—any god—without having to believe in religion. Maybe they weren't as clearly linked as he had been led to believe. If there really was a God, was she Episcopalian?

Buddhist? Voodoo priest? Does God even notice religion? Does she care? Does it matter?

Maybe...maybe...there was a spiritual peace Jason could connect with, whether it made sense to anyone else or not. When it came to the great forces of the Universe, he was used to feeling like a drooling monkey anyway, so maybe feeling that way with some type of god at his side would at least be a step in the right direction.

He wasn't exactly converted, but for the first time he could remember, Jason decided that he would sit back and listen for the voice of God, and find out if the man in the sky actually had something to say.

"Talisman," Jason said, reaching for that Great Spirit. "Talisman."

Chapter 57
The Magic Button

The Eastern Sphere of Eternity—Horizon Terrace
Milky Way's Public Unveiling: T-Minus 11 Days (Eternity Standard Time)

Behind Brigsby's oblong head, Donald looked through the enormous penthouse window 717 floors above his own condo in Horizon Terrace. He watched the Andromeda galaxy—like a giant magenta pinwheel—rotate in its magnificent counter-clockwise swirl.

Donald turned around and pointed at the large, flat-screen television mounted on the wall opposite the window. "You told me to do it!"

Brigsby threw his hands up against the everlasting sunlight. His spindly finger shadows radiated across the hardwood floors. "Donnie, Don, darling...are you out of your mind? Why do you even watch that twittering nonsense?"

"It's *your* show! Look! It's on right now!"

Brigsby stared at his image, seated on his stool, encircled by a spotlight. He led Donald to the couch, its back facing the window. "Sit," Brigsby said. "Take a minute."

Donald's hands were sweaty; his armpits itched. But he nodded, letting his jaw unclench. "Yeah, okay," he said. "All right."

"Now...you know I like to talk," Brigsby began, almost a foot shorter than Donald, and dressed in white pleated pants and a baggy yellow shirt with oversized cuffs. "And you know I like to talk to different people in different ways."

Donald shook his head, as always, in awe of his friend's audaciousness. It wasn't lost on Donald that Brigsby, ever the showman, orchestrated the room's stage dynamics. That while Donald was seated—on the couch, lower than Brigsby—with his back to the window, he was also facing the television. The big screen.

Brigsby, meanwhile, stood above him—and with an unobstructed view—could admire his own reflection staring back in the window. Yet beyond the window, the Andromeda galaxy was in the distance...swirling. And then there was Milo's Smear—that permanent nothing.

And behind Brigsby—facing Donald—was his prerecorded television persona, holding court in the background, creating an aura as if he, Brigsby the Magnificent, were omnipresent. Brigsby reflected. Brigsby on replay. Brigsby live.

"You can't take my show seriously," he said. "You *know* that. Better than anyone. Do I play to the masses? Of course...but, honey...listen—that's just show biz."

Okay. Donald smiled. *I give in. I'm listening.*

"I like living in this building," Brigsby continued. With his open hand he alluded to the vast penthouse. It included a two-tiered mahogany library, an all-purpose rumpus room, a gourmet kitchen, and a full spa with steamed rocks, live tropical plants and a cascading waterfall. "I like the things money will buy."

The talk show host sat beside Donald and put a soft, wrinkled hand on his knee. Brigsby lowered his voice to just above a whisper. "But in the end, all I really do is tell people not to worry so much. To have a little fun. To enjoy each moment as often and as thoroughly as they can. That's it. That's all I do. It's no more complicated than that."

Donald didn't argue, because wrapped inside Brigsby's insatiable bluster was a tendency to make sense. And as if on cue, sensing Donald's acceptance, Brigsby snapped back to center stage. He just couldn't help himself.

Brigsby. You kill me.

"But you know why they really watch me? Because they think there's this secret, magic button somewhere, one that will fix their problems and make them rich, fabulous superstars." Brigsby offered a gluttonous smile. "Like me."

Donald chuckled at Brigsby's shameless vanity.

"And yet they're all so wrapped in fantasy...they don't realize...everybody has the same wish they do."

Even before Donald could ask, Brigsby answered the

question.

"They think *I* know where the button is, and that if they keep watching my show...I'll tell them. And that maybe, just maybe, they and they alone can press it, too. They want more, they want better and they want it now. So what I give them," Brigsby said, turning on his heel and then, with both hands open and palms up, gesturing to his image on the giant flat screen, "is the next best thing. An hour a day that makes them feel like they're more special than anyone in Eternity. That's why they tuned in today...and why they'll come back tomorrow and tomorrow and tomorrow, or whatever that silly little playwright will be on about. It's the hope that there's one easy answer for all the questions big and small, and that they'll get it for free."

"Yeah." Donald chuckled. "I liked that bit on combating crotch rot."

Brigsby nodded. "Indeed. We still get calls about that one." He stopped. "Hey! Are you getting cheeky with me? Ooh. You spunky little devil. I like to see it in you."

"I don't know," Donald admitted. "I was looking for a quick answer...like you said. I don't know what I expected to hear."

Brigsby sipped. "We've known each other a long time, have we not?"

Donald recognized the joke between them. Waiting for the punch line, he stood up, smiled. Donald may have towered over Brigsby physically, but he still felt diminutive before the charismatic performer. "Yeah," he said. "We have."

"So how long's it actually been now?"

Donald delivered his line. "Too long," he said.

And then Brigsby finished it. "Way too long."

Brigsby let Donald settle in, as he was a compulsive fixer of *other* people's problems, a character flaw he couldn't seem to shake. But when given advice, Donald often became either defensive or amused. It was his way of holding the confrontation at a distance.

Yet Donald would hear everything Brigsby had to say, and think about it—one of the traits Brigsby most loved about him. Donald would take time to contemplate, rather than just rolling the words through his mind as if they were pointless and unconnected. Donald was actually so close to making a leap in his own spiritual development that Brigsby could barely keep himself from saying so. But it would have to wait. Donald had a very real problem that needed immediate attention.

"So." Brigsby poured a blue martini. He took a sip. "Mm. Want one?"

"No." Donald chuckled. "I'm fine. So what am I going to—?"

"Ah, yes! Your plan. Well." Brigsby clenched his teeth, craned his head. "Eesh. That's...some strategy you've got there."

"I think it'll work."

"I'm not totally sure why, but, yes, I'm getting that.

"Look. All I have to do is—"

"You told me already, but I need to say this out loud...just to confirm that I understand you." The bespectacled talk show host took a sip and then cleared his throat. "Ahem." Brigsby smacked his lips. "In a week's time, during your...*vacation*... you're planning to walk back into the...what did you call it?"

"CB—"

"Okay. Yes, yes. The CBM warehouse. Right. So...you're going to stroll into the CBM warehouse as if it were just any old day. Just a regular Donnie's-going-to-the-office-and-doesn't-have-a-crazy-plan-to-ruin-his-whole-life kinda day. And then you're going to stand on one of those electro ladder gizmos, and climb up to the slot on the shelving unit where your missing jar is *supposed* to be, but currently...is not."

Brigsby stopped. Donald nodded affirmatively.

"Dandy. Then—and this is my favorite part—you are going to *pretend* to slip on the ladder, and during your *pretend* grasp for safety, you're going to *accidentally* knock four or five nearby jars to the ground. Upon impact, the jars will smash into itsy-bitsy pieces, as the CBM warehouse is the only concealed area in Eternity where the jars are actually breakable and the contents can do no damage whatsoever. That's because of the containment field or...something else I care nothing about."

Brigsby drew a breath. "Have I got it right so far?"

Donald nodded again. "Ye—"

"Yes, darling, that's just fabs for you. A nod will do. Brigsby's talking." Brigsby sipped his martini, and then smacked his lips again. "To cover your tracks, you will then rely on the emergency clean-up system to collect the undiluted cosmic building material and the glass shards, and dispose of them accordingly. That way, nobody will ever know that your original jar was missing. The idea...*ahem*...is that you'll camouflage your *first* blunder with a second *fake* blunder. And according to you...the concept for this plan comes at my suggestion."

Siiip.

"Is that it? You're going to make a mess, make the big boo-boo go all bye-bye?"

Donald nodded.

"Interesting," Brigsby said. "Interesting....Insane, but interesting." There was silence between them. "You really got that from my show. Huh. I never saw that coming." Brigsby refilled his glass. "So...where's your lovely bride going to be during all this cloak and dagger?"

"Actually...at a mandatory seminar about safety and protocol."

Brigsby tipped his glass. "Mm. Well done."

"Naturally," Donald began, "I'll be a little late."

"Or you won't be back at all."

"Yeah, well...I'm trying not to think about that."

"No." Brigsby circled his finger around the rim. "I'd imagine you wouldn't."

Chapter 58
The Sound of Motherfucking Music

Salzburg, Austria—International Youth Hostel
Wednesday, September 14, 2005, 8:32 p.m.

Jason held out for Theo as long as he could. But after three long days in Prague while wrecked with flu—battling the heat and humidity and mosquitoes and a hostel just far enough away from the city center that the trips back and forth alone almost had him in tears—Jason decided to cut his losses. Taking off made him sick in his soul, like he was tossing Theo aside. Ditching his friend. But he just couldn't take it anymore. He had to get out of Prague.

Like Hank said, you meet people in one city, lose them in the next. You never know why. You just have to move on. Even when you don't want to.

Having endured yet another miserable overnight train trip, Jason made his way back into Western Europe, to Austria, snagging the last remaining bed at the *International Youth Hostel* in Salzburg, which turned out to be just what he needed.

Jason showered, and slept through the night, when his intense fever finally broke. Tired but on the road to recovery, he spent the next day at the *Hohensalzburg Fortress*—he thought the torture chamber was especially cool—and then stopped back in the hostel dining hall. There he made quick friends with Clint and JoAnne—mates, but not lovers, from Brisbane, Australia.

Accompanying them was Jelena, a petite brunette from Lithuania; Kristof, a gray-faced computer tech from the Ukraine; and Shannon and Maura, second-year students at Manchester Metropolitan University, close to where Jason's adventure had begun.

With night falling, gas lamps and candles dimly lit the

dining hall, now filled with backpackers. Empty beer glasses littered their table. Jason downed another pint.

Clint had a rugby tattoo on his forearm. He had a heavy Australian accent. "So, Jason. What sorta Sheila makes you crack a fat, mate? A giant rack, with nipples like sausage patties?"

"Uh." Jason was warm and lightheaded. "I guess I'd have to say—"

"Any woman I marry's gotta swallow and do anal. If not, the wedding's off. But not before I have a go at all the bridesmaids."

"Clint." JoAnne slapped his arm. "You're such a beast."

At twenty-nine, Clint was two years younger than JoAnne, herself a year divorced from an alcoholic math teacher. Clint put his head on her chest. He looked up and smiled. "But you love me anyway."

"Never like that, mate. I don't hump with dogs."

"Rowf rowf!" Clint barked. "Rowf!"

JoAnne laughed. Clint laughed, as did Kristof and Jelena, Shannon and Maura. Jason did the same. He looked around the table, feeling grateful. That he felt warm inside. That he had good company again. A community. Losing Lilly, and then Theo, crystallized for him just how much he valued the bond between good people.

"When you get back to Manchester, come see us for a proper visit," Shannon said. Maura agreed. "It'll be brilliant. You can stay with us. We've got loads of room."

"Rowf rowf! You hear that, mate? A fucking threesome! You girls are all right."

"Clint!" JoAnne slapped him again. "Just ignore him, girls. He's all bark."

"Oh, I bite, all right. I'll bite you anyplace you like. Rowf rowf!"

Jason blushed. His nads tightened up. He turned to Shannon and Maura. "Yeah, that sounds good. I'll be back in Manchester in a few weeks."

Shannon had straight brown hair, pouty lips and a baby face aglow with the radiance of a young girl becoming a woman. She wrote down her contact information and gave it to Jason. "We'll be gutted if you don't visit. And maybe we'll come to New York.

We've never been."

Maura's long black hair dangled below her shoulders. Her eyes were green. "New York would be brilliant."

Jason was overrun with hot flashes just then and a bulge that required covering. "Yeah, definitely. Come any time you like. There's no place like it."

"That was terrible, yes?" said Jelena, who until then had been attentive, but quiet. "With the nine eleven. So sad."

Clint put down his pint. "That must've been shit, mate. Bloody fucking awful."

And with that the table fell silent, the only quiet group in a room full of revelry.

Jason was not used to being asked about September 11. It was all but understood among New Yorkers that the attacks destroyed their ideas about what life should be like, that they just couldn't watch any more news footage of those massive towers crumbling into piles of dust, as if their spirits had crumbled with them, and had never come all the way back.

Americans at large had struggled since, and New Yorkers especially carried on with a sense that there was nothing left to say about that day, that there was nothing more they wanted to say. At least, not out loud. Jason welled up. "I don't like to talk about it."

"You were there?" Maura grabbed Jason's thigh. "Were you scared?"

They all leaned forward, awaiting details. For Jason to recount the horror of that awful morning, when he passed through Hell's Kitchen on his way to see the orthopedic surgeon who operated on him years earlier. Jason was supposed to have been in Buffalo, but his elbow had swollen up unexpectedly, and was facing a possible second surgery and rehab.

Jason remembered a clear blue sky draped over Manhattan that morning. Until just before 9 a.m. it had been the template for a lifetime of perfect mornings.

Already amped just for being in the city, Jason walked out

of a deli on West 43rd Street with an almond poppy muffin and NesQuik chocolate milk. A green van with a yellow *Donatelli Plumbing* logo stenciled across the side was parked on the street. The driver's door was open. Morning talk came over the radio.

Two hefty plumbers sat on the rear bumper drinking coffee from Styrofoam cups. New Yorkers bustled. At the corner of 42nd Street and 9th Avenue, a policeman wore an orange mesh vest over his blue uniform. He directed traffic. He wore white gloves.

Through the radio the broadcaster announced the time—8:52 a.m.—and then said in a calm voice that just a few minutes earlier a plane had crashed into one of the towers at the World Trade Center. Jason looked up just then. The sun was warm on his face. But the news didn't sound quite right. He figured it must have been a mistake.

"It started out as a beautiful day," Jason said, "but it didn't end that way." The table fell silent again, no one quite sure how to be. But only for a moment.

"You get over to that castle today, mates?" Clint slammed his hand on the table. "Now *that's* a fucking fortress, yeh? I almost crapped myself walking up that bloody hill."

"No doubt girls," JoAnne said. "Crocodile Dundee over here whinged the whole time. Talk about an earbashing!" She mocked Clint. "Jo-Aaaaaannnne. It's too faaaaar. I'm tahy-ered. I'm thuhr-stee. This is shit. Let's go baaaaack."

"That was a brilliant view," Shannon agreed, her British accent getting Jason all riled up. "You can see the whole city, with the river on one side, the mountains on the other."

"They film *Sound of Music* there," Kristof said. "The movie, yes?"

Jason smiled. *The Sound of Music*. He never saw it.

"So here's to it, mates." Clint raised his glass. The others did the same. "Here's to *The Sound of Motherfucking Music*."

After another round of drinks, the party broke up. "Cheers, thanks," Maura said. "We're off to bed. Heading back tomorrow.

It's crap. Another year at university."

"You can't leave," Clint said. "You just got here."

"I'm knackered," Shannon said. "But it was lovely meeting you."

Jason took out the paper to confirm their details. Maura whispered in his ear, her hand on his shoulder. "Room nine. Wait five minutes, then come say a proper goodbye."

Those were some loooong five minutes. Jason sweated each tick of the second hand, until finally he finished his pint. "Um... thanks, guys. I'm gonna crash out."

Clint wasn't having it. "Where you going, mate? We still got drinkin' to do!"

Jason stood up straight, smiled. "Rowf rowf," he said, and then winked at Clint. "Rowf rowf."

Chapter 59
Luck of the Irish

With some kindly help from the Manchester girls, Jason was fully recovered from his separation anxiety, flu and malnutrition. His first threesome was as good as advertised, minus a few awkward bumps—including an elbow he took to the eye. He also discovered that women can be pretty darn accommodating when it comes to giving directions. It was most appreciated. Twice.

Refreshed—and more experienced—Jason was ready for Amsterdam. His plan was to take the 20:18 train, sleep all night, arriving 8:57 the next morning. He would then check into *The Band Wagon*, which his guidebook said was "friends to all," and although there was "no smoking in the rooms, you'll inhale enough walking through the lobby."

Having learned his lesson, Jason arrived at the *Hauptbahnhof* train station at 6:44 p.m., almost three and a half hours before his train was due to depart.

Standing outside, he looked back at the hostel. The snow-capped mountains were striking against the setting sun. Jason took a mental snapshot. A camera wasn't necessary for this one. Inside the station, the corridor was clean and empty except for a teenager sitting on the polished floor. His back was against the wall.

Alan Flaherty was heading back to Ireland, ending his first trip away from home. "Me mum'll go mad if I'm not back by tomorrow, ya know?" Flowing with an East Dublin accent, his voice was friendly and unassuming. "She says eighteen is too young to be off on me own, but me da said to go for it."

"Yeah." Jason sat next to Alan. "Moms tend to worry."

"But for good reason. We're always up to no good."

They shared a smile. "So what are you up to next? Back to school?"

"Oh, yeah. My first year at college. Me da insisted, like? He wants me to be a doctor? A foot specialist? And get rich in America? He says you're golden if ya stick with feet. Everybody's got 'em and they always hurt. Me da wants to retire on me. Kinda like his own private dole."

Jason laughed, his own feet sore and blistered. "A doctor. Cool."

"Yeah...I don't know. I'm a bit squeamish, if ya asked me."

Jason nodded. "When I go for a blood test, I make a deal with the nurses. They let me look away, and I promise not to puke on the floor."

Alan laughed. "A man after me own heart."

Jason sliced a piece of cheese. He offered some to Alan.

"Cheers, mate. But no, thanks. I can't eat any more cheese, like. One more bite and I'll get cancer of the arse. I haven't shat right in a week."

Alan wrote out directions to his parents' house, street by street, from the Dublin train station leading directly to his doorstep. "Dublin's just a wee ferry ride away from Manchester," he said. "Come any time. Me mum'll feed ya good and proper, like."

"I just might. Hey...you been to Amsterdam? You know... you hear the stories."

"Sorry, mate. Never been. But I'm hoping to. Maybe on me next trip."

Jason leaned back against the wall. He closed his eyes and smiled. And then he heard a strange but familiar noise—a *flap flap flapping* of the board—like a train was about to arrive. Or depart. "Oh, God. Dude! What time is it? What time!"

Alan checked his watch. "It's almost half eight. Yeah. About eight twenty."

"Hold on." Jason rifled through his bag for the mangled train schedule. "Salzburg...Salzburg...got it!" Jason ran his finger along the page. "Amsterdam. Am-ster-dam. Come on. Where the hell are you? There!" Alan recoiled. "No," Jason said, and felt his panic subside. "This is right. Departs twenty eighteen, arrives eight fifty-seven."

There was a *Kr-pssh!*

"What did I...?" Jason suddenly felt as he had recovered a fumble in overtime, ran it back for the winning touchdown, celebrating in front of eighty thousand fans, only to realize he sprinted in the wrong direction, spiking the ball in his own end zone.

"Holy crap. *Eight* eighteen! *Eight*. Not ten! Eight eighteen!"

Jason had calculated earlier—incorrectly—that 20:18 was 10:18 p.m., rather than 8:18 p.m. The last train of the night heading north just left the station. He put both hands against the wall. "Damn."

"You could always go back to the hostel. Just take a train tomorrow?"

"It's booked for the night. They told me before I left. Why do I keep doing this to my—?" Jason shook his head. "No.... Not again."

Jason flipped through his schedule. He was getting to Amsterdam. Tonight. One way or another. He thumbed through his maps and timetable, running his fingertip along the long, curvy lines, tracking his path city to city, country to country. It would work. He could make it work.

From Salzburg he would take the 21:27 train horseshoeing west underneath Switzerland, passing through Lyon, France, and then arching north, arriving in Paris at 9:31 the next morning. There he would switch trains, traveling northeast into Belgium, riding the 10:20 to Brussels, arriving at 13:17. He would transfer to the 13:29 train, into the Netherlands, through Maastricht, and then head north up to Rotterdam, and then finally a quick zigzag northeast to The Hague and Utrecht, before arriving in Amsterdam at 16:34, or 4:34 p.m.

Aware that he was adding seven hours and almost five hundred miles to the trip, it was nonetheless important to Jason that he find his own way to Amsterdam. He didn't care how long it took, just so long as he got there.

"Good luck, mate. You'll always have a bed in Dublin."

Jason smiled and slung the disfigured rucksack over his shoulder. That familiar tug of weight once again reminded him that he was carrying his own load. That it was *his* journey to make, his choices. That tomorrow, like every day, would be a new day.

He reached for his crotch. Money belt check. Because you never know.

So after making his way down the next corridor, Jason let out a little laugh. The train was waiting for him on the track. The doors were wide open.

9-15-05

Hey Hank,

Got stuck in Prague with some crazy flu, but I'm in the Salzburg train station now, off to Amsterdam. Ooooh. Crazy. And last night I met two Manchester girls who were pretty cool. If you get my meaning.

Had a blast in Budapest before that. Met a girl there, too. And no...there's been no love, so just chill on the lectures!

I was traveling with this guy from New Zealand, and he was a really cool guy—really cool—but we got split up, so I'm on my own again.

You were right about not getting attached. It's funny how you think you're going one place...then WHAM-O!...you don't know where the heck you are or how you even got there. I'll buy the first beer when I get home. Take it easy.

Jason

Chapter 60
Waiting for the Man

Auckland, New Zealand—Two miles from Bastian Point
Friday, September 16, 2005, 2:18 p.m.

Roger looked over his shoulder. But he knew better than to doubt her. Carla was right behind him, pedaling around the bay as it sparkled in the sunshine. Maybe she couldn't go stride for stride, but she wouldn't bail on him. She would never do that. Roger had been taken with Carla since the day they met.

"That's a sweet board," she had said that day at Piha Beach, forty-five minutes west of Auckland. The surf was pumping. "Nice long board. That's a nine-footer, yeh?"

Kneeling in the sand, Roger looked up to find Carla in her wet suit hugging her from hips to chest. She smiled. Roger found it easy to focus on her body. How her brown hair fell in front of one eye, covering a patch of freckles that spread across the ridge of her nose. How her blue eyes sang against her pale skin.

But it was her gentle way that ultimately disarmed him, as if the world she viewed rotated on a different axis.

Time, she once told him, is precious. She said every second past is a second gone forever. And while Roger couldn't argue with her logic, he felt just a little bit stupid, as she seemed to be telling him something he should already know. That he was missing some fundamental truth that hung all over him like ornaments on a Christmas tree.

Roger wasn't sure why she said the things she did. Maybe it was being an only child, maybe it was growing up with her grandfather living in the house. But whatever the reasons, Roger didn't know anyone like Carla. And while only seventeen, he was at least sharp enough to realize that girls like her were one in a million.

Roger and Carla navigated the bicycle path along the city outskirts, and then made their way up to Bastian Point. Downtown Auckland was in the distance. The sun shone warm on Roger's face, yet goose bumps rode up his arm. The wind came off the water. It sent a chill down his spine.

He decided. He had something to tell Carla, and like she said, he was running out of time. A blue whale, who visited him in a dream, told him to take that seriously.

Across the bay to the north was Rangitoto Island—a volcano six hundred years dormant and whose name essentially translates as *Bloody Sky*.

"Oi!" Roger felt a sudden, crushing slap on his shoulder. His bones ached upon impact. It could only be Davey. Short, tan and unusually hyper for a New Zealander, Davey was a ballsy sort, especially under the constant protection of his brother, Aputa.

Aputa was the leader of the Cougars, who had a small, but profitable marijuana trade on the North Island. Emblazoned on each of their backs was a cougar tattoo that stretched shoulder to shoulder, the head wrapping around their midsections.

Davey helped them out, running only minor errands, but was kept away from the dirtier Cougar business. Aputa didn't want his little brother getting roughed up. Davey just wasn't the type. But he was smart enough to know just how much of Aputa's legend to spread around. Davey would never say for sure that his brother had killed three men who insulted their mother, but he wouldn't deny it either. Maybe it happened, maybe not. You can ask Aputa…if you like. But I wouldn't.

For Aputa, business was business—you did what needed doing, and you did it efficiently and with little fanfare. Family was another matter.

"Oi! Ro-*ger*! My main man."

Roger and Davey slapped hands and gave a chest-bump hug. Davey, no Cougar himself, raised his eyebrows and grinned.

"Who's your little friend?"

Roger's heart thumped away. "This, uh, this is Carla, my uh...g—"

"Carla, yeh? You're a sweet one, aren't you?"

Carla offered a tight-lipped smile. She nodded.

Roger pulled his shoulders tight. He tried to keep himself from shaking. *Girlfriend.* He couldn't say the word. Not even to himself. But he wanted to. He really did.

"Got a special treat for you," Davey said. "Over there. By the car."

"Oh, yeh?" Roger looked toward the small parking area. "Who's that?"

"That?" Davey smiled and took a drag on his cigarette. He blew smoke out his nostrils. "That...is the maaaan. That's fuckin' Rasta Bond, mate. The legend. *That's* Rufus. He made a special trip to do some business, yeh? Wanna meet him?"

Roger looked over at Rufus, and then at Carla, who was leaning against the rail, staring at the Rangitoto volcano. He wondered if either, or both, were about to explode.

We shouldn't be here. I'm such a scrotum. And yet...

"Fuck, yeh," he said. "Let's go meet the man."

"So, mate." Davey inhaled the fat end of joint. Roger rolled down the passenger-side window to let the smoke funnel out. "You gonna be all right, like, with your girlie there? She seemed kinda pissed when she took off."

Roger wondered the very same thing. "Oh, I dunno. She's..."

The best girl I know. But I'm losing her. I blew it.

"She's just a little wound up. We were gonna have the whole day to ourselves, yeh? But it was only gonna take a few minutes here. What's the scruff about?"

"Mate, mate, mate." Davey slapped Roger's thigh. "You can't be thinking here," he said, tapping his forehead. "You gotta be thinking here." Davey poked Roger in the chest. "Your girl... she doesn't care you picked up some weed. She's fucked off you broke the deal."

"What deal?"

"You just said. It was supposed to be just you two, and you didn't tell her about this. You said something earlier, heh, maybe she's with you now. You ask me, no girl's worth the hassle. But you like this one. And sure as I'm fucked on this shit...she's fam-bam-damned at you!"

Roger stared through the windshield at the Rangitoto volcano.

Come on. Just explode. Torch me with hot lava. Just fucking explode.

"Yeh. Kinda."

"Oh, mate. You're more fucked with this girl than I thought."

Sober as his Aunt Carol, Roger's mouth grew clammy nonetheless. In his mind's eye he saw himself open the car and chase after Carla. He saw himself take off on his bike, peddling as fast as he could, riding and riding and riding with the *Rocky* theme music in the background until he wound up on her doorstep.

Roger saw himself standing there—saw himself pull Carla close—until finally their lips were pressed together. And he saw himself hold Carla, feeling that if he never let go, that would have been just fine with him.

Roger saw himself leave the car. Roger saw himself get on his bike. There was no reason to stay, every reason to go. He shouted in his mind.

What are you waiting for, dickhead? Go after her! Now, dickhead! NOW!

And yet something held him back. "So...what about Rufus?"

Yep. Definitely a scrotum.

"Yeh, yeh. I lost my head there. Quality shit, mate. Woo! Rufus. Right. So, your dad's still into all that World War Two shit? The guns and helmets and Nazi crap?"

"Yeh. He's got a whole collection. Wait....Why?"

"Me and Rufus got to talking...well, I did most of the talking. He's not a real chatty fucker, I'll give you that. But turns out he's got a German pistol, two Nazi fuck medals and a tobacco tin. He wants to sell or trade 'em, like anybody would want the crap anyway. Still, he says he's leaving New Zealand next week. Says this is his last trip here and wants to unload the stuff right and proper. I dunno, mate. He's a bit creepy, if you ask me."

Davey looked around. "But don't tell him I said that. He's like Aputa. Very touchy about his reputation."

"Don't worry. Your secret's safe."

"Sweet. So? Think your dad'd be interested?"

"No way, mate. I'm not bringing Rufus over. My mum would freak out, yeh? She just started this massive cleaning fit, like she'll die if she doesn't get every molecule of dust. I dunno. She goes for like a week straight. I just stay out of her way."

"No worries, mate. It'll be sweet all around. Your dad gets more of his stuff, I get in good with Rufus, and we all have you to thank for it."

"Oh, I dunno," Roger said. "I...dunno."

"Don't worry, mate. It'll be in and out, like a fly in a cow's ass. Real quick-like."

Roger shook his head, exhaled. He looked at the volcano again.

Just explode already.

And before he could change his mind, Roger agreed. "Fuck it, then. Tell him next week. But not until Friday. Seriously. My mum's getting her hair done that day. It's like a present to herself for all the cleaning. She'll be gone all day. We'll have the place to ourselves. But make sure it's *Friday*."

Davey smiled, gave Roger a playful elbow. "You're a real mate. Friday it is."

"Yeh," Roger said. "No problem."

Please explode. Right. Fucking. Now.

Chapter 61
Welcome to Amsterdam

Amsterdam, The Netherlands—The Band Wagon
Friday, September 16, 2005, 5:12 p.m.

Jason was soaked from the torrential storm battering Amsterdam. He threw his sopping clothes onto the floor next to his bed, the bottom of a pair of bunks, in a room full of bunks, on the second floor of *The Band Wagon*.

While feeling awkward and anxious upon arriving at each of his previous destinations, Jason felt oddly relaxed now, as if he had found a way to commune with the gods of ritual. Pack, unpack. Train stations, hostels. Indeed he was in a new city in new quarters with new people, but he found comfort in the consistency of it all, feeling that his surroundings were familiar somehow. And in a way, they were.

His immediate concerns were a hot shower, dry clothes and a hot meal—and extracting the soggy boxers wedged in his butt crack.

Jackie Pellington, or John Pellington III, sat on the next bed. He was the twenty-four-year-old son and only heir to John Pellington II, the owner and CEO of Pellington Airlifts Inc., the third-largest private helicopter service in the United States.

Sporting an odd, disaffected smirk, Jackie wore black jeans and a maroon jacket with white frilly ruffles extending past his wrists. His arms were draped across his chest in a quasi-hug. His fingernails were painted black. His long, bony fingers pet his sides.

"Sweetie, I don't mean to state the obvious, but a rain slicker is supposed to keep you dry." He peeked at Jason's exposed navel. "Not that I'm complaining."

"Thanks. I'll make a note of it." Jason's fingers were shriveled and pruned. "It's got a rip in the back."

While his level of map reading had improved, Jason's skill

was still hovering just a notch below sock puppet. He somehow managed to stretch a ten-minute walk from the train station into an hour-long scramble in a thunderstorm.

Jason had had an otherwise uneventful journey from Salzburg, with the exception that an old woman—for reasons he never ascertained—yelled at him incessantly in French on the leg between Paris and Brussels.

"Not to worry," said Jackie's top bunkmate, Omar. "This should warm you up." A short business student from Puerto Rico with a well-groomed goatee, Omar was huggable like a human Smurf. He handed Jason a fat, burning joint.

"Uh," Jason said. "I don't think you can smoke up here."

The dormitory-style room, filled with an international gathering of backpackers—and a lingering cloud of pot smoke—let out a collective roar.

"You're so *cute*." Jackie crinkled his button nose. "You'll be okay."

Jason nodded, and then laughed at himself. He mimed putting on a dunce cap, the lit joint between his fingers. "Uh, der-der. I'm in Am-stuh-damn. I wunduh if dey got duh weed heeya."

His fellow bunkmates laughed, which got Jason laughing so hard until he finally clapped his hands once, dipping his head. He looked up, and saw a collection of smiles. He took a long, deep drag, and with the joint between his fingers, held it up, toasting his hosts.

Kaff! Kaff! Kaff!

"What the fuck is this?" Jason felt a giant rush to his head. He leaned forward, his face beet red. He unholstered his finger guns. "Watch out boys and girls. Big J is on the scene." He cocked his thumb triggers and made the *chk chk* sound.

His bunkmates roared with laughter once again.

"I wonduh if they got duh weed here," one of them said, laughing.

"Uh-yuh," another said. "I sure dink dey do. Uh-yuh, uh-yuh, uh-yuh."

Omar took the joint from Jason, who leaned back on his bed, pounding the bottom of the top bunk, helping to shake out his cough.

"Welcome to Amsterdam," Omar said. "Nice to have you aboard."

The rain since past, Jason followed Jackie and Omar along the slick cobblestone roads. Smaller canals appeared black beneath the night sky. They crossed a stone bridge arching over one tree-lined canal, and then ambled down two short alleyways compressed between a Japanese fusion restaurant and a bicycle repair shop.

Jackie's long flowing stride made it appear as if he were ice skating. "So…you seem to be feeling better. It doesn't take a lot to get your mood on around here."

With a plate of falafel, three pints of Heineken and a hit off a red bong having sufficiently warmed him, Jason stumbled along. "Mmm, yeah. You could say that."

"Well, good. Omar and I found this wonderful little place last night. Actually…no. That's where we *met*. I think you'll get a *bang* out of it."

Jason raised his eyebrows. He sighed. "What's it called?"

"The *Ball and Tickle*." Omar let out a sheepish giggle. "*Tee-hee-hee*."

As they wandered the medieval city, Jason was suspicious of the silhouettes that seemed to emerge from the darkness and into the street light, and then disappear. But it wasn't until they crossed another stone bridge that Jason got his first glimmer of the Red Light District—like a glowing beacon calling all heathens into the heart of Sin.

Short buildings were lined side-by-side as far as he could see, which, in almost any other neighborhood of almost any other city, would have been pastry shops and jewelers, hair salons and shoe stores, cafés and booksellers.

But not in the Red Light District. Not in Amsterdam.

They came to a window. Behind it, a busty blonde in high heels and fake eye lashes was standing on a platform, lined with red cushions. She wore a black, see-through teddy and a black garter. She rubbed her hands over her body. She licked her lips

in a most unsubtle fashion. At the base of the window was a
neon light. It was red.

Window after window, the women varied in shapes and
sizes. Tall, leggy blondes. Short, stocky brunettes. Redheads.
Chunky women, skinny women. Curvy women, flat women.
White women, black women. Asian women. Women with bad
gums and crooked teeth. Women with no teeth. Teenagers.
Grandmothers. Midgets. Amputees.

Until Jason finally saw those women—living, breathing human beings—displayed behind glass, for rent, he
hadn't formed a picture in his mind of what he might find in
Amsterdam. He just assumed that it would be more...fun, like
seeing the neon lights of Las Vegas. Only these weren't the kind
of slots that interested him.

"You see anything you like," Jackie said, "just holler."

"No, thanks. I'll pass."

"Suit yourself, sweetie. Maybe this is your thing."

Jackie pointed to a row of clubs. Bouncers stood outside,
handing out flyers. Above them, on the marquis, were signs
advertising the club's specialty: *Live fucking. Girls on girls.* The
next several clubs offered multiple variations. *Guys on girls. Guys
and girls on girls. Guys on guys. Gang bang. All-male gang bang. All-
girl gang bang. Dogs on girls. Guys and dogs on girls.*

Jason wanted to take a live-and-let-live attitude about it. To
each his own, and all that jazz. But rather than just a passing
interest in the river of naughty, Jason felt sick and ashamed, as
if a cold, creepy aura draped over the Red Light District. As if it
draped over *him*. It felt like more than Sin. It felt *evil*.

Jason didn't consider himself a goody-goody by any means,
but it didn't take long to figure out that the Red Light District
definitely was not for him. For as much as he had wanted to
walk on the wild side, he now very much wanted to be safe at
home watching *Seinfeld* reruns.

After rounding the corner, they came to a brightly lit shop
that sold XXX DVDs, leather masks and various sex toys, including chains, whips and edible panties, as well as lubricants, butt
plugs and a wide variety of other penetrating objects.

"We'll swing by on our way back," Jackie said. "I know just

the thing for you."

"Look," Jason said. "Are we almost—"

Slumped against the wall, a ghost of a dude in a black leather jacket rocked in place. His bloodshot eyes sank into their dark sockets. "Heee drips oh wee...heee drips oh wee..."

"What? I don't..."

"Es, trips, blow, weed. Es, trips, blow, weed..."

Jackie looped his hand through the crook of Jason's arm, and led them around the corner. "Sweetie. *That* is a drug dealer. You mustn't converse with them. They're icky."

Jason looked over his shoulder as Jackie took them deeper into the darkened heart of Amsterdam. The cobblestone roads bustled with activity and yet seemed perversely quiet. The cold, mossy canals shimmered in the darkness. "Icky," he said. "Right."

The bright neon sign of the *Ball and Tickle* glowed above the road. Jason could hear a chorus shouting from inside. Something about a girl named Alice. "Oh, good God." He dipped his head, and then reached for the door. "I need to get drunk."

Jackie stopped before entering. He straightened the collar on Jason's shirt. "Now *that's* a good idea. I think you'll do just fine."

Chapter 62
Picture Perfect

The Eastern Sphere of Eternity—Horizon Terrace
Milky Way's Public Unveiling: T-Minus 11 Days (Eternity
Standard Time)

There was a picture in Donald's mind. And it was perfect. Sure, the picture changed as he and Danielle grew closer, but the picture was always beautiful. Most things can be given or taken away, Donald figured, but some things you get to keep forever. They're yours.

For as long as he would be in this life, Donald knew that in the quiet calm of that place deep inside, he could always close his eyes and see Danielle. Just being. His love.

"You still with me?" Brigsby waved a hand in front of Donald's face. "You know...your life, your existence. Nothing important."

"What? Huh? Oh. Yeah. I'm here."

"You sure you won't change your mind? You know I support you, Donnie. But this is a bit bold. For anybody. Smashing those jars to hide your mistake? Have you considered just, you know...*confessing*? Honesty is quite disarming. It catches people off guard. It's a real hoot."

"You don't understand." Donald stood up, still staring at that perfect picture in his mind. "It's my fault. We had strict orders to keep Earth in prime condition. But Danny and I, well, you know, when...we were together, I..."

He went to the window and stared at the Andromeda galaxy. It swirled. Brigsby reflected in the glass. Milo's Smear—that permanent nothing—was in the distance.

"I swung my arm around and felt a thud. I just figured I bumped into Danny's knee, but I sent the jar off the ledge. At first I denied it, because I was embarrassed. But now, when I blame myself...Danny thinks I'm covering for *her*. I'm not."

Donald shook his head, his own image reflected back at Brigsby. "I tell her not to worry, that everything will work out. But when she sees me smile...it's only so she doesn't see my shame. I did this to her. To us."

Donald turned to face Brigsby, who, for the first time in all their years together, offered no response. "Don't just stand there. Say something. You're making me nervous."

Brigsby looked into his glass. "You love her that much?"

Donald nodded.

"Then tell her what you told me. She's your wife. She'll understand."

"I can't. She's more than my wife, Brigs...she's my girl."

There was a silence between them, but not emptiness.

"So why tell *me*? If you came to me right away...*maybe* I could've helped out. But now...this is way beyond me."

"I know that. But I owed you an apology. Face to face. I put you in a bad spot. Lawrence is *my* boss...but he's *your* friend. He wasn't too thrilled to take us on in the first place. You should have seen him that first day. He was pretty nasty toward me."

Brigsby put his hand up. "Oh, don't worry about little ole m—"

"Plus," Donald continued, feeling sorry for screwing up with Brigsby, but not *that* sorry, "when I get redistributed, or whatever else The Big MOU does to me when this blows up in my face...I want you to take care of her for me. I'm going to take full responsibility. I want you to make sure Danny gets a fresh start. It's the last thing I can give her."

"You've got a lot more to give than y—"

"Just promise you'll look out for her when I'm, well...wherever I end up. Just promise."

"Of course," Brigsby said. "I promise."

Donald nodded, hugged his friend. His final goodbye. "So, any advice before I go?"

Brigsby gulped down the last of his martini. "Yes," he said. "Indeedy I do. And I can't believe I'm saying this, but, please, whatever you do...don't watch my show...ever...again."

Chapter 63
The Wrolen Library of Organic Beauty

The Southern Sphere of Eternity—Lambert Falls City
Milky Way's Public Unveiling: T-Minus 11 Days (Eternity
Standard Time)

Emma was engulfed by magnificence.

The buzz surrounding the Milky Way galaxy—its unveiling less than two weeks away—was far greater than Emma anticipated. She was getting the very real sense that the stakes would be on a scale few in her position had ever experienced, and that once the public got a taste of what was possible, the frenzy would be far beyond her capacity to control it. And yet she never expected *this*.

The Wrolen Library of Organic Beauty was not just a structure dedicated to the keeping of written works, but was considered the very epicenter for divine inspiration.

Sitting across from Emma in the crisp night air, high up into Lambert Falls City, Jacques Abladeujé was dressed in a tan suit, white collared shirt and no tie. The sides of his wavy brown hair were gray. He would need to shave again soon. Emma liked that.

Jacques was the senior vice president of Renolo Enterprises, a subsidiary of the Galactic Particle Plant, owned by Marcus Dünhauser, Sr.

Emma's problem with Jacques was the one problem she had been avoiding all along. That he was only there about business. To use *her* to make *himself* money. A smile stretched across his face. His blue eyes twinkled.

On the table between them, a candle flickered. Its flame would never extinguish.

Surrounded by the downtown banking district, the library was a narrow stone building more than two hundred stories high. It housed every published work in Eternity.

Yet the utmost beauty resided on the penthouse floor, the highest point in Lambert Falls City. The penthouse elevator opened into the Reading Room, a glass-encased den with a pointed ceiling. It housed only the rarest editions in Existence.

Outside was an L-shaped terrace. Three small tables were well spaced for privacy. Drinks only. Reservations extremely limited. Emma and Jacques shared a bottle of wine.

In a red skirt and tight, black blouse, Emma walked to the balcony. She looked over the ledge, staring at the long row of traffic as it scurried below in turns and loops, like little red and white comets she had designed for the heavens time and again. Emma smiled, wondering if Jacques thought she was just a poseur, or if she actually belonged.

The stone edge was smooth against her fingers. The wind blew through her hair. She crossed her arms, to hide a shiver. She didn't want to appear weak. The city lights sparkled in the darkness. Emma could hear Lambert Falls churning in the distance.

Beyond the city limits, Emma could barely make out the snow-capped Baldamere Mountains, the most fantastic formations in the Southern Sphere. They hovered along the city outskirts like bulldogs protecting its master. Emma found them especially imposing, their true girth cloaked in the cover of night. Loyal beasts hiding in the darkness. Emma could almost feel them breathing, hear them growling.

What else don't I see? What else is waiting for me?

And yet above them all, in its fantastic glory, was the Andromeda galaxy. Purple around the outer edges, the inner swirls faded into magenta, finally spiraling into its black center—a funnel into the Universe.

There was the distant flow again, that low rumble, like two stone gears in constant motion. She squinted, reaching up, as if she could touch the galaxy—like swooshing her hand in a bath as it filled with water. Even Emma had never considered such beauty.

Two copies of the contract were flat on the table. Jacques signed both copies. A gold pen was on top, brimming in the wake of the flickering candle. "This contract will open doors." He swirled his drink. "This will, how do they say...put you on the map?"

Emma nodded to her cleavage. "I'm already on the map. Just read the signs."

The brisk mountain air breezed beneath the table, rolled against her legs and up her skirt. Her black silk panties were snug around her waist. She squeezed her pelvis.

Beginning at the gold pen glowing in the candlelight, her gaze made an elongated swoop. Up toward Jacques and then over his shoulder to the planter filled with red roses, to the white-peaked mountaintops. And above them still was the Andromeda galaxy. It swirled against the black canvas, the underside of the Universe. Swirling. Milo's Smear—that permanent nothing—was in the distance.

Emma held the pen. The weight of it felt significant. Important.

Jacques raised his glass. "The price is fair, no?"

Emma looked around, considered it all. "Yes," she said. "Quite fair."

And yet still she hesitated. Signing the contract would mean agreeing to design three more galaxies, including a star system to support new life, for which only a select few were commissioned. Emma would be denied few opportunities. But with such standing would come few moments for privacy. To be anonymous.

Her life, while hers, would never entirely be her own.

Emma signed her name. The ink flowed easily as the pen

rolled across the page. A final *scritch*—the last "e" in Emmaline looped back—finalizing the deal.

"Oh, yes, my Emmaline." Jacques massaged his glass. "You have made us happy. The twin moons of Dimitri Minor—and the nebula, especially—was most elegant. And now, with this Milky Way you have given us...you have outdone yourself. It will be received with the glory of open arms. We are all most impressed."

Emma raised her eyebrows. "We?"

Jacques nodded. "Yes. Me. *I* am impressed. But then, you are most impressive." He folded his copy of the contract in half and then again, fitting the enveloped paper into his inside jacket pocket. He slid Emma's copy across the table. She stuffed it in her purse.

The overhead lights reflected off the glass panes of the Reading Room. Two red roses behind Jacques swayed in the cool breeze.

Emma stared up at the bounty of stars, as if salt had been sprinkled on a black cloth. She could feel the pulse of the white-peaked mountains, the whooshing of the falls and the low rumble of that hypnotic swirl, as if she were about to be swallowed up into the mouth of purity itself. She leaned back in her chair.

"Does this inspire you?" Jacques said. "They remind us just how small we are, but also that to dream of greatness brings us closer to it. If you don't believe in something greater than yourself, how do you become greater than you are?"

"What if you're just holding on?" Emma suddenly became ill with vulnerability. It wasn't like her to speak this way.

"Ah, yes. You do not believe in the greater being...that we simply are." Jacques smiled, and then gestured at the surrounding beauty. "For to become *who* you are, is to become greater than you believe yourself to be. Despite what you would like others to think, my Emmaline, you are far too worried about how history will see you. You would be best served to focus on how you see yourself."

Emma's gut seized. Nausea shot to her head. And while she couldn't see the mountains, camouflaged in the darkness, she knew they were out there. She trembled inside, despite her attempts at defiance. She forced a smirk. "And how's that?"

"First...as a designer of galaxies. The most talented to grace us in the longest while." Jacques tipped his glass. "Second...as a very beautiful woman."

Emma ran her tongue along her bicuspids. "And third?" She became dizzy, as if the Andromeda galaxy was not swirling above her, but within. She could hardly breathe.

Jacques emptied his glass. He set it on the table. "As a woman who must seduce every man she meets, lest she fall and realize that all along...she has been trying to seduce herself."

Across the flickering candle, Emma stared at his breast pocket. The contract had been signed. Her life, while hers, would never entirely be her own.

Chapter 64
Private Tour

Auckland, New Zealand—Auckland Museum
Saturday, September 17, 2005, 11:09 a.m.

The Lydia situation was extremely delicate. George needed her to feel a mixture of desire and safety, so he suggested at the end of their last talk that they meet again, at this very spot, knowing that he would have to move quickly after that, as Emma was undoubtedly deep into her own efforts.

One more meeting to cement Lydia's trust. Then the jar.

The spectacular New Zealand oceans were a far cry from the stagnant, mossy canals of Amsterdam. But jealousy had been George's undoing in the first place. When he lost sight of his limitations. When he let temptation distort his priorities. When he fell victim to his own vanity.

"This is a lovely country," he said while admiring another red-crowned parakeet. George and Lydia had bonded over one last time. To his good fortune, he found another. "I'm really taken with its beauty."

"Yeh, it's all right. I could use a change, though."

"I think we all feel that way from time to time. That's why I'm here."

Lydia raised her eyes to meet his. "How's that?"

"The museum." George pointed through the slight forest, all but obstructing their view of the marble building with four pillars in front. "I own an art gallery in Amsterdam, but city life...it has worn me down. New Zealand quite appeals to me. I'm speaking with the curator about presenting some pieces I own. I could arrange a private tour."

Lydia clutched the front of her blouse, bit her lower lip. She tried to hide a smile. It didn't work. "Oh, no. I couldn't. I—"

"Don't be silly. Invite your family, of course."

"I don't think they'd be interested. Besides...Theo's away

again."

"Oh? Where's the young man off to? If you don't mind my asking."

Lydia sighed. "We just got a postcard from Venice. He said he'll be gone at least another month. But with Theo...I never know what he's up to. Even when he's here."

George took no pleasure in deceiving her. But there was little time to waste. There would be others. "Come to the museum... if you like." Only to his surprise, George truly longed for her company, worried she might decline his invitation. Like Lydia, he was lonely. "Two o'clock. I think you would enjoy it."

Looking at the parakeet, the George part of him thought the bird was much like himself, admiring its natural cloak—allowing it to remain out in the open, yet still invisible. "He's very sophisticated, our little friend. He possesses such grace and ability. We shouldn't be fooled by his size. He's quite a survivor."

Looking at the parakeet, the Angelique part of her thought the bird was much like herself, a fabulous, multi-colored tease—making a statement without uttering a sound.

"And what's fascinating about him," George continued, "is that while his green body camouflages him, he's an exquisite fellow." He pointed out the yellow streak on the bird's head and the small red dots on the side of each eye. George also noted its beak, whitish blue with a sharp black tip. "It's like a fake fingernail. Only you never see that kind of detail on a falsie—"

Too much, too much.

"Well...I mean...my point...is that he's tremendously well ornamented...for someone trying to stay hidden."

But I've got to get in there before Emma. I can't take that chance.

Lydia nodded. "There's so much in front of me. I never really notice."

George squinted as sunshine caught his face. "We often don't," he said, breathing slowly. Slowly. "But that's what the little fellow's counting on."

Chapter 65
To Catch a Thief

Amsterdam, The Netherlands—The Band Wagon
Saturday, September 17, 2005, 11:45 a.m.

Jason awoke feeling depressed, murky and hollow, his energy replaced with spiritual backwash. He wiped the drool from his mouth. His hair was mussed into a fishtail. The room was spinning. From another bunk came a quiver of sadness.

Shin was a twenty-three-year-old marine biology major from Shimonoseki, Japan. He had been traveling alone, and after five weeks in Europe, was excited to see his girlfriend again. "My passport," he said. "It is gone. And my money. I have only ten Euros left."

Not long after Jason arrived in Amsterdam, Shin had told everyone about Tomiko. How he was planning to buy her a ring. How his hands shook in a good way when he thought about it. How his girlfriend was like a perfect flower for his heart.

Jason held onto the look on Shin's face when he spoke about Tomiko, and wondered if somebody would ever admire the look on his face, gushing about the love of *his* life. But none of that seemed to matter now. During the night, six lockers had been robbed. Shin was supposed to leave for Japan later that day. Outside, the sky was one dark cloud.

"I got robbed, too," Omar said. "But nothing major. Just my knapsack."

Shin held his money belt open. It was empty. "What is it I do? Now I cannot go home to my country. I am all alone."

"We'll help you," Jackie said. "I'm sure we can—"

"No. I go to embassy now. It take three week to get new passport. I don't know where I will stay. I go alone. Goodbye."

The bunkmates, some leaning against their beds, some beneath their blankets, remained quiet as Shin collected his bag.

Jason wanted to reach out to him, to do…something, but all he could offer was his quiet remorse. His heart was as heavy as the sound of Shin's footsteps as he walked down the stairs and out of their lives forever. Jason wanted to pull the covers over his face.

There was a collective hush, a helplessness. With so many people coming and going, they would never find out who stole, who violated them. And it wasn't lost on Jason that maybe the thief was still among them. What better way to stay hidden than to be out in the open?

Was it Jackie? Nah…that doesn't make sense. He's loaded. Or Omar? He doesn't seem the type. But maybe…yeah…maybe it was the drummer guy from Antwerp. Or the tattoo guy from Frankfurt. Or the art student from Colorado. Or maybe the thief is long gone. Or maybe it was someone who works at the front desk or mops the floors or…

He reached for his crotch. Money belt check. Because you never know.

Finally, Jackie broke the silence. "I know. Let's go to the Anne Frank House."

"Oooh," Omar said. "That sounds like fun."

Jason and Jackie looked at him.

"Oh…well," Omar said. "Maybe not fun, but…you know."

Jason climbed the stairs of the Anne Frank House, where the young girl and her family hid from the Nazis, before being betrayed and shipped off to the concentration camps—where she was exterminated. The house had undergone some repairs, but was almost entirely unchanged since the Nazi occupation, except that it had also been turned into a museum.

A black-and-white photograph hung on the wall leading to the second floor. Nazi soldiers led a mother and her small children through a back alley. Rubble was scattered in the street. The corner building was demolished. A black cloud billowed from the engine of a burning car.

"That's awful," Jackie said. "It's just hard to imagine."

Jason felt queasy as he stared at the slats in the floor, and then at the very wooden wall panels Anne Frank must have leaned against all those years before, hiding from absolute evil. *"I saw two Jews through the curtains yesterday,"* she wrote in her diary, December 12, 1942. *"It was a horrible feeling, just as if I had betrayed them and was now watching their misery."*

When they ascended to the second floor, Jason stopped by a window, letting Jackie and Omar walk by. From there, he could see into the courtyard, the one he had read about in *The Diary of Anne Frank.* Where she would look out and imagine a world beyond those walls, where one day she could be a whole person again, and not just a Jew in hiding.

There was a tall gray tree in the courtyard. Its branches stretched far into the sky. It was just as Jason envisioned back in the eighth grade, when he read about Anne. It was as if she was still in that house, as if she had never left.

"I just...," Jason said. "I can't..." He pushed his way back out of the museum. When the cool air hit him, he almost toppled over. He leaned forward against a lamppost. He gagged. He breathed in, then out. In, then out. A slight mist fell.

Jason walked back toward *The Band Wagon,* sickened by that unfathomable reign of horror. The enthusiasm he had mustered since Salzburg was gone. He wanted to go home. Where the Nazi ghosts did not linger. Where he could be safe among the familiar. Where he could close his eyes and make those monsters go away.

So that when he looked ahead through the mist, as the cars drove by, Jason saw, standing on the corner, there, in Amsterdam, someone he feared would never be a part of his life again. Someone whose own ghost never left him, as much as he tried to forget.

But more than anything else, Jason was overwhelmed by the remarkable gesture, one that both baffled and dazzled him. He threw his arms open. Smiling and with eyes clenched, Jason was reunited with someone who, deep down, he had felt destined to find again. Somewhere, some way. He just absolutely knew it.

PART III

I GOT YOUR MUFFIN RIGHT HERE

Chapter 66
The Great Ohhhmmmmmmmm

Amsterdam, The Netherlands—Outside the Anne Frank House
Saturday, September 17, 2005, 2:03 p.m.

There was a blast of white light. There were streaks of scream-ing fluorescent color. There was the sensation of being swal-lowed by a tornado. And then there was friendship. Lots and lots of friendship.

They both felt the flash that time. Hell yeah, they did.

Jason could barely speak. "What are you doing here? I'm just...this is...I mean, wow. Just...wow. How'd you even find me?"

Theo was wearing those same beat-up moccasins and blue-and-green pullover. "I dunno. You wanted to see Amsterdam, so I took a chance. We saw *The Band Wagon* in your guidebook, yeh? I just had a feeling you'd be here. I can't explain it."

Jason looked at Theo, and blinked, and while it may have taken his eyelids only a second to close and then open again, it was like wiping a squeegee on a windshield, sponging away a translucent layer of grime. The result was that he was now able to perceive a world more textured and nuanced than he ever noticed before, but one that had actually been there all along.

Jason was stunned by the notion that Theo had trekked thousands of miles—on a whim—just on the chance he *might* be here. So Jason looked at Theo, his friend...really looked at him...in one way bewildered and honored and overwhelmed with gratitude, and in another way not at all surprised, because that was Theo.

Would I have done the same? Would I have taken that chance?

"What?" Theo laughed at Jason's laughter. "What?"

And Jason kept right on smiling. *I would. I really would.*

They came in from the rain, checked Theo into *The Band Wagon,* and then caught up with Jackie and Omar, who stayed an extra hour at the Anne Frank House, and looked every minute of it. The four bunkmates agreed to find a quiet diversion, to unwind, and as came as no surprise to anyone, Jackie knew just the place.

Jason had never been to a hash bar. And given that Hell would have to freeze at least ten times over before he would bungee jump, skydive or vote Republican, for him, this was extreme living. He stood at the bar while Jackie and Omar took seats at a table near the open café windows, each drinking a pint. Theo ordered a hefeweizen.

Jason examined his ganjanic options displayed beneath the glass countertop, deciding between Nederhash (hash made from Dutch weed), Hydro (weed grown using hydroponics), and Hashish (imported from places unknown). This was to be the first joint he ever bought, so he wanted to pick just right. "Third from the left," he finally said.

Two beers down, the foursome passed the joint, and after just a few minutes, there wasn't a wide eye among them.

"So, dude," Jason began. Warm, elongated waves rolled over him.

Ohhhmmmmmmmm...ohhhmmmmmmmm...ohhhmmmmmmmm...

"Theo," he finally said. "What the hell happened to you in Budapest?"

Ohhhmmmmmmmm...ohhhmmmmmmmm...ohhhmmmmmmmm...

"Dude, I mean..."

Ohhhmmmmmmmm...ohhhmmmmmmmm...ohhhmmmmmmmm...

"...how did you miss that train?"

Chapter 67
Circular Logic of the Puzzle
Book Maze

Budapest, Hungary—Keleti Pu Train Station
Sunday, September 11, 2005, 10:33 a.m.

A week before finding Jason in Amsterdam—and just hours after losing him in the first place—Theo sat on a wobbly metal chair at the *Keleti Pu* train station café in Budapest. He ate a cheese sandwich Lilly bought him.

It was the least she could do, she said. Only Lilly had introduced herself as Liz. Elizabeth was her full name, explaining that it even said so on her passport. Theo wasn't sure why she needed to clarify her documentation, but he was too annoyed to care.

Lilly—calling herself Liz—was painting again. Sports themes. Tennis. But she wanted to incorporate the athleticism of competition with the nuance and scope of the European cultures. Liz did a sketch for him. In it, Theo was eating his sandwich at the very table he was leaning on, except the tabletop was like the head of a tennis racket, and instead of cheese, a long piece of netting dangled from the roll.

"That's good." Theo smiled despite himself, feeling a sudden flash of color in his mind, and though they were becoming less intense, more subtle, he had a sense they weren't warnings so much as signs. "Yeh, really good."

"Thanks. I just got back into it. I had some...trouble...you know. Life got kinda complicated, but I'm getting it together."

Theo nodded politely, but behind those steady eyes he was blood-boiling furious. Yet rather than vent that rage at Liz—whom he did not know was Lilly, Jason's Lilly—he just sat there quietly picking at his food. He nodded.

"I got a little distracted for awhile," she said, "but I met this woman in Arizona...this like...totally *amazing* woman, and she's sponsoring me here. She said 'Lil-Liz.' She said 'Liz...Liz, go to Europe. And when you come back, you'll paint a masterpiece.'"

Inexplicably, Theo saw Lea just then, as if she was right there with him, wearing her safety helmet with the miner's light in front. Her face was vivid for just a moment, so close and real he could almost smell the beetroot on her breath. "Oh, yeh?"

"I couldn't believe it. But when I found out who she was... it made total sense."

Theo put his sandwich down. "What do you mean? Who—?"

"So who was your friend? Again, I'm *totally* sorry. Seriously. I'm just..." Liz rolled her eyes at herself. "I'm such a total spaz like that." She forced out a laugh, craning her neck so that her breasts jiggled. "My brains and my body are hardly ever in the same place. It's like they start at opposite ends of those puzzle book mazes..."

Theo nodded, trying not to stare at her breasts—they were right there, after all—round, ripe and freckled, hoisted out.

"...figuring they'll meet in the middle, but at least one of them always seems to take a wrong turn and get stuck some- where. By the time they find each other, the maze is wrecked and I have to start over."

As Theo sat there staring blankly, nibbling on tiny pieces of his roll, he knew he *should* be tempted to jam his face in between her melons. But there was something about Liz that made him shake it off, like he was staring at a mirage. Except Theo knew the illusion wasn't with her.

Theo had been anxious and deflated ever since he watched Jason pull out of the station. Only Theo wasn't supposed to get worked up over things like this. He was a private guy with private thoughts and couldn't talk to other people about them because he hardly made sense, even to himself. But he could talk to Jason. Theo didn't know why, but he could. And it wasn't just that they had been separated. It was why.

Did I really need to whiz in the station bathroom? Not the train? Really? I couldn't have waited just five more minutes?

Indeed, the station facilities were more spacious. And when you spend so much time in cramped quarters, you crave mobil- ity whenever possible.

But as much as Theo wanted to blame Liz for knocking him flat on his back, he knew that getting split up had been a possibility, and exactly what happened. Deep down he wanted that challenge. That thrill. Was he resourceful enough to actually track Jason down across the continent? A part of Theo was trying to explore the Waitomo Caves all over again, not so much to *hang out* with Jason, but to *find* him.

While Theo sat there, in his mind's eye seeing himself run from train to train, city to city, country to country, reality set in. *What if I can't find him?* Theo could always look up Jason in New York, or e-mail him someplace now and hope to get a response. *But what if things aren't the same? What if I split us up for good?* He knew he was making a terrible mistake. He stood up from the table. "I have to go. I'm going to find Jason."

Liz stumbled, cleared her throat. "I'll, uh...I'll come with you."

11-09-05

G'day Mum,

Sorry I missed your birthday, but I got you a nice present in Berlin.

My money's been holding out, and I still haven't made it to Portugal. Tell Dad I want to see that whirlybird ready for flight by the time I get back. It's about time that thing got off the ground.

And let Roger know I'm having a whale of a good time. He'll know what it means.

Theo

Chapter 68
The Faith in Faith

*The Southern Sphere of Eternity—Starlight Designs
Milky Way's Public Unveiling: T-Minus 4 Days (Eternity
Standard Time)*

Lex was on a mission. Indeed, with another three galaxies now officially under contract and the Milky Way unveiling only four days away, his already considerable salary was about to double, if not triple. Indeed, he had moved into a balcony apartment with a view of the Grand Lion River, upgraded his wardrobe, bought a black convertible, and as a result of Emma's—and by extension, his own—rising status, he could land a quality table at almost any chi-chi restaurant.

And indeed, he clearly established himself as the No. 2 executive at *Starlight Designs*, having quietly encouraged Tyler to make a design suggestion to Emma, who fired him before he could finish speaking.

But Rufus. Motherfucking Rufus.

Lex didn't know who the bastard was, or why Emma brought him into their lives, but he wasn't going to watch Rufus stroll into her inner sanctum while he sat around like her lapdog begging for attention.

Six pints of beer, three shots of something related to pineapple and a small square tab of chemical fun were all coursing through him. Lex fumbled for the keys to the office, which he dropped on the sidewalk—twice—before making his way inside. A half moon hung from the night sky.

Lex stumbled into his office and closed the clear glass door. He leaned back in his chair. From his trousers pocket, he removed a red tin, and from it pinched a tiny white pill, which he swallowed. Lex then laughed his drunken, hallucinated laugh, a laugh quite similar to the laugh he laughed the night he was fired from *Quality Galaxy Fabrics*, right before Emma found him facedown in a pile of discarded peanut shells. The night before she saved him.

"Oh oh oh oh uh-oh. Another bad night for *Lexie*-pooh. Lexie-pooh is getting all bad-bad again. Uh-oh, uh-oh."

He powered on his computer. The flat screen's glow cast shadows on the wall. He began typing, such as he could, barely able to make out the letters on the screen.

Deeer Emmer,
Yooouuu, do yu evn know me Emmer?? Becaiuse Iknoww youuuu and yu know what I see? I sse yyou andI see mee and I seee him!!!!!!!!!!!!!!!!!!!

Lex swiped at his computer, but missed, falling sideways.

"Ohh. *Tsch.* See? Lexi-pooh on the floor again." He sighed, tugging his tie. "Now I gotta pee." With that, Lex pulled himself up, unzipped his fly. And while staring at the moonlight as it rolled in through the half moon window, he urinated into his wastebasket, which, he would remember in the morning, was cross-hatched, and not solid. "Ohhh...no." He laughed. "Got pee-pee on my hands."

Lex staggered to the kitchen. With the warm water cascading off his fingers and onto his leg, he turned toward Emma's office. He could see a dim light come from behind the frosted glass door.

Tiptoeing with intoxicated grace, Lex stood beside the door, open just enough to peer inside. A thin beam of light streaked across the otherwise dark hallway. Lex put a finger to his lips. "Shhhh." He almost choked holding in his giggle.

Lex leaned into the outer door frame. He could see Emma sitting on the floor, her back against the desk. Rufus sat adjacent to her, against the wall. A full-color rendering of the Milky Way hung above him. The only light came from a lamp on Emma's desk.

"I don't think he likes me," Rufus said. "I think he's jealous."

Emma dropped her hands. "Don't worry about Lex. He's not wired to be top dog, but when it comes to managing the daily grind...he's got that nailed. I just gave him a push. And if not me it would have been someone else. He just needs to trust himself a little more. He's afraid to be his own rock."

Lex then heard something else surprising, from someone who surprised him.

"Do you tell him?" Rufus said. "Does he know you think that way?"

Emma shook her head. "No. I don't tell him."

"Can I ask you—?"

"You're my only real friend. You can ask me anything."

"Why don't you tell him that you are lonely? That a woman with dreams and ambition is something most people do not like to see, and whether they admit it or not, would relish in seeing you fail?"

"You've been talking." Emma unfolded a paper clip. "I've been hearing this a lot lately."

Rufus chuckled. "Always so afraid to need someone, to have faith."

Emma snapped the paper clip, tossed it in the bin. "Faith in what?"

"In faith," Rufus said. "As you told me once when I most needed to hear it, you have to trust that believing in other people is better than only believing in yourself."

"I believe in *you*," Emma said. "I always believe in you."

"Just as I believe in you. But we cannot be everything to each other. We tried. We just do not fit that way. No two people can."

Lex heard nothing now except for the sad, steady beats of his own heart.

Boom-buhm, boom-buhm, boom-buhm.

"I know," Emma said. "But I'm not ready to have faith in anyone else. Do you...you know...?" She looked away. "...have faith in anyone?"

There was silence. Lex licked his lips. He waited.

"No. It has not worked out so far, but I am trying."

"Oh, yeah? So who's this mystery woman?"

Lex felt his heart speed up again. His hands were sweaty.

"Her name is Angelique. She has a nightclub act. We just met."

Lex pumped his fist in victory.

Emma got up, straightened her skirt and then took her place behind the desk. The wheels on her chair rolled against the hardwood floor. She fumbled with some papers. "I have a lot to do for the unveiling." She looked up, but only at the rendering of the Milky Way, the image she would be most associated with for the rest of her days. "I think you should go."

Rufus stood before her now, separated by more than just the desk. "Don't be mad, Emma. My heart is still with you. But I have to let someone else in. I have to try. What if today were to be my last? Who would comfort me but you?"

"I really have this work," she said.

Rufus nodded. "Your day has come. I will be there to smile on you, as always."

Before Lex snuck away, he saw what he otherwise thought impossible: a stream of tears rolling down Emma's face. And for a moment, Lex felt compassion for her. And as much as he hated to admit it, for Rufus.

"I know you will." Emma wiped her eyes. "But you still need to go."

Chapter 69
Training Day

It was her first time back since the Milo warning. With the auditorium sloped upward like a giant shoehorn, Danielle sat in the 349th seat of the 2,013th row, just off center, approximately two-thirds to the left and slightly below the middle. Present, but nearly invisible.

Illuminated with fluorescent lime bulbs underneath, a curved, white countertop stretched from end to end of each row. Gray carpeted stairs on both sides extended from the platform level all the way to the top of the auditorium. There were no windows. The overhead lighting was dim.

Bound manuals were set on the countertops, one in front of each employee. The covers read: *Safety and Protocol: CBM Operations, Management and Procedures*. The bottom right corner was marked by the following:

Authorized
The Minder of the Universe

For a facility that stored every drop of cosmic building material in Existence, the CBM Center was a nondescript building on a lot two miles off the main road. From the outside, the industrial facility did not appear particularly tall, wide or long, and was desperate for a hosing down. There was graffiti and mud splatters on the outer walls.

Donald walked through the parking lot, empty but for a few stragglers. The sky was passing through its cranberry stage, fading into a darker maroon. He always enjoyed this phase, especially by the beach, with Danielle, listening to the ocean's *whoosh*.

But the sky seemed more foreboding now, like the heart of the cosmos had been sliced open, smeared with its own blood. And while Donald believed the sky would eventually fade to purple—it always had—perhaps it wouldn't this time. Maybe it would remain bloodstained forever. Maybe his destiny was such that for all his days he would look up, seeing nothing but dark red—his all-encompassing guilt.

Alone, Donald approached the security booth. He shuddered as his foot scraped along the asphalt, feeling that his presence was unmistakable, magnified as the brilliant yellow sunshine beamed down on him. Only on him. A red tag hung from his neck.

Danielle looked behind her, to the top row, and then at the bottom, thinking the speaker would have been impossible to see if not for the tremendous screen behind him, his image projected a thousand times larger than he actually was. Or else each attendee could look upon a shrunken image of him on individual video screens that extended up from each countertop. Giant master or tiny voice. Or both.

The meeting was mandatory for all day-shift CBM employees. The auditorium was filled to capacity. Donald was not in attendance.

So that when Danielle closed her eyes and saw herself snuggled in her husband's nook, she could feel his warmth as his chest would rise and sink with each easy breath.

Donald nodded to the security guard, as he had done every day. From behind the window, the guard glanced at the security pass, paused, and then returned the nod.

There was a *click* and a *buzz*, followed by a metal *clank*. The cross-hatched metal gate opened. Donald walked through. The gate *clanked* shut behind him, locking him in.

As he came upon the warehouse, Donald couldn't help but be aware of just how much his left knee itched. He stopped, reached down to scratch. So that when he closed his eyes, he had a singular picture in his mind. And it was perfect.

Lawrence stood at the podium. The CBM warehouse manager cleared his throat. He held a long pointer.

Danielle looked side to side, behind and below. She kept hoping Donald would show up.

The CBM center consisted of three sections. In front was the shipping warehouse, in back were the executive and accounting offices, and there was the CBM warehouse, neither in front nor in back, above or below, next to or around, inside or out. It was accessible only through a service elevator in the basement, leading to a room that did not register on a blueprint. You were either inside the warehouse, or you weren't.

"It has come to our attention," Lawrence said, "that perhaps we have not been serving you well." He addressed them from behind the podium, so very far away and below, except that his image was projected on the massive screen behind him. The auditorium fell silent. "While we should be striving toward a common goal, it appears that we have become...disjointed. Yes, that's it. Individuals working separately, but with no sense of belonging. Without community."

Danielle scribbled on her manual: *Community. Community my ass.*

She smirked. But when she picked up her eyes, Lawrence

was staring at her, both through the giant screen and her individual video monitor.

"From what I can gather," he continued, "you don't put much stock in my words."

Danielle's eyes drew wide, certain that Lawrence was talking only to her. Feverishly, she erased the last line.

"I don't blame you," he said, "because I wouldn't believe me either."

Chapter 70
Where's Waldo?

Eastern Europe—Somewhere Between Budapest and Prague
Sunday, September 11, 2005, 1:49 p.m.

Headed on the 20:26 train as it rumbled along from Budapest to Prague, Lilly wouldn't use his name. She said *him*, or *your friend*, or *your buddy*, but not *Jason*.

Sitting across from Theo as he disappeared in his guidebook, Lilly wondered if he noticed, if he was suspicious of her. Her heart beat faster and faster.

But how could he know what I'm thinking? Is he waiting for the right moment to spring it on me? To mash me into emotional pulp? To expose me for the fraud that I am?

Lilly—posing as Liz—looked out as the telephone poles sped by like the seconds of her life. One second. Then the next. Then the next.

Theo reasoned that if Jason wasn't on the Charles Bridge, then maybe he would be in a nearby hostel. So Theo made a list, starting with the hostels closest to the bridge and then expanded the radius. He had ten in all. He would stop at each and every one if that's what it took.

With the train chugging along, Theo was hoping to ditch Liz, and not because she was either nervous and hyper or oddly silent, but because she was there. It was *his* quest to find Jason, not *theirs*.

Lilly didn't want to see his face, didn't want to remember. She distorted Jason into this generic torso with his head blotted out, like a confidential mob witness doing a TV interview. Lilly wanted to hold onto the *idea* of Jason, to a feeling *about* him, but suppress it, keeping it at a great distance, on the outermost edge of her consciousness. The final, smallest moon in the deepest orbit around the farthest planet of her heart.

Their train sat for an hour, until finally it was sent back to Budapest. Someone said there was a track fire. Lots of damage. "Oh, this is fucked," Theo said.

Back at the *Keleti Pu* station, he thumbed through his time-table. They could take a train to Vienna, then switch to another in Prague. "It leaves in...," and he counted on his fingers, "we've got about two hours."

"Won't that take longer?" Liz said. "Maybe we should just stay here and wait. It's a major line. They'll have to fix it."

Theo had the feeling that Liz didn't want them going to Prague, that she wanted to stick around Budapest, just not alone. This was his chance to break free. "Maybe," he said. "I dunno. No. Fuck it. I'm going to Vienna. Yeh. That's it."

"Why don't we eat first," Liz said. "I'm starving."

Theo looked at his watch. His stomach growled.

Lilly—posing as Liz—watched over Theo as he slept in the bottom bunk, back at *Your Best Days* #14. He was covered in sweat, wrecked from food poisoning. He had been in the bathroom for more than an hour. Bad borscht.

"You just sleep," she said. "You need your rest. We'll wait it out."

Lilly went to the pub. She stared at the Mona Lisa, just not *the* Mona Lisa, wondering if the old gal had ever gotten herself into such a fine mess. Lilly watched smoke rings dissipate into the crimson air. "I'm Only Happy When It Rains" by Garbage was playing on the sound system. Lilly slugged down a shot of tequila.

Pushing those memories down.
Keeping the faces far away.

By the time they finally made their way into Prague and set foot
on the Charles Bridge, at noon, Jason was nowhere to be found.

Lilly exerted all of her might to keep from trembling, knowing that Jason could come walking up at any moment, unaware
that he had already left the city. "Maybe...he just never made it.
Or maybe he already left. You said he was sick."

"He was definitely here," Theo said. "He made it."

"How do you—?"

"Because," Theo broke in, although Lilly could see that he
wanted to say even more. "If he says he'll do something, he does
it. You can count on him."

"Yeah," Lilly said. "I know what you mea—"

Theo looked at her strangely.

"I mean...you know...from the way you talk about him. It
just sounds like...you know. Like...you wouldn't go to all this
trouble for someone you can't trust..."

Oh, god. He knows. He totally knows.

Theo nodded. "Yeh," he said. "True."

They leaned on the ledge of the Charles Bridge, staring out onto
the Vltava River. Dark like chocolate milk, it flowed through
the arches of the gothic bridge that connected Old Town and
Malá Strana. They shared a pack of salt and vinegar chips.

After three days and no Jason, Theo was getting tired.
Disheartened. Lilly could see his crumbling resolve. Time to
make a move. "You know," she said finally, "I can't believe I
didn't make the connection."

"What's that?"

"Oh..." Lilly turned away. She gnawed on a chip. She saw
a pair of tighty whities in the muddy water, caught on a fallen
branch. "Never mind. Forget it." She dusted the salt from her

hands. The crumbs fell to the river. "You wouldn't be...it's just too—"

"No," Theo said. "What?"

"So, like, this woman I know from back home? The one I told you about? Emma? I can't believe I didn't think of it before, but..." As predicted, Theo was interested in her proposition. He needed something to feel good about. "She wants someone right away. She never stops bitching about it. 'My garden is so neglected, blah, blah, blah.' She's got money like Bill Gates and decorates like Liberace. And from what you've told me, you're just what she's looking for."

Lilly dangled a chip over the muddy river. Unconsciously, she pressed her tongue against the roof of her mouth. Pressing. Pressing. She watched Theo as he looked about the bridge. People holding hands. Artists doing sketches. A guitarist with a hat at his feet.

"You want to see a picture?" Lilly said. "I can show you."

Theo had been so sure he was going to find Jason. Just sure of it. When Liz had asked how he knew Jason had already been there, what he wanted to say was: *Because the colors swirling in my mind tell me so.*

But it was becoming impossible to ignore the truth: he wasn't going to find him. And Theo knew it was his fault. So he thought about floating in the still, cool waters, underground in the Waitomo Caves. His favorite place in the world.

They found a cyber café on their way back to the train station. They logged onto Emma's Web site.

Liz was pushing hard. "It looks great, right? Isn't it beautiful?"

Theo sat on a bar stool, staring at the screen. He felt Liz's hand on his shoulder. The monitor displayed a pillared mansion and a three-tiered fountain. "It's awesome. Um...what's the pay?"

"A thousand now, a thousand when you get there, and then you can work out the rest. All cash. Plus plane fare there and back home. I can't believe it took me this long to think of it. You should totally do it. You'd be great."

"Oh, I dunno," Theo said, although two thousand American dollars was worth double that in New Zealand. For that kind of money, he could rebuild his greenhouse and plan another trip around the world. He felt Liz squeeze his shoulder.

"I think you'd be fantastic," she said into his ear.

"I...uh...," he said.

Lilly felt uneasy with her hand on Theo's shoulder. *Am I really like Emma says? Am I a...?* She pressed her tongue against the roof of her mouth again, feeling as if she would break through into her brain at any moment. She looked at Theo as he craned his neck to face her. She smiled. "It's a big decision, definitely. But you get involved with her...your life's never the same. Trust me. There's no one like her."

And thank God for that.

Lilly could see that Theo was fidgety, debating his options.

"I," he started. "I..."

Just fucking do it already!

"Uh...," Theo said. "Well...yeh. Okay."

"Really? You will?"

Theo nodded. "Yeh. Fuck it. Let's do it."

"Oh! This is great!" Lilly hugged him from behind. "I'll tell Emma."

"Okay. I gotta pee." Theo lumbered off to the bathroom.

Lilly's hands shook. "Wine," she blurted out, cried briefly, and then wiped away a tear. "Ride wine."

She signaled for the waitress, who took the order. Lilly then reached for her bag. Leaning forward, she raised her head, only to clunk it on the bottom of the table. "Ow. Shoot." She winced, kicking her foot in frustration, but in doing so, knocked over Theo's knapsack. Lilly picked it up. One of the pockets was open halfway. She stared at the dangling zipper like a cat in the grass, stalking a bird as it flew by.

Lilly glanced inside. She could see a plastic bag sticking out from underneath Theo's baseball cap. She reached in to get it. But then she stopped. "I just...no. Stop it. Cut it out." She zipped the pocket closed and held the bag close. She waited for her drink. Hugging the bag. Waiting. Waiting. And then she unzipped the pocket.

Theo stood over the sink. He stared in the mirror. He splashed water on his face. *Am I insane to go with her? But America, yeh? Fucking America.* Theo hesitated then, a final respect to Jason. His friend. *I tried, mate. I really did.*

And when Theo made his way back, he snatched his bag from Liz.

"It was an accident," she said. "I couldn't help but notice. What is it?"

Theo scowled, disgusted with himself. *Serves me fucking right. I knew it.*

"I'm...I'm sorry," Liz said. "It fell open and I..."

Theo opened the plastic bag, and for some reason, felt defiant in showing her what was inside. What had gotten him started in the first place, but had become more burden than treasure. "Here," he said. "Look." There were six pictures in all. One each from different angles. Pictures of an item. A special item. A glass jar.

"What, uh...what is it?"

"Something I found."

"It's nice." Liz squinted, as if afraid he was going to belt her in the face. "Where is it?"

Theo looked at her. His heart raced. His throat became tight and dry. "Someplace safe," he said, and went silent, ashamed for having doubted his instincts, for bailing on his friend. For giving up.

I can still find him. There's still time.

The words echoed in Lilly's mind: *Someplace safe.* And suddenly the gears in her mind found each other, spun effortlessly.

"Ohhhhh," she said. "Oh." Lilly felt like Theo was wearing a T-shirt with an arrow pointing in her direction, reading: *I'm With Useless.*

Emma doesn't want Theo. She wants the jar.

Totally. Fucking. Useless.

Yet somehow, despite her humiliation, Lilly couldn't help but think that maybe it was just what she needed. So she started to cry.

"Hey." Theo lifted his rucksack. "Are you...?"

Why am I feeling bad for her? Screw her.

And still he reached for Liz, rubbed her back. Gently. "You okay?"

Lilly squeezed her eyes shut until she saw colored rings pulsing against the blackness in her mind. She pressed her tongue against the roof of her mouth again, as if she would break through and make her head explode once and for all. And then a strange thing happened.

"I'm gonna look for Jason. I know where he is. At least I think so."

"Really?"

Theo looked at Liz as she raised her head. Her eyes were messy with tears and remorse and something else he couldn't quite decipher, and yet he seemed to understand perfectly. And for the first time since they met, Theo liked what he saw. "I just do," he said. "I just do."

Lilly stared in Theo's direction, but in her mind's eye all she could see was a barreling figure and her dog, their faces blotted out, until finally they just faded away. Emma no longer mattered.

Lilly stared in Theo's direction, but in her mind's eye all she could see was Jason's face again, her heart dancing with an extra *thumpety-thump*. She saw Jason because she let herself see him. Because she wanted to.

And as Lilly stared in Theo's direction, in her mind's eye she could see one other man. The one she missed most of all.

Chapter 71
I Can't Believe It's Not Butter

The Southern Sphere of Eternity—Titan Hall
Milky Way's Public Unveiling: T-Minus 11 Minutes, 54 Seconds (Eternity Standard Time)

Emma stood on the marble platform of Titan Hall, above the crowd. A long planter of roses stretched out before her. The waters of Titan Lake glittered beneath the morning sun. The sky was lime green. The sun was golden and warm. "I'm a fucking rock star," she said to herself.

Behind her was the entrance to Titan Hall. Its four fluted columns projected dignity and strength. Grandeur and power. "This is fucking great."

It was an amazing sight, as an almost endless sea of Eternitarians gathered below on the great lawn, along the lake. The constant murmur sounded like a pack of squawking gulls.

Mohpmohpmohpmohp...wahh...sshhhhhhhhhhhhhhh...oooshhhhhhhh.

The media clustered along the staircases on both sides of the platform. Cameras clicked. Video recorders whirred. Microphones dangled.

Standing at the podium, Emma realized that if she blurred her vision by crossing her eyes, she could morph the crowd into a massive amoeba. It was like butter smeared on a green bagel with a giant blue hole in the middle. And when she relaxed her vision, they were people again, with hopes and dreams, worries and pain. She liked them better as an amoeba.

Emma repeated this—transmuting them from crowd to condiment, condiment to crowd—biting her bottom lip to keep from guffawing at the power she had over them.

Clear...people. Blurry...butter.

Clear...people. Blurry...butter.

The slew of reporters, most notably from *Top Galaxy Design*,

Cosmic Designer Digest and *Galactic Fabric Review*, gathered with their little notepads open, eager to take down every last word that flowed from Emma's lips.

Emma craned her neck, only to see Lex standing slightly behind and to the side of the podium, swallowing yet another one of his little white doofus pills. Next to him was Jacques Abladeujé, an arrangement Emma was sure had Lex in a twist.

Jacques nodded at Emma, and then gestured to the crowd. Rufus was standing at the tip of the giant amoeba, rooting for Emma, as always.

She shuddered a wondrous, goose-bumpy sensation. And finally her throat drew tight and dry, knowing as she looked down that never again would Rufus hold her. And that without him, her only friend, she was nowhere. She was lost.

Emma smiled at Rufus. She raised her eyebrows. It was the closest she had ever come to saying the words *thank you.*

Jacques had already introduced her. He announced that based on her stupendous work—both on the Blue-Bubbled Dumbbell Nebula, and the newest, most spectacular galaxy in eons, which she was about to unveil—Renolo Enterprises signed her to design three new galaxies, the largest contract ever awarded to an independent firm.

Indeed, Emma could feel the collective surge of energy. But for a moment, the chatter seemed to go quiet.

In the distance she could see the reflective tips of the Titan Towers. And like a wink from the heavens, in the shade of a single white cloud they all went dark...one...two...three...and then, as the cloud drifted away, the tips sparkled again...one...two...three.

Surrounded, Emma took them all in—the media, the giant amoeba, the towers—and wet the very lips they clung to, wondering what it would be like to vanish from that most grandiose stage, to never face that pressure again.

Unbeknownst to everyone, Emma clenched her pelvis, once, and then again. It reminded her that this single moment—perhaps her very last as such—was about her and her alone, and that the forthcoming frenzy would be about them and what they wanted from her. That the spectators were waiting for someone, anyone, to give them a purpose. To give them hope. And that they would be merciless and unforgiving if they were disappointed.

Inhaling the sweet scent of anxiety and roses, of thrill and moisture, Emma breathed in and then out. In...then out. In... then out.

She looked out at the giant amoeba surrounding Titan Lake. She looked up at the lime green of the morning sky. She felt the golden sunshine on her face. Her destiny would wait no more. "Time to kick their asses," Emma said finally. "It's show time."

Emma addressed the crowd, that giant, faceless amoeba. "...when I told them you were sick of being spoon-fed the same galaxies. When I told them they could fool themselves, but that they couldn't fool you..." Emma saw the crowd grow silent. The media was frozen with awe.

She had them.

"...they knew, deep down, I was right."

She so fucking had them.

Emma unfurled her brow, and then allowed the masses to come into focus, the cluster of individual faces yearning for more, for a voice to carry them forward.

"I stood right in their offices," she recalled, and pointed to a high-rise on the other side of Titan Hall. "I looked them square in the eye. I told them they were all just perpetuating the nonsense of their own gospel. That they had lost their way, convinced they should think *for* you, instead of talking *to* you."

And with that, a massive purple laser beamed from each of the four pillars behind her and into the lime green sky. They ultimately thinned into four points. Together—one each beginning at the four corners—the purple lasers burned a rectangle into the heavens.

Oooh, the audience said. *Click-click,* the cameras went. *Aaah,* the audience said.

"And finally," Emma announced. "Here it is." Adrenaline blasted through her like rocket fuel. She pointed to the giant rectangle. "The Milky Way, ladies and gentlemen. And the centerpiece of it all. The Solar...System."

The rectangular outline filled with blackness. The size of a football field, the canvas was so close that the crowd, the press...even Emma herself...scrunched their necks, ducking, like this monolith might descend and crush them into humus. As if the sky itself had fallen.

From hidden speakers came a low, steady introduction:

...*RUMBLERUMBLERUMBLERUMBLERUMBLERUMBLE-RUMBLE*...

A keyboard bass note reverberated up their legs, along their spines and down their arms. The spectators uttered gasps of excitement and wonder. They turned to one another, inspecting their hands, feeling the energy channeling through them.

And then, as Emma had expected, the sea of onlookers came under a collective hush. Their attentions were drawn once again to that enormous black football field, with her out in front of Titan Hall, on the marble platform, as if conducting an orchestra.

Thousands of tiny white stars announced themselves with a flash. They appeared against the blackness like microwave popcorn crackling inside the bag, slow at first...*pop...pop...pop*...and then a little faster...*pop-pop...pop-pop*...and faster...*pop-pop-pop-pop-pop-pop-pop-pop*...until finally it was a frenzy of stars vegetating the image of this new galaxy, a fireworks display celebrating the future, rather than the past.

The keyboard bass note grew louder and louder. Hairs on necks stood up. Penises hardened. Breasts tightened. The vibration connected everyone to everything. The ground was shaking. The buildings were shaking. The audience was shaking. They wondered if they were in the midst of creation itself, which, of course, they were.

...*RUMBLERUMBLERUMBLERUMBLERUMBLE*...

KA-BOOM!

The audience leaned back. Their eyes went wide. They gasped and gawked at the black monolith. It appeared, like a mammoth doorway, about to unleash the enormity of the Universe on the other side of Eternity.

And in the center blackness, a thousand tiny stars peppering the background, the greatest star of all finally flashed before them. Its luminescence evolved from a billowy white to a soft yellow, and then thicker, thicker and thicker still, until a deep, rich, tangy yellow exuded warmth and life. Pride and power. The single perfect sun for this most perfect star system.

The audience cheered and cried. They hugged and roared with applause. And then from the speakers came another ground-shaking thunder.

...RUMBLERUMBLERUMBLERUMBLERUMBLE... KA-BOOM!

With an outstretched hand, Emma introduced the first planet, which she named after the first diamond of Organic Beauty. The scorching planet erupted before them. It fell into a close orbit around the sun. "Mercury!" The audience clapped and roared again.

...RUMBLERUMBLERUMBLERUMBLERUMBLE... KA-BOOM!

The second—a large, yellowish-white planet—appeared and fell into its own, wider orbit around the sun. "Venus!" The audience roared again.

...RUMBLERUMBLERUMBLERUMBLERUMBLE... KA-BOOM!

Emma then announced the next planet. Rather than name the blue and green orb after the third diamond of Organic Beauty—Earth, as should have followed, and approved by The Minder of the Universe—she gave it the only name in Existence that could desecrate the ceremony.

"Emma," she shouted, declaring the planet's moniker. "Emma."

The giant amoeba let out another series of oohs, aahs and whispers, suspecting—correctly—that Emma had called an audible, that she had made a statement that could not be unmade. Designers were forbidden from naming a planet after themselves. Ever. No exceptions. Emma knew as much. She simply chose to ignore it.

Lex's jaw hung open. Jacques Abladeujé shook his head. Rufus smiled, and then closed his eyes.

Following each subsequent *KA-BOOM!* Emma introduced the other six planets, named after the remaining diamonds of Organic Beauty—Mars, Jupiter, Saturn, Uranus, Neptune and Pluto, which, after much deliberation (and a best, two-out-of-three rock, paper, scissors) made the final cut. The nine planets fell into place. More than one hundred moons orbited them. An asteroid belt maintained in a final outer orbit. And in the center of it all was one glorious sun.

Emma basked in the majesty of her design. She put both hands on the podium, straightened her back. She offered a confident smile. Saliva was clammy in her mouth.

Okay. Here we go. I had my moment.

"The Solar System," she said. "The Milky Way. Are there any questions?"

With the roar of the audience, the press erupted with a hailstorm of comments, including: *Do you think there will be fallout from naming a planet after yourself?*

Emma took a breath, allowing herself one last look at her creation. At the giant amoeba. At Lex. At Jacques. At Rufus.

And before she could answer, there was a blast of white light. There were streaks of screaming fluorescent color. There was the sensation of being sucked through a tornado. And there was a body. A big, fat body.

Chapter 72
A Part of Everything, the Whole of Nothing

*The Northern Sphere of Eternity—CBM Training Center
Time Elapsed Since Milky Way's Public Unveiling: 14
Seconds (Eternity Saving Time)*

"But things change," Lawrence said. "When I woke up this morning and received word...I held my anger. Again I reminded myself why it is important to clarify...to elaborate...to *fortify* our overall philosophy. Because if we don't understand the goals of the organization, how can we participate with consistency and determination?"

There was a collective murmuring. Heads turned. There was shifting in seats. This wasn't what they expected. "But then I thought...fuck 'em. I've been clear and specific throughout."

Again there was a ruffling of papers and murmuring, but when Danielle thought about the only question that mattered to her—*why did all this happen to me?*—and when she considered the answer, she frowned, as there seemed little point in asking.

Donald held his security pass, considered the responsibility attached to it. He knew what it would mean to step inside the elevator, to hear the gears and cables stretch and pull, to feel himself traveling—although not up or down, side to side, forward or back, but moving nonetheless—and then have the doors slide open again.

His heart was a panting dog. His heart was a fire alarm.

As he reached up toward the scanner, in his mind's eye Donald saw himself walk inside the CBM warehouse, much as he had done day after day, and stand upon the electric ladder, punching into the arm control the row and section designated for the storage of his jar—a jar *he* lost on *his* watch. And when the automated platform took him to his destination...rising...rising...rising...he would stare at empty space.

And as he had done day after day, he would see a disappearing horizon, as if the shelves were curved, stretching into infinity. And as he had done day after day, he would consider himself just so very small. Insignificant. And yet so wonderfully important.

"The truth, and I can't emphasize this enough...is that every last one of you were this close...," Lawrence made a pinching gesture, "...*thisclose* from being redistributed. You aren't our first group of engineers, and you won't be the last. You're certainly not the best."

Danielle picked up her head. She looked side to side.

"You were given particular instructions about your CBM jars. You were told how to store them, the power they contain, and in no uncertain terms, the consequence for losing them, or, their unauthorized use." Lawrence sighed. "Apparently...I haven't been clear enough. Because another jar has gone missing."

Danielle felt her heart beat slow and heavy. *Forget it, baby. Come back.*

"And now the jar's galaxy—one of the newly approved models—is on the verge of total collapse. Unless we repair it in time, the Milky Way will be ruined. The Minder of the Universe is beside himself. I've never seen him so upset. His anger is astonishing."

There was a hush. Danielle's shoulders drew tight, unaware that Lawrence's ex-wife—the Milky Way's designer—would wind up sitting in a motel room on Earth, in Yuma, during the early stages of the planet's cosmic destiny, searching for the very item Donald and Danielle were terrified would ruin their lives.

"I can see...," Lawrence said, pinching the corner of his eyes, "...that review is in order. So. Once again. *What will happen if you lose your CBM jar?*" No response. "Come, come, people. If you can't say it, you can't face it. And if you can't face it, well, working here will be the least of your worries. Let's try again."

Danielle felt her breaths pull quick and tight. Petrified, she mumbled over and over. *"No no no no no no no no..."*

"What...will...happen?"

There were muffled responses. *"...ish...byoo...shun..."*

"Come, people." Lawrence tapped for emphasis. "Ree... dis...trih..."

"...bution?" they finished.

"That's it. Redistribution. Now say it with me."

Reduced to your base elements, scattered throughout Eternity and then soaked into the cosmic fabric, reappearing somewhere, sometime—a part of everything, and yet the whole of nothing. Complete identity disintegration.

"Redistribution," they said in unison.

"Right," Lawrence said. "Redistribution. And what a thing it is."

Staring at the scanner, Donald knew that the guts were just a configuration of microchips and wires, and that even though he had scanned his security tag on that very screen day after day, this time he was convinced the machinery was alive. That it was watching him. That the scrolling, infrared light could read his thoughts. Maybe even his soul.

Maybe it could read his guilt. How he laid awake every night, petrified that his wife's heartbreak would plague him across time. That no matter what was to become of him, he would carry that psychic scar forever. And that maybe he deserved it.

But he knew that his panic was just a way to delay the inevitable, as if distracting himself from punishment would be the same as escaping it. He shook his head, could almost hear Brigsby's voice, warning him to avoid foolishness, encouraging him instead to unburden his soul. And accept whatever came next.

Donald held his eyes open—he was certain of it—yet all he saw was darkness. He let himself drift into the recess of his mind, drifting...drifting...drifting. And in his sense of drift a warmth came over him. Comfort. Soon he felt himself rock on his heels in an easy, gentle rhythm. The tension in his body faded away. He breathed easily. He was ready.

Donald scanned the security tag. The red light flashed once, again, and then again. There was the familiar sound of a bolt and a heavy motor. *Clank. Whiiir.* As expected, the message appeared, only it was different from ever before. His heart fluttered. His throat went dry. He tried to swallow, but there was no moisture. His worst fears realized, he scanned the tag again, just to try, but the same two words materialized: *Access Denied.*

So that Donald could hear only one word: Redistribution.

"Lucky for you," Lawrence said, "The Minder of the Universe, more so than anyone, knows that Eternity is imperfect. That the Universe is imperfect. That *we* are imperfect."

Danielle's eyes widened.

"When last we convened, at the forefront of discussion was the damage caused by Milo, your former associate, and that he was to serve as an example of poor discretion. Yet on his way to being processed for redistribution...there's quite a bit of paperwork...regrettably, Milo eluded our team, and accessed the CBM warehouse. He stole five jars and disbursed them into the Universe."

Danielle grabbed the counter with both hands. *Wait. What the fuck? That's not...*

"We've...dealt with him. He has been redistributed. Milo is gone....But the damage he caused is considerable....Such a mess."

Danielle's heart thundered.

"And yet as much as it pains me to say it, Milo's ineptitude and cowardice...," Lawrence held his thought in place just then, Danielle once again certain he was talking to and about her, "...may have been a boon in disguise. Milo did us a favor."

Huh?

"By stealing those jars..."

Oh no.

"...by ruining our efforts..."

No no no.

"...what Milo made clear is that our infrastructure needs work. There are gaps in the system. We need to fix them. And we will."

I'm the gap. I'm done...

"On a more personal level, he also reminded us that a few bad apples...or even just a single disaster..."

Here it comes.

"...doesn't mean the entire batch is rotten.

Say what now, muthafucka?

"It would be unfair to *automatically* lump you together as being equally useless. Some of you, I must say, have done fine work. You should be proud." Lawrence took a sip of water. "That said...and I suggest that you hear me on this...I have a stack of Redistribution forms on my desk this high." He raised his hand above his shoulder. "They are *complete, signed* and ready for *immediate processing*. The only thing missing...is your name. And I'm ready to fill those fuckers in."

Danielle shook.

"Before we conclude for today, let me leave you with one last thought: you are involved with the design, creation and maintenance of the Universe. Your responsibilities are of the highest magnitude. It is not your *right* to be here. You are not *owed* this opportunity. But seeing as you *are* here...your experience with the organization is very much up to you. It can be great, it can be awful, it can fall somewhere in between. We've laid out the rules of conduct, provided training, and given you the tools to succeed. If you need assistance...ask. If you have questions... ask. We will help you. It is in the organization's interest to support you whenever and however possible. It is the only way for us to accomplish our goals."

Lawrence took a breath, then let it out slowly.

"But if you hide from your mistakes...if you violate the orders passed down by The Minder of the Universe...the consequences will be extraordinary. There will be no one to save you. And in those final moments, when you are confronted with yourself, only then will you realize the opportunities you've squandered. It will be too late."

Donald leaned his back against the elevator. He scratched his upper lip with his bottom teeth. "Well," he said finally. "So much for that."

And with that admission he started back down the tunnel. His first step landed firmly. Confident. But then his knees buckled. He collapsed against the wall. His breath quivered, waiting for The Minder of the Universe to come upon him with vengeance and fury. And after Donald's molecules were demolished and scattered throughout the ether, would Danny be next? Would The Big MOU transform his wife into a slug, as she feared most? And if so, with a slug's brain would she be burdened anyway with the memory of this life and all they had thrown away, cut off from each other forever, left in the mud?

Donald's chest drew tight, his heart beating faster and faster until he almost blacked out from fear and shame, knowing he had failed as a man. As a husband. That he failed to protect them from themselves. Their good fortune had literally fallen away, not because they were unlucky, but because the euphoria of sudden success blinded them from what they knew so well. That nothing of value comes free or easy. That they had to earn it, and keep on earning it.

And yet he forced himself to continue, to take another step. So that when he made his way through the tunnel again and out into the sunlight, and then nodded again to the security guard, who nodded back, Donald strode across the parking lot. He took one step, then another, then another.

The exit in sight, Donald felt a tugging on his spirit, as if a massive *whoosh* funneled through him. A vanishing. Only it wasn't as if *he* vanished, but the CBM center. Just behind him, he sensed a flash of white light. Streaks of screaming fluorescent color. Being swallowed by a tornado.

But he refused to look back. Because even though he knew that any single step could be his last in Existence, Donald had to believe he would make it home anyway. That he would be with his girl once more. And that as long as they were together, hand in hand, whatever came next for them would be all right indeed.

Chapter 73
The Demarcation Line

Auckland, New Zealand—Barnes Residence
Thursday, September 22, 2005, 1:49 p.m.

Lydia invited George back for coffee because she just couldn't bear to let him walk away. Surrounded by windows on three sides, they sat at the kitchen table, facing each other. A thin beam of sunshine split the table down the center, safe zones of a demarcation line—Lydia on one side, George on the other.

"I'm heading back to Amsterdam to meet a young woman," George said. "She's a painter, from America. I'm hoping she'll do a show in my gallery. It'll be my last one."

It unnerved Lydia, feeling so attached to him already. But with each moment she became more convinced that George knew the path to her salvation, as if he had read the book of her life many times over. She could feel in her bones that relief was within her reach. George was her last chance. "Oh, yeh?" she said. "Why's that?"

"It's a complicated world. You must keep many people satisfied, all in the hopes they'll pledge you money...enough to stay open just a little while longer. And then you're on to the next one. And then the next. It's endless."

Lydia stared down the length of her home, through the sun-soaked kitchen and into the carpeted hallway at the back end of the house. There were two bedrooms on the left—one for each of her mysterious, determined boys who had once clutched at her long strands of hair as she rocked them to sleep—and one on the right, where she shared a bed with her husband, her high school sweetheart, who was out back, and seemed to think of her less and less as the days passed them by.

"What will you do then?" Lydia finally said. "Will you be all right?"

"Actually...I'm hoping to open a nightclub. In Auckland. I

have a very talented...performer signed on."

"Oh, yeh?" Lydia's face was a warm raspberry. She curled her toes. She rubbed her hands beneath the table. "What does she do?"

"Angelique? Well, she sings a little, dances a little....She makes a spectacle."

Lydia let slip a reserved smile, but there had been a time when she would laugh so hard mucous would blow from her nose. When she used to steal the newspaper from the old man next door and draw lewd smiley faces on page eleven, just because.

There had been a time when she would sneak out into the night while her parents listened to George Gershwin on the radio. When she would meet her boyfriend, Oscar, before they became two dissolving masses that happened to get mail at the same address.

And Lydia thought just then of a postcard Theo had sent a few months back, just when she thought her eldest son might never write her again.

9-25-05

G'day Mum,

pretty knackered now. Been sitting in a café in Berlin watching this old guy have a feed. He's choking down sausages like you wouldn't believe! It's funny how you get to like sitting still sometimes when you're always running around. Say hi to Dad and Roger.

Off to who knows where.

Theo

George sipped his coffee. "Lydia, can I ask you something?"

"Yeh, yeh. Go ahead. Please do."

"Do you need to make amends?" George took a shallow breath. He felt his heart race and slow in direct correlation with Lydia, whose glow of attention morphed into what he expected—fear and confusion. "To yourself? Do you ever feel like you owe yourself an apology?"

Lydia's look turned curious. "For what?"

"For denying the chance to live the life you want, rather than the life you have? For avoiding the tough decisions, the painful conversations? That has certainly been true for me." George leaned forward, folded his hands just shy of the demarcation line. "But the more you avoid them...the more that inner voice tracks you down. Hunting you." George sat back. "It's a persistent little bugger, is it not?"

Lydia nodded. A tear welled up. "Yeh. I know that feeling. I feel it right now."

This time, George offered his hands across the forbidden barrier. "Then apologize to yourself. Set free whatever's inside you. You deserve it."

Lydia raised her head. The tears began to flow. Reluctantly at first, then more securely, she took his hands. Warm. Soft. And safe.

"The problem," George said, "is that we tell ourselves all these little lies...day after day, year after year...no matter how sick they make us feel, like we're drowning in the sea of our own shame."

Lydia was bawling now, her face red and puckered.

George whispered. "And yet it is amazing how quickly we can forgive ourselves...once we admit the truth." He shook Lydia's hands—one, two, three—trying to joggle away her grief and jumpstart the possibility of joy. He felt an unexpected tug of altruism toward Lydia just then. To save her somehow. To reawaken her spirit. "It's like the greatest orgasm you could ever have...only...you get to keep your clothes on."

Lydia laughed a little, but turned serious again. "I'm afraid."

"I know. But you can do it."

"I can't. All those little lies...the ones you said...they're my glue. They keep me from going crazy."

"Or maybe...they're tearing you apart."

Lydia went still. And whether she realized it or not, she let go of his hands, those little hands, much as she appeared to let go of something far more significant. "Yeh." She sniffled and then wiped her face on the duckling apron. "Maybe."

George walked behind Lydia. He squeezed her shoulders as she inhaled. He left his hands there as she breathed out. Still connected. "Good," he said. "Good. Now..." George sat down, offered a handkerchief. He leaned forward at the table one last time. "...There's something we need to discuss. And it's very, very important."

Chapter 74
Catch Me If You Can (Reprise)

Prague, Czech Republic—Charles Bridge
Thursday, September 22, 2005, 1:50 p.m.

Lilly stayed in Prague for another week. She spent most of that time drunk on cheap wine and feeling as sorry for herself as she ever had—which was really saying something—until finally she sobered up and made her way back to the Charles Bridge.

And as she scanned the city and people around her, she saw them for the very first time. As if Jason, Theo and Emma were characters on some TV sitcom she had seen once a long time ago, but couldn't quite remember anymore.

Lilly stood against the ledge, no longer terrified that she might meet someone who would tap into her guarded heart. For the first time in a long time, she actually wanted to meet such a person. She had one particular person in mind.

Will he forgive me? Will he take me back?

Hearing giggles, Lilly turned to watch three small children jump up and down as a sketch artist, standing behind an easel, handed them caricatures.

Lilly smiled, remembering the hours she spent in the high school art room, swirling the soft bristles on her palm. How mixing her paint was like meditation, losing herself in the rhythm of the brushstrokes. How she could channel her spirit onto the canvas the way she could never do with words.

"Yeah," she said, and then cried a happy little cry. She closed her eyes and felt the sun on her face. "I think he will."

But can I forgive myself?

And Lilly thought just then about a painting she worked on years ago but never quite finished. One she knew was the beginning of her evolution as an artist, rather than just a painter. With just a few brush strokes left she threw a tarp over it. She hid the canvas in the back of the garage, behind an old ten-speed bicycle and a stack of cardboard boxes with baby clothes her mother could never seem to throw away.

Lilly hadn't thought about the painting since that day, when she buried it along with some essential part of herself that would never totally disappear, no matter how much she tried to distance herself from it.

In her mind's eye she could see the painting now. An old Italian villa overlooked the ocean. Mountains curved along the coastline. Lapping water stretched out into the distance. Along the villa was a slotted, stone balcony. It surrounded a section of grass that led to a garden blooming with flowers of every color. Above it all was the sun.

And in the back of the garden was a stone gazebo. It was draped in shade. And next to the gazebo was a stone bench, a compartment beneath the lid. From inside came a small hand. It belonged to someone who believed that magic only exists if kept locked up and then sprinkled like fairy dust. Someone who needed to understand that speaking her dreams aloud wouldn't make them disintegrate, but enable them to come true.

From within the compartment came a blast of white light. There were streaks of screaming fluorescent color. Orange leaves swirled into a little tornado.

Lilly stared at the river. Her tears flowed. "Yes," she whispered.

I forgive me. I'm ready to come out.

Lilly felt a tapping. She looked down to see one of the children, a young girl wearing a green dress and ribbon in her hair. The child handed up her caricature.

Lilly smiled back. "For me?"

The girl nodded, then scampered away, hiding behind her father's leg.

"Thank you." Lilly pressed the gift against her chest. "Thank you."

Lilly wiped her face. She ran across the Charles Bridge, back to the Internet café. As the tears stung her eyes, she realized that her life would always have uncertainty, but maybe if she worried less about what *might* happen and focused on what was happening now, maybe what scared her most wouldn't be so scary after all. And that if she let go of those horrible secrets, maybe something wonderful would take their place.

Before Lilly made her way to the airport, she had one last e-mail to send. One she had been putting off for a decade, but one she couldn't imagine waiting another minute to write. She sat down at the keyboard. Her fingers clacked the keys. The letter began:

Dear Daddy...

Chapter 75
The Minder of the Universe

The Southern Sphere of Eternity—Brigsby's Loft Apartment Time Elapsed Since Milky Way's Public Unveiling: 37 Minutes (Eternity Saving Time)

Lex crashed his convertible into the NO PARKING sign outside Brigsby's loft apartment. Following Emma's press conference, the media swarmed him with questions to which he had no answers. Brigsby was the only person who would understand the pressure.

There didn't need to be an announcement. Lex already knew what happened to Emma. Everybody knew.

"Well, well." Brigsby held the door with one hand, a blue martini with the other. "I thought you would have been here sooner. My goodness. Emma." He raised his glass. "That was quite the showstopper."

Still buzzing from his little white doofus pills, Lex paced across the near-empty apartment, shaking his head, his hands in the air. He went to the bar and poured himself a blue martini. He slurped it down. The aftertaste made his eyes water.

"She's banished, right? I didn't just hallucinate that?"

"Hu-ho. Well…I can't say if you're hallucinating or not, but, yes, Emma has been banished. To Earth, in fact. As you obviously know, that's what the third planet was supposed to be named. Is named. Some delightful irony, don't you think? If only she'd just said the right—"

"Whu…wait. Hold on. Wait a second. How do you know she's been banished to *Earth*? This just happened. How could you possibly know that?"

Brigsby sipped his drink. "Mmm." He wiped his lip. "How indeed?"

"Well," Lex began, "I guess…"

Before he could finish his thought, Lex felt as if he had been thrown over the side of an ocean liner. As if a violent storm thrashed him about the rough waters, flipping him end over end, then sideways, then back and forth. Lex felt as if his lungs were filling with water, the pressure caving in the roof of his thoughts so that only blackness surrounded him. Only blackness. But on the verge of passing out for good, Lex felt himself making his way back to the surface. Where he could breathe again.

"Does it make sense now?" he heard a voice whisper. "Do you see?"

Once again, Lex felt his lungs tighten. His heart raced. He was panicking now, the end of his life seeming more like the beginning of his death, as if some force wasn't just choking out his last breaths, but choking him out of Existence as he knew it.

Lost beneath the watery recesses of his subconscious, Lex was overcome with a sense of emptying. It was as if his mind… no, it was more than his ability to think rationally…as if his *soul* had finally relaxed, exhaling after a lifetime of holding its spiritual breath. His body went limp. Whether induced by chemicals, karma or both, Lex accepted his fate. The storm was gone. There was just Lex. And Brigsby.

"You mean, *you're* The Big MOU? You're The Minder of the Universe?"

"Well…you could say that. You'd be wrong, but you could say it. Although it actually does have a nice ring to it."

"I, uh…" Lex shook his head. "This is freaking me out."

"Relax, Lex. Relax. Here, have another drink."

Lex took the glass from Brigsby. He sipped at first, then swallowed it all. He wiped the blue dribble from his chin. "I don't understa—." The room started to spin just then, slowly at first, and then faster faster faster until all Lex saw was black, his mind spiraling like that great cluster in space. He vomited an inky pool of blue and yellow.

"Okay," Brigsby said. "No more for you. I'll take that."

Lex fell onto the couch, staring straight ahead, uncertain he was even breathing. There was puke on his cheek. And before Brigsby could offer a handkerchief, Lex threw up again, cried a bit, and then threw up once more before finally passing out.

Lex awoke, smelling like his own vomit. "Maybe it does make sense," he said in a sort of waking trance. "People watch you every day."

Brigsby sat on the coffee table, facing Lex. "But do they listen?"

"They're always talking about you."

"I know." Brigsby wiped Lex's face with a handkerchief. "There. Got it. But what do they say? 'Brigsby said this, or Brigsby said that.' And so what? What does it matter?"

Lex held his hands in his lap. His voice was shallow. "I don't know."

"I keep hoping they'll just boo me off the stage. That they'll just switch me off. But the thing is...the more ridiculous I become, the more they tune in. I can't figure it."

Lex was returning to a more active state of consciousness. He forced himself to blink. "Why don't you just cancel yourself? You know? Retire?"

"That would be the easy way out, wouldn't it? I could disappear from public life, but then what? I would be replaced faster than anyone could forget me. The answer isn't to give up, Lex. It's to keep looking."

"For what?"

"A-ha! Yes! That's a great question. But the truth is, my frazzled friend...I don't know what you're supposed to be looking for. That isn't for me to decide."

"But you're The Big MOU. The Minder of the Universe. You're the—"

"I'm not the *one*, Lex. I'm not."

Lex sat up, got a whiff of his yak. The scent was like a paramedic's ammonia stick. "You just said you're The Big MOU."

"I didn't, actually...but if I am?"

Lex sighed, shook his head. "I don't understand."

"If I'm this creator, this...Minder of the Universe...or whatever you're calling me...then what? What is it you think I should do?"

Lex felt his heart speed up. Tears came to his eyes.

That's not fair. Why are you doing this to me?

"I don't know," he said. "I just figured that...you know...you keep us all together. You hold Eternity in one piece. You protect us."

Brigsby chuckled. "Oh, Lex. Me? Hold it together? That's delightful."

Lex wiped a tear. "Don't laugh at me. That's fucking bullshit."

"I'm not laughing at you, Lex. I'm sorry. It's just that...I'm always amazed at how much faith people put into what they think I might be."

"Then what are you?"

"What if I'm not The Big MOU? What if I'm not *The* Minder of the Universe, but just one of many? You know, like middle management, overseeing my own little slice of Eternity? The whole thing is *way* too big for me to handle on my own."

"I don't—"

"Think a minute. What if I answer to someone, or something, who answers to someone, or something, and on and on? And what if we're actually assigned in threes, but live among the masses, to know them? I'm just saying. What if?"

"I'm not sure I—"

"Are you sure there's just *one* force that keeps Eternity together? Are you sure there's just one hand on the master switch?"

Lex felt his hands clench. His breath grew short and tight. He was petulant now, his heart lumbering like the steps of a drugged giant.

B-BOOM!...B-BOOM!...B-BOOM!...

He shook his head. "No, I'm not sure."

"Do you need there to be just one? One being, one force, one...Minder of the Universe? Do you feel safer believing in one, great, benevolent master? That everything will be all right if you just have faith?"

Lex stared at this frumpy daytime television host who, apparently, doubles as the creator of Existence. "Yes." Lex exhaled long and slow. He closed his eyes, breathed in. Breathed out. And again. Tears streamed down his face. "I'm scared. I need to believe."

"Then that's what you should do. Sometimes it's better to *believe* in something than to be right about it. Being right is hardly ever enough. And it hardly ever happens. Trust me on that. Don't worry about being right, Lex. Just focus on being you."

Lex woke suddenly from a dream and then scurried to the motel door, in Yuma. He let out a low whine and started barking... *woomph...woomph...woomph*...as a drunken couple stumbled into the next room and had sloppy, noisy sex.

Eyes wide and tail wagging, Lex downgraded his sense of urgency, accepting that his temporary home was, for the moment, cleared of danger.

But what still troubled him was the increased frequency and clarity with which he was hearing sounds he had never picked up on before: the snap of a twig; the tiny thud of a bluebird that falls from its nest; the motel attendant farting into his swivel chair.

And it wasn't that Lex minded—he was fascinated by his auditory powers—but he was beginning to worry that he might soon forget he had ever walked on two feet. That ultimately he would become Lex the dog, and not Lex, this new identity permanently replacing the other.

He curled back into a ball, and then lifted his snout. He breathed in the bitter, salty sweat puddled on Emma's back as she slept on the bed. And as he finally closed his eyes, he fell back into dream, one of the last memories he had of his old life, one he was beginning to think may have never actually happened, seeming stranger and less coherent by the Earthly day.

"So," Brigsby said. "We just have one more thing to resolve."

Although rattled that Brigsby was The Minder of the Universe, or *a* Minder of the Universe, or whatever was overlooking Existence, Lex felt surprisingly alert. "Emma."

"Right. Emma. That naming stunt was so very *her.* I told her not to."

"Wait. You told her...? When did you tell her? I didn't even know you knew her. Although, I guess you kinda know everything."

"Not everything." Brigsby chuckled. "I know some things... a few things. And, yes. I do know her personally. I didn't mention that?"

"Must have slipped your mind."

"That's my bad. She used to be married to Lawrence, the warehouse manager at the CBM plant. He's a friend. Emma and Lawrence divorced about a year ago. They still get along. Sort of. We had dinner last week. Your friend George set it up. My, how he seems to know but everyone. He's quite resourceful."

"I knew she'd been married. I only knew his name."

"Yes, well, you never really know what someone is thinking or feeling, do you, Lex? You have to want to get close, and they have to let you. And just between you and me..." Brigsby whispered. "...Emma's a bit of a scaredy cat when it comes to love. She tends to, you know...overcompensate."

Lex felt like the very doofus Emma said his pills amplified.

No. What's dumber than doofus? A loser? A fool? A foolfus. Yep. A fucking foolfus. I'm always getting suckered. I guess I always will.

"Does she know that you and I've met?"

"No, no. It's our little secret. Sometimes it's better to keep mutual acquaintances apart...something George is starting to forget."

"How so?"

"Well...it seems that George is quite fond of you, if you hadn't noticed. And to get into your good graces, he was prepared to tell *you*...about *me.* The great introducer."

"You mean that you're the...?"

"Right. That I'm the..."

Lex was flattered—and overwhelmed. "So he knew all this time?"

"Yes, he knew. More people know than you'd think."

"Where's George now?"

Brigsby smirked. "I think you know."

"You mean...like Emma?"

"Mmm...you could say that. Although...I've given him a chance to come back. I do that on occasion. We'll have to see how resourceful he really is. He'll have to find something important. And he'll have to decide just how badly he wants what it will bring him."

Lex sighed, dizzy with revelation overload. "Now what?"

"Well, my good man, we have to decide what to do with you."

Like being dunked in ice water, Lex was now alert and focused. "Stay here, sounding like a crackpot if I tell anyone what I know, or go with Emma, keeping what I know to myself, even though she would almost definitely believe me if I told her."

"Right again. Well done. It's your choice. But you do have to choose."

Lex felt some courage, and even more surprising to him, he voiced it. "Why do I have to choose? I thought you decide? I didn't make this happen. It's not my fault."

"Fault implies blame, Lex. And blame implies punishment. You haven't done anything to be punished for. But you do need to accept responsibility for yourself. You have to decide who you want to be. I can't do that for you. You may not want to believe this, but I don't have that kind of power. And even if I did, I wouldn't choose for you anyway. What would be the point? All those lives everywhere...they'd be useless."

"And if I go down there, to Earth...there's no coming back?"

"Well," Brigsby said. "There's always a miracle."

"I thought you didn't believe in miracles."

Brigsby sipped his drink. "A miracle is something positive and unexpected, Lex. The degree isn't the issue. Whether you choose to notice them is up to you."

Lex sat quietly. And before he sank into his comfortable zone of self-pity, trying to figure out why he needed to be scraped off the floor once again, he laughed to himself. *Fucking foolfus. Fuckin' A.*

Lex poured himself a drink. He let it settle in his mouth. It was the last time he would be able to appreciate such nuance in quite the same way. "I'll go with Emma."

Brigsby's eyes went wide. "Huh. I figured staying was a no-brainer. See, Lex. I don't know everything." He shook his head, and then hesitated. "...Can I ask why you're going? I'm...not sure I get it."

The question that haunted Lex his entire life came into focus just then: *Am I a leader or a follower?* He wanted to be one kind of person, but couldn't escape that he was another. *I'm a follower. And I'm okay with it. Besides, if Emma knew about this, she'd burst a blood vessel. My punishment and my reward, all rolled into one.*

"Actually...I'd rather not say."

Even though he figured Brigsby could read his mind, keeping a secret from The Minder of the Universe was as much control as Lex thought he would ever have over anything.

My reasons are my own. Even if they're wrong. At least they're mine.

Hearing Emma snort and roll over, Lex's long, pointy ears shot up, reminding him once again of where he was, and why. And while he couldn't see the wrinkled face, a single name lingered in his mind: *Brigsby.*

"Had to make me a dog. Ha-ha-ha. He-he-he. What a fucker."

From outside the motel room came the faint scent of chicken-fried steak, French fries and enough gravy to drown a busload of children. Lex contemplated maneuvers to snatch a helping. But before he could remember what he had been dreaming about, he licked his chops, put his paws over his eyes, and fell back to sleep.

Chapter 76
Pack Your Bags

The Eastern Sphere of Eternity—Horizon Terrace
Time Elapsed Since the Milky Way's Public Unveiling: 3 Days
(Eternity Saving Time)

Danielle leaned on the rail of her condo balcony. The sunshine blazed orange against a scarlet sky. A cloud formation took the shape of a squid wrapping its tentacles around an ocean liner.

She couldn't believe it. She couldn't fucking believe it.

A tear tumbled down her cheek, off the balcony and then into the wide expanse of Eternity. It evaporated into the ether, returning to its essence, a part of everything once again. From behind, two arms wrapped around her waist. She could feel warm lips on her neck. The tiny hairs on her earlobe tingled. "Mm...Hi, Baby."

Donald held her snug in that way he did, reminding her that no matter where they were, she could always close her eyes and fall back on her heels, and he would be there. Not holding her up, but holding her. "I wasn't sure you'd be back," she said. "I just didn't know..." Danielle reached behind her, grazed the side of his face. *Yeah. It's really him.* She turned to face her husband, Donald's presence exuding a warmth greater to her than the distant sun. She squeezed him tight. "Oh, Baby. Oh..."

Donald whispered in her ear. "We have to go."

Danielle shuddered. *It's all over.* "So we outta here? We leavin'?"

"Well." Donald led her back inside. "Kind of."

Danielle felt the sun on her back, afraid to take even one more step inside, as if the sun protected her somehow, safe under the clasp of Eternity. Letting the rays slide down the back of her leg—like turning her back on faith—Danielle wanted to speak with conviction. But she could only eke out a tight whisper. Her knees buckled. She clasped her husband's hand. "Don't mess with me. I ain't got the heart for *kinda*."

They sat on the couch. With his finger, Donald rubbed the top of her hand, letting Danielle know that the language they used to define the context of their lives no longer applied. That they were about to get knocked about again. Only *this* time there would be no muthafuckin' *next* time.

"I just heard," Donald said. "We're being re—"

"Oh, mutha..." Danielle shed more tears. "Don't say that word. I can't handle it. I can't, I can't. I just can't."

"No. Oh, no. Don't cry, Baby. It's not re—"

Danielle looked toward the scarlet red of the afternoon sky as it waved in off the balcony. Her heart raced to that awful place deep inside, thinking that if she leaned over and let go maybe she would fall into an endless dream, where the only thing to do was stare into the eyes of her man until there was nothing left but the grace of his love.

"Honey." Donald turned her head. "Re*assigned*," he said. "Re*assigned*."

"I knew it, I knew it. I muthafuckin' knew it." Danielle jerked up and paced the floor. She shook her hands as if air-drying her nails. "We're so fu—" She stopped, then looked to her husband. She felt a surge in her chest. "Wait. What you say?"

Donald stood up. "Reassigned," he said. "Re*assigned*."

Danielle looked toward the balcony once again. Only this time, the scarlet shining red on the floor was like a pathway to freedom. "Reassigned?"

Donald's eyes were open wide. He smiled. Husband and wife stood there for a moment, just looking at each other. Until they broke into dance, chanting their new favorite word over and over and over.

Fuck-in' re-assigned. Uh! Fuck-in' re-assigned. Uh!

"But how, Baby? Where?"

"Guess," Donald said.

"I ain't in no mood for guessing, muthafucka. Tell me whe—"

Donald handed her an official company document. It said that, based on recent events, their talents were better suited for inspecting the CBM warehouse security and communication systems, and that in a week's time, they were to report to their new post. Level 3 clearance.

"Muthafucka," Danielle said.

"Yep. Muthafucka."

Danielle felt a need to confess, to tell her husband that she'd gone to see Brigsby, and asked for help. "You think he did this?"

"Honestly. I really don't know."

"You gonna ask him?"

Danielle watched her husband as he looked around their high-rise apartment, as if for the first time he saw it as theirs, and not on loan.

"Nah. We belong here. I don't care who did what."

The words Danielle had wanted to hear all along. "Wait!" She slapped him on the arm again. "What's with the packing? You said we leavin'."

"Well...I figured we could use a vacation before we start the new job. Four-day cruise to the Edge of Forever. First class all the way."

Danielle leaned into her husband, feeling that the love she'd had for him all along was now cemented in her heart forever.

"Oh...and Danny...I just have one small request."

"Aw...wu'zat my widew pumpky wumpky?"

"When we get back, can we, you know...maybe...get some new furniture? Something a little less...I don't know... leopardy?"

Danielle kissed her husband flush on the mouth. Her plump, juicy lips cushioned against his. And then she pulled away just enough so that their eyes met. She smiled, and let out a little laugh. "Not on your life, muthafucka. Not on your life."

Chapter 77
No Sé

Spain—63 Miles South of the French Border
Thursday, September 22, 2005, 1:51 p.m.

After leaving Amsterdam, Jason and Theo spent three days wandering the cobblestone roads of Bruges, a gothic town forty-five minutes north of Brussels. They smoked a joint beneath the massive arms of an old windmill, ate warm Belgian waffles with the syrup baked right into the dough, and drank giant glasses of cherry beer as the drizzle carried on and on and on.

They spoke little during the long train ride now, not because they had little to say, but because they didn't want to say it. Their time together was coming to an end. Soon it would be time for goodbye.

Jason leaned against the window as the train sped south along Spain's eastern coast. He was excited to arrive in Barcelona and help Theo finally find out about his jar. He *owed* Theo, after all. Jason knew better than to separate in a crowded place, especially a train station, in a foreign country, and on a tight schedule.

But he was a NO person still struggling to become a YES person. Jason had said *yes* an awful lot for him those last few weeks, but under stress, sick with flu, hungry and exhausted, old habits kicked in. *Did I really need to lie down that bad? Couldn't I have held out another five minutes?* Jason wasn't used to YES. He was still fighting an addiction to NO. And like any addict, there was no cure for temptation.

Reuniting with Theo helped Jason reclaim his center, reenergized him when he needed it most. But what lay before him now was something larger still.

Unable to shake the hovering cloud of his impending adult

responsibilities, Jason was mired in an elongated pause, caught between now and then, unwilling to commit to either, yet leaning against both. The thought of having to stand before a room of teenagers every day made him tight in the chest.

Theo struggled with his rucksack. He clipped the black support belt around his waist as the duo stood outside the Barcelona train station. Theo was not accustomed to prolonged companionship.

And while he could not shake the hovering cloud of their impending departures, Theo thrust his thoughts into finding them a place to sleep. It would be their last stop together, so he wanted to make it a good one. Jason's Eurail pass was about to expire. He had to be back in Manchester in three days for his flight to New York.

Theo consulted his guidebook, and with his almost Zen-like confidence led them to the La Ribera section of Barcelona, tracking down a hostel with arched doorways cut from stone. Elaborate tapestries hung from the walls. Ceiling fans circled slowly.

"Hey." Jason smiled. "This place is wild. Nice choice. Mate."

The desk clerk ran her finger down the register. There were two dorm-style rooms with one available bed each. It seemed almost fitting, Theo thought, as if the gods were reminding them that their paths were beginning to diverge. That they would soon have to retire to their separate corners of the Earth.

Jason and Theo wandered through the narrow canyon of buildings off La Rambla, the city's main shopping thoroughfare. The buildings were close in, shading them from the sun, yet allowing a cool Mediterranean breeze to stream through.

Jason felt a comfort in those canyons, an intimacy he was unaccustomed to. The shops and pubs and restaurants were lined one after another, the opposite sides of the streets hardly ten feet apart. The confined, familiar space brought people together rather than forcing them, which got Jason thinking about those things he would rather forget.

"Thing is," he said. "It's hard to be an American right now. Before nine-eleven, we had this swagger, this confidence, like the madness of the world was out *there*, away from us, that it would never really touch us. That it *couldn't* touch us. But after the towers went down, and with every bomb that goes off somewhere, even though hardly anybody says it, we know we'll never feel that invincibility again. But we never were invincible. It just seemed that way. Kind of a silly thing to think, I guess." Jason shook his head. "That world we used to know....It's gone."

Theo nodded. "You Yanks really got in over your heads this time, yeh? In New Zealand, we're this tiny speck nobody notices. We just keep our heads down while the world goes ape shit around us."

Jason chuckled. "Yeah. Back home, we always churn so hard, grinding ourselves down. Work-work-work. More-more-more. Now-now-now. We pretty much live for the weekends. But here...people just seem to live. I dig this two o'clock siesta thing."

They searched the canyons for more than half an hour, looking for the one person who would identify the origin of Theo's jar. After navigating yet another series of alleys, taking them toward the Port of Barcelona, they doubled back, finding themselves walking in a square.

"Is this place even here?" Jason scanned the numbers above the doors. There was a small park on the corner. "I don't see it."

Theo studied Alberto's note: *Vincenzo Italia. de la Guárdia. Thirteen.*"I dunno."

Jason approached an old man in a brim hat who was whistling loudly and off-key. "Uh, excuse me," Jason said. "English?"

The old man stopped. "Sí, yes."

"Beautiful. Do you know this place?" Jason took the note from Theo. "This is the right street, right?" He enunciated it phonetically: *Day-la-gwar-dee-uh.*

"Oh, sí. Sí."

"Dude." Jason elbowed Theo in the ribs. "This is it. We found it."

Theo's eyes widened.

"Pietro no here," the old man said. "Shop close three years ago. Pietro gone."

Theo did not physically collapse, although he may as well have.

"Gone?" Jason said. "Do you know where?"

The old man shook his head. "No sé," he said. "No sé."

Jason offered his sympathy. "Sorry, man. Looks like a wild-goose chase. Maybe we just missed it."

Theo looked down one end of the alley and then the other. He stared up at the sky, now covered in a blanket of dark clouds. He took a series of deep breaths, measuring his own resolve. Those streaking flashes of color, the pulling on his mind, the hallucinations. Ira and Howard. George. The tugging on his soul. They seemed to crumble within him.

"Well?" Jason said. "What do you say? Do we keep looking?" He studied the note again, and then handed it back to Theo. "I'm game if you are."

Theo had been drawn across the world, looking for answers, and now that he was finally in Barcelona, he felt no closer to finding them than when he first left Auckland more than seven months earlier. If anything, he felt further away than ever.

"No," he said dejectedly, folding the paper in half. "It's over."

Chapter 78
Walk in the Park

Yuma, Arizona—Top Joe's Finest Motel
Thursday, September 22, 2005, 1:52 p.m.

Seated on the closed toilet lid, Emma stared at a long, greasy strand of sautéed onion as it dangled from her double bacon cheeseburger. She held it up to her mouth. She watched the grease drip to the floor. Her mirrored reflection stared back.

I'm coming home, Lilly told her over the phone. *And there's no Theo. Do what you want.*

Emma typically soothed her pain with sex, validating her beliefs that any failures she endured were not of her doing. She had learned to adapt on Earth, anesthetizing with food instead. But she was forced to lock herself in the bathroom or else have Lex begging at her feet.

There was an emptiness in her, one that bore deep into her spirit in inverse proportion to her waist, as if she was actually eating her way into the hole in her soul, and not out.

Emma's tongue was covered with the dry paste of saliva and torment. She straightened her posture, able to see herself in the mirror, and though her face was hidden by the burger, her loneliness was completely exposed.

Her hands clenched. She fought the compulsion to shove the food into her mouth, feeding the beast inside until finally she dug her fingers through the soggy bread and meat and toppings and mashed them against the mirror—not just into the glass, but into her own reflection. Into her. "NO!" She shouted it over and over, each howl long and ferocious until finally her throat was as coarse as pummeled cinderblock.

Emma barreled from the bathroom. *SLAM!* She snatched her walking stick. She grabbed the room key off the table.

Lex circled around, fearful of another beating, but looking for the burger. "Where are you going?"

"For a very. Long. Walk. Got a problem with that, fuckhead?"

And just as that single word came out of her mouth—
fuckhead—Emma became dizzy. She stumbled, wanting desperately to reach out into time and space and yank back all
the nasty things she'd said to Lex. She had lost control of
herself, made excuses for becoming less than she was. Emma
had been swatting away her guilt like a Ping-Pong ball in a
wind funnel, shooing it into the swirl, only to have it blown
back in her face.

She tried to build an empire by knocking down those
around her, by reminding them that they were unworthy of
her, when all along she was demonstrating that maybe she was
unworthy of them. While Emma had complained about those
who wanted to see her fail, she had done nothing to help others succeed. She forced her way up through talent and will, but
her self-imposed exile while *in* Eternity led to her banishment
from it.

She sat on the edge of the bed. "I was so close," she
whispered.

Lex took a cautious step toward her.

"I'm just...I'm so..." Emma sighed, cried a little. "...Do
you...you know...want to...go for a walk?" She cried a bit more.
"With me?"

Lex hesitated before answering. "Really?"

Watching his tail wag, Emma realized that for the remain-
der of their days on Earth, Lex would forever be a dog—a
canine. That those days would be far fewer for him than for
her, and that unless she participated in the positive outcome of
their lives, her own final days would be lonely indeed. Emma
felt more tears well up.

"Yeah." She rubbed the inside of his ears. "That would be
nice."

"Sweet. There's this new signpost I've been meaning to
check out."

Accepting that the CBM jar would never find its way to her,
Emma smiled, wiped her face and then grabbed a plastic baggie
off the table. Lex led the way, stepping out into the sunshine.
The door closed behind them.

And even though Emma had designed the Milky Way,

representing a force behind this planet far greater than anyone would ever know, her remaining days with Lex now felt bigger and more important than any of it. "I've been thinking," she said. "You know those cybercafés we've been going to? I know how we could start a chain. *The Starlight Café*. This is what I have in mind..."

Chapter 79
Have You Seen the Muffin Man?

Auckland, New Zealand—Barnes Residence
Thursday, September 22, 2005, 1:53 p.m.

Roger had Carla's hand in a sweaty grip outside his house. But the front door—one he had opened and closed literally thousands of times without consideration—now seemed daunting. Imposing.

He finally took Davey's advice and decided—fuck it—today would be the day for Carla to meet his mum. Now even. If she wanted. Carla wanted. But now that the moment arrived, Roger wasn't ready to face it. He took a deep breath. The sun was obscured by a patch of clouds.

Roger played the scenario in his mind. He would walk through the door and announce that, *yes, this is Carla, my...girlfriend. That's right. I said it.* But in making such a declaration he would also be confessing—to his mother—that he actively thought about sex, and having sex with *this* girl. He would also be confessing—to his mother—that he longed for the soft, gentle touch of a girl, *this* girl, and that they would all have to find a way to be okay with it.

"Just...like, let me get it all started, yeh?"

Carla extricated her hand. "Easy, killer. I'm sure she's very sweet."

By the blips of his watch, Roger knew that it took no more than three seconds to extend his hand to the knob, twist it, and then open the door. Yet his heart revved with such intensity, he felt that perhaps he would flood his system and pass out.

"Uh...Mum." Roger led them into the living room. He craned his head as if he would somehow be spared the initial shame of his mother watching him with a girl, *this* girl, like when he was a child, thinking that if he covered his eyes and couldn't see you, then you couldn't see him. He smelled cinnamon muffins baking in the oven. "Mum, I want you to m—"

Roger already was in mid-palpitation when he saw his mother at the kitchen table, her hands awkwardly pulling away from a short, handsome, well-dressed Taiwanese man.

"Roger, my goodness." His mother shuffled and then stood up, took two coffee mugs and put them in the sink, far from her guest. She dried her hands on her duckling apron. "I didn't hear you come in. Roger...this is George, yeh? He's a—"

Caught between a smear of shame, anger and thrill, Roger thought *he* was the one about to introduce *his* secret friend.

"Greetings, Roger. I'm George. Please don't be—"

There was a loud knock at the door. Roger flinched as if a gun had gone off. He saw Davey's face pressed against the screen.

"Oi, mate. G'day." Davey let himself in. "Was in the neighborhood, like, and figured I'd drop by. Hope that's all right, yeh?"

"Uh," Roger said. "Wh—"

"Oh, yeh. I brought someone."

Roger swallowed hard.

Carla. Mum. George. Davey. And now?

In his mind, Roger repeated the singsong: *I-don't-see-you, you-don't-see-me. I-don't-see-you, you-don't-see-me.*

Davey made the introductions. "You remember Rufus? I know we was supposed to come tomorrow, like, but turns out he's gotta shove off tonight. I didn't think your dad would mind."

Rufus nodded. "George. I didn't recognize you without your pumps."

George shrugged. "Sorry about that. I just assumed you knew."

"Eh?" Davey turned to Rufus. "This your mate?"

"We're...acquaintances," George said. "From back home."

"Well ain't that a yank on your chain." Davey turned back to Roger. "So, mate? You finally introduced your girlie. What do you say, Mrs. B?"

Carla. Mum. George. Davey. Rufus.

"Oh, uh...fine David, fine. I wasn't expecting all this company. Let me get some tea started. I've got muffins in the oven."

Roger was on the verge of freaking out in a way that would very much *not* cement his reputation as a man amongst men. "Davey. Come here for a second. I wanna—"

"Actually," Rufus said. "I'd like to wrap this up. It has been a long trip and my destination is not...easily accessible."

"Well, my dad's just outs—"

Rufus removed a shiny black pistol. He cocked the hammer. Roger, like the others, went suddenly still.

Carla. Mum. George. Davey. Rufus. Gun.

"It's a World War Two Walther P38 German pistol. We can make a trade," Rufus said, "or we can get unpleasant. I suggest you give me the jar, and that you do it quickly."

Davey was not impressed. "Oi! Mate. Are you off your lid? What's with the gun? You're gonna blow someone's head off, yeh?"

"The jar," Rufus repeated. "Get it now."

Roger's heart and mind raced with equal ferocity.

I-don't-see-you, you-don't-see-me. I-don't-see-you, you-don't-see-me.

He felt underwater again, submerged in a dream he hadn't completely understood until now. When a blue whale named Howard told him two things: don't let your girl slip away, and when you're standing in your kitchen surrounded by strangers, do as you're told. Roger was able to compose himself. "How did you know about that?"

"You've held it in your hands," Rufus said. "I could tell just by looking at you."

"Rufus," George said. "You're being rude. Perhaps you can just—"

"This doesn't concern you...Angelique. There's no other way. They couldn't possibly understand, and I have no capacity to explain."

"They might surprise you. The Rufus I knew wasn't so rash."

"I'll get it," Roger said. "It's right—"

George cut in. "No. We've got it here. Lydia, would you mind?"

Roger's eyes lit up as his mother opened a cabinet above the sink. She removed a green duffel bag. There was a noticeable sag at one end.

"It was in Theo's greenhouse," she said. "Behind the plant spray."

"But...," Roger started. *No it wasn't. That's not where I put it.*

"I'll take that," Rufus said. "And then I'll be off."

"What jar, mate?" Davey looked at Roger. "What's he on about?"

"It's nothing. Don't worry about it."

"Nothing, my balls. Oh, sorry, Mrs. B. But that's a load of s.h.i.t."

"The bag," Rufus said. "Hand it to me."

Roger took the duffel bag from his mother. He considered his options: grab the gun (die of gunshot wound); run (die of shame); fall down and cry (also die of shame); give over the bag (live with shame).

Roger looked at George, whom he wanted to pummel into Kiwi paste and yet hug for just being there. He looked to Carla, who got more than she bargained for, and then to his mother, who wore an expression of love and worry that he had never seen before but was probably there all along. Time to make a decision.

"Yeh," he finally said, and handed the bag to Rufus. He would apologize to Theo when he got home. "Here you—"

There was another bang at the door, followed by the entrance of a large, tattooed biker, and then another, and another and then four more still.

"Aputa?" Davey said. "What the fu...eff are you doing here?"

Aputa pointed at Rufus. "Looking for this chum. Whoa! Gun!"

The Cougars all removed guns of their own, pointing them squarely at Rufus, who was no longer in command. "I'll take that," Aputa said. "Somebody ain't playing right."

Bing!

Aputa scanned the kitchen. "What was that?"

Roger shrugged, surrounded by his girl, his mother, a gang of drug dealers and some dude named George. "I think the muffins are ready. Want one?"

Chapter 80
Finders Keepers

Barcelona, Spain—Dos Libera Hostel
Thursday, September 22, 2005, 10:49 p.m.

Jason already felt his head nodding in rhythm to *Vertigo* by U2, drawn toward the open archway up and to the left. A glow of orange light thrust out into the stairwell.

Theo heard about a hostel that hosted parties every Thursday night near the eastern end of La Rambla, not far from where Pietro should have been...but was not. The sixty-meter monument honoring Christopher Columbus was nearby. The column jut up in the middle of a traffic circle, directing travelers into the heart of the city.

Jason stopped halfway up the staircase and turned to Theo, who was muttering to himself and laughing. "What's so funny?"

"Oh, I dunno." Theo put his palm against the wall. "I was pretty bummed, yeh? I had no idea what Pietro would say...I didn't even care...I just wanted to find him. I've been going so long. But now...I feel like the weight's off me, yeh? Maybe some things we aren't supposed to find. Maybe some things just find you."

Jason nodded, and in his mind's eye saw Theo on that street corner in Amsterdam, just waiting. "Yeah," he said, "they sure do."

In a room full of partiers in various stages of sweat, inebriation and undress, Jason took two beers from the señorita tending bar. There was a bowl of chips on the counter. The smell of salsa burned Jason's nostrils. "Last night together," he said, and clinked bottles. "Let's make it count."

As the beer went down cold, Jason wanted to say something to Theo, something he felt worth saying out loud, lest he never say it at all. That for all his days, Jason would remember how his own acts of foolishness had almost derailed their friendship, and that Theo had rescued it from the fire, when he stuffed reason in an old trunk and scoured the continent for him anyway, going purely on instinct. On devotion.

For reminding Jason that you never lose faith when a friend of substance comes into your life. You never let them slip away. "Oh, hell." Jason embraced Theo. "Thanks," he said, and patted Theo on the back. "Thanks for not giving up on m—"

There was a blast of white light. There were streaks of screaming fluorescent color. There was the sensation of being sucked through a tornado. And then there was a party. A loud, wild party.

"Dude." Jason shook his head. "That's it." He looked at his beer, put it on the bar. "You felt that, right? That flash, that color? That...tornado thingy?" He looked at the beer once more, then back at Theo. "What the hell was that?"

Maybe it was the music, maybe it was the beer buzz or maybe it was the half-dressed women, Barcelona or their circumstances in total, but Theo felt an energy that lifted his spirits more than he had felt in a long, long time.

So without censoring himself, he told Jason what he truly believed but hadn't until then said out loud to anyone—that the jar he found deep in the Waitomo Caves just might contain some sort of heavenly or even cosmological element...perhaps the very essence of the Universe...and that, for whatever reason, he was meant to find it. And that ever since, he had been having hallucinations, like rocketing through the center of the galaxy.

Had Jason heard what he thought he heard at any other time, in any other place and under any other circumstance, he would have testified under oath that Theo had quite clearly poured himself a heaping cup of crazy and then gone back for sprinkles.

But between the circuitous journey Jason had followed over the past month and those tripped-out hallucinations, he couldn't dismiss the possibility—as insane as it sounded—that maybe Theo was on the level. But a Universe jar?

Come on. I mean, it couldn't be true...could it?...Could it?

Jason looked at Theo...really looked at him...seeing those hesitant eyes staring back, and though there was laughter and pulsing music all around them, they faded away.

Is he just fucking with me, or is he out of his mind?

Behind those eyes was a message: *I know this sounds insane, but I'm serious. This is real. Don't give up on me. This is real....This is real.*

Jason felt tight in the gut. Not because Theo was yanking his chain, but because maybe he was telling the truth. And if the jar really did contain molecules of the Universe—the essence of everything in Existence—then he was being asked to make a decision.

But what am I supposed to do?

Rather than as philosophically abstract, Jason started thinking of the Universe just then as a tangible realm, an actual place forged with magic and mystery, myth and superstition, danger and possibility.

And then he realized something important about himself—that he was now looking at the Universe from an altered perspective compared to even a few weeks earlier. That it all wasn't just some pool of milk more sour than sweet. That maybe the Universe really was some boundless, intricate mechanism with cosmic coils and springs and gears that unfold in just such a way. That it isn't all random or pointless.

But either way, Jason was starting to figure that Hank was right after all. That he should try to enjoy himself as thoroughly and often as he could, because maybe the gears were meant to thrash apart tomorrow, or even tonight, or maybe they would churn forever. But since he wasn't likely to ever find out which, why not maximize on the time he had left?

A month earlier, Jason couldn't have imagined standing where he was now. But having made it this far, he couldn't imagine standing anywhere else.

Theo stood before Jason and, for just a moment, considered telling him that it was all just a joke, that they should have a good laugh and forget the whole thing. *A Universe jar? Easy, mate. I'm taking the piss.* But Theo didn't want that. He wanted Jason to believe him when he said that maybe the jar really did contain something beyond them, that its immense power had affected him in ways he was unable to articulate. And that he wasn't as bat shit as he sounded.

So when Jason let out a thundering laugh that had them both doubled over in hysterics, Theo was relieved. Not because Jason thought it was funny, which he did, but because the laughter came from someplace very different indeed.

Jason felt a tap on the shoulder. And when he turned around, greeting him was a short, curvy girl in her early twenties, with black hair, blue eyes and olive skin. A cluster of permanent acne scars rolled over her cheekbones.

"Excuse me," she said. "Are you American? I heard your accent."

Jason liked what he saw. Her energy was remarkable. "New York. How—?"

"Me, too!" She slapped his arm playfully. "You're the first person I've met here from back home."

"Same," Jason said above Duran Duran. "What's your name?"

"Anna." She extended her hand. They shook. "Nice to meet you."

"...Her name is Rio and she dances on the sand..."

Jason felt another blast of adrenaline. And while he again had that woozy sensation, that pull of familiarity and excitement, he also had a peculiar sense of safety and calm, as if there was nothing to worry about. Which, of course, there wasn't.

"...Just like that river twisting through...a dusty land..."

He looked over to Theo, who tried pulling away from a

drunken Austrian dude with a booming laugh, spilling his beer as he tugged Theo by the arm.

"So where'd you get this scar?" Anna touched Jason's elbow, holding her hand there long enough to signal an invitation toward intimacy. "It looks painful."

"...And when she shines she really shows you all she can..."

Jason laughed a laugh layered with understanding, experience and humility.

"What?" Anna offered a smile. "What's so funny?"

"...Oh Rio Rio dance across...the Rio Grande..."

"It's kind of embarrassing," he said. "Do you know anything about Whiffleball?"

Five beers and two tequila shots later, Theo leaned against the wall. He studied Jason sitting in a wicker chair, with Anna on his lap. They were kissing—subtle, gentle— enjoying the sensation of first contact, lips against lips, fingertips against fingertips.

Theo knew that for all his days he would have a friend, that if he could trust Jason with the biggest, most off-the-wall secret he had...he could trust him with anything. And it wasn't just that Jason believed him, but that they shared those...hallucinations...those blasts of white light, those streaks of screaming fluorescent color. Other than Roger, how could anybody comprehend what Theo had been going through?

And so he admired his friend. A friend he would visit. In America.

Theo made himself that promise. One day he would feel consumed by the spirit of the Grand Canyon. He would motorcycle across the Golden Gate Bridge. He would stand in the center of the Brooklyn Bridge and gaze out onto New York.

Maybe they would even do those things together.

Theo made himself that promise. It wasn't a matter of *if*. It was a matter of *when*.

Chapter 81
Have You Seen the Muffin Man?
Part II--Electric Boogaloo

Auckland, New Zealand—Barnes Residence

Thursday, September 22, 2005, 2:18 p.m.

Lydia and Carla served the tea and muffins. "It's nice to meet you, Mrs. Barnes, although it's not exactly how I pictured it."

"Indeed, dear. You're very sweet." Lydia then glanced at Roger, who looked at the floor. "We'll deal with him later."

"Ooooooh," Davey said, "you are soooo busted."

The Cougars, each holding little white teacups with a rose pattern along the sides, started chanting. *"BUS-TED! BUS-TED! BUS-TED!"*

"Enough!" Aputa barked. "Let's finish our business, and let these nice people get on with their lives. Rufus. *Tt-tt-tt.* You really shouldn't play with guns, right boys?"

Again, the Cougars shouted. *"YIP-YIP-YIP-YIP-YIP-YIP-YIP-YIP-YIP!"*

"But to not even load it..." Aputa pulled the clip out of Rufus' gun and showed the room that it was empty. "Tell 'em the rules, boys."

"No bullets, no GUN! Or get your ass up out and RUN!"

"No bullets, no GUN! Or get your ass up out and RUN!"

"All right, boys. All right. Rufus was supposed to make a delivery this morning, but when he didn't show up, and I saws him driving off with little brother here, well...I gots to figuring he was up to something. He got our money, but he ain't delivered our package. Now, that doesn't sound like very good business to me at all."

"Mister Aputa," George said.

"*Mister,*" Aputa repeated. "You hear that boys? Mister. I like that."

"Ooooooooooh," they said in unison. "Mi-stirrr. Ooooooooooh."

"So the ways I see it," Aputa said, "either you give me the package you promised, or you hand over that little green bag of yours. And then we take you for a drag."

"I have what you want. It's in the car." Rufus tried to stand, but the smallest, yet strongest of the Cougars put a hand on his shoulder. He forced Rufus back into his chair.

"We'll check the car," Aputa said. "Sit tight."

"No. You have no idea what you're dealing with."

"Well, well, well." Aputa stuck his gun in Rufus' ear. "This ain't really the time for *no*, mate. You can either say *yes* on your own, or we can help you. Your choice."

"Aputa," Davey said. "This is my mate's home. Mrs. B is our host."

"My apologies, Mrs. B. It's just that, as you can see, we've got a bit of a situa—" Aputa looked about as a low, yet unmistakable vibration started up through the floor. And then, coming from the distance, they all heard a loud *THWUB*.

And then another *THWUB* and another *THWUB* and then *THWUB-THWUB-THWUB-THWUB-THWUB-THWUB-THWUB*... until finally the vibrations became stronger and stronger. The floor rumbled. Walls shook. Teacups crashed to the floor. Pictures dropped to their sides.

Aputa shouted. "What the hell?! There ain't no earthquakes here."

The rumbling grew deeper and louder and louder still. The ceiling fan came loose. Wind and pebbles slammed into the windows from the outside.

...*THWUB-THWUB-THWUB-THWUB-THWUB-THWUB-THWUB-THWUB*...

We woke the jar, Roger thought. *We have to get it out of here.*

Aputa shouted. "Everybody outside! Now!"

In the confusion, Roger grabbed the duffel bag from Rufus, who himself was dragged outside by two Cougars. Roger took Carla by the hand, Lydia in tow. The house shook to the point where they thought it would completely break apart.

...*THWUB-THWUB-THWUB-THWUB-THWUB-THWUB-THWUB-THWUB*...

Ducking beneath the whipping wind, they could see that the rumbling did not come from earthquake, tornado, plague or apocalypse. Instead, they saw these massive whirling blades slice through the sky as a giant, motorized beast hovered overhead. And seated behind a glass bubble was Oscar Barnes.

Roger shouted. "GEORGE! Watch my mum, yeh? I gotta get rid of this." George nodded. "Carla." Roger kissed her. "Ready to ride?" And then he strode forward. That is, he tried to. Before his left foot even touched the ground, he was jerked back like a dog on its leash. He landed on his ass beside a row of bushes. Dust swirled in his face.

When Roger looked up, the most dangerous and violent of the Cougars—Pooky—was standing above him, blocking out the sun. Pooky appeared as an immense shadow, his edges alighted by the rays. One of his very large hands was coiled into a fist. Between Roger and the shadow was the green duffel bag.

As Pooky leaned down for it, his black T-shirt came into view. In white letters, it read: *It Ain't My Fault You Suck This Much.* "I don't think so, mate! That's our payday, like. I'll be taking tha—"

Before Pooky could finish, Roger scrambled on the lawn, grabbed the duffel bag and then rolled behind a tree Theo had planted a decade earlier. The branches were thin, but it was a barrier nonetheless.

Carla was a few feet ahead, shielding her eyes from the whipping dirt and leaves. George and Lydia were huddled by the house. The remaining Cougars had Rufus near the motorcycles. Aputa stood in front. The helicopter was descending upon them.

...*THWUB-THWUB-THWUB-THWUB-THWUB-THWUB-THWUB-THWUB*...

"Playtime's over," Pooky shouted. "I'm gonna wipe my dog's ass with your skull!"

"Carla!" Roger waived her toward Theo's truck. "Go-go-go!" And then he made a break for it. But his trip, such that it was, ended much the same as his first stab at getting away—abruptly. Quick and powerful, Pooky tackled Roger, who hit the ground hard. His head took the worst of it.

Pooky leaned over. "Gimme that!" He grabbed the bag and

held it up, signaling to Aputa, who nodded. With that, Pooky turned to Roger, his free hand drawn into a fist. He zeroed in on Roger's forehead. "And this is for being such a little cock fucker."

With the *THWUB-THWUB-THWUB* overhead, Roger closed his eyes.

I-don't-see-you, you-don't-see-me. I-don't-see-you, you-can't-hurt-me.

But if Roger knew anything, he knew that Pooky could definitely see him, and that the pain would be very real indeed. "Let's get this over with." But as he prepared for the inevitable crunch against his head, Roger heard a wild, yet familiar voice.

"Fuck that, you asshole!" Davey barreled Pooky to the ground, jammed his knee between the back of the biker's legs and into his crotch, crushing ole lefty, keeping the much bigger and stronger Pooky face down in the grass.

"Go, mate." Davey handed Roger the bag. "Aputa's gonna have my ass for this. And this guy's gonna fucking kill me. You better run. Sorry about the mess."

Beneath the swirling helicopter rotors, Roger piled into Theo's truck, where Carla was waiting with the engine running. They sped off from the driveway.

Yet before the Cougars could head after them, Oscar settled the helicopter on the front lawn, blowing half the gang to the ground, and into the bushes. Their motorcycles toppled like dominoes. During the melee, Rufus managed to crawl out from Theo's rose garden, climb into Davey's car and speed after Roger. After the jar.

"Sorry about all this," Roger said to Carla. "I had no—"

"Just drive! But nice intro, mate. Very romantic."

Roger was leading them to Rotorua. Also known as "Sulfur City," the lake town was layered with bubbling mud pools, gurgling, hot springs and, most importantly, gushing geysers. He needed to get rid of the bag. Permanently.

They drove as fast as Theo's truck would take them, first along Highway 1 and then southeast along Highway 5. Roger and Carla were in the lead, followed by Rufus in Davey's car, and then the Cougars, on motorcycles. Davey rode with Aputa.

After that peculiar day at Cathedral Cove—after their underwater hallucination—Theo instructed Roger what to do, just in case. "Theo's gonna owe me huge for this."

After almost three hours on the road and with the needle falling dangerously close to *Empty*, Roger and Carla curved around Lake Rotorua, and finally to the small town of Tikitere, or *Hell's Gate*. Sulfur emanated from the soil and muddy pools like a mist of rotten eggs. They pulled into a gravel parking lot, with a large sign out front:

HELL'S GATE. HOME OF THE HOT GEYSERS. BEWARE EXTREME HEAT.

Roger and Carla jumped the turnstile. They ran along wooden platforms, taking them in a zigzag pattern up and around the gurgling, steaming mud pits. They made their way through the crowd of tourists waiting for the centerpiece geyser—the Devil's Eye—to erupt, as it did roughly every twenty-three minutes.

The New Zealanders respect the land, believing it to be sacred and honorable. Throwing garbage was like spitting at Mother Earth. And even though there were a dozen signs prohibiting it, Roger was about to discard the bag into the one place where it could never be found again.

"You sure?" Carla asked.

"Have to." Roger pointed at Rufus, followed by Davey, Aputa and the Cougars. "Or else it's just more of this." He shrugged. "Fuck it. Here we go." Roger swung his arms. He hurled the bag into the air. It soared over the sacred ground in a long, high arch, momentarily shielding him from the sun. And then it dropped from the heavens, finally landing in the molten sludge, sinking...sinking. Gone.

There was a loud slurping sound, followed by a steaming *bloop!* Rufus and the Cougars stopped, transfixed as the molten earth swallowed the bag whole. And then right on schedule, the geyser erupted, shooting higher and more spectacularly than anyone had ever remembered.

Aputa grabbed Roger by the scruff. "You *ain't* supposed to do that."

Roger nodded quickly. "I know, I know." He gestured at Rufus.

"Yeh. Okay. But you're gonna come back here." Aputa lifted Roger off his feet. "You're gonna work off your debt to us Kiwis. That's no bullshit. You don't mess with the land. The gods don't like it, and neither do I. It's our home, mate, not a dump. We're gonna work out a little program for you with the bastards that run this place. However many hours they say, that's how many you work here for free, doing whatever crap job they give you. Got it?"

Roger's feet dangled above the platform. "Okay, okay. Fine. But what about them?" Two security guards approached, hands on their nightsticks.

"Don't worry. We'll handle it."

"And what about—?"

Only Rufus was gone. It was as if he simply vanished into the ether.

Aputa let Roger go. "Don't know, mate. Don't know. Lucky for you he had our package where he said. I think we've seen the last of ole Rufus...although, I don't see where he could have gotten off to."

Carla took Roger by the hand. "We should get home. Your mum'll be worried."

Aputa winked, started to chuckle. "Your mum, huh? You are so gonna get it, mate. You are so gonna get it."

Chapter 82
Closing Time

Barcelona, Spain—Libera Section
Friday, September 23, 2005, 2:43 a.m.

The rain fell. Hard. The hostel closed at 3 a.m every night, locking its doors until 7 a.m. They would not open in between. Not for emergencies. Not for anything. It was 2:43 a.m. Time was running out.

Drunk on beer and Anna's perfume, Jason ran his fingers through his hair, moppy from the downpour. The raindrops were thick as dollops of pancake batter. "Think they'd lock us out?"

"I dunno," Theo said. "I'm pissed as a fart."

"Do you know the way back?"

Theo shrugged.

"Yep," Jason said. "Me neither."

"Wait!" Theo dashed into the street. "I remember! This way!"

They ran to the traffic circle as cabs drove by the Columbus column. Headlights blinded them beneath the black of night.

Once again, Jason found himself in familiar territory, relying on Theo to navigate their way, when quite unexpectedly Jason stopped running. He didn't understand why—only that it was necessary. That he needed to remain still as the rain poured over him.

He felt a great rush to the head. For the moment there was no darkness, there was no traffic. There was no rain and no Theo. Jason was overcome by a sudden wave of fear, as if some greater force—maybe even the hands of the Universe itself—held him in a cloak of anticipation, preparing for a physical and emotional contortion.

Something's coming.

Jason leaned against a lamppost. A car splashed him. He

hunched forward, let his head drop, bracing for the purge. Only instead of salsa and beer foam, he expelled a breath that made him woozy and disoriented—one that had been working through his psyche for years.

"I don't want to do it," he said finally.

Theo yelled over the monsoon. "What's that? I can't hear you!"

"I'm not going to teach!"

Despite his schooling, somewhere along the way Jason stopped asking whether a choice he made when he was eighteen still made sense for him at twenty-four. All along he had been telling himself that teaching was a noble profession, that he would be making a difference.

And he did like teaching, even loved it at times, feeling that when he was at his best, he was really something to see. But teaching was a considerable responsibility for a young man who was only just beginning to appreciate the experiences his life offered. He had ignored that his ideas about the world at large... about himself...were no longer the same as they once were.

Soaked down to his boxer shorts, Jason realized that along his pursuit to *become* a teacher, he forgot to ask himself if he still wanted to *be* a teacher. And while it saddened him to give up what had been such a large part of his world, he was surprised at how easy it was to let go. "I'm done!"

"Oh, yeh?" The rush of water cascaded on the pavement like bacon stips sizzling in a pan. "Why's that?"

"All these years...I never gave myself any options! I couldn't see myself doing anything else! It sounded good, but the truth is...I just don't want it!"

"You just figured that out?"

"Yeah!" Jason shrugged, wondering if those jar-induced hallucinations helped him find his way, or if he would have gotten there regardless. "Who knew?"

"Great!...What are you going to do now?"

Jason raised his hands to the rain. "No clue." Never before had Jason felt so damn good about the unknown.

Theo led the way down one street, made a left down another, until finally they were back before the Columbus monument, the old explorer pointing the way. Theo had another blast of recognition. "Oh! I know!" They stomped through puddles, making a left through a courtyard, and down a narrow street. Amid the thunderous downpour came a church bell warning that their time was about to expire.

Claaaaaaaang! Claaaaaaaang! Claaaaaaaang!

"Hold it." Theo jammed his foot over the threshold, his foot crushed behind the weight of the massive door. "We're here. Hang on."

The desk clerk opened the door. "You are late." She pointed to the grandfather clock in the lobby. It denoted 3:01 a.m. "You should *not* be late."

"You're right." Jason peeled off his shirt, then wrung it out. "I'm not teaching anymore. What do you think about that?"

Theo and Jason started laughing. The clerk shushed them.

After a deep sleep—and the hostel's morning changeover of backpacker tenants—Jason sat on the floor next to his bunk. He rummaged through his money belt, pulling out the litter of receipts and ticket stubs he had accumulated over the past month. With Theo in the next room, Jason sorted them into neat piles, and then unpacked and repacked his rucksack, giving him a sense of control. Soon, he would leave Theo behind.

And yet Jason smiled a quick little smile, thinking that perhaps it really was time to go. That he could handle much more than he thought. Jason could map out a plan to Manchester. He could do it alone. He was ready.

Rather than start back across Europe, find his way into Bangkok and then finally New Zealand, Theo decided to remain in Barcelona for a few more days. He had an open-ended ticket, so there was no rush. He would be home soon enough.

Instead, Theo borrowed Jason's rain slicker and headed into a storm. There was one more thing to take care of first.

With time before his train departed Barcelona, Jason wrote a postcard to his sister.

9-23-05

Hey Jill,

As much as it kills me to say it—you were right. This trip was just what I needed. (I know, I know. Put it in secret storage for a later date).

I'm heading out of Barcelona in a few hours even though my clothes are still soaked from last night, but that's a whole other story...with a few sidebars to it.

I'll probably be home before this postcard, but I thought of you just now. I'm packing up for England, and I found something you gave me. Remember the keychain? ASK ME IF I CARE.

I do. More than ever.

Jason

Theo pulled the hood back. The rain let up. He walked up and down *de la Guárdia*, needing to know if Pietro was really gone. If Theo was going to fly back across the world, he wanted to make sure he hadn't given up too soon.

He studied the note for any secret codes that may have been embedded in the text. Did he need to read it backwards? Upside down? Hold it to a mirror?

No, no and no.

After examining the entrance to his unlucky thirteen, Pietro's long vacated shop, Theo sat in the doorway, playing with pebbles he picked out of the cobblestone street. He closed his eyes, hoping the answer would appear, except that when he let his mind drift, all he wanted was to sleep. To stop chasing a dream.

Theo tossed a pebble to the street, then another. When he reached for a third, he noticed something scratched into the old brick. He got down on all fours to see it clearly. It read: *Theo. Sorry about the mess. George.*

Theo shook his head and chuckled. His smile was wide.

Standing in front of the subway station, Jason's rucksack felt lighter somehow. And yet somehow heavier. The sky was dark. "So," he said. "I guess this is it."

Theo nodded. "Yeh," he said.

And then there was silence between them, neither wanting to take the first step, leading them in opposite directions.

After awhile, Jason sighed. "So," he repeated. There was a rumble, and then new rain. A businesswoman fanned her umbrella. "I guess that's my cue. God doesn't want us to be dry."

Theo let out an uncomfortable laugh. Jason did the same. And then they hugged it out, two friends going their separate ways. And though they both anticipated it, there was no blast of white light. No streaks of screaming fluorescent color. No sensation of being sucked through a tornado. Only friendship. Lots and lots of friendship.

Jason started down the stairs, leaving his friend behind. But just before he headed into the subway station, he turned around instead. "Fuck it," he said, and started back up. "I got an idea."

Without needing an explanation, Theo thought exactly the same thing.

Chapter 83
Two-Fers

Theo stepped out of the cab, thinking that his home looked bigger somehow, for the first time noticing its significance. Its magnitude.

Nobody knew he was coming. And while Theo was correct in assuming that when he walked through the front door he would ultimately find his dad sitting cross-legged at the kitchen table with the newspaper spread out, he never would have predicted what was in his father's lap: Theo's mother.

"Theo, my boy!" his father said. "When's you get in, yeh?"

Lydia leapt up and smothered Theo with kisses.

"Just now. Hi, Mum. What's going on?" Theo's parents were in the same room. Together. Smiling. His dad threw a bear hug around him. Startled, Theo resisted at first, unaccustomed to his father's embrace, but finally accepted it for what it was. Love.

"Have a good trip, then? We missed you, son. Good to have you back."

"Uh, good to be home…Dad."

"Hey! Assmonkey!" Roger slapped his shoulder. "Look who's here." Carla was right behind him. "This is my girl, mate."

"We just love Carla." Lydia gave her a squeeze. "She's a doll."

"Mum." Roger blushed. "Come on…"

"Before you get bonkers on me…this is Jason. From New York. From America."

"Hiya Jason." Lydia kissed him on the cheek. "Welcome to our happy home. Isn't Theo something?"

"Uh," Theo said, baffled. He looked to Jason, and shrugged. "I'm a little…"

"Indeed," his father said. "I think you oughta sit down."

Sensing there was much he had missed during his time

away, Theo took a seat at the table. He accepted a glass of juice from his mother. They were all staring at him, as if they knew something he didn't.

"Oh, I can't take it," his mother said. "We just love *her*, too."

"*Her?*" Theo heard the toilet flush. He looked down the hallway. And when the bathroom door opened, out came someone he had all but forgotten about. "Lea. What are you—?"

Theo had not seen her since back in Waitomo, when they shared a hallucinatory sexual experience far beyond the limits of their flesh. When he felt as if he had been ripped out of his skin. When his spirit had been set free to roam the limitless shores of Existence. When he woke up in a motel room to find her gone. When he decided to troll the world in search of answers that now seemed far less important than the questions.

Lea looked just as he remembered. Except for the rosy glow. And the significant bulge in her midsection. She patted her stomach.

Theo's eyes went wide. His hands started to shake.

"Hi, Daddy." Lea pressed her lips against his cheek. "Wanna feel?"

"I...," Theo said. "Wu...uh?"

"Twins!" his mother blurted. "Can you believe it? Girls! Finally!"

"Two for the price of one," his father said. "Well done, mate."

"Yep." Roger slapped his shoulder again. "You're gonna have two stinky butts to wipe. Oh, man, this is gonna be sweet."

Jason's eyes went wide. "Twins? Dude..."

Theo held his juice. It was yellow. And then the room went black.

Jason sat on Theo's bed. He had a call to make. "Hey," he said into the phone. "Guess where I am?" Theo's bedroom faced the yard. A breeze came through the open window. Posters hung on the wall, one each of Bob Marley, Led Zeppelin and Kylie Minogue.

Through the phone came the *clack* of Hank's lighter. "New

Zealand. Obviously. How you like them Kiwis?"

"Wait...how did you know that?"

"Caller ID, Kid. Get with the twenty-first century. So...good trip?"

"Yeah. Awesome. But I want to—"

"Hang on a second. Someone wants to say hello."

Jean was on the call. "Alright, Jason. Having fun, yeah? Hank says you've been having quite the time of it."

"Hi, Jean. It's been great. But, uh...what are you doing there? I mean..."

"Ohhh...I think Hank played a fast one, didn't he?"

Hank inhaled on a cigarette. "Okay...you got me, Kid." Exhale. "You asked me once what I gave a horse's hairy nut about. Well...you're talking to her."

"Always so charming," Jean said. "I'm just the luckiest woman alive."

"Look, Kid. So maybe I pushed you to Manchester to help me get back in touch with my number one girl, here....What are you gonna do? Two for the price of one."

Jason chuckled. "Why am I not surprised?"

"So," Hank said. "You find yourself a nice lady friend or what?"

Jason blushed, and then picked up the set of waterproof boots next to Theo's bed. They were heavier than he thought they would be. Theo's hardhat was tipped on its side.

"Oh, you did, you dirty dog. You scored. Now we're talking. That's...Wait! You didn't fall in love, did you? Tell me you didn't." Hank took another drag. "Kid's a hopeless romantic. Can't help himself."

"Just like you, Dear." Then to Jason, "I'm sure she's a sweetheart."

Jason smiled. The bed squeaked. "Don't worry. No love."

"Really?" Hank said. "Swear it to the man upstairs?"

Jason shifted. "...Well..."

"I knew it!" Hank slapped his hands together. "I knew it!"

"Okay, okay. Maybe I got a little carried away at first, but I'm all right now." But just for a few seconds, Jason's heart sped up, wondering whatever happened to Lilly, and if by some act of cosmic lunacy, he would ever see her again. And then, with ease, he let her go. "But, yes, I did meet a sweetheart. I'm seeing her next week. She lives in New York. Her name's Anna."

"That sounds brilliant," Jean said.

Jason examined Theo's closet door. Tacked up were postcards from all around the world, including new ones from Amsterdam, Venice and Bruges, cities they had toured together. "So what do you think, Hank? You gonna behave this time?"

"Yeah. I'm not getting any younger, you know. Next week we're heading out west for a honeymoon. My girl's never seen the Grand Canyon."

"I've always wanted to go," Jean said. "Although your mate insists that we pop over to Yuma. Wherever that is."

Hank chuckled. "Got an old friend I want to visit. Kinda feel like I owe him. He's starting to forget things. Figure I should swing by at least one more time."

"Cool," Jason said. "I'll see you when you get back."

"Definitely, dear. Definitely. Mr. and Mrs. Hank B. Monroe. Come any time."

Jason picked up a framed picture of Theo, Roger and Oscar standing by the helicopter, and then through the window, looked at the metal contraption perched on the lawn. The rotors were enormous. "Wait....B? What's the B stand for?"

There was a slight pause, and then another *clack* of Hank's lighter, followed by an inhale of cigarette smoke. Exhale. "Brigsby," Hank said finally. "It's Brigsby."

Chapter 84
Ocean View

The waters of Cathedral Cove sparkled below them. Jason held a strap in the helicopter cabin, having a grand old time. Theo was still in shock. Roger shouted above the sound of the swirling rotors. "Don't worry about it, assface! This baby can handle it. Right, Dad?"

...THWUB-THWUB-THWUB-THWUB-THWUB-THWUB-THWUB-THWUB...

As Jason took in the shoreline...the trees growing out of white rock; the tunnel boring through; surf rolling onto the beach...he wasn't sure if he was looking forward or thinking back, as if all moments in time existed simultaneously. And yet as a scattering of memories over the past month flooded his mind—Grey suit's help; his Italian train buddies; the Grand Canal; Lilly's red wine; the Salzburg crew; Sven's bath house; his Hungarian grandmother; Jackie and Omar; Theo's Amsterdam corner; Anna—Jason smiled, realizing that the boundaries of time and space and dimension were dissolved by all the people he encountered, forever linking them to him, and him to them.

Ten miles or ten thousand. What did it matter? Plane, train, bus or cab. Just get off at a different stop. While he had barely ever wandered beyond his own neighborhood, Jason was now eager to travel again, to see what else was out there.

Tokyo? San Francisco? Mexico City? He wanted to see them all. Even by helicopter. And New Zealand? Of course, New Zealand. He already made it.

Oscar called from the pilot's seat. "Here's as good a spot as any. I got clearance."

...THWUB-THWUB-THWUB-THWUB-THWUB-THWUB-THWUB-THWUB...

Jason looked with curiosity as Roger opened a panel in the metal flooring. He reached in and handed Theo the jar, wrapped in a blue towel. "It's been here the whole time, just like you said. Amazing, yeh? When I walked in, I thought Georgie there was scamming on Mum. But he's kind of all right...you know, for a dude who wears a dress." Roger chuckled, then held out the wrapped jar. "I don't know how, but he knew this thing was gonna cause trouble. He told Mum to stash the bag with something, yeh? So she used that honey jar on my dresser. The one filled with pennies. Biker dicks had no idea. Bag sank right off."

Roger snapped his fingers. "That reminds me." He unfolded a flyer for *GenderBender*, a new nightclub opening in downtown Auckland. There was a picture of Angelique. "George said we can come any time. On the house."

"Yeh," Theo said. "I've seen this bit."

Roger tapped Jason on the shoulder. "So...I'm kinda young to be an uncle, yeh? Looks like he'll be grounded awhile. No more trips for him."

Jason smiled. "Yeah. Maybe. I bet he'll find a way out there anyway. He seems to have a knack for it." Roger nodded in agreement.

Theo hadn't said two words all morning. "I had a weird feeling something big was headed for me, yeh? I just didn't think it would be this..."

Oscar called back. "You boys ready with that thing?"

...*THWUB-THWUB-THWUB-THWUB-THWUB-THWUB-THWUB-THWUB*...

Theo looked at Jason. "So...what do you say, mate? Want to do the honors?"

Feeling part of Team Kiwi, Jason unfolded the towel, and took his first look at Theo's jar. *The* jar. Never in his wildest dreams did Jason even consider so much as riding in a helicopter, much less with the essence of the Universe in his hands. Yet there he was.

With a nod to the Barnes boys, who nodded back, Jason flipped the towel. It sent the jar plummeting toward the water... falling...falling...falling...until finally the cause of so much commotion landed with a silent *splash*, and sank beneath the ocean, buried, perhaps, for all time. Although deep down, they knew it would be a part of them forever.

Ira looked up from the ocean depths. There was plankton between his gums. "Hey, Howie. You ready? Look up. Look."

Sinking toward them was a small object, drifting into focus. Bubbles floated up in a long trail behind it. "Hey," the great whale said. "Right on time. Brigsby was right."

Ira extended his flippers. The jar landed in his grasp. "That old boy never misses."

Howard let his enormous tail wave up and then down. "So what do you think he's up to? Think he'll visit? It's been a while."

"Not sure." Ira held the jar out before him. "Let's find out."

He opened his mouth. Out came a short sequence of dolphin clicks and clacks, the very harmonic frequency for unsealing the jar.

Beneath the New Zealand waters, there was a blast of white light. There were streaks of screaming fluorescent color. There was the sensation of being sucked through a tornado. And there was lots and lots of...

Jason smiled at Theo, and in that very moment, made a promise to himself. He would come back to New Zealand some day. To see his friend. Together they would journey again. And when they did, Jason would arrive with only what he brought, but leave with so much more.

Some things we aren't supposed to find, he thought. *Some things just find you.*

About the Author

Russ Colchamiro is the author of the mysterious, action-packed space romp *Crossline* and the hilarious science-fiction backpacking comedy *Finders Keepers*. He is now at work on the *Finders Keepers* sequels, scheduled for publication through Crazy 8 Press.

Russ lives in Queens, N.Y., with his wife, two children, and their gregarious dog.

For more on Russ' fiction, you can visit him online at www.russcolchamiro.com, like his Facebook author page at www.facebook.com/RussColchamiroAuthor, and follow him on Goodreads, and Twitter @authorduderuss. He encourages readers to email him at authorduderuss@gmail.com.

Hotdog pilot Marcus Powell has been selected to test Taurus Enterprises' *Crossline* and its newly developed warp thrusters, which, if successful, will revolutionize space travel as we know it. But during his psychedelic jaunt across the stars, Powell is forced into a parallel universe, where he finds himself at the center of a civil war he may have been destined for all along!

Teamed up with a gorgeous, trigger-happy rebel leader, a pot-smoking Shaman, a crafty pie maker, and a weary soldier who hates his guts, Powell must survive a cross-country rescue mission and his own trippy vision quests long enough for his wife and young daughter to outsmart Taurus' reclusive CEO, whose own secrets may prevent Powell from ever making it back to Earth.

From author Russ Colchamiro, *Crossline* is a hallucinogenic, action-packed romp across time, space, and dimension that asks the question: once you cross the line, can you ever really go back?

DuckBob Spinowitz has a problem. It isn't the fact that he has the head of a duck—the abduction was years ago and he's learned to live with it. But now those same aliens are back, and they claim they need his help! Can a man whose only talents are bird calls and bad jokes be expected to save the universe?

No Small Bills is the hilarious science fiction novel from award-winning, bestselling author Aaron Rosenberg. See why the NOOK Blog called it "an absurdly brilliant romp"—buy a copy and start laughing your tail feathers off today!

You thought you knew about King Arthur and his knights? Guess again!

Learn here, for the first time, the down-and-dirty royal secrets that plagued Camelot as told by someone who was actually there, and adapted by acclaimed *New York Times* best-seller Peter David. Full of sensationalism, startling secrets and astounding revelations, *The Camelot Papers* is to the realm of Arthur what the *Pentagon Papers* is to the military: something that all those concerned would rather you didn't see. What are you waiting for?

Inside the old House called Tanglewood are the Doors: too numerous to count, made of the wood from the Norse World Tree Yggdrasil, leading to every time and place that ever was— or ever could be. A few rare children have the ability to step through such Doors. They are the Latchkeys, the Wardens, the protectors of Tanglewood and its Doors. But now many of the Doors have gone missing. And many have splintered. Those missing pieces must be restored for the Doors to be returned. And Splinters can be anywhere and assume any form. Almost like they don't want to be found. Read all about the Latchkeys and their exciting, thrilling, spooky adventures to places that were, places that might have been, and places that almost could be!

At the age of thirty-eight, Zeno Aristos has quit the NYPD and is trying to figure out what to do with his life. Then someone close to him is kidnapped by dark and cryptic forces. The deeper Zeno digs, the more he realizes he's dealing not with a mere earthly adversary but with an entity steeped in the deepest and most malevolent of ancient mysteries.

In *Fight the Gods*, Michael Jan Friedman takes a major creative step beyond the *Star Trek* novels, comic books, and television scripts with which his name has become synonymous, and braves the sinister rooftops and mystical back alleys of urban fantasy. Whatever you think you know of him or of his work...you ain't seen nothin' yet.

Meet Vince Hammond. He has a secret that, if his mother finds out, she will absolutely kill him.

No, he's not dating a girl she'd hate. No, he's not gay.

He's a vampire. And Mom is a vampire hunter. And all of his friends are vampire hunters. And his fiancee is a vampire hunter, and so are his future in-laws.

Need an antidote to every other vampire novel out there? Then you're going to want to be *Pulling Up Stakes*. After putting a silver bullet in werewolves in his classic *Howling Mad*, *New York Times* Bestseller Peter David now sinks his teeth into vampire lore, with bloody good results.

London, 1593. Christopher Marlowe, playwright, spy, and renowned womanizer, is desperately working on what could be his greatest play. But inspiration eludes him, until a chance encounter with a dark temptress rekindles his passion and the words start to flow with that famous passion.

But forces are arrayed against Marlowe. Something doesn't want him finishing, and Marlowe suspects there is a foul, unnatural agency at work. Can the incandescent playwright stop the chaos before it overwhelms the entire city?

This new occult thriller from bestselling authors Aaron Rosenberg and Steven Savile combines Elizabethan theatre, ancient mythology, and ageless seduction to create a dark, gripping tale that is both as old as time itself and wholly original.

FOR THIS IS HELL

AARON ROSENBERG & STEVEN SAVILE

It's 2012. Maxtla Colhua is an Investigator for the Empire– an Aztec Empire that successfully repelled Hernan Cortes in 1603 and now stretches from one end of what we call the Americas to the other. But now it is the Last Sun, and someone has decided to punctuate it with a series of grisly murders reminiscent of the pagan sacrifices of ancient times. Can Maxtla find the killer before his city is ripped apart? Then he has to locate the missing star of a burtal Aztec ball game, the idol of millions. But to do that Maxtla will have to challenge the most powerful men and women in the Empire—or see the streets run red with blood.

Aztlan is a pair of murder mysteries set in an exciting world that never was but could have been!

On the Damned World, it's every man for himself. Only it's not just mankind who inhabits this crumbling, desolate world. Twelve very different species, creatures out of Earth's mythology that live on the land, in the sea, and underground, vie for survival in a hostile land. Humanity is nearly extinct. But now the Twelve Races have discovered that their own fortunes are inextricably linked with the remnants of the human race.

As a result, a young slave girl named Jepp may hold the key to the future of the world. But can she and her new companions survive long enough to save everyone . . . or will they damn the world instead?

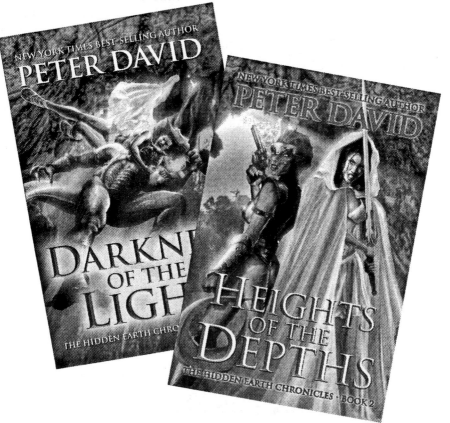